DRAGON TRIAD

THE COMPLETE DUET: MOTH & FLAME

LANA SKY

MOTH

Moth

Moth By Lana Sky

Copyright © 2020 by Lana Sky
All rights reserved.

No part of this publication may be reproduced, distributed, or transmitted in any form or by any means, including photocopying, recording, or other electronic or mechanical methods, without the prior written permission of the author.

This is a work of fiction. Names, characters, businesses, places, events and incidents are either the products of the author's imagination or used in a fictitious manner. Any resemblance to actual persons, living or dead, or actual events is purely coincidental.

ACKNOWLEDGMENTS

Thanks so much to everyone who supported this draft along the way, including the many beta readers who provided encouragement! Please keep in mind that this story includes dark, graphic and explicit content matter that may not be suitable for readers under the age of 18—or for readers who are uncomfortable with the following subject matter: explicit sex, mentions of sexual abuse, mentions of domestic abuse, and graphic depictions of violence.

We're lied to as children. Monsters aren't found in the closet or under the bed, and nothing portrayed in horror movies could ever do them justice. The awful truth became obvious to me at an early age. Real monsters lurk inside of *everyone*—from a kind elderly grandparent down to the very people who tuck you in at bedtime.

We all have demons inside, waiting to emerge when least expected. The only effective weapon against them is denial. Close your eyes, count to ten, and endure the worst of the assault. Suppress the pain, the anger—the fear.

You *breathe.*

Eventually, the horror fades, and you convince yourself it was all just a dream.

Until the lies stop working. The nightmare becomes a reality, corrupting every aspect of your life.

Your mind.

Your body.

Your soul.

Until the person you see in the mirror becomes the scariest monster of all. In vain, you try running away.

But you never can.

There is only one choice left—live that pretty, fragile lie and craft the walls of your own ignorant little cage around you.

Like a moth dancing on the edges of a flame.

MUSIC SPILLS from the club's brick façade, providing a fitting soundtrack for this busy city street. My nerves aside, I can't deny that the place has its own unique brand of ambiance. Loud, pulsing notes form the bulk, grating against my eardrums. It's not my preference, per se—more along the lines of the punky sort of stuff that Mara listens to. Vulgar on the surface, but when the chorus hits, the guitar riffs give way to surprisingly deep lyrics.

It's the juxtaposition, she explains whenever I raise my eyebrow at the noise seeping from her headphones during our bus rides to campus. *You should study it more, Hannah. A few curse words might spice up your writing enough that you'll make the international news next time.*

My cheeks heat at the prospect as I lean against a grungy brick wall paces away from the actual line snaking inside. I'm out of sight here, and there's no one to stare as my hand falls to the knitted bag hanging from my shoulder. I curl my fingers into a fist just to keep from reaching inside for it—it being a crumpled article from four weeks ago. Sure, the article itself had been buried within one of the most well-read local imprints from my small town, but it featured a short story, written by none other than Hannah Dewitt. Or, in this case, Hannah *Matthews*. Not that using my mother's maiden name helped obscure my identity any. Everyone from my parents to those in my hometown knew instantly who wrote it.

The narrative conveyed in the few short paragraphs transcends any pseudo-identity I might hide behind. A spine-chilling horror or as my creative writing professor deemed it—a story of betrayal and violence.

And death.

Mara had snorted the first time I showed her the article. *"You really carry that around with you?"* she'd asked, but her voice had touched on that awed, reverent tone artists reserve for those weird universal quirks we all understand. She just got it.

That feeling.

That pride.

That fear.

After three months of being her unofficial best friend, I'm convinced she loves testing our mutual fears more than any other bonding activity. Our fear of rejection. Isolation. Of the unknown.

Like venturing out to a club on the outskirts of downtown at a time inching dangerously close to midnight. It's one of the most reckless things I've ever done, even if I haven't gathered up the nerve to go inside yet. I'm here, and that's the important thing. All for the sake of research—how can I write about the human experience without…well, living?

The first step? Break free from my cage—a task easier said than done. Warily, I dig through my bag for my phone. It might not be a cage in the literal sense, but its pink case resembles nothing more than a pretty shackle, linking me to an owner, though he's miles away. Several unread messages dance across my home screen, none of them from Mara:

Where are you?

Where are you?

Where are you?

My fingers tremble as I hastily compile a reply. *At home. Like usual, lol.*

A new message flashes across the screen as if the writer knew my response by heart, ready with his own counterpoint. *Is your webcam still broken?*

I swallow hard and desperately try to ignore the unease unfurling in my belly. *I can do this.* I went over the plan a million times, fine-tuning every detail, such as insisting the security camera he'd installed in my apartment had spontaneously combusted this morning. It's a harmless lie on the surface, but it set the groundwork for my fragile confidence. I'm ready for anything.

Yeah, I finally reply. *The battery died, remember?*

Sweat slicks my palms as I wait for a response. A heartbeat later, my phone vibrates with an incoming message.

Call me then.

Enjoy Santa Barbara, I insist. *Don't worry about me. I'll be fine without you for just one night.*

Call me, Hannah. Now.

I sigh and bring the phone to my ear. It barely has the chance to ring before someone picks up on the other end. "How are you doing?" my brother demands.

"I'm fine, Branden." I try my best to keep the strain from my voice. "Now enjoy your vacation. Promise—"

"I can barely hear you…" Static disrupts his words. I just get shouted snippets. "What the hell is that noise?"

"N-Noise?" My heart stops beating. As if from miles away, I interpret the music pulsing in the distance. *Crap.* He must be able to hear it even through the phone. Turning, I spot a nearby alley and hurry down the cramped space until a dumpster blocks my path. At least here, some of the noise fades.

"Sorry, I was…watching something on the television," I say, cupping my hand around the receiver. "I turned the volume down."

"You think you can live by yourself in an apartment and have the TV that loud?"

I grit my teeth at the disapproval in his tone. "It's not that big of a deal, Bran. I'm sorry—"

"Take a picture," he demands. "Right now. Your cell phone seems to be working okay if you can't use the webcam. I need to see your smile."

"Branden." I'm blinking too rapidly to ignore the prickling sensation building behind my eyes. It's such a stupid reason to cry. I've prepared for this, too.

"Just one," he goads in that tone that makes the outrageous sound reasonable. Sane. "So that I can make sure you're safe."

"I'm honestly fine," I whisper in a half-hearted attempt to placate his paranoia.

More static rattles the feed from his end as if he pulled the phone from his ear. "Kaitlin! Pack up. We're heading back tonight—"

"Fine." Sighing, I hold up my cell phone and take a picture of the brick wall before me. The shutter sound echoes loudly enough for him to hear it. "Cheese," I mutter as I flick through my recent photos and select the one I took right before leaving my apartment. My finger shakes as I hit send. "Satisfied?" I ask, knowing that within seconds he'll be able to see the image—me, supposedly safe and sound, lounging on the couch in my pj's while smiling wide.

"I'm just looking out for you, Han," he finally replies. "I still don't get why you left. I'm just trying to protect you. You know that. And I'm sorry...for what happened the other day. You should have told me you weren't coming sooner." His voice hardens the way it does when he's thinking too long and too hard. Usually, about the past and all the ways I've screwed up under his watch before.

"I just want you to enjoy this time with Kaitlin," I croak. "That's all."

In theory, my moving out was supposed to be our chance to start over. Put some distance between us. Cut the cord…

If anything, he's started to strangle me with it.

Only because he loves me. He does.

"Night, Bran." I know better than to hang up until he grunts out a muttered goodbye. Only then can I rest assured that he won't show up outside my apartment in the middle of the night.

Hopefully.

But I've survived, and as I return my phone to my bag, I refocus on the task at hand—not chickening out of my— technically first—night out with a real live friend. Ever.

Not even Branden can make me turn back now.

Squaring my shoulders, I face the club entrance, no less intimidated by the sight of the line than I was before.

What had Mara called this place? Eccentric. *"It's the best! Really grunge. The kind of place where you'll find an underground DJ as often as a drug dealer."*

Fortunately for me, there don't seem to be any drug dealers among the scantily dressed women and men who make up the bulk of the line—not that I would honestly know the difference. Still, something won't let me scurry from the alley and join them just yet.

Fear? Branden isn't the only reason I'm hesitant to go headlong into a nightclub, in a strange neighborhood with a "friend" I've admittedly only known for a few months. But part of my New Year's resolution is to live a little. Stop dwelling in my bubble. Stop living life under Branden's discretion.

And, most importantly, grow as an artist…

Inhaling deeply, I force myself to advance the few necessary steps it takes to join the end of the line. My hands shake as I rummage through my bag for a card Mara gave me. Neon blue, it proclaims the club's name in a bold black script— *Dragon's Head.* When I flash it to the bouncer, he barely gives me a second glance.

And I'm in. Dorothy is no longer in Kansas, but the real world is a dizzying collage of neon lights and crushing music. Dark walls and a press of bodies make this realm so very different from the cloistered, closeted spaces I'm used to. One overriding thought weighs on my mind as I inch my way forward, but I'm smiling the more I mull it over. *Branden would kill me.*

But at least then he wouldn't be able to *control* me anymore.

In this place, control seems to be a foreign concept entirely. Mara hadn't been lying. Beneath the grime and decay, the venue oozes creative allure in spades. I have to physically stop myself from dragging my journal from my bag and writing down snippets of inspiration. I can't help it. Poetry lurks in the flickers of bright light and lingering shadow. Stanzas beg to be written about mysterious figures lurking on the outskirts of the dance floor.

Every person here has a story to be told—people watching, in less flowery terms, sure. Either way, this is much better than sitting at home watching old movies in my ratty pair of sweats.

I do my best to meld within the crowd, craning my neck back to take everything in. The high rafters riddled with metal scaffolding. The brick walls illuminated in muted reflections of the pulsing lights. Color abounds, and I almost miss the flash of pale skin as someone grabs my wrist, spinning me around.

"You came!" Mara Chan stands before me, dressed to kill in a black minidress that hugs her curves. Her long black hair hangs loosely down her back, and her light makeup enhances her pretty features and almond-shaped eyes.

She could have easily chosen to be a model rather than an English lit major.

And in her shadow, I instantly feel underdressed. "I thought you said this was casual?" I have to shout just to be heard above the music.

"What do you mean?" She eyes me with a frown and shrugs. "You look great."

Great—as in *boring*. My beige sweater—speckled with white bunnies—and a conservative brown corduroy skirt are admittedly the most risqué items in my wardrobe. Even so, Mara waggles her eyebrows.

"Relax! You have that sexy librarian thing going on. Now, let's dance!" Grabbing my hand, she pulls me out to the center of the dance floor. "The music tonight is fire!"

I spot a DJ in the corner, curating the pulsating, energetic beat that seems to switch on a dime, keeping every dancer on their toes.

It's an electric atmosphere far different from what I see portrayed on television. Yet my worried, niggling fears meld with the flourishes of the music…

Branden would kill me.

Kill me.

Kill me.

"Hey, buzzkill!" Mara giggles even though she's forced to shout near my ear. "Loosen up! I'll get us some drinks."

She scurries off before I can follow, leaving me adrift amid a sea of writhing bodies. I grip my bag with both hands and try not to panic—a feat made ten times harder as paranoia sets in, nibbling away at my fragile resolve.

Branden would kill me. He will kill me. He's on his way here, sensing that something is wrong. He'll find me here and then kill me.

He'll…

Stop controlling my every moment because he is my brother, not my keeper. I mentally chant the thought as fiercely as I can until it sinks in—a little bit.

Until I remember his explosive reaction when I backed out of the beach trip he spontaneously planned to start this week—a full month earlier than when he usually takes his vacation. *You're so fucking selfish, Hannah.*

You hate me, Hannah.

You're just like them.

Like them.

You'll abandon me too.

I flinch as a dull ache resonates through my right arm. I'd started to clutch it with the opposite hand without realizing it. I stop and refocus on my surroundings.

It's too beautiful here to worry.

Neon lights bathe the room in alternating plumes of color. Yellows. Reds. Greens. They transform the space into an almost mythical realm where the clubgoers around me shift and mutate at random. A girl grinding against a male companion glows pink, then blue before appearing normal again for a split second. She catches me staring and winks, gyrating her hips.

My cheeks flame as I push my way past the dancing couple, hunting for Mara. I don't see her over by what seems to be the only bar in the back corner. Neither do I spot her long hair swaying in the nearby vicinity. Confused, I keep going, making my way through the club. On my second trip around, I spot a flash of dark hair along a section of booths cordoned off by a neon blue velvet rope. Two massive bouncers guard the opening I assume to be the entrance, and Mara stands beyond them, inside the section.

One look at her and I stop short. Something's wrong. Her arms are crossed, her chin jutting defiantly.

And three men eye her from various positions spread out along a row of black leather couches. I inch back a step as an invisible alarm in my brain goes off, making my chest constrict. It's the way they're looking at her. Like a piece of meat on display.

Ravenously.

I love you, Han. The memory plays on the fringes of my consciousness, threatening to unfold in full. *No one cares about me like you do. No one...*

I close my eyes. Shake my head. Ignore. But when I refocus, I find myself inching closer to that corner, straining my ears to hear above the music. This far from the DJ, and the beat isn't anywhere near as overwhelming as before, but their voices are so loud I can understand every word. It's as if they don't care who might hear them.

"Your daddy's been falling behind on paying his debts," one of them says. A man maybe in his thirties with a goatee and thinning black hair. "Lucky for him, there are plenty of ways for what he owes to be paid off." He strokes his chin while eyeing Mara up and down with an expression of narrowed, hungry eyes that makes my skin crawl. He zeros in on her bare collarbone and licks his lips. "I'd pay it off myself. Just ask me nicely."

Mara says something I don't catch because the laughter of another man cuts her off.

He's older than the other two, his features weathered. Worn. A set of gold chains dangles from his neck, obscuring the collar of his black shirt. He sits sprawled out, his legs splayed, one hand palming the center of his dark jeans. "With a face like hers?" He purses his lips and raises a finger stacked with gold rings. "One night, tops."

He and the first speaker laugh, trading knowing looks.

But the third man draws my attention. He's seemingly the youngest, judging from his full head of jet-black hair, but the other two sit angled toward him. Every now and again, they glance in his direction as though to seek approval.

Rather than join in their taunts, he one-handedly tosses a small object into the air. Bright orange ombre, square-shaped… A lighter. He juggles it without looking at Mara, choosing instead to scan the room but in a way that reminds me of one of my father's hunting dogs. Alert. On edge. Vigilant.

Absently, he swipes his free hand through his hair, revealing just how long it is—enough to brush his shoulders in jagged waves. Too long. The wayward strands obscure his eyes until it's too late. I can only stare as they dart from some distant corner to…me.

He sits forward, snatching the lighter from the air. Then he snaps his fingers once, drawing the attention of one of the bouncers. He points at me and crooks his finger in a silent command. *Come here.*

A heavy hand falls over my shoulder not even a second later, shoving me forward. I don't resist. I don't scream. It's like some internal switch is flipped in my head, controlling my limbs and ceasing all thought. My only driving force is instinct, which lays out a familiar framework. *Don't think. Don't scream. Don't fight. Obey.*

As if from underwater, I hear Mara say, "Leave her out of this! This has nothing to do with her—"

"Shut the fuck up," the man with the goatee snaps.

It's like I blink, and I'm here—in this space without any real recollection of moving. My arm is throbbing, my breaths slowing. In some ways, it's like falling into a well-worn routine. I go numb, turn my brain off. Endure.

You're so fucking selfish, Han. You'll leave me eventually, won't you? You will…

"You wouldn't be playing games with us, Mara?" the younger man asks, and my brain ceases every thought to fixate on him. His voice is soft, like a snake's hiss—but deeper too, resonating with the strength of a roll of thunder. Pocketing his lighter, he gestures to me—to my bag, I realize.

One of the bouncers snatches it from my arm and hands it to him. Holding my gaze, he digs through it slowly, withdrawing its contents one by one. My journal. My pink leather wallet. A white case containing my birth control pills. My jade green pen that I borrowed from the Paper Crane, the bookstore I work at—his eyes scan the wording on it, and he scoffs. Finally, he retrieves my cell phone.

He weighs the device on the palm of his hand and then swipes through my home screen.

"What are you doing?" Mara cries, her voice higher than I've ever heard it. "That's hers! Leave it alone. She has nothing to do with—"

"I'm making sure that you wouldn't be dumb enough to do something reckless, Mara," he says in that unnerving tone. "Like bring a little friend to record our friendly conversation."

His cold gaze flickers from her to me and back again. "She's not from around here," he says as if that alone proves his suspicion. "Hanging around you. Zhang? Looks to me like a nosy little bitch."

"She lives here," Mara hisses, her voice hitching. "She just moved in, and she works for Mr. Zhang. I was just showing her around—"

"She's not dressed like it," he counters, eyeing my sweater skeptically. "No. It looks to me like she ain't dressed to party. More like to poke her fucking nose around where it doesn't belong. A reporter?" He snatches something from my bag—the article scrap. "This you?" he asks me.

"It's just an article *about* her," Mara insists. "She didn't write it—"

"I wasn't talking to you," he snaps. "Let the little bunny speak for herself. Are you a reporter, bunny? You smell like one—" His nostrils flare pointedly. "But I'm not sure."

His eyes zero in on my face, piercing and impossible to avoid. It's like he sees through me, his gaze slicing to the innermost parts of my being. To those emotions I've learned to turn off. Impulses I've fought to smother.

He stares and stares, all the while toying with my cell phone.

Then he drops it, only to reach for my journal next. Boldly, he flips it open, lowering his gaze to the first page.

At this point, my control snaps. I step forward, straining the grip of the bouncer who tries to stop me. My lips part, a plea slipping out, violating one of my internal, concrete rules—*endure.*

I break. "Don't!"

"Let her go. You can leave." The younger man waits until the bouncer complies and returns to his position outside of the barrier.

"Rafe," Mara pleads, "just leave her alone—"

He holds up one finger, and it's like time stops. I freeze solid, unable to move. Once a few seconds pass, he sits back and leisurely turns the page as if he has all the time in the world. To violate my deepest thoughts and innermost secrets. Gawk at my rawest, unedited writing. Delve into my brain unbidden.

Again, I feel my mental reins strain. "Stop…"

He doesn't. I don't think he even hears me. Casually, he licks his finger, then turns the page. Licks. Page. Reads, seemingly riveted by what he's seeing—and that's the worst part. The fact that makes my cheeks catch fire and my nails sink into their respective palms.

The pretending.

His two seatmates snicker, rolling their eyes. "Knock it off, Wei."

"We're interested in buying ass, and he wants to read some fucking little diary—"

"You can go." He inclines his head toward Mara, who grabs my hand, surging for the exit. "Not her—" I feel his gaze on the back of my neck, locking me into place. "She stays."

"The hell she is!" Mara snaps, whirling to face him. "Leave her alone! I mean it, Rafe. Or I'll call the police. Your issue is with my dad. Then keep it that way—"

"And tell them what?" He sits straighter; his tone honed like a whip. "That your daddy likes to rack up his gambling debts when he isn't managing that little restaurant of yours into the ground? That he's dug too deep of a hole to come out? Or that his daughter has to play snitch to save his neck? Come on, Mara, I thought you and your family enjoyed living in a safe, peaceful neighborhood. Keep running your mouth, and it won't stay that way for long."

Mara stiffens at the barely concealed threat. Her fingers tighten around my wrist. Tighten...

"Though, you know what? Call the pigs," the man goads, his laughter cold. "I hear a few even like girls like you, too. Ask around. Or maybe you can go work for Gino and learn firsthand? At least then you'd get paid for it."

Mara's face pales as she lets me go. "You'll be fine, Hannah," she insists, but she hurries from the enclosed section without me. "I'll be watching. I won't take my eyes off you. I promise."

As she fades from my peripheral vision, my brain does that thing again. Shuts off. Focuses on the most important actions to perform at this moment—breathing. Standing. Staring.

The younger man is still watching me, his head cocked as his fingers continue to molest the pages of my journal. That violation stings more than any other. He's carelessly wandering over words he couldn't possibly understand. Mutilating phrases that have literal blood, sweat, and tears mingled within the ink. He's mauling me with every swipe of his fingers.

And I can't even look away. His eyes hold me captive, sparkling the more my irritation grows. Like he knows every thought I'm thinking. The hate I'm feeling.

And he's relishing in all of it.

"Go." He inclines his head, but again, he isn't speaking to me.

The two men beside him share a look, but they stand, shaking their heads incredulously. "Damn. You always did have the weirdest fucking taste," the one with the goatee murmurs, barely audible above the music.

The other man isn't as subtle. He raises an eyebrow and looks me over, then he cranes his neck to seek out Mara standing along a nearby wall. "You traded *that* piece of ass for this?"

"I said, fuck off." The younger man doesn't take his eyes off me. His tongue traces his lower lip in a quick strike. A threat? Or a warning?

"Go," he repeats without shifting his focus. "And leave the Chan girl to me."

The goatee man hisses through his teeth. "Greedy fucker. You want them both?"

"You heard me." He utilizes that iron tone again and doesn't move an inch until the two men finally leave the section. Then he sits back and crooks one finger at me. "Come here."

I don't move. There's something about being trapped like a deer in the headlights. When every muscle contracts, paralyzing you, it's impossible to react logically. Or think. At least until something more alarming snaps you from the daze.

Like him literally snapping his fingers. *Thwack!*

I flinch, but my body obeys my commands again. I cross my arms and square my stance, making myself as small of a target as possible. I should run, but I can't. My eyes won't leave my bag. My journal. My conscience.

It's the one possession I can't bear to give up.

"G-Give it back."

"She speaks." Amusement flickers through his angular features, making me jump. His eyes are more expressive than most people's. Like a predator's. It's almost too easy to tell what he's thinking, but you're only ever seeing half of the tale. Hunger, yes, but its presence alone is no predictor as to when he'll finally pounce.

"Hop this way, bunny." Again, he crooks his finger, but the motion carries a swiftness that wasn't there before—a command lurking in the deliberate twitch of his knuckle. "Come here. Unless you want me to call your little friend back over."

I sense it's not a threat. He means it. He'll dangle Mara's welfare like a shiny toy, expecting me to jump for it.

Because I will. My feet are already propelling me toward him. Maybe it's genetic, this inherent cowardice. This need I can't shake to always go along with any plan, no matter how terrifying. *Always.*

I'm the girl perpetually depicted in horror movies. Gullible, manipulated by everyone.

By Branden.

By strangers.

By these instincts hardwired within my psyche.

To approach the figurative killer without making a sound. To find the safest spot away from him and sit, not that he seems to mind. He copies the posture of his friend, sprawled out, unconcerned. I notice he's wearing the same dark, unremarkable clothing as the others, but one detail makes his ensemble stand out in a way theirs didn't. My gaze fixates on his left arm, bared by a short sleeve, and I realize why.

Colors drip over the pronounced muscle, embedded in his skin. Ink? Reds. Indigo. Black. They form snippets of a scene mostly hidden beneath his shirt. The only solid detail I can make out licks down the length of his forearm in writhing tendrils—flames.

"Eyes up here, rabbit," he warns, snapping his fingers. *Rabbit?* As his eyes flicker over me again, I realize what he meant. *Me.* As a joke?

Or a crude reference to my sweater? I glance down, eyeing the beige wool speckled with innocent white bunnies that seem to glow in the dim lighting.

"Cat got your tongue, rabbit?"

I say nothing, pursing my lips, ignoring reality. There's an art form in silence—in shrinking down within yourself until the real you is just a blip. A memory. Completely untouchable by anyone…

Until he touches me.

The flesh of his fingertip is alarmingly soft. I almost don't realize it's happening at first—the brief, persistent contact disrupting my loose curls—until my nerves become electrified with his touch. Alarmed, I flinch back, nearly lurching off the couch entirely. Before my eyes, his fingers float, denied a taste of my skin.

He chuckles, leaving his hand unmoving anyway. Dark, his eyes trace the outlines of mine, hunting for a way in. I blink to keep him out, but I fail.

His smile catches me off guard, and our gazes lock. Amusement glints across the dark irises, but there's no malice. He's a child playing a game merely to thwart boredom, and I'm just a toy. With nothing better to do, he's dangling me by my puppet limbs, watching me flail—all for the sake of entertainment.

"I'll make you a deal." He lifts my notebook from his lap, brandishing it just beyond my reach. "Read me one of your little stories, and I'll let your friend off the hook for tonight."

He wants a response. Demands one. His silence feels deliberate this time, nibbling away at my nerves until I have no choice but to pry my lips apart. Speak. "Why?"

He raises an eyebrow. "Her daddy owes a shit ton of money, rabbit." He chuckles when I flinch at the nickname, hating how it sounds in his voice. A husky, teasing whisper on the verge of a growl. *Rabbit.* "Letting her go without a warning would be a mercy bestowed out of the kindness of my bleeding heart."

He winks, prompting me to go against my instincts once again.

"Why is that her problem?" I croak while glancing at Mara. Lurking on the periphery, she hasn't left me at least. Her eyes meet mine, wide and frightful, and she waves toward me in a frantic motion. *Run!* As if leaving would be so easy.

"Why?" His harsh bark of laughter draws my attention back to him. He forms a fist and props his chin onto it, probing deep with those merciless eyes. "I don't know what cul-de-sac you skipped out of, but here in the real world? We pay for the sins of others, whether related to us by blood or not. It's the way the fucking cookie crumbles. You suffer for Chan, and she'll have to bear the weight of her daddy's gambling addiction."

It sounds like something a movie villain would say, but in a sense, he's right. I know that better than anyone. Be them the sins of a father, or a brother…some of us are destined to live out our lives tainted by the crimes of others. No matter what we do, they haunt us.

Constantly. My phone buzzes, the screen lighting up, and even from here, I know who's calling. *Branden.*

Laughing, the man picks it up from the couch and glances at the home screen. His already permanent smirk stretches. "Should I answer it?" he ponders, inclining his head toward me.

He's baiting me.

But I bite, lurching forward even as I clutch at the edge of my seat with both hands to keep from really moving. "Don't."

Am I even worried for myself? No. Maybe Mara instead? Or my fragile freedom. This space. Branden would stop at nothing to drag me back into the cage he's built around me and lock it shut for good if he suspects for a second that I'm not playing by his rules.

In some ways, this man *should* answer the call. Once he's done with me, Branden would burn this place to the ground…

But I wouldn't wish his wrath on anyone.

"Don't."

He chuckles again, stroking the outside of my phone with his thumb. But for all his games, his eyes keep flicking toward the screen, reading the name I've programmed in for my brother—Bran <3. The heart is symbolic, but he wouldn't know that.

He lifts his thumb, letting it hover over the touch screen. When he lowers it, I suck in a breath. Rather than the green answer button, he strikes the red one to dismiss the call instead.

Relief escapes me in a sharp exhale. Branden will just call back, irritated that I didn't answer, but already bored, the man drops my phone into my bag and shoves it aside.

With little effort, he reclaims my journal and flips it open to a different page. I recognize the various scribbled lines—my latest piece, the rough draft of an essay assignment. The single essay that may or may not decide if I continue school next semester.

"You write about lying a lot, rabbit," he remarks while scanning my words. "Maybe you really are a fucking reporter? *Lies spilled like bated breaths. Suffocation inevitable. Drowning…*" Smirking, he looks up, forcing eye contact. "What's a bunny got to hide from?"

"Why do you care?" I rasp. Internally, I'm more shocked that he could make that kind of assumption from a few words scattered throughout.

He chuckles, seemingly amused by my reaction. "Deceiver. Falsifier." He's rattling off my various scribbled titles by heart. "You must have plenty of secrets to tell, rabbit."

"And you must be really bored to pick on some random girl over a journal."

"So she bites as well as speaks." He raises an eyebrow, another wry smile playing over his mouth. "I'm curious, rabbit…" he tells me, leaving the implication dangling so that I'm forced to ask.

"Why?"

He sits back, stroking his chin. "Why you have those sad, fucking bunny eyes." A newer emotion makes his eyes narrow further—annoyance. "A normal person would have run by now, rabbit. They would have made good on their threat to call the police. Otherwise, they'd be crying. Begging. You haven't done a fucking one of those things—" His teeth flash, his gaze piercing. "Why is that?"

I clench my jaw shut, but a reply slips out regardless. "I guess you just like terrorizing people—"

"And you haven't answered my question." He sits forward again, bracing both of his hands on his knees. Then he lunges.

I don't even have the chance to react before he's beside me, his arm thrown over my shoulder, his breath on my throat. Then ice. Cold. Sharpness…

I recognize the feeling, and I go rigid, picturing the size of the blade he must have tracing along the very edge of my windpipe. Nothing too large. A pocket knife? He holds it there teasingly, daring me to pull away.

But I don't.

I can't. All I can do is flex my fingers, grasping at the air. It's all I can *ever* do.

Suffocate.

But I'm used to my tormentor demanding silence—not this.

"Read." My book lands open on my lap, the page a scribbled poem. I'd written it months ago, and the pain I'd felt then still leaps off the page, bled into every swirl of ink.

Haunted by darkness, shrouded in guilt. In deception, salvation found…

"No." Speaking makes the blade press in. Scrape. But more words escape unbidden, impossible to keep in. "Get off me—"

"Read." His impatience disturbs me more than any threat, mainly by what it reveals. He doesn't want to scare me. He's having too much fun provoking me. "In deception, salvation found," he recites for me, his tone pompous with mock bravado. "From golden bars. Deceptive beauty—"

"Stop."

He doesn't.

"From chains formed of secrets linked by fear. Freedom's price paid with the blood of another." He chuckles, tapping the knife against my throat. Once, twice. Never hard enough to cut, just enough to sting.

"You're not afraid of me," he murmurs near my ear, his voice impossible to ignore. "Not one fucking bit. You've seen a much worse monster. I want to *meet* that monster. I want to know what makes a little rabbit like you so damn hard she doesn't flinch when a man presses a knife to her throat. I want—" He breaks off, shifting his gaze to the crowd. At the mouth of the section, a slim woman is talking to one of the bouncers. She's young, her dark hair kept at bay with a glittery butterfly-shaped hair clip, her outfit a modest shirt and jeans that make her seem more out of place than I do. A snippet of what she says reaches us, mutilated by the pounding bass.

"…need to speak to Rafe. It's important."

"Shit." Rafe's eyes narrow, and he shoves me aside, rising to his feet. "Looks like we'll have to cut this short, bunny."

He walks past me, heading for the section's entrance—but in his grasp is my journal. Its cover glints in the neon lighting as he takes the woman's arm and melds into the crowd with her.

And I can't even muster up the energy to chase him.

My hand paws at my throat, following the sting of his knife as his words echo in my brain. *I want to meet that monster. I want to know what makes a little rabbit like you so damn hard she doesn't flinch when a man presses a knife to her throat…*

"Hannah!" Mara exclaims from beside me. I jump. It's as if she appears out of thin air to grab my wrist. I only have enough sense of mind to gather up my belongings and shove them into my bag before she's dragging me after her through the dance floor and out of the club entirely. As the fresh air displaces most of the noise, I finally realize that she's been speaking to me this whole time.

"I'm so, so sorry. Those assholes… I knew they came here sometimes, but I wasn't thinking. I'll make it up to you, I promise. I know! Come to my spoken word tomorrow. It will be a nice, quiet night—"

"You don't have to apologize." Again, it's one of my instincts. I'm the one who spews out the apologies in the end.

Unwilling to play along, Mara just shakes her head. "Bullshit! I do. And I'll owe ya one for life. Just… Just don't tell anyone about that shit, okay?" She eyes me warily, biting her lower lip. "Rafe is a total dick, but he's harmless if you don't piss him off. Think of him as more of a gatekeeper. Living around here, you were bound to meet him anyway."

I don't miss the resignation in her voice. "Who is he?" I ask.

"Just the local, resident asshole," she says. "Let's say his uncle commands a lot of respect, and Rafe thinks he's hot shit just because he handles business for him."

"Business?"

She rolls her eyes. "Being a dick to all of the local business owners so that they pay him. All so that he and his merry band of assholes don't become bigger dicks. It's not as dramatic as it sounds." She swipes at her cheek, and I stare in alarm.

We're nearing the intersection that joins this backstreet with the main road. It's brighter here, and I can make out the telltale smudges disrupting her once perfectly applied eyeliner. She was crying—she was that scared.

"Are you okay?" I place my free hand on her shoulder, sensing the slight tremors wracking her slender frame. "Mara—"

"Rafe and those guys... They're just punks, alright? It's nothing." She faces ahead, squaring her shoulders even though her grip on my wrist remains so tight her nails are digging into my skin. "Don't worry about them. They won't mess with you again. But damn, girl... You have balls; I will say that."

"Huh?"

She shoots me a funny look. "I've never seen anyone stare him down like that. It was as though you weren't afraid of anything. And he *liked* it. All the dumb bitches around here throw themselves at Rafe, but I've never seen him get a hard-on like that without anyone flashing their tits at least." Genuine awe taints her tone, and I shake my head, my cheeks burning.

"Yeah, right."

"Yeah. I'm right," Mara says without missing a beat. "It's a good thing you're a nice, wholesome girl. It's better if you stay away from him. Though, he is cute." She frowns, her eyes narrowing. "If he weren't such an asshole, I'd even let him ink me."

"Ink?" I feel my cheeks heat further. Despite my designation as a twentysomething, modern-day slang isn't my forte. "Is that a weird way of saying hook up?"

"No. He runs a tattoo shop downtown, though he's exclusive about who he takes as a client. It's invitation-only as though he's some kind of '*illustrious artiste.*'" She makes finger quotes. "I did hear he was a good fuck, though."

In my brain, those facts don't negate his obvious instability. Certainly not enough to explain the genuine appreciation coloring her voice. "Good sex makes up for him being a psycho?"

"Of course not." Mara sighs and tucks a strand of hair behind her ear. "I'm not a slut or anything, Mother Theresa," she mutters, her frown apologetic. "I just have *eyes*. Some of us can't be innocent little virgins who cast judgment on the rest of us sinful mortals."

"I'm not judging you," I say.

"*Sure*, you aren't." She raises an eyebrow. "You're such a cliché. The sheltered, sweet writer girl who loves to people watch, sneering down on the fuckups of us normies. Let's be honest, you wouldn't even be friends with me if I weren't such a pushy bitch." She crosses her arms, convinced of that fact. "I don't even know a damn thing about you, other than you write morbid short stories about monsters and drowning people. If I didn't know any better, Dewitt, I'd assume you were ashamed of me."

It's my turn to play skeptical. "Says the girl who impressed so many professors on campus that they've practically begged for you to take their classes next semester." Meanwhile, I had to rest on my grades to score the next credits I need. "I'm the idiot who banked all of my hopes on one program."

"Well, there is that," she concedes, beaming. "But it's not like you don't have a shot at entering the Fenwick program next year. I haven't even bothered to apply, and don't give me that look. Anyone would kill for that internship."

"Like I really have any chance of winning," I say with a forced laugh.

"Yeah, right. Your shit is so good you've already made the paper. I'm sure you'll ace the entry essay. What's the topic again?"

"Inner demons," I say, recalling the assignment that's been plaguing me since the semester ended. "We're supposed to describe a narrative during which we faced an inner demon—"

"But with fancy descriptive prose. You're the queen of that. If anything, tonight just gave you plenty of inspiration to draw from. 'Inner Demon' could perfectly fit Rafe Wei-

Shen," Mara declares with utter conviction. The tears have already vanished, and she's back to her usual self. "Anyway, about tomorrow. Promise you'll come?"

"I have to work. Mr. Zhang wanted me to stay late tomorrow to help close up the store."

"Oh, come on! It'll be great. You can trial balloon your essay!" She delves into a vivid description of how much fun it will be—how exhilarating—much like she had to convince me to come with her tonight. Though I barely register her words, I nod along anyway.

I'm too busy staring at the object clutched within my fist as if it appeared there by magic. Or… if I'd stuck my hand into a certain "punk's" pocket and took it while he was distracted.

Stole it.

The brilliant orange ombre lighter looks more beautiful up close. Too lovely to belong to a monster—though one is etched onto the front of it in gleaming, brilliant gold.

A snarling, fire-breathing dragon.

Not all monsters are destined to be bad in the end. I'll save this one.

Or at least protect it from its original owner's reach.

H*ell.*
Cigarette smoke.

Ash.

I can still smell him right up until the second I open my eyes…

Then poof. He's gone like magic, and a new day begins fresh.

I've always been good at compartmentalizing things since childhood. With a little determination, scary events become nightmare fodder easily ignored during the daytime. When I wake up, thoughts of strange men and their taunts are a long-forgotten memory.

It's how I cope.

As is rifling through the old shoebox tucked beneath my bed the second I lift my head from my pillow. A yawn stretches my mouth as I feel along the floor for the box, drag it out, and tug aside the lid. One by one, I grasp the objects inside it.

The first is just an old newspaper clipping, the headline unoriginal—Local Girl Found Drowned in Lake Beaver. I set it aside and run my fingers over the items resting beneath it. An old piece of taffy long past its sell-by date. A handful of unopened ChapSticks. Two never-used bottles of nail polish. A gold bracelet decorated in tiny, delicately crafted ivory daisies. And finally, the newest member of my collection—a gold lighter that feels dangerous when held after the others.

I take my time observing the shape of it in the pale dawn glow. It blazes against my yellow bedspread, the most eye-catching detail in my sparsely furnished room at the moment. I start to return it to my box, only to place it on my nightstand instead. It's too bold to belong with my other trinkets. Maybe looking at it will remind me to get some new décor.

Anything, really.

I sigh as I take in the narrow space, devoid of any posters or pictures. Just books, most of them damaged stock foisted onto me by my boss, Mr. Zhang. I think he took pity on my lack of thrifting success and decided that volumes of history and literature make for better clutter anyway. Apart from my bed and a small nightstand, the only solid piece of furniture is a thrifted wardrobe in the corner that I fell in love with for its peeling-white-paint-over-old-wood aesthetic.

Yawning again, I march over to it and fish out a plain sweater and jeans. As I get dressed, I glance out of the window and admire the grungy, trash-strewn street below. This part of the city is already bustling with workers scurrying off to their nine-to-fives and the homeless men who troll this block with their belongings piled into shopping carts. A lazy sun teeters over the horizon, barely visible beyond a sea of skyscrapers, and I feel a smile tug on the corner of my mouth. It's days like this when I love living here the most, right in the thick of it all—the human condition. It may not be the safe, cloistered existence I lived on my family's estate, but in so many ways…

It's better.

At least during the few moments of the day when I can forget that Branden moved to this city when I did almost two years ago.

Sighing, I enter my closet-sized bathroom and wash up. I'm in the middle of towel-drying my hair when I hear my ringtone going off. My heart pounds as I creep into my room and fish it from my bag. The remnants of masculine fingerprints are still smeared over the touch screen—larger than my own, oval-shaped, and marred with unfamiliar ridges. A shudder runs through me as I wipe them off with my sleeve. Then I answer the phone without really scanning the name flashing across the screen.

Only one person would ever call me this early anyway.

"Hey!" I roll my eyes up to the ceiling even as I force pep into my voice. "Yes, Brand—"

"Hello?" The crisp, feminine tone doesn't belong to my brother, and every muscle in my body goes rigid. "Is this Hannah Dewitt?"

"Who is this?"

"So, this *is* you. Hannah, do you remember me?" Her voice triggers a memory. A woman with streaky makeup and tears streaming down her face as she screamed at me from behind a police barricade. *"You know what happened!"* she'd shouted. *"Just tell the truth! Stop protecting him! What did he do to Alexandria? What did he do to my daughter?"*

I rip the receiver from my ear as if the act alone can make her disappear. Vanish the same way I had to. Branden had to. "I'm sorry—" I swipe at my home screen, attempting to hang up. "You have the wrong number—"

"You know who I am," the woman declares, loudly enough that I can hear her despite the phone being several feet from my ear. No matter how hard I swipe to make her silent. "I saw your story in the paper. It was good." She waits as if expecting me to respond.

I don't.

"Hannah…" She sighs. "I really just wanted to talk to you. About Lexi. Remember her?"

Finally, my finger moves properly and hits the red button, ending the call. I drop the phone and sink to my knees, practically crawling under my bed in search of my box. I go through the ritual of removing the lid and palming every object over and over again. The article. The ChapSticks. Nail polish. Everything but the bracelet at first.

The cherry-flavored pink balm was from a convenience store near the border during the trip from Pennsylvania. Dad drove me the entire way, and we didn't say a single word. I don't think he even looked at me once. Bran had blown up my cell phone, and I'd made eye contact with the bored, pretty cashier behind the counter as I swiped this from a display just below her line of sight.

The pearly nail polish was from a gas station last week. But those memories can only distract me for so long before I find myself reaching for another object, twisting the cool metal between my fingers. This stupid, fucking bracelet…

There's a word for how I got every last item in this box—stealing. Though, I think of it more as…anchoring. Little things to tether me when it feels like I'm spiraling, and nothing short of screaming can bring me back—tiny little things no one would ever miss.

Either because they never noticed them in the first place, or because they aren't around anymore to care.

Or they're a deviant asshole who doesn't deserve to own them.

Slowly, I return the bracelet and my other trinkets. Then I shove the box under my bed and start to pace, scrambling my thoughts into the semblance of stanzas. Phrases. Coherence.

I can't control the direction they take—a dark path through two black eyes and stern, pink lips. A voice like crackling embers—*I want to know what makes a little rabbit like you so damn hard she doesn't flinch when a man presses a knife to her throat...*

The answer is easy. Numbness.

Emptiness.

A pit in the core of my being that I dump every ounce of emotion into. A pen and paper are the only keys to releasing them.

Soon, I'm pawing through my end table drawer for a notepad, then pouring out a series of lines onto the page. In some ways, writing like this always feels like bleeding —purging.

As my pen scratches away, I find myself glancing up, spotting the object nestled on my nightstand beside my lamp. The tiny golden dragon laughs at me, its embossed eyes gleaming.

I don't take my eyes off it as I scribble a title across the top of the page. *Liar.*

Maybe the man from the club had a point? Most of my writing centers around deception. Cheating. Lying.

It's emotionless.

Numb.

They're the only other states of being I'm good at embodying.

That, and being invisible. Safe. Unnoticed—until last night.

I eye my rabbit sweater lying on the top of my hamper with a pang of self-consciousness. *It looks to me like she ain't dressed to party. More like to poke her fucking nose around where it doesn't belong. A reporter?*

My outfit for today is even more muted, plain, and simple. To help lessen the effect, I drag a brush through my hair and arrange the strands around my face. It's no use. I'm still the same old Hannah with dark brown waves, green eyes, and a forehead obscured by a curtain of blunt bangs. In defeat, I adjust my sleeves, tugging them down to my wrists to hide anything that might counteract that boring image.

As the fabric runs over my right forearm, I jump. It's sore, throbbing if I focus on the pain for too long. So I ignore it, letting my hands fall to my sides as I enter my narrow living room.

It's neat, consisting of a battered couch, an armchair, and little else. Peeling beige paint coats the walls, creating a somewhat cozy atmosphere—minus the hole beside my door.

It's deep—a crater in the drywall, exposing the wooden guts beyond and part of the exterior.

There goes my deposit, a part of me remarks.

But I'm rubbing my arm again, unable to tear my gaze from the gaping, yawning hole.

Not until the musical ping of my cell phone accepting an incoming message cuts through the air.

You must have gone to bed early, Branden wrote. *Text me when you wake up. I know you work today. I miss your smile.*

A sigh escapes me as I reply—*I'm awake.*

Have a good day, he responds not even a second later.

I look up, eyeing my door. One of my first installations to this place when I moved in was a series of locks in addition to the deadbolt the door came with—four of them, all in a row.

Two sliding chains.

Two exterior deadbolts.

I undo them one by one and grab my bag before slipping out. They won't be enough—already, they haven't stopped their intended deterrent from getting in.

They never do.

CHAPTER THREE

Mr. Zhang is the nicest boss I've ever worked for. Admittedly, he's the only boss I've worked for, but I wouldn't trade him for any other. A kind, elderly man who immigrated to the US back in the 80s, he's a true bibliophile with a killer sense of humor to boot.

And he's been the most welcoming fixture since I moved to this neighborhood, letting me dive into the depths of his shop unrestrained. After barely a month of working for him, I'm already in love with every inch of the dusty old space.

In his world, Shakespeare shares a shelf with a series of adult-themed comics. Bronte and fashion magazines occupy the same vicinity, and books of poetry are sprinkled throughout the contemporary literature section like Easter eggs. Far too often, someone's innocent search for a book on the history of the San Francisco area brings him or her to a section also containing volumes of the Kama Sutra.

In a nutshell, it's paradise.

But paradise doesn't attract many customers these days. I don't have to be an accountant to know the shop is firmly in the red, and that Mr. Zhang continues to spend as though it isn't. The lack of sales contributes to a growing phenomenon I've noticed ever since I started working here. Some days, I'll come in to find an envelope wedged within the doorway. Mr. Zhang never tells me what they contain, though, with the arrival of each one, he closes up the shop a little earlier than usual.

After last night, I think I have a grimmer picture of what might be happening…

Let's say his uncle commands a lot of respect, and Rafe thinks he's hot shit just because he handles business for him.

No. I shake my head to clear it and refocus on the day ahead of me. It'll be a good one. Safe. Normal. A few hours of work, then Mara's spoken word, and no thoughts of the man from the club. Or Branden.

Just peace.

Teeth gritted in determination, I set my sights on the direction of the Paper Crane, and I'm only a block down when I hear a loud, musical smash that destroys my hopes in one fell swoop.

My pulse quickens before I even reach the storefront. At first glance, it looks like Mr. Zhang's fortunes may have changed overnight. A small crowd is gathered around the large window, showcasing our newest arrivals. Only now, half of the glass lies scattered over the pavement.

I can't seem to stop staring as my brain attempts to process the sight. The jagged edges of the hole create a dangerous landscape around the empty space. Piles of books lie scattered on the pavement, a soft breeze ruffling their pages.

And it finally sinks in. *Broken.* My footsteps falter as I scan the area for a wayward rock or a baseball bat. Anything that could cause so much damage. *Ha!* A part of me scoffs. *You know what really caused this…*

Or who.

"That old fool never learns." Behind me, an elderly woman mutters under her breath. "You can't toy with the triad. They always get their money back one way or another…"

My quickening heartbeat surges, the thrum of it swallowing her voice as I keep walking, eventually coming across a poor battered tourist handbook. Its glossy cover, featuring a photograph of the Golden Gate Bridge, has been marred by a dusty footprint, its shape dented. I stop short, stooping down to snatch the book from the ground. My fingers shake as I dust it off. Mr. Zhang wanted me to display these in the front, convinced they would attract new business.

In a way, he may have been right.

More people litter the sidewalk to gape at the mess than I've seen here at any one time other than rush hour. But rather than compliment the front display, they chatter mindlessly, speculating on what might have caused the disaster.

"Somebody pissed the bastard off," another woman murmurs.

"Let's hope he doesn't do more than just break the window…"

I swallow hard, letting their noise fade to a hum as my focus fixates on the charming brick-fronted building that has become my haven. Cautiously, I tuck the guidebook under my arm and approach the shop's entrance. The emerald green door is swinging awkwardly on its hinges, creating an eerie soundtrack to the scene awaiting me within. A masculine voice reaches my ears as I cross the threshold, but it isn't laced with Mr. Zhang's heavy accent.

"You've been missing payments," the man says, his snakelike hiss unsettlingly familiar. "Rather than show your gratitude for that mercy, it looks like you've been running your mouth. Mingling with reporters? We've let the lapses slide, but no more. I've decided that your 'protection' fee has doubled, in addition to what you already owe for your little 'hobby.' Bring the money to me by midnight. Until then, consider yourself closed."

"I-I can't! I don't know what you're even talking about. What reporter?" Mr. Zhang argues. He stands on the other side of the showroom floor, which I have to blink repeatedly just to recognize. Books are scattered all over, and entire shelves have been knocked out of the bookcases.

"I know some nosy bitch has been here," that guttural voice replies. "Don't lie to me."

"I'm not!" Mr. Zhang's wire-rimmed glasses perch crookedly on the edge of his nose, though he does his best to thrust his chin defiantly into the air. "And I will pay what I can. I've already told Mr. Shen that I just need more t-time—" He says something else that I can't understand. Another language.

The man facing him from the other end of the store laughs. "I don't give a fuck. Things have changed. Consider this a renegotiation of your 'loan.'"

It takes me only a second to recognize him. The muscular body, clothed in a leather jacket and dark jeans, creates a harsh silhouette, but that deep voice resonates in my skin. The owner of my new dragon-faced lighter.

He's leaning against a display of journals, holding a book open in the palm of his hand. Even from here, I can tell what it is. *Emily Dickinson's My Letter to the World and Other Poems*—the illustrated edition. It just so happens to be the only copy in the entire store—something Mr. Zhang had ordered at my request. My name is even written on a pink sticky note that the man absently rips off.

I'd saved up scraps from my last paycheck to afford it, but this monster has already damaged the precious collection. His fingers paint the pages red—courtesy of the blood dripping from his knuckles. At least now I have a pretty good idea of just what caused the damage to the window.

"Midnight, Mr. Zhang." He sighs while turning the page he's on. "I really am sorry it has come to this, but that's why you should be careful who you associate with—"

He breaks off, but it takes me a second to realize why. His dark eyes are in my corner, narrowed into slits. Mr. Zhang seems to notice me at the same moment.

"Y-You can go home today," he stammers, shaking his head. "We're closed. She's leaving," he insists to the other man. "She's leaving."

Rafe doesn't buy the lie. With a decisive *snap!* he closes the volume of Emily Dickinson. "Right on cue," he grates through clenched teeth. "The nosy little bunny rabbit."

Mr. Zhang frowns. "She works here."

Rafe cocks his head, stroking his chin. "Does she now?" He brandishes my book, unconcerned by the damage he's done. "Is that true, bunny?"

I say nothing.

Eyeing the blood he's smeared over the cover, I have the strangest thought. I wish I'd brought his lighter with me. One flick, and he'd go up in flames along with the defaced pages. A part of me flinches at the viciousness. Murder a man over a stupid book? *Yes.*

Because he picks his way through the carnage of the bookstore with a calm that betrays an unsettling familiarity with violence. More than that, he's relishing this moment and savoring the fear and every glimmering bit of broken glass.

What had he called me? *Rabbit.*

Well, he's a dog too damn cocky to care what carnage he may cause whenever he gnashes his teeth. That power is all he has.

It's all he craves.

I've spent my entire life learning how to navigate people like him, but I break the most important rule. I react.

"Why are you here?" I hear myself croak.

Shock distorts his features, disrupting the hard, chiseled expression. He almost appears human for five seconds. "Well, well, well," he murmurs. "You do work here. Maybe you're not a reporter after all?" But it's all an act. He saw my pen when he went through my bag. I know he did.

That's why he's here.

"Still, you've been behind on payments, old man," he says to Mr. Zhang. "It's time you caught up." Smirking in that cold, callous way, he turns and approaches the door, heedless of the crowd gaping beyond it. The lack of police presence makes me question if anyone even called them. Deep down, I know the answer. They haven't, and they won't.

"Midnight, Zhang," Rafe tosses over his shoulder along with an address. "Meet me there with the money. Or close up shop. Permanently."

I stare after him for what feels like an eternity before a series of thuds makes me turn to Mr. Zhang. He's clinging to a nearby bookshelf, knocking over the few remaining books from the display, his eyes bloodshot.

My chest tightens. I feel like I should turn away. Leave. Something about his reaction is so personal—private. I can't imagine what it's like to witness years of hard work reduced to scattered paper and broken glass.

"Are you all right…?" I start to approach him, but he shrugs off the hand I place on his shoulder.

"Go home!" He makes it sound so easy, but I don't even know what "home" is anymore.

My apartment is a cage where I'm lucky to find four hours of sleep, especially now. It feels like the moment I step foot over the threshold, everything I've been keeping in will spill out into the open.

He'll know.

He'll come.

He'll rage.

You disobeyed me, Hannah.

You failed, Hannah.

You need me, Hannah.

Lately, the Paper Crane, with its bright yellow walls and soothing scents of crisp paper, feels like the only place that comes close to deserving that term—*Home.*

But in one cruel moment, some sadistic bastard has waltzed right in and demolished any remaining peace I may have felt.

"This is my fault," I blurt out, setting the guidebook down on a crooked shelf. "Let me help you. How much money do you need?"

"Too much." He shakes his head. "The store is closed."

"*How* much?" I press. I have a few hundred in savings—though I doubt it would even be enough to cover the cost of the window repair, not to mention the damaged inventory.

But I'm not naïve. This won't end, even if he does pay. The man, who terrorized two women in a club and pilfered a copy of Emily Dickinson, doesn't strike me as the type to cease his demands for money, even if the Paper Crane does close.

Men like that don't read. They don't appreciate art. They steal and destroy, and he'll probably toss that book in the first trash can he comes across. This has everything to do with power.

"Maybe we should call the police?" I suggest. Then I realize how stupid I sound, and I snatch my phone from my pocket, swiping my thumb at the screen. "What am I even saying? I'm calling them now—"

"No!" Mr. Zhang worriedly eyes the broken window and the now dispersing crowd. "No police. That will just make this worse," he insists. "It's fine."

"Then at least tell me how much money you need." I don't know why I'm pushing this so hard. At worst, I'll have to find a new job, and that should be where my concern ends. I shouldn't feel so damn invested. So…angry.

But I am.

"He only did this because of me." Fury prickles in my bones like electricity, causing my fingers to tremble. It's so bad that I have to return my phone to my pocket or risk dropping it.

"Don't worry," Mr. Zhang continues to insist. "Don't worry—"

"A thousand?" I blurt out, taking a stab in the dark. "Five thousand?"

Mr. Zhang's eyes lower to the floor, and he shakes his head. My heart sinks.

"Double?" I have a feeling that it might even be *more* than that. How anyone could expect a single elderly man running a middling bookshop to come up with that sum of money in less than twenty-four hours is beyond me.

Then again, that's probably the point. To taunt and tease and set down impossible ultimatums, knowing they don't have a hope of being fulfilled.

That's how monsters get their way.

"Go, go!" Mr. Zhang commands, tugging at my arm. "Go now! Take the rest of the day off."

I allow him to shove me gently through the front door. I even manage to wave goodbye before heading back the way I'd come, but I can't forget what I've seen. Or *him.*

The memory of those dark, mocking eyes detracts from what is otherwise a beautiful day with a clear blue sky speckled by only a few clouds.

The sunlight is gossamer-thin, like a veil thrown over a nightmare. I keep seeing him everywhere. He's every man with broad shoulders passing by. Every discreet figure sporting a head of black hair or fathomless ebony eyes.

My paranoia grows with every step I take. Is he the figure leaning near the opening to an alley up ahead? Or the person across from me, crossing the street?

Or are people like him just roaches who scatter in the face of light…

"Watch out!" An unseen hand cinches my forearm and yanks me backward. I rock on my heels and glance down. I was only inches from stepping off the curb into the moving traffic.

"What were you daydreaming about, Hannah?" I turn to find my rescuer beaming, her black hair falling over the straps of her bright orange sundress.

"Mara?" I finally recognize my surroundings as the busy block housing the Chan's restaurant. Mr. Chan stands in the doorway, scanning the people passing by. I suspect it's almost time for the lunch rush, which explains why Mara has a stack of flyers tucked beneath one of her arms.

"Have the day off?" she asks.

"Y-yeah." I cross my arms over my chest and try to seem nonchalant. "Um…sort of."

"Sort of?" She gives me a funny look before shaking her head and reaching for one of the flyers. She holds it out for me to read. *A Night of Poetry (and free drinks)!* "Don't forget about the spoken word tonight. You coming? I promised you noodles on the house, and I plan to deliver."

A part of me wants to say yes, but thoughts of poetry only conjure a harsh voice proposing a single question—*You write about lying a lot, rabbit. Why is that?*

"Hannah?" Mara snaps her fingers beneath my nose. "You spaced out there for a minute. You're coming tonight, right?"

"I'm not sure. Maybe…"

"I've decided you are." Mara shrugs. "You have to. You can have anything you want off the menu on the house. Shit, not now—" She breaks off, glancing over her shoulder.

My eyes follow the same path, over to the front of the Chan Noodle House, and land on a tall figure looming over the smaller frame of Mr. Chan. The stranger's black hair clashes with the red awning shading the restaurant entrance.

Rafe.

Beside me, Mara stiffens. "I have to go—"

"It's him again," I rasp. Apparently, I'm not the only one he decided to visit today. He's speaking to Mr. Chan, his words inaudible. "Is he threatening you? You should call the police—"

"No," Mara says, her teeth clenched. "Just leave it alone, Hannah. Anyway, I'll see you tonight if you're coming to the spoken word."

When she approaches the two men, the taller one turns, and our eyes meet. My stomach clenches in recognition, but his expression reveals nothing as he brushes past Mara and disappears into the crowd. I can only watch as the Chans duck inside the noodle house while my mind grapples with what just happened.

I start for my apartment, but I don't even go a block down before I smell it.

Smoke.

"You can't keep clear of things that don't concern you, eh?" The closeness of his voice startles me. I stumble forward a few steps, but I can't resist turning to face him.

In the ten minutes since he terrorized Zhang, he's managed to wrap his injured hand with a rag, but blood is already seeping through the gray fabric. My book is nowhere in sight, and I eye his pockets, searching for its distinct shape against the leather.

Thus, my earlier theory is strengthened. He's already trashed it.

"You wouldn't be following me, now would you?" he taunts before I can respond to his original question. "Reporter or not a reporter? You certainly scurry around like one."

I clench my jaw shut and eye my surroundings for an exit. If I shift a little to the right, I could slip past him and race for my apartment. Yet despite how my toes flex in my sandals, I never move.

He's standing just far enough away from me to prevent arousing alarm in any nearby bystander. Regardless, he's so close that I feel the body heat wafting from him anyway. And he's so tall that I have to crane my neck just to see his face clearly.

"Not so talkative today, huh?" His lips twitch. He almost seems disappointed. The same way a cat gets bored when the mouse it's toying with doesn't fight back. "All that courage seep away overnight, rabbit?"

Leave, my intuition warns. I press my heel to the pavement, shifting my weight to move. I don't know why my lips part, a question spilling from them. "Where's my journal?"

He chuckles. "Where it belongs, bunny. In the fucking trash."

I grit my teeth as a flush of alarm creeps into my skin. Is he lying? I can't tell from his sneer. Anger festers, biting through my usual resolve, and another question springs to my tongue before I have the sense to choke it down. "Where's your lighter?" I blink, mortified by the shift in my tone…mocking?

His eyes widen and narrow as a dawning realization flits across his features. "Little bitch..." He sounds angry, but a contradictory smile shapes his mouth, stealing my breath. "*You* wouldn't happen to know, would you?"

"No," I lie in a rush.

"I think you do." He eyes my hands as if I'd be stupid enough to dangle it before him. Though maybe I should flick the flame in his face and see how he'd react to having the tables turned...

A pang of alarm makes me frown, and I back up another step. This isn't like me. Because of *him*. He feeds on these dark thoughts I'm not used to thinking. The hate I'm not used to feeling.

At any other moment, it's so easy to suppress it all.

But he's like a flame licking at the thin wick linked to my control. One taste of his fire, and I can't slow the blaze.

"If I do know where it is..." I lick my lips, meeting his gaze. "I don't think you deserve to have it."

"Oh, really?" Within an instant, he's towering over me, his eyes like black coals. "And why is that?"

I stare ahead, desperate to ignore the heat of his breath on my cheek. He still smells like coconut and cigarette smoke. Forbidden. Wrong. But my nostrils twitch to take him in anyway. "Because...you'll only use it to terrorize people."

"Terrorize. Is that what you think I do, rabbit?" He almost sounds unsure. As if he's traumatized so many people that he can't really be sure of the lasting damage—or he just doesn't care.

"Yes."

He's standing way too close now. Other people are forced to maneuver around us, casting us strange looks as they do.

"So then why should I stop now?" His breath sears like the blast from a furnace, and I take another step back, nearly bumping into a woman sporting a designer purse and an irritated glare.

He follows, still laughing. Taunting. "You stole from me, didn't you, rabbit?" he murmurs. "What are you going to give me to make up for it?"

"Nothing. I'm not afraid of you."

"You should be," he taunts, his smile ripe. "Do you know the only time a rabbit screams? When it thinks it's going to die. There any truth to that?"

"Is that a threat?" I cut my gaze to his bloodied knuckles.

He copies me, but the emotion I catch flitting across his face isn't triumph—far from it—and I hate myself for noticing it. Unease contradicts his entire image, at least until he blinks, and all traces of emotion vanish. "Fair is fair," he says, flattening his mouth into a cold, hard line. "So, what are you willing to trade?"

"T-Trade?" I back up another step. "Like hell would I ever make a deal with you."

"Not even to save dear old Mr. Zhang?" His tongue shoots out to wet his lower lip. "No… A girl like you. You may not be a reporter, but you play in the slums for 'enrichment,' is that it? You'll run back to your little McMansion like a good girl when shit gets real. So, go on. Run…"

His eyes narrow as he glances over my head. Confused, I turn and catch a flash of telltale blue fabric mingling with the crush of pedestrians a block down. The closer the figure approaches, the easier it is for me to make out the silhouette of a uniform I know well—an officer, but not just anyone out on patrol.

"Bye, bunny." Without another word, Rafe shoves past me, bumping my shoulder hard, and lumbers down the street in the opposite direction.

I catch myself watching him—staring. He moves without a care in the world.

While I falter, trapped in the path of a man who frowns when he spots me. "Hannah? What are you doing down here?"

"Hey, Liam," I croak.

Tall, with a head of brown hair, the officer approaches me. "Hey." He looks me over, his eyes narrowing. "Your brother know you're out here?"

I force a nod. "I'm working today."

He frowns. "We got a call from that part of town. I'm on my way there. Everything okay?"

"I don't know. I… I'm on break. I have to go."

"Alright, well, look out for yourself." He continues his patrol as I scurry beyond his range of sight.

Despite the blazing sunlight, I'm numb down to my fingertips by the time I finally reach the block where my apartment building is located. However, it isn't long before determination washes through my veins and banishes the coldness away.

You'll run back to your little McMansion like a good girl when shit gets real, won't you? So, go on. Run.

It's stupid to get involved. It *is*. I desperately try to tell myself that as I fish my cell phone from my pocket and dial a number I know by heart.

A charming baritone answers on the second ring. "Hannah, pumpkin?"

"Hi, Daddy." I'm near the entrance to my building now, but rather than head inside, I pace the strip of concrete in front of the door.

"Hi, darling. I have a meeting in a bit, so I can't talk long."

"I know it's a little late notice, but…" I swallow hard before blurting my request out in a rush. "I need some money."

"Are you in trouble?" His tone deepens with concern.

"N-No!" *Yes.* "Unless…you count not being able to purchase the new Michael Kors purse before they all sell out 'trouble.'" I wince at the lie. "It's nothing serious, I promise."

"Kors…a purse?" Suspicion laces his every word. "Since when are you interested in fashion?"

I glance down at my vintage sweater, cargo pants, and sandals—all found at a thrift shop for less than ten dollars total. "Since…now?"

"How much do you need?"

It seems way too easy, and my stomach churns when I spout off a random figure. "Ten thousand."

"Done," he says before I can even start to feel guilty, and somehow, his trust makes it so much worse. "I'll make some calls, and it will be in your account within the hour."

"Thank you."

"And…how are things?" he adds. "With you and Bran?"

"Fine."

"And school?"

"We're on summer break," I say, though I feel we had this same conversation the last time I spoke to him. And the time before that. His reply even sounds the same.

"Oh, that's nice, honey."

"I plan to submit for an internship in the fall," I add, mainly to hear myself talk. Acknowledge my achievements out loud. "I could shadow an editor for a while. Learn what it takes to be published—"

"Do you think that's a good idea?" Daddy questions. For once, he's actually listened, but his reaction also isn't that much of a shock. "What does Branden think about it? He's been good, lately, Hannah. Moving out there has been good for him—" He pauses as if waiting for me to argue, but I don't. I never do. "I know you have your hobbies, Hannah. I know they're important to you, but try not to dig up the past too much. It hurts us, you know. Me…your mother… Branden. I know you're proud of your story, but we are still fielding questions from nosy neighbors who are reading into it more than they should."

"It was one article," I say softly, but the guilt cuts deep. Even a vague short story invites judgment. Annoyance. I mourn the loss of my journal now more than ever—the one place I could store my thoughts without being judged.

"Darling…" He sighs. "Think of your brother. You know what it's been like for him—all the rumors. You've always been his champion, honey, and he's always been yours. People will take any little thing they can twist to fit their narrative."

"I'm sorry," I say for what has to be the tenth time since the article was first published.

"I know. Anyway, you can count on the money being in your account by tonight."

I don't question how he can possibly arrange the transfer on such short notice. My father and money are enigmas to me—but, for once, his cavalier attitude toward it plays in my favor.

"Thank you, Daddy."

"Anything for my princess. That's what family is for," he insists. "We *help* each other, no matter the cost."

And I know what he means.

Either monetarily, or with our very souls, we pay the price of being family.

I get ready for bed robotically, dressing in my comfy sweats and braiding my hair into two plaits. My reflection in the bathroom mirror stares back at me warily until I finally turn away.

Entering my living room, I lounge on my couch directly across from my small television, and the tiny, broken device propped on top of it.

With my arm extended, I smile and snap a selfie with my cell phone. Then I send it to Branden with a quick message. *Long day, heading to bed early. Night!*

His reply takes only seconds to come. *Good night. I'll have Liam drive by to check on you. He saw you in town earlier. You know I don't like you wandering the streets outside of work.*

I swallow hard and compose a reply. *Just got some lunch. Night!*

It's like an invisible timer ticks down as I stand and turn off all the lights but the one in my bedroom. In the semi-darkness, I sneak to my window and wait, watching the street. Ten minutes later, a patrol car cruises by, and I know its driver is looking up, searching for my floor. He'll expect me to wave, so I do, smiling brightly.

He flashes his lights in a silent greeting and then drives off.

And the second he's out of view, I strip my sweats and change into a sweater and jeans. Then I grab my bag and slip from my apartment, creeping down the stairs as if Branden can hear me all the way from Santa Barbara.

It's surprisingly quiet out at this time of night. Shadows lurk on the street corners, and I can almost hear them whispering "idiot" as I creep past.

The same old worry crosses my mind. Branden would kill me if he knew. That is, if some criminal or thief doesn't beat him to the punch.

What the heck am I doing out here? On what? A savior mission?

Or a suicidal one…

Thankfully, I'm not completely naïve and have a can of pepper spray in my bag. My cell phone is at the ready in my pocket, with my thumb hovering over the speed dial for emergency services.

It's not enough. A phone call won't stop a knife or a gun.

Or a man capable of smashing glass with his bare hands.

The fragile peace of mind gives me the strength to keep walking, though. It isn't long before the distinct shape of the Paper Crane comes into focus. Shadows drape the broken storefront along with ribbons of bright yellow caution tape that glow in the light of a nearby streetlamp. Before I even reach the front door and tug on the handle to find it locked, I know Mr. Zhang isn't here.

Disappointment gnaws at my stomach. Or maybe it's more like *desperation*?

What am I even doing out here? I should leave. Go home. Search through the local job listings.

Instead, I turn on my heel and find myself wandering down the block in another direction. The events of the day unfurl in my mind, and one tidbit of information stands out. Before I can talk myself out of it, I'm already typing what little I remember into the search engine on my cell phone.

The address turns out to be on the other side of town, nestled among a bunch of abandoned warehouses. I think it's near Fisherman's Wharf, but this area isn't dominated by the glitzy markings of a tourist trap. I don't know what to expect when I approach a building with graffiti scrawled across its brick façade. A glass door only reveals a shadow-covered hallway beyond, but it's unlocked, and a smell like wet metal itches my nose when I cross over the threshold.

"H-Hello?" My voice travels on a seemingly endless echo. A dead end? This place is abandoned, obviously. I start to turn back just as someone answers from the darkness.

"…I'm trying," a woman insists, though she isn't speaking to me. Her voice is soft, betraying her age. Young. Early twenties? "But you don't know what it's like. It's not like I can just walk away."

"Why can't you?" a gruffer voice replies. Rafe. "Just turn the bastard in for prostitution, and break whatever fucking hold he has over you. You said he texts you? That's evidence."

"It's not that easy," the woman says. "I'm sure he uses a burner, especially now. After what you did… He's fucking insane. I have no idea what he's going to do now. They all probably know I'm the one who—"

"You did the right thing. That's it."

"Did I?" the woman questions. "I can't hide from him forever. Whether or not you want to play the role of hero, I have to go."

Light footsteps start in my direction too quickly to evade. Up ahead, a slender figure rounds an unseen corner. Dark hair spills down her shoulders, obscuring the neckline of her tight, pink minidress. Smoky makeup enhances the shadows that shroud her face, and the only detail I can make out clearly is a sparkly bit of material glinting in her hair. A hair clip?

The closer she comes, the clearer it is to make out—a tiny silvery butterfly.

"I hope I wasn't interrupting anything," she calls back to Rafe, eyeing me up and down as she walks by. "It looks like your next damsel in distress is already here."

She leaves as I struggle to place her. She's familiar, but how?

I don't have long to contemplate. Low with impatience, a voice calls from deeper in the building, "In here."

My heart races as I fumble forward and feel along the wall for another door. It opens easily onto a hallway where a pool of yellow light floods from a doorway a few yards down. Soon, my surging pulse is the sole sound I can hear above my footsteps. *Thump.* Step. *Thump.*

Observing my surroundings provides a minimal distraction from the building fear. The walls are a faded cream, and a flickering fluorescent bulb hanging from the ceiling barely casts enough light to illuminate half the room.

But a thousand faces stare back. Most of them gawk from various pieces of paper in all sizes affixed to the wall. Lined paper. Faded parchment. Canvas…

Drawings. They take up nearly every inch of available space like windows into a twisted psyche. One that views the world in vibrant shades of light and shadow. The artist's style is distinct with bold, sharp lines and painstaking detail.

As much as I cringe from the descriptor, my brain keeps cycling back to one word, over and over. *Beautiful.* I'm left gaping like an idiot until something new draws my gaze.

In the center of the room, beneath the glow of the lamp, stands a figure not composed of ink or charcoal. His back is to me, and I assume his shirt is the wadded bit of white cloth lying on the floor a few feet away. Chiseled muscle sculpts his shoulders, giving definition to the impressive red and black dragon tattoo spanning the length of his upper body. Its ruby-colored eyes burn into my own, its fiery breath blazing down his left forearm.

"Huh." His voice draws my gaze back to his face as he takes me in with a single glance over his shoulder. "It's you. How did I know it would be you…?"

I recall the quip the girl sent his way and feel my cheeks flush. Just how many "damsels" are waiting in line to visit him tonight? Though the topic of his previous conversation didn't sound like it revolved around sex. More like he was trying to convince the woman to do something…

And she was afraid of someone.

"I assume you're here for a reason," Rafe prompts, snapping my attention back to him.

I relinquish my grip on my phone and fish a stiff envelope from my purse. "H-Here's your money." I jab it toward him when he doesn't move. "Take it. Now you can leave Mr. Zhang alone."

"Zhang…" With deliberate slowness, his eyes fall to the envelope, and he sneers. "Oh, little rabbit. You struck me as the type."

My hand trembles, causing the envelope to waver back and forth. "The type to what?"

"To take it upon your good-natured soul to beg *Daddy* or some rich uncle for the cash." He turns back to the canvas with a dismissive shrug. "Tell Zhang that his payment is still due."

"You can't…You can't do that—"

"Why not?" He turns to face me fully, and I flinch.

His scent of coconut without the blood strikes me first. My eyes register his appearance second. There's a small, white bandage taped over his battered knuckles. Unconcerned by any pain, he holds my gaze with an intensity that chills me right to the bone.

"You made this about me, didn't you?" I counter. "I'm not a reporter."

He scoffs.

"And you only picked on him to prove a point, right?" I raise the money again. "Well, this is me, fixing it."

"You have no clue what you've stuck your meddling nose into, rabbit," he taunts in an almost pitying tone. "I suggest you leave."

Only then do I notice what he holds in his left hand. It's slender, and I flinch instinctively. A knife? No. A long stick of wood with a vibrant red tip that matches the stripes of paint streaking the canvas behind him. A paintbrush.

"Tell me something," he adds before I can obey his command. "You came all the way here, carrying this much cash." He nods to the envelope. "For Zhang?" He chuckles when I nod and runs his free hand through his hair. From behind a wayward lock of it, those dangerous eyes cut in my direction. "Are you alone?"

I take two hasty steps back. Then another. "N-No." My eyes drift to the exit, and I can tell from the way he smiles that he suspects the truth. "I'm not."

"Let me guess," he muses, playing along. "That boyfriend of yours is lurking outside, huh? Bran with the heart?" He practically scoffs the nickname. "Maybe you should scream for him now, rabbit—"

"My boyfriend? Y-Yes." I seize upon the lie. "He's waiting for me. He knows where I am. And… he's a cop."

"I'm shaking, rabbit." The mocking tilt to his mouth steals my breath away. I back up even more while he starts to advance, trapping me within the sliver of space right before the door; a stack of framed canvas is all that blocks my path.

"It's not just money that Zhang owes," he says, his breath hot on my face. "It's respect. Loyalty. If he wants to hire even a little nosy bunny, he knows better than to not go through me. The money is a mere *token*." I can't move without touching him now because he pins me in with his bulk alone. "You want to pay for him? Then offer something that means more to you than money."

My arm falls dejectedly by my side. "What do you mean?"

I *know* what he means, and my chest heaves beneath my thin, navy sweater. Knitted cotton isn't nearly thick enough to protect against his gaze.

He looks at me all wrong. That dangerous way…

A fox eyeing a delicious rabbit.

"Take a guess," he dares. My senses scatter as he leans in close and brings the paintbrush up to leave a dab of red along my cheek. I jump, though it's little more than lukewarm paint. "I think you know what," he murmurs, flicking his gaze down to my chest. "Something *important* to you."

He makes his intentions very clear when he waggles his eyebrows.

"Fuck you." I put everything I have into making my voice sound as scathing as possible.

"Fuck me." His smile widens as he traces his bottom lip with the tip of his tongue. "Now there's an offer I might consider—"

"Get away from me!" I try to push past him, but his hand latches on my forearm.

"Not so fast."

My brain stalls. Self-preservation replaces every ounce of fear. Endurance fails. Nothing matters but getting away, and I resort to the dirtiest of tactics I know. Hollowing my cheeks, I spit in his face.

"The fuck?" He rears back, swiping at his jaw, and I succeed in shoving past him, my eyes on the door.

Before I even go a single step, he grabs my shoulder and yanks me back. My arm flies out and strikes a pile of paintings, sending them toppling, but the clamor doesn't faze him.

"Would you?" He tightens his grip until I wince. All trace of mocking is gone from his tone, and it's icier than ever. "Would you trade yourself to pay Zhang's debt?"

"Let *go* of me."

"Answer the fucking question. Would you?" The choice is too dangerous to even contemplate. So he spells it out with a sneer and a whisper. "Fuck a stranger to save an old man?"

"I said, let go of me!"

"Just admit it," he goads, unconcerned by my struggle. "Because I think deep down, you knew what coming here alone really meant, rabbit. What was it?" He lowers his mouth to my ear. "You wanted to earn your Girl Scout badge? Do your good deed for the day? Girls like you are all the same. You want to save the world but run scared shitless when you discover that protection comes with a price. The others learned their lesson. But with you? Maybe I'll make an exception—"

Pepper spray. I reach into my bag, but he surprises me by backing away with both hands raised before I can activate the nozzle. Another coy smile distorts his lips. "Careful. Don't do anything you'll regret."

"You too." I stare at the bandage on his hand pointedly. "Don't touch me. If you think you can use Mr. Zhang as a bargaining chip to assault me, you can think again."

My bottom lip trembles, undermining how intimidating I might seem. God, I can't breathe.

Trade. Trade. I hate that he's right. Money alone would have been too damn easy. Even Mr. Zhang had alluded to the truth that his debt went way beyond a few dollars. *Blood money.* And if it all wasn't paid tonight, then what fate might await an elderly man too terrified to even call the police? What might the bastard before me obliterate next beyond the glass of a display window?

The thoughts won't stop coming. One. Right. After. The. Other.

But I'm not shaking in the face of them.

Again, I feel like my blood is boiling, feeding off the rage only he has ever inspired in me before. It's…intoxicating.

"You couldn't just leave it at stealing books? Though I doubt you even know how to read. You want to add r-rape to your repertoire?" Disgust laces my tone, along with flecks of spittle that strike his bare chest. "You're pathetic!"

"Again, the little rabbit speaks." He strokes his chin, eyeing me through a heavy-lidded gaze. His intentions are harder to read this way, his motives impossible to guess. "The way you run your fucking mouth… I bet you really *are* a screamer, rabbit."

I recoil against a nearby table. "You're sick!"

"I am." Another laugh rumbles from his chest as he shrugs. "I don't know about rape. But I'll tell you what I *really* want." He comes even closer this time. By sheer willpower, I bite back a scream when he reaches out, snagging the hem of my shirt with fingers streaked with scarlet paint.

"I want to play, little bunny. An hour," he proposes as cool air ghosts my belly. Winding his fingers, he lifts the hem of my sweater higher, higher… "You're mine. I do whatever the fuck I want to you. You can't say shit after. By tomorrow, Mr. Zhang can consider himself debt-free, and you get to skip away happily, having done your good deed for the day."

I skirt the rim of the table behind me, nearly tripping in my haste to back away. "Get the hell away from me—"

"That's the offer." His tone dares me to challenge him. "Accept. Or Zhang gets his fucking knees broken the next time he misses a payment. How is that for a deal?" He smiles as I feel the color drain from my face—but that was his aim. To horrify. His tone lacked conviction, the words falling flat as if he's dished out the same threat a million times.

"Why can't you just leave him alone?" I sound so childish, so plaintive, wailing about injustice to the face of a criminal.

He scoffs. "Let's cut the bullshit. Don't pretend he's the reason you're even here. Because he's not, is he?" He advances, casting a shadow that drenches me in darkness. "No. I saw your face when you ran your mouth back at the shop. You get off on this shit, don't you? This is *fun* for you. You write in that little fucking notebook, but you aren't used to bitching out loud, is that it?"

Fun. My cheeks flame. Arguing with him isn't even worth the battle. I eye the money in my hands instead, then turn on my heel, scrambling for the door.

"You aren't afraid of me," he continues as my steps falter. "No… I think you're just as curious as I am to find out. What will it take to make the little rabbit scream?"

"Not you." I don't even know where the words come from. So bitter, so damn angry, they don't sound like me. *You aren't used to bitching out loud, is that it?* "You're pathetic."

"And you're a desperate, bored little suburban girl dying on the inside. Is this how you get your kicks?" I jump as movement catches my peripheral vision. His fingers snag a tendril of my hair and tug, forcing me to face him. "I'm giving you every chance to leave now, rabbit."

Running is what I should do because it's what I've always done. When it comes to Branden. The world. Everyone.

I don't know what makes him so different. What it is about his gaze that consumes my interest, making it impossible to shy from? Or his taunts unbearable to endure…his hatred so electrifying that I'm buzzing with it.

"You're disgusting," I rasp.

"So prove it." He takes another step, palming my hips without an ounce of hesitation. I jump, cringing at the feel of his heat leeching through my sweater, but he doesn't back away. "Be a good little martyr, then," he taunts against my ear. "Run away. Scream. I'll wait."

He does so patiently, his hands unmoving.

And it's the worst thing he could do.

There is no brutal groping. No harsh contact meant to intimidate. He merely lets his fingers settle against me as if daring me to pull away. React.

But I've spent so long training myself to endure that I've forgotten how to feel. And he feels…

Wrong. Too warm. Hot. Burning. Sizzling. Hateful.

His eyes narrow as if he's reading my mind, and he angles his jaw, his lips parting. A gust of his breath rustles my hair, enhancing my perception of every ounce of flesh laid bare before him.

Before I can regain my senses, his fingers flex, yanking me closer, his eyes cutting down to my chest. I feel my hands twitch to shield myself, but they never move. And he just stares, raking me over with that impassive gaze. He lets his hand graze lower until he finds the sliver of space where the sweater's hem meets my skin.

And he teases that strip with the tip of his nail, watching avidly as I flinch. Twitch. But it isn't until his brows draw together that I realize what has him so confused.

I'm not pulling away.

So he shoves his hand beneath the sweater entirely, shocking my flesh with a scalding assault of heat. I jump in my rush to cringe from his reach.

But he just chuckles.

"You'd let me do whatever the fuck I wanted to do, wouldn't you?" His tone is mocking enough, but a frown tugs on his mouth, betraying his true emotion—irritation.

His rabbit won't resist the feral teeth bared for her throat.

"Fuck yeah, you would." Bored, he turns away, shrugging his shoulder dismissively. "Hop away, rabbit. We're done."

"W-What?" Looking up, I catch him lumbering across the room. Once again, I cease to exist to him. My actions no longer matter—not even when my fingers snatch something from his table as if of their own accord.

"I said leave," he snaps as my hand slips into my bag, depositing a scrap of paper inside. "Zhang can consider himself cleared…for now. I'll collect my payment later."

"What do you mean?"

He scoffs. "I mean you should scurry away before I change my mind, rabbit."

I don't challenge him this time. I just run, powering forward until I'm outside, hurrying down the street. Only when he's safely in the distance, do I find myself withdrawing the slip of paper. My hands shake as I unfurl it, but I'm forced to smooth it out against the side of a nearby building to appreciate the image in full.

A laboriously sketched dragon rages, seemingly alive though formed out of ink and bold lines. Its eyes meet mine unflinchingly, proposing a question I'm not brave enough to answer.

You'd let him do whatever the fuck he wanted to you, wouldn't you?

I crumble it into a ball and start toward a nearby trash can. In the end, I return it to my bag instead. As I head home, I grit my teeth, desperate to ignore that niggling question.

Would I have?

My racing heartbeat provides the answer my pride refuses to acknowledge.

Given his personality, I'm sure I'll find out soon enough.

CHAPTER FIVE

It's amazing what a shower can do. Soothe aching muscles, and wash away the dirt and grime left by a stranger's groping fingertips. Lies, too. The spray of water even disguises the tears spilling from my eyes, and for one brief second, all my worries disappear into a wad of terry cloth and soap. Once the water shuts off, however, they find me again.

The second I step into a towel, the ping of my cell phone becomes a chilling reminder of the hell my life has become. My hand shakes as I snatch the device from the counter where I left it. The screen flashes with a predictable message from Branden. *Good morning. Text when you're awake. I miss your smile.*

But there's another lurking beneath his from a number I don't recognize. *Please, Hannah. Lexi deserves justice. Please call me.*

I block that number without a second thought and change into a sweater and jeans. When I enter my living room, my phone lights up again, a text message from Mara this time. *Missed you last night! Wanna go out tonight?*

I don't answer. Instead, I leave my building and head to the Paper Crane. It's still boarded up, the broken glass replaced with plywood. A crude, handwritten sign on the door proclaims *Closed indefinitely*, with a list of nearby bookstores to visit instead.

Because even in his own dire straits, Mr. Zhang still can't ignore the quest for a good book.

Rather than obey the sign, I cut around to the side alley and approach a door I've only ever entered through on my very first day when I came to interview for the job. I knock once to silence. Then again.

It's chilly out despite the sun blazing down. I'm forced to wrap my arms around myself as I pace the narrow space before the door. Finally, its hinges squeal as it's cautiously opened from the inside. "What do you want?" A pair of wary eyes peeks out from the thinnest crack.

"Here." I reach into my bag and withdraw a battered envelope. "It's probably not much, all things considered, but it should be enough to at least help replace some of the stock. Here. Take it."

He doesn't. "You should leave." The thin crack vanishes as the door slams shut.

I watch the envelope of money tremble over the filthy concrete below as my hand wavers. "I want to work. I can pick up trash. Whatever you need," I say to the silence. "I… I need to work."

The tremble of desperation in my voice can't be faked. Hours in the bookstore have become a welcome escape for me. Otherwise, nothing prevents me from sitting in my apartment and staring into space as Branden stares back.

"Please…"

I don't know how much time passes before those rusty hinges squeal again, and someone gingerly pries the money from my grasp.

"You're a good girl." Mr. Zhang sighs as he opens the envelope and starts to count the assorted bills inside. "Too good. You want to work?" He jerks his chin toward the front of the shop. "Go in, and you start fixing up. You're right, this isn't much…" He pockets the money, but then his lips part in a quick, warm grin before I can truly feel any guilt. "But it's enough for the window, at least. Here. Go."

He fishes something else from his pocket and tosses it to me. I barely manage to catch the shop keys. "They're spares," he says. "You can help me organize everything for the insurance adjusters when you have the time."

I nod, fighting a grin. "You've got it."

When I circle back around to the main street and duck beneath a lazily hung string of caution tape, I find that the inside of the shop isn't much better than the day the damage was inflicted. Sighing, I toss my bag behind the counter, open the utility closet, and set to work.

Some of the books are damaged beyond salvation, but I can't bear to throw them away. Instead, I set them aside in a careful stack near the door that soon towers over the smaller pile of books worth selling.

Broken glass litters nearly every surface, and I don't have a chance in hell of moving any of the heavier shelves by myself. Still, it feels good to help in *some* way.

With diligent effort and the aid of a broom, little by little, some semblance of peace begins to rebuild itself.

"Hey." I glance up from a dusty volume of Dickinson's complete works to find Mr. Zhang standing before me. He's wearing his gray bowler hat and maroon sweater. "Time to go," he says. "You did good." He eyes the neatly swept floors and stacks of books scattered throughout with a thoughtful shrug. "Help yourself to something to read tonight. You've earned it."

Once he leaves, I stand from my crouched position beside one of the damaged shelves and stretch out the cramped muscles in my legs. Darkness casts swaths of shadows over the majority of the shop, and it almost resembles some secret stash of forgotten tomes. The mainstream novels on the central display are the dusty histories of some lost king or queen, their glossy covers ageless in the twilight.

It's the perfect atmosphere to write, and my heart pangs for my journal. Luckily, I spy a pile of printer paper that I can make do with, so I circle around the counter for my bag on the hunt for a pen. I've barely touched the fabric when the bell above the door sounds, catching my attention.

"Sorry," I say, "we're closed."

The intruder's smell reaches me first—coconut—before my eyes find him slouched against the entrance. I lunge for the nearest light switch and flick it on, throwing his body in stark relief.

"I thought you'd wised up, rabbit." There's a rough quality to his voice that rides my spine in an unsettling thrill. Amusement? "Yet here you are, still hopping around."

"You're trespassing," I croak, still toeing the threshold of the dingy back room where we keep new books along with outdated computer equipment and a few plastic trash bags full of broken glass waiting to be taken to the dump.

"I'm protecting my investment," he replies on a sigh. "Zhang's debt didn't magically pay itself. For all intents and purposes, I own this place."

I frown in confusion. Is he implying he covered the tab himself?

Without explaining, he steps inside and props the door open with his knee. Then he slaps something onto the topmost half of it above the welcome sign.

"What are you doing?" I skirt the counter and creep forward as close as I dare. On top of the peeling emerald paint is a small circular red sticker. It's surprisingly detailed with a black fire-breathing dragon in the center.

"I'm keeping my word," he says, letting the door slam shut. But he's on the wrong side of it, spinning around to face me. His mouth twists into something that could be a smile, but it just illuminates the dark circles lurking underneath his eyes. "Don't look so surprised, bunny," he chides. "This place is still under my protection. And I expect it to earn back every penny." He runs a hand through his hair, turning to the nearest lopsided bookshelf. "I also expect the workers here to do their fucking jobs."

As I watch, he crosses to the fallen shelf and lifts it easily, attempting to slot it back into place. He grunts, his forearms straining with the effort, but eventually, he assembles it properly.

Then he crosses to a stack of salvaged books.

It's almost surreal to watch him place them haphazardly onto the shelf in the wrong positions. There's no method to his madness, and when he arranges a popular romance novel next to a critically acclaimed thriller, pride can no longer keep me silent.

"That goes over here," I blurt out before moving the book to its correct spot on the other side of the shop.

Either he doesn't hear me, or he doesn't really care, seeing as how he never stops his careless stacking. I don't know why I find myself following in his wake to either tweak the placement or to stare in shock when he manages to place something in the right spot.

Soon, one stack becomes several. He reassembles more shelving units, and eventually, we've restocked the rest of the undamaged merchandise.

"Why are you here?" I direct the question from over my shoulder, hoping he won't answer.

Because he'll leave.

"I'm asking you the same question."

"I *work* here."

"For how long? All things considered, I own this shop now, rabbit. I prefer my employees to have more spine."

With a sigh, I turn to face him. The shadows paint his skin, turning him into a patchwork creation of darkness and light. My eyes don't know which part of him to settle on first—or how to interpret this man who's made up of so many contradicting hues of ivory, silver, and ebony.

In the end, I pick his hair, as the pure, harmless black seems to be the least threatening element to focus on.

"Ask me what you *really* want to know," he demands. His voice catches me off guard. It's too guttural, his breath searing the nape of my neck as I turn my attention to the opposite end of the room. Anywhere but him. "Ask it."

"You said I owe you a debt," I croak. "What do you want?"

"What do you think I want?" He takes a step closer, but there's a dangerous edge to his tone—a demand he hasn't uttered out loud—yet.

I lick my lips, desperate to stall. Combat him. Anything. "I think you want to annoy me. What are you, some kind of criminal?"

I look back just in time to catch his eyes narrowing—it's not the question he expected. Nonetheless, he has an answer ready. "Maybe I am, rabbit. But that wouldn't scare you, would it? No…" He leans in, his nostrils flaring as if he can smell the truth on my skin. "You love knowing that I'm some dirty little fiend you can sneer down your nose at. It makes it easier to play with fire if you *know* you'll get burned."

I turn away, hissing through my teeth. "You don't know me—"

"Don't have to. It's written all over that pretty face," he interjects. "You can never hide who you really are for long, *Hannah*."

I glance back to find his eyes on my name tag pinned to my sweater. It's the first time he's actually called me by my real name, but his voice catches over the syllables, distorting the pronunciation. Harmless Hannah transforms into something else. Something guttural and dangerous.

"But judging from the shit you wear, that's all you're good at doing. Hiding."

I self-consciously finger the hem of my sweater. It's even thicker than my bunny one. "So now you're a criminal *and* a fashion expert."

"Better," he corrects. Another step and his shadow cuts my body in half. "I'm a criminal who can fucking read."

He reaches into his jacket and withdraws an item he either carries around for moments like this, or he brought with the sole intent to seek me out—my journal.

"Give it back." I reach for it, but he dangles it just beyond my reach, letting the pages sway.

"You want it, rabbit? Where's my lighter?"

I stiffen, reaching into my pocket. A part of me despairs at relinquishing my one bit of leverage over him, for about a second. Even the thought of him pawing through my journal again makes me relent. "Here."

I present it on my palm, and he snatches it. Juggling my journal, he grabs a cigarette from his pocket, then flicks the lighter one-handed and ignites the end.

Shoving the lighter back into my hand, he turns for the door.

Confused, I stare down at the ombre object before returning it to my pocket. As I do, my head swivels in his direction, tracking his retreat. "Wait! Give me my journal—"

"Come and get it, bunny. Hop this way." He inclines his head for me to follow before he exits the shop entirely, letting the door slam.

I ignore the barb, preferring to focus on the obvious. I should leave. I am. Returning to the counter, I grab my bag, then I approach the door and cautiously pull it open. He isn't lurking outside it.

Instead, he stands across the street, leaning against the entrance to another building—a run-down coffee shop I sometimes grab lunch at.

Determined to stay focused, I start down the block. A few more paces, and I'll be home. But above the hum of traffic and passing pedestrians, my ears catch a distant, high-pitched whistle.

Don't look. I won't…

It's too late. My chin tilts, bringing him within my line of view again. He's still leaning against the doorway with a smile playing on his mouth, visible from here. It's smug, containing a dare that lurks in the tilt of his lips. *If you aren't scared, then prove it. Come here.*

And I should be scared.

"Hey!" someone hisses as my steps falter, forcing them to maneuver around me. "Watch where you're going!"

So I watch, not taking my eyes off a smirking figure as I stumble into a crosswalk, drawn in his direction despite myself. With every advancing step, my brain struggles to rationalize the action. This is just a stupid show of pride—no, a singular quest to regain my journal. Nothing more.

As if reading my mind, he fishes the book from his jacket and flips through the pages with a knowing grin.

I walk faster, gaining on him within seconds.

"Give me my journal back." The words come out breathless, made even more pathetic by the desperate attempt to pretend I'm not affected. My chin juts, my jaw squared. *You don't scare me.*

He terrifies me. His body dominates the narrow entryway. Tall. Imposing. I'm one step away from digging through my purse for my pepper spray.

"Not yet, rabbit," he warns as if reading my mind. "I need you to hop a little farther." His voice is softer now, but no less unnerving as those dark eyes flicker along my jaw. He's sizing me up—attempting to figure out just how much I'm willing to do. More, it seems. Always *more.* "Come on."

He starts inside, cutting across the narrow dining room. A cashier freezes behind the counter, tracking him with her gaze, but she doesn't call out in alarm. This must be a usual occurrence.

Without confessing, she turns her attention to me. "You're blocking the way for our customers," she says softly.

"S-Sorry." I scramble out of the way, but once again, I'm moving in the wrong direction. Toward him, not away. He's still just within my line of sight—a shadow darting across a crowded, busy kitchen and then down a hallway leading to a set of rickety stairs. They go up and up at least four flights or more.

I'm panting by the time I finally reach a partially opened door that leads to fresh air and a spacious strip of asphalt beneath the open sky. It's an unexpected view. I have to blink to adjust to the shift in lighting from the harsh fluorescent interior.

We must be on the building's roof, and a moment of shock distracts me from my quarry. Below, I can make out the streets intertwined like a maze, their streetlamps casting alternating red and green glows. It's beautiful. Quiet. Secluded. Up here, the only light comes from an orange bulb positioned directly above the door.

A circle of light that Rafe steadily leaves behind, approaching a shadowed section on the other side of the space.

"Over here, rabbit." He leans against a brick wall that must house another entrance, though I can't see any door from here. "Hop." With a wave of his hand—the hand I can make out holding my journal—he beckons me over.

I come close enough to snatch it, and this time, he lets me.

The familiar weight of it settles against my palms, and I nearly sigh in relief. "I'm leaving," I rasp, pivoting on my heel.

"You won't." He inhales on his cigarette, making the end glow a brilliant orange. Then he holds it from his mouth and exhales a cloud of smoke into the air. "You're a predictable, little bunny."

His next breath sends a tendril of smoke drifting directly toward me.

I cough, my eyes watering. "I am—"

"You won't, for the same reason you scurried back to Zhang's shop or why you skipped right into my place. I could say you crave danger, but that's not it, is it?" He shoots me an appraising glance and shrugs. "No. You're just numb. Bored *and* numb—" He shakes his head, watching his breath clash against the ebony sky. "Welcome to the club, rabbit."

Clutching my journal to my chest, I eye the door, then take a step.

He chuckles. "I read your little journal. Writing?" He scoffs at the moniker. "Those scribbles ain't anything special. Just a lot of bitching and moaning."

My cheeks flame, and something makes me pry my teeth apart, spitting out, "And you're such an expert?"

"I am," he says. I look over my shoulder to find him nodding, his eyes closed. His head pressed against the brick, face tilted toward the sky. "More than you, amateur bunny. I know one requirement for good sappy shit? Emotion. *That's* what you sorely lack. Your shit is drier than a virgin's pussy."

I feel my eyebrow shoot up as I shove my journal into my bag. "And I'm sure you've written tons?"

He smiles as though he predicted the question. "And if I say yes?"

"Then…" I lick my lips and try to sound convincing when I can't even bring myself to meet his gaze. His hair sticks out at awkward angles. A messy fringe of it keeps falling in his face no matter how many times he impatiently bats it away with the back of his hand. "Show me."

He scoffs. "Fine." Setting his still smoking cigarette on the railing, he pulls away from the wall. "But you asked for this, bunny."

He moves so fast that I barely process the moment he grips my forearm and shoves me against the brick wall. A heartbeat later, my arms are pinned above my head, and his face looms mere inches away from mine. My heart sputters as I cringe in anticipation of the pain I should be feeling.

Crushing fingers. Brute strength.

I wait…but the only sensations to register are his touch. His hot breath on my lower lip, his scent flooding my nostrils, his heat…prickling between us.

"What are you doing?" I croak, painfully aware of his nearness. "G-Get off!" I feel my knee twitch, but he shifts, ensuring any target I could assault is well beyond my reach.

"Relax." He deliberately adjusts his grip to trap both my wrists in one hand while the other slides down to my hip, ghosting around to my lower back. "You asked me what I've written. Feel for yourself." Presumably, he's referring to his fingers, skimming my body uninvited. Each individual digit flexes against my muscle and bone, imparting their rough, scarred, and calloused texture.

"Feel you groping me?"

"No. I don't scribble my thoughts into a fucking notebook. I don't work on paper, bunny. I work in flesh." With the tip of what feels like a forefinger, he traces an invisible design against my skin. My thoughts spin, unable to interpret the lightning-quick motions. Words? "My 'writing,'" he murmurs, letting his hand fall. "Blood and pain. Ink. The only shit that makes a real mark."

"Ink…" My gaze darts to his chest. Beneath his collar, I can see the hint of the intricate designs I know span his torso. "A tattoo? Like you know anything about art?"

But he might. The drawings scattered across his warehouse contradict me, as does the dragon etched into his skin.

Rather than say as much, he chuckles again. Up close, his almond-shaped eyes aren't entirely fathomless. A hint of silver glints off each pupil, reflected from the distant streetlights. The glow makes him look more serious than he should. Thoughtful.

"I do," he counters gruffly, raking his eyes down the front of me. "I know it's more than spewing out a bunch of pretty words. My 'art' is in pain. But what about you? Can you even describe one little emotion, *rabbit*? What this feels like?"

My chest heaves as I fight to suck in air, but every breath I take is tainted with the stench of him—cloying, endless smoke. Again, I try to squirm from his reach, but he tightens his grip. "It…It feels like I'm being assaulted."

He laughs. "See what I mean, bunny? That little brain of yours only knows how to scamper. Run. You can't even fucking describe what you're running *from*."

"Get off. I'll…I'll scream," I manage to threaten between pants. My nails dig into the wall to reinforce the boast. "I swear, I will."

"Do it."

I suck in another breath.

"Do something useful with all that panting." With one hand still braced above me, he reaches over and brings something to my mouth. "Inhale."

Smoke irritates my nostrils as the sensation of wet material prods my lower lip.

"Take a hit," he says. "Don't play scared, bunny. I can see it in your fucking eyes. You don't give a shit. Breathe."

My mouth opens, and I inhale when he lowers the cigarette. My nostrils itch with the bitter flavor.

"Good," he grunts. "Now, exhale."

It hurts when my lungs manage to fully empty again. Fear is like a vise, fighting to constrict them. But I can't deny the smug satisfaction I get by breathing a cloud of smoke directly into his face.

"Maybe that will loosen you up," he taunts without batting an eyelash. "Why is it so fucking hard for you to describe what you feel?" His voice is too controlled. Too level. "Not your surroundings. You write a lot about a fucking cage, but how does it *feel* to be trapped?"

"I don't know," I rasp as he returns his cigarette to his mouth and takes a drag. "How does it *feel* to destroy a book shop or terrorize an old man?"

"Good," he says, his next breath feathering my throat. "That's what you expect me to say, isn't it? It feels good to be bad, bunny rabbit."

"Yes."

"Tell me something. Does *he* appreciate your little hobby? Your boyfriend?" He laughs again, but the sound is decidedly colder this time. "Don't answer that. Describe me instead. Describe me with your writerly words."

"An asshole. A creep. A fucking liar,'" I snipe. "There. Satisfied?"

He lets me go, turning away. "I've been called worse. I bet you have too, rabbit."

I bite my lip. Have I? Yes. The words echo, distorted and muted by memory. *You're so selfish, Hannah. Fucking selfish…*

"I'm leaving now," I say, struggling to sound like I mean it.

"Not before I get to critique your assessment." He whirls to face me, stroking his chin. "A creep. Asshole. Well, I am all of the above…except that last thing. I'm not a liar."

I meet his gaze again, but the darkness I find there is unwaveringly steady. He's telling the truth, or at least he thinks he is.

Which strikes me as strange. Out of all the attributes on that list, I wouldn't expect him to deny that one.

"You never lie?" I ask, still holding his gaze.

"No," he says. "So think carefully about whatever you're going to ask me next. Make sure you can sleep with it."

I do. The air catches in the back of my throat as I open my mouth, and ask, "Why pick on me?"

He laughs. "I told you." He moves slowly, giving me every chance to escape his advance. When I don't, his hands return to my hips. "I want to know what makes a rabbit scream."

One by one, he spreads out his fingers, and I'm riveted by the sight of them—long and slim, streaked with dirt. Or paint? Gradually, they slip between the denim of my jeans to connect with my skin. Greedily, seeking more. More. Once he's gained enough leverage, he tugs.

I inhale, raising my hands. "S-Stop—"

"No," he growls, yanking me to him. "Close your eyes."

Something in his voice reaches past my logical brain, the part of me I've listened to my entire life. He goes deeper.

"Feel," he commands in a tone that ripples down my spine. "What does this *feel* like? Tell me, and I'll stop."

Softness mingles with a slightly rougher texture. Definitely paint. Warmth from the fingertips traces a blazing path over my chilled flesh. Down, down, down…

"Breathe, rabbit," he urges, his mouth near my ear. "I won't hurt you. Unless you ask me to."

"S-Stop—"

"You *stop* with the fucking words," he counters. "Show me."

I know what he's doing. I can feel the tension tugging on the clasp of my jeans. Hear the rasp of the zipper coming undone. My heart races, throat thickening.

Is this fear? *Yes,* I decide as the air sticks to the inside of my lungs. "It feels bad," I tell him.

"Bad," he echoes. His warm breath sears me and wetness chases the sensation. I startle, my eyes fluttering shut. Feel? His mouth. Lips…parting over the hollow of my throat.

"I was right, wasn't I?" he murmurs there, the words like smoke fanning smoldering embers. "You'd let me do whatever the fuck I want. But not because you're afraid. You're just too fucking numb to give a shit." He pulls back, and my eyes open slowly, taking in his ripe, smug smile. "That's no fun. I hate to tell you, rabbit, but you'd be a bad fucking fuck."

My cheeks flame. "Like you'd ever get the chance."

"Like you'd know what to do with my cock," he spits back. "You can't even use that pretty tongue properly. Tell me something emotional, bunny. Maybe then I'll believe you aren't some dry, nosy little reporter."

"Well, you're a criminal," I spit back. "Aren't you?"

"And if I am? I don't even think you know what that fucking means."

"I know it means you're pathetic."

He slaps a hand playfully over his chest. "Am I? A pathetic criminal. Tell me something I don't know."

"And…you're talented. A-At drawing," I admit. He flinches at that. Has he never heard that before? There's probably a good reason. "Yet, you beat up old men for money."

"And you hide behind your fucking little journal, obscuring your truth with pompous titles like Deceiver. You may snipe at me, little bunny, but you hide from the monster who's made you so numb, don't you? How did that story go again?"

"Get away from me." I push him.

He shoves me back, letting his weight pin me flat. "I'll tell you," he says. "Someone was so damn terrified of the monster on her tail that she 'deceived' someone else into taking her place. That's the shit you wrote, isn't it? *Freedom's price paid with the blood of another.* That little bunny watched another victim get bitten in her place, didn't she?" Our gazes lock as I'm forced on my tiptoes when he pins my wrists above me.

My breaths feather as my mind shies away from the memories invoked by that particular story. The same one printed in the local paper back home. The same one haunting my every waking moment.

"You can't even admit it, can you?" Rafe demands. He restrains me for a full second more before letting me go, but the freedom doesn't last long. Almost instantaneously, he snatches my waist again. "Tell me, bunny…" He grazes me with his palms, chuckling when I shudder. "How hard can *you* bite?"

I grit my teeth. My hands are free, so I should hit him. I try, but they swipe uselessly through the air. My lips part instead. "I dare you to find out."

A tilt of his chin is my only clue as to just how horrible a mistake I've just made. "Challenge accepted." He moves in too close. Too fast. His lips are on mine before I can react, pressing, parting. And…

He tastes like ash—vile and revolting—but then his tongue slips between my lips, carrying a different taste along with it. Sweet. Spicy. Conflicting flavors that catch me off guard.

I'm so stunned, I can't seem to bite down like my instinct warns I should.

Like he *wants* me to—because this is a test.

"I'll tell you how you feel, rabbit," he murmurs into my open mouth, sounding irritated as I remain frozen. "Jumpy. Like a virgin. Like no one has ever fucking touched you like this before. And they haven't, have they? Not your boyfriend. Not anyone."

Fabric kisses my hips—my jeans inching lower, guided by his ruthless touch. My attempts to stop him end with my fingers gripping his forearms, nails drawn. I let them dig in, scouring lines into the flesh. It must hurt.

But he doesn't stop.

He groans, letting his fingers catch more of me—but not in retaliation. "You feel soft." His voice thickens in a way that makes me shudder. It's too deep. "I bet you taste sweet. Like flowers or some shit…"

As if to feed that curiosity, he lowers his hand. Breathless, I press my thighs together, trapping his fingers between them. He flexes them anyway, grazing more of my inner thigh each time.

I stop breathing. Thinking. As he claimed to want all along, there is only feeling… His heat, sinking into my skin. His palm, sowing that invisible fire with one stroke. Then another.

Again.

"S-Stop—"

"Why?" he counters. "Because it feels good? Look at me, rabbit," he commands when my gaze drifts down, watching his fingers disappear beneath my fly. "You want me to stop?" His free hand snatches one of mine, forcing it down to his wrist. "Make me."

I grip him tightly, letting my nails bite into his skin.

And I feel.

Everything. Creeping, searching fingertips. Flexing muscle and bone. Bold, hungry curiosity. All of it connected to a creature I can't control or anticipate.

He's not the monster I spent my entire life training to fear.

This beast asks for permission first. "Show me how to touch you," he commands, but his voice sounds bitten out. Angry. Irritated. He has to make me move. React.

Show him.

I try to push him off, but somewhere between my hand and my brain, the signals mix up. I push. He pulls.

I gasp.

With every move I make, he interprets the motions in all the wrong ways. Like I'm goading him. Telling him how. Pressure here. There. Lower…

My panties are a teasing barrier, the lace dragging over my skin, warmed by his touch. Over and over again. With every stroke, my breaths feather, and my brain shuts down.

There's no room for shame or alarm in the tiny sliver of consciousness I have left.

Just breathing. Sensation.

Survival—whatever it takes to play his game. He *toys* with me, letting his fingers drag over the gusset of my panties, teasing me with their weight—the pressure. The inherent wrongness their presence brings…

"W-Wait," I rasp, struggling to remember…something. This is wrong. Just when my senses start to return, he flexes his wrist, stroking along the flesh between my legs. Just once.

And my nerves go haywire. My hips jerk, then my lips part, allowing a startled sound I've never heard myself make before escape.

An answering growl revs in his throat. "Shit…" He bucks against me, splaying my legs around his hand—all chance of escape vanishes. I can't move, and any air in my lungs dissipates, leaving me devoid of a scream.

In silence and tension, I suffocate as one thick finger hooks beneath the lace shielding me, letting him underneath without permission. I flinch, gripping his shoulder, my mouth open, my throat dry.

I swear a refusal forms on my tongue.

Only to die in the face of his startled grunt as his finger continues its search of me unabated. "You're wet?" He says it like it's some rare, terrible, dirty thing. Something so unexpected, it makes him press his mouth against my shoulder as if to keep the confession inside. But he can't. *Fuck.* You're so fucking wet…"

"S-Stop!" My face is on fire, embarrassment so thick I cringe, clamping my knees together. But then I see his face, how those eyes are unfocused for once. As if from miles away, I hear him grunt, then feel his fingers twitch again. Stroke. Caress.

Ignite.

My head rears back against my shoulders, my eyes staring toward the sky. I stop thinking. Caring.

It feels…

Good. So damn *good.* It's as if every stroke feeds some inner part of me I never knew existed. Every bit of friction enhances my perception, alerting me to each nerve connected to my spine. Every quivering bit of muscle drawn taut by his touch.

"Fuck…" His mouth attaches to my neck, his teeth scraping as in punishment. I'm making him reckless. Ruthless. With unsteady motions, he cups me against his palm. Rubbing. Harder. More. *More.*

When our eyes meet a second time, I quake. My throat dampens, every inch of me thrumming with an awareness that I'm on the verge of something horrible. Vital. Some distant, looming thing only he can bring to fruition.

He accepts that duty with his teeth bared, eyes narrowed with focus. His free hand snatches my waist, forcing me to arch my back and give in to him. One of his feet kicks mine, nudging my legs farther apart.

Taking advantage before I can regain my senses, he slides one rigid finger inside me.

My body clamps down, resisting him at first. He has to ease his way in, forcing my inner muscles to relax around the invasion. Relent.

A million reactions go off all at once. Sparks. Fireworks. Cliché, stupid words that cease to matter in the face of the pleasure that has me gaping. Gasping. Icy, harsh brick bites at my scalp as I writhe, forced to grip his forearms for stability and to keep my sanity. At the same time, my hips move of their own accord, rocking, taking.

And he steadily thrusts his hand, giving me dose, after dose, after dose…

"Fuck." All at once, he pulls away. Dazed, I stagger against the wall, grappling against the brick for balance. My knees are quivering, my stomach jelly, my pants around my ankles.

A persistent, throbbing ache resides in my belly. It's too much. Unbearable.

My eyes latch onto his fingers, glistening in the dim glow— but then he clenches them into a fist. And when I look up at his face, the expression hits like a bucket of ice water.

He's not laughing anymore. Instead, he fixes me with a glare that sends my already scattered thoughts spiraling. *Anger?*

It's the only way to explain those cold, empty eyes. "Fun's over, rabbit."

He turns away, snatching his still burning cigarette from the railing. He sticks the end into his mouth and heads for the door, shoving his hands into his pockets.

Woodenly, I refasten my pants. "What... What happened?" I hear myself croak, barely recognizing the sound of my own voice.

He says nothing, and that silence haunts me long after he vanishes through the mouth of the staircase. By the time I make it down to the street level and stagger all the way to my building, that silence persists, numbing me to everything else.

The fear that Branden could find out.

The enormity of what I've done—what I let happen.

None of those concerns can break through the cloud obscuring my thoughts—because some part of me still craves an answer from him. Even once I'm in my bedroom, long after I've shut off the lights.

In my head, in my dreams, my nightmares...

I'm still waiting for it.

CHAPTER SIX

When I wake up, shower, and get dressed, I'm determined to fall back to my old habits and put my talent for endurance to the test. That means ignoring everything that happened.

It doesn't exist.

My mind is a blank slate as I leave my apartment and head straight to the shop. Mr. Zhang isn't inside when I use his keys to unlock the door, but I get to work anyway, finishing up the tasks I'd already started. The monotony helps—up to a point.

I sort new inventory and prepare the insurance paperwork, but between filing, my inner thighs chafe together. I cling to the edge of the counter, gritting my teeth in a vain attempt to suppress the memories. His touch. His taste. His taunts. *You are so fucking wet...*

Desperate, I snatch up more paperwork and newer books, drowning out the thoughts with busywork. I pretend.

And the fragile lie holds up until the doorbell chimes and an unwelcome visitor barges in, heedless of the sign proclaiming we're still closed.

I do everything I can to ignore him. I clear all the backlogged inventory from the storeroom. I meticulously take stock of all the damage for the insurance records. I try to breathe, aware of his gaze on the back of my neck.

Rather than issue a taunt or a threat, all he does is watch me.

He watches my fingers shake as I struggle to rearrange the bookshelves. He watches how my eyes dart around the room—in any direction but where he stands. And he watches the way *I* watch him from the corner of my eye—a living shadow, lurking by the doorway.

We play this silent game for so long that it comes as a shock when he finally speaks. "It's closing time, *rabbit.*"

I glance up. Somehow, the day's given way to early evening without my noticing, darkening what little light seeps in from the lone windowpane in the door. Otherwise, I've been working in near darkness all this time. Long shadows stretch across the floor, swallowing him whole.

Without a word, I shove my cell phone into my pocket, grab my bag, and attempt to slip past him, but it's too cramped in the entryway. He has no trouble grabbing my wrist the second I'm close enough. "I said it was closing time," he declares gruffly. "I didn't say you could leave."

I wrench away from him, but he releases me, laughing as I scramble to put distance between us. "You shouldn't be here," I croak, aware of him on my heels. "Go. I'm leaving."

I lock the door behind me and pivot opposite his position. I don't even know which direction I'm heading in, just that I need to move. Get away.

"I shouldn't be a lot of things, *rabbit*," he chides, still following me. "Like be turned on by a bouncing little bunny. But I was, and I think you were too."

My cheeks flame as my body betrays my entire day's worth of effort when I remember. I can still feel him, the remnants of his touch and his kiss—that pleasure. Increasing my pace, I stagger around a passing man with a briefcase, desperate to get away.

"Leave me alone." I take a risk and dart into the street, barely missing an oncoming car. The driver honks at me, cursing from the window. But when I look over my shoulder, he's still standing on the curb.

In triumph, I gladly turn my brain off, letting myself move aimlessly, though it's getting late. I'm starving, I realize, as my stomach rumbles.

I didn't take time for lunch because he watched me work all day and never left. To unnerve me? Threaten me further? Or wait for another moment to crowd me into a corner and shove his tongue down my throat.

Only to walk away again.

I stop short, my chest heaving. Standing in the middle of the street as the evening foot traffic flows by, I realize that maybe I haven't let myself really process it until now.

He kissed me.

Touched me.

But I didn't make him stop. *Liar,* a part of me snarls. *You didn't want him to stop…*

"My apologies, bunny," a man rasps against my ear, jarring me back to the present. "If I didn't make myself clear before…"

I jump, pivoting on my heel, but his bulk is already there to block me in. His fingers encircle my wrist again, holding tight—but not the way I'm used to. Not hard enough to hurt. Just burn, branding the sensation of his fingertips into the flesh.

"That wasn't an invitation." He tugs, forcing me around the next corner and down the street. Only when we're halfway to the next intersection, do I remember how to make my legs move. I dig my heels in, yanking at his grip.

He sighs, then releases me, only to slip his arm around my shoulders, muscling closer the more I cringe from his reach.

"Get off—"

"You need to learn how things are done around here, bunny," he says, his tone level, posture confident even as people turn to stare. "Unless you've changed your mind about helping out Zhang?"

He slows his pace, waiting for his threat to register. When it does, I stiffen, though I don't know why I'm so surprised. "So, you are a liar, after all."

He shrugs. "Nah. I'm playing it straight, bunny. There are aspects of the business you need to learn. It's just how things are done around here."

He withdraws from me, but only because he expects me to follow of my own accord this time. There's a twisted grace in the way he moves, commanding attention. Yet anyone approaching gives him a wide berth while avoiding eye contact.

Watching him approach the next crosswalk, I feel my jaw clench in annoyance. He's halfway across the road when something makes me follow. Maybe guilt?

I dragged Mr. Zhang into this mess. I can't leave him now.

But I reach into my pocket and palm my cell phone, keeping it close just in case. I don't come any closer to Rafe either, keeping at least twenty feet of distance between us. He doesn't look back, though, as if he's that damn sure I'll follow.

When he finally slows, I scan our surroundings and see a slightly busier street near the heart of downtown. A music shop dwells in the building across the street next to a sandwich place. As for the building he's entering now?

A scarlet fire-breathing dragon spans the length of a black awning, guarding a modest storefront. INKED reads the shop's name in a simple utilitarian script. When I come close enough to peek beyond the door as he opens it, I make out a shadowed, though clean interior.

"In," he grunts, inclining his head. He enters without waiting for me, though, letting the glass door slam behind him.

I deliberately take my time, lingering just beyond the storefront. Rather than books displayed in the window, an array of photos line a black velvet backdrop. As much as it stings to admit, they're impressive. Eye-catching images inked onto random body parts make up most of the display, spanning various topics. Symbols. Faces. Intricate designs.

I observe each creation and find myself musing on the artist's intentions behind each one. As I stare, the storefront ignites. He's turned a light on inside, allowing me to view more of the interior from here.

Many of his design choices are unsurprising. Black walls. Polished floors of hardwood. More drawings hanging behind glass frames. *They* draw me inside in the end—not him.

He leans against a wooden counter, his gaze tracking my every movement, but I don't give him the satisfaction of claiming my attention. It's my turn to play the role of a silent intruder. Clutching my bag to my chest, I eye the closest row of drawings, etched in ink. The subject matter spans almost everything imaginable under the sun from soaring dragons to dancing flames, roses, and Chinese characters.

Moving from frame to frame, I'm aware of my lips parting. It's becoming harder to school my expression. Shock slips in before I can help it, widening my eyes. I catch sight of my reflection in a sheet of glass and sigh in defeat. There is no disguising that I'm impressed.

I could write the artwork off as cheap, lazy, typical designs, but they aren't—and that's the worst part. They're intricate, each one reflecting some unique quality deserving of notice. Emotion? That elusive feeling he's taunted me about. He expresses some form of the concept on every page from the watchful gaze of a vengeful dragon to the guarded stare of a wary tiger. Pretending he didn't draw every one would be easy, but the style is distinct and loud like him, I grudgingly admit. Each stroke of ink and charcoal conveys bold confidence for everyone to see.

Despair unfurls in my chest, but it's entirely unexpected. Jealousy? Maybe acknowledgment because I could never write so indiscriminately. It's why my father doesn't see this as anything more than a silly hobby and why Branden won't take my attempts to stand on my own seriously.

I've become so good at being numb that I've let it stifle the only other passion I possess.

But *he's* stifled as well, a realization made apparent in every piece of artwork. How? They're all here, locked behind glass. Without bothering to ask, I suspect he's never shared them beyond this space. Beyond his skin—or anyone he may tattoo.

This place is his journal, and he's just as secretive with it as I am with mine.

"Your mouth is open, rabbit," he taunts when I'm halfway around the shop. "I'm surprised you aren't waggling that pretty little tongue—"

"And I'm surprised you spent all day stalking me." I cock my head to shoot him a cold glance. To my chagrin, he winks. "Don't you have a job?"

"This *is* my job." He lifts his arms, gesturing around us.

"It's pretty empty," I point out.

"Because I don't take just anyone," he counters. "My services are invitation only. But that's not what you meant, is it?"

I turn around to find him standing closer than expected. His eyes bore into mine, his body heat an oppressive wall that drives me back against a wooden surface—a desk, I realize. Beside it is a sturdy leather swivel chair, presumably where people sit while having a tattoo applied.

"Why did you bring me here?"

"For business," he says. "I've decided how you can repay me, rabbit. From now on, if you work for Zhang, you work for *me*. That means you come when I call. When I say jump, your feet leave the ground."

"How?" I croak, though I don't think I want to know the answer.

"You bring me Zhang's payments from now on," he says. "On time, bunny."

"Payments?" I frown, my nostrils flaring in anger. "I paid, remember? That's what you said—"

"You paid off *that* debt," he corrects, raising an eyebrow. "Don't tell me you're that naïve to think he won't rack up more?" He lowers his gaze, raking me over. "Especially when he has such an eager little bunny to do his bidding."

I cringe at the assessment, but I don't argue. "How do I pay?"

"With money. He'll give it to you, and you bring it to me," he says as though it's obvious. "Unless you want to offer up something else...?" His eyes deliberately linger over my chest, and he chuckles when I cross my arms, blocking his view.

"I'm leaving." I turn for the door, shoving it open.

"Hop away, bunny," he taunts. "The view from the back is just as nice as the one from the front."

I freeze mid-step over the threshold, preventing the door from fully closing.

"What now?" he prompts, his tone cutting. "If you have something to say, rabbit, then don't be shy."

"Fine. You mock my sexuality like it's a game," I hiss as I turn to face him. "Like I'm some stupid prude. Like it's funny. But yesterday? I wasn't the one who ran away, was I?"

He blinks, his jaw tensing. Something indecipherable darkens his gaze and hardens his expression. "Ran away?" he echoes softly. "Or refused to fall for your little trick?"

"Trick?" I'm so confused by the word choice that I step forward, entering the shop fully. "What are you even talking about?"

"I'm talking about *you*, bunny." He crosses his arms, eyeing me with a scoff. Real anger seeps into his voice, deepening the gruff baritone. "Letting me think you'd want it. Get carried away. All so you could turn around and cry assault the moment your boyfriend noticed a pretty little hair out of place? I'm not that fucking desperate for ass. I'm not some toy you can play with, either."

I hear myself laugh, and I barely recognize the strangled, mocking sound. "You thought I was the one playing games? So all that crap about feeling? Bullshit! You came after me, remember? Though you're right. Someone like me could *never* want someone like you." My lips sting. I never talk like this. Ever. No one else has ever pushed me to this point. "This is all just a game to you, but you don't even have it in you to back up your own stupid words. You wanted me to feel? Well, the only thing I *feel* for you is pity."

He should take offense to that and puff up with anger, but he doesn't. His brow furrows instead, an eyebrow arching as if he can't believe the suspicion unfurling in his own head. It's too incredulous that he has to utter it out loud. "You wanted to fuck me *that* badly, bunny?"

I pivot on my heel as my cheeks burn. My hand fumbles for the door, yanking it open.

This time, his steps echo like a gunshot, gaining on me by the second. "Answer the fucking question."

As I stagger out of the shop, my lips part before I can stop them. "I guess you'll never find out."

I lunge, practically jogging across the street to get away. When I look back, he's watching me from the entrance of his shop, his gaze unreadable.

But at least he isn't smiling.

He isn't laughing, either—but my victory is short-lived. He's still watching when I turn away and head down the street. With every step, I feel his gaze on the back of my neck.

And it lingers there during the entire frantic trip to my apartment.

CHAPTER SEVEN

I wake up to the sound of my cell phone pinging. Dazed, I grab the device from my end table, but when I read the message on the screen, alarm rips away the dreamy haze of sleep.

Call me when you're up, Branden commands, skipping his typical morning greeting. *We need to talk.*

My heart sinks. I scramble from beneath my blankets and stagger to the bathroom, desperate to stay calm. Think. With my eyes on my reflection, I brush my teeth and comb my hair—anything I can do to stall.

I last ten minutes. Ten sweet minutes of peace, during which I attempt to build my fragile resolve. When I finally gather up the nerve to call, he picks up on the second ring.

"Morning." His voice is so hard, I stiffen. The baritone cracks the way it does when he's irritated.

"Morning," I whisper in response. My bare feet carry me into the living room where I sink onto the couch, drawing my knees up to my chest. "What's up?"

"Tell me, what do you know about Rafe Wei-Shen?"

Rafe. At the sound of that name, my thoughts topple like bricks. So much for my resolve. It shatters, and in the resulting chaos, all I can do is croak out, "W-Who?"

"Tall guy," Branden iterates coldly. "Dark hair… A member of the fucking triad. A gangbanger." His voice gets deeper, his words harder. "Likes to exploit locals for cash or worse. A person someone like you should never associate with."

My heart rate increases, pounding through my veins. "Branden—"

"Do you know him?"

"N-No." I shake my head to enhance the act despite his camera being broken. He isn't here. But in so many ways, he *is.* I can even see him, puffing up, his fists clenching, eyes flashing. As always, his face would be the mask of calm no matter what, providing deceptive reassurance that all was well.

Until it wasn't.

"You don't?" He pauses as if giving me the chance to come clean. A growl conveys his disappointment when I don't. "Then why did someone I know see you in his fucking shop last night?"

Alarm surges through me, and those worn old instincts return in full force. Only I can't remember which one comes first. Enduring? Or being silent?

"I…"

"Don't lie to me, Hannah." Static laces his voice, transforming it the more I listen. My brother becomes a stranger in an instant, snarling into my ear. "What the hell were you doing there?"

"I… I was with Mara," I croak, letting my brain come up with the lie. It's a bad one—this isn't like me. It's as if someone else is in my head, taunting me with what to say. *Use those words, bunny.* "She wanted to get a tattoo but chickened out. I promised I wouldn't tell anyone. She begged me to come with her—"

"Funny," Branden hisses, unconvinced. "My informant didn't mention anyone else was with you. Just that you were in his shop. Alone."

"I-Informant?" I feel my brow furrow at the word choice, and I forget my cowering act. "Are you… Were you spying on me?"

Would I put it past him? The answer lands like a punch to my stomach. *No.*

A spy would be nothing outside of his camera. His texts. His constant phone calls.

Just another bar to add to my cage.

"No," he says with a sigh. His tone shifts, losing the hardened edge, and he's my brother again, feeling guilty at having been exposed. "Of course not, Han. Just… Be careful who you associate with. That guy? The bastard's got a rap sheet longer than one of your little poems. He's dangerous. It's because of him that I'm on fucking suspension—" He breaks off, but my curiosity grows. He never mentioned why he suddenly got "time off" a full month earlier than when he usually takes his trip. I hadn't thought anything of it before. But now?

Suspension…

"Besides," he says, "you don't need a tattoo. You're perfect the way you are."

Perfect. That word sticks in my throat, choking me. "Bran… I have to go."

"Fine." He sighs, still trying to regain his calm but authoritative tone. "You're working today?"

"Yes."

"Then I'll have Liam stop by and take you out to lunch. He'll be out on patrol."

Liam. His partner, now turned spy? I'm not brave enough to ask. Or even argue. "Won't he be busy?" I say instead.

Branden grunts out something that could be interpreted as a laugh. "Too busy to show his partner's baby sister around town? Let him. Just… don't run your mouth about anything silly." His voice slips again—a warning. Something *silly.* Like home. Our lives before moving here. His past. "Try not to talk his ear off. He's been bugging me to meet you."

"Branden—"

"This way, at least I know you're safe," he insists, letting the implication hang between us as subtle as a storm cloud. I can guess what he doesn't say. *Because if I don't, I'll come back now.*

"Okay," I whisper.

"Bye, Han," he tells me. "Have a good day."

I hang up and get dressed, cycling through various items of clothing until I look at myself in the mirror and freeze. Around me lie piles of discarded garments—my typical favorite sweaters. Left behind is an old sundress I bought on clearance last year, that I don't even remember wearing before now. It's thin, a pale yellow linen that hangs on my frame. Simple, but at least it's devoid of bunnies. Not that anything, in particular, is shaping my current desire for change.

Or anyone.

After brushing my hair, I leave my building for the heat of the early morning. Summer is already creeping in, displacing the crisp spring chill with blazing sunlight. I could take it as a good omen. That today will be a step in a new direction, despite Branden's invisible collar, choking away what little freedom I have left.

Today, there will be no Rafe, at least.

No more games.

Just fresh air and the depths of the bookstore to look forward to. I hold on to that hope until the second I approach the Paper Crane. When I take in the storefront, my optimism plummets, dashed to pieces on the sidewalk. A lone figure waits for me, leaning against the entrance.

He switched up his outfit today, as well. Rather than a scruffy leather jacket, he's paired his jeans with a gray T-shirt that stretches tight over his muscular forearms. By design, I suspect.

One could assume that his intimidating attire is in the wash—but there's a method to his seemingly simple style. He doesn't really catch the average pedestrian's notice, and they scurry past him, innocently oblivious.

But those who *do* see him find it hard to look away. Impossible. Much like spotting a panther blending in with his surroundings—once you discover the predator hidden amongst the leaves, the whole tree disappears, and you know no other reality than as prey.

"Morning, bunny," he says, eyeing me up and down.

I turn my back to him and unlock the door to the shop. "You shouldn't be here."

"I thought we had this discussion," he says, following me inside even though I try letting the door shut behind me. "I *own* here, bunny."

"I'm busy." I scramble to put distance between us by positioning myself behind the counter. For whatever reason, he doesn't follow and instead chooses to lean against a wall of bookcases.

"Tonight?" he wonders in a tone that catches me off guard. Cautious? I sneak a glance in his direction, but his expression is carefully blank and reveals no answers. "You better not be, bunny. I've decided to cash in on that favor you owe me."

I frown and risk breaking my concentration by turning to face him fully. "What favor?"

He cocks his head, a sly grin shaping his lips. "The one you earned by skipping away with Zhang's debts miraculously paid. I've decided it's time you repaid *me*. With interest."

I scoff and set my bag onto the counter before dragging an old logbook Mr. Zhang uses for inventory toward me. I heft it open and find the page with the latest entries. One by one, I go through each item, trailing my finger along the page as a guide. Maybe I hope the renewed focus on my work will make him vanish.

In theory, it should be simple to ignore him, but I can hear his slow, heavy breathing. Smell his most recent cigarette from here. Taste his spice on my tongue.

Finally, I sigh in defeat and look up, meeting his watchful gaze directly. "I don't have any money."

He raises an eyebrow. "Did I ask for money?"

"I don't have anything else you might want either," I snap.

"I doubt that…" He pointedly eyes the neckline of my dress, making me shift uncomfortably. It's cut differently than my tried and true sweaters, displaying more of my collarbone and a glimpse of the flesh beneath. I can't stop myself from crossing my arms over my chest, and he flashes that dangerous grin in triumph. "In fact, I can think of a few things you could offer—"

"Get out." I slam the ledger shut and turn away as if just telling him to leave could make it true.

But he doesn't. Neither does he creep toward my corner to drill in his taunt—and that's the worst part. I have to endure him, but without the tools I'm used to utilizing. Silence and the safety of my own head don't work where he's concerned.

His breathing is too noisy, grating, and raspy. His scent is overpowering, sneaking into my lungs with every inhale. Around him, my thoughts don't form the protective wall I'm used to hiding behind. They fracture. Splinter.

And he breaks through easily.

"I want to see you hop, bunny," he murmurs, just when I think I might scream to counteract his presence. "Without the dowdy little sweaters or the boring little mask. I want to prove you wrong. I didn't run last time. I just gave you a taste. It's up to you if you want more but with no excuses. No chance to cry assault."

I bristle at his tone, wrapping my arms around my waist even tighter. If I hope to find comfort in the action, I don't. His gaze slips beneath the barrier, creeping over me without permission. I can practically feel his gaze rasping along my skin. "What are you talking about?"

"Tonight," he repeats. "Dragon's Head. You can even bring your little friend if you want."

Dragon's Head. The name conjures the image of neon lights and raucous dancing. "The club?" I frown. "Why would I go there with you?"

He laughs, and his steps resonate along the floor. Alarmed, I turn to watch him move, but he takes his time, giving me every chance to cower and back away.

I don't recognize the way my breathing hitches as he comes closer. How my nerves tense as he raises his hand, deliberately inching toward my cheek.

"D-Don't touch me—"

"I have touched you," he reminds me. "Don't kid yourself into believing you don't want more."

"More of what?" I force myself to meet his gaze only to regret it.

I wish his eyes gleamed in that mocking, cruel way, but their stare is flat and empty. "More of what could happen the next time I have my fingers inside you."

My hand flies out of its own accord, landing across his cheek. *Hard.* My gasp is louder than his startled grunt, my eyes widening at the violence—and the swiftness of his reaction.

His free hand cups his smarting cheek, but the other snatches my wrist, wrenching me around. I scramble to brace myself against a bookshelf as he pins my arm against my back. A heartbeat later, he steps in, his breath hot on my throat.

"Not nice, bunny." There's no real anger in his voice—a fact that makes me shiver. No. Because he's too busy sliding his other hand down my thigh and grasping a handful of my skirt. "Let's cut to the chase. Why I'm really here. I want to hear you say it…" He lets the silence linger, just long enough to have me squirming with anticipation. His pulse is racing, palpable through his fingertips, thrumming through the thin linen of my dress. "You danced around it the other night. Now admit it, you would have let me fuck you on the roof that night."

He scoffs when I don't reply. I'm too disgusted to. Horrified.

Because, a part of me taunts, *he's telling the truth.*

"Do you need a reminder?" My eyes seem riveted to the contours of his hand, those fingers perpetually stained with ink. They toy with the yellow fabric, daring me to question or scream or fight.

Anything.

I go silent instead, watching as if observing a stranger. This moment… It's almost like it *is* happening to someone else. Another woman who doesn't seem to care as a thug swipes his thumb against her bare thigh. Worse, she bites her lip, alarmed by her own reaction to him. A scream isn't the sound she's choking back. A gasp slips out regardless, and he travels higher, dragging up her skirt with every dangerous inch gained.

Higher.

Higher…

"Hannah?" A knock on the door shatters the moment—almost too surreal to be happening. But no. It is. Dazed, I gape at the door, spotting a familiar figure peering through the glass. "Hannah? You in here?"

"I have to go." I lunge for my bag and trip, landing hard on my knee. The pain has me gritting my teeth, but the stabilizing force on my arm withdraws. When I turn around, he's already gone, disappearing down the side hall that leads to the back entrance of the store.

"Hannah?" Liam tries the door handle this time.

I stagger to my feet and snatch my bag, practically racing through the door before he can come in. I nearly run into his chest, forcing him to grab my shoulders just to steady me.

"Whoa! Where's the fire?" He smiles, his expression warm.

I can barely muster up a grin in return, and the expression slips the second I spot a figure melding into the crowd paces ahead. He doesn't look back, his posture proud, movements leisurely. As if I don't exist.

Even as his heat still radiates through my skin.

"Hannah?" Liam waves his hand in front of my face until I turn my attention to him. "You ready to go?"

"Y-Yeah." I lock the shop door and allow him to lead me down the opposite street.

"How about we get out of this neighborhood for a while?" he suggests, and I trip over the curb. The language is distinctly Branden's. Does it bother me to know that he set this up, weaseling his way into my life even while miles away?

If it does, I can't tell.

I'm too numb to.

CHAPTER EIGHT

L iam takes me to a café in a slightly more upscale part of town. The artsy, rustic scene for rich kids getting their art degrees while renovating old houses on their parents' dime. It's the kind of place my parents assumed I'd move to, but Branden always hated.

I try to push him from my mind as we grab lunch at a small, cozy café where the pleasant beige walls and bright lighting reduce everything else to a distant memory.

"So, what made you come here?" Liam asks. He's still in uniform, catching odd looks, though our booth is at the back of the shop and mostly out of sight. "All the way from Pennsylvania?"

"Branden asked me to," I blurt out, only to realize that he didn't mean "here" literally. Here, as in far from home, in a strange city that I moved to on a desperate whim and a vain quest for freedom. "I liked the English lit program at the college," I quickly say, my go-to response to similar questions.

He chuckles. "Your brother makes your hometown sound like something out of a storybook. I'm surprised you left."

I *had* to. But I don't say as much out loud, squirming in my seat as sweat dribbles down my neck. Is this a test? Branden's way of ensuring his hold on me lasts, no matter who I'm with… Though he isn't the only reason I'm on edge. The truth is something I've learned to smother and obscure. It's the only way to live with it.

But for one little second…

The pain hits me like a sucker punch, wholly unexpected. Do I miss my old home? More than anything. At least the memory of it, how it used to be before the chaos and the pain and the darkness that drove us both away.

"I'm sorry," Liam says, frowning. He fumbles for a napkin from a dispenser in the center of the table and hands it to me. Only now do I realize that my cheeks are wet. "I didn't mean to upset you."

"You didn't." I smile wide to prove it, though my lips tremble at the corners.

"At least you have Branden," he points out. "That's one hell of a big brother who would move all the way out here just to keep an eye on you. I'm not sure I'd do that for one of my kid sisters."

His smile is so painfully genuine. He really means it.

"Though, I will say the guy doesn't chat much. You wanna hear his nickname around the station?" He cups his hand around his mouth and winks. "The vault."

"Did he ever tell you about Lexi Winacott?" I blurt out. Panic drains the color from my cheeks. What the hell am I doing?

"Not that I recall." Liam shrugs. "Is she an old girlfriend or something? I knew getting to know you better was a good idea." He winks again.

But I'm shaking.

Deep down, maybe I could rationalize the slip of the tongue as accidental due to stress. Or spite. Branden puts so much effort into controlling my life. How would he like it if the tables turned?

And it would be so damn easy to turn them—or break the damn table entirely. One word. One phone call. One name.

Lexi, a pretty brunette with blue eyes who skipped into the path of a monster. Lexi, who witnessed something she shouldn't have. Lexi, who's dead because of me.

All I have to do is open my mouth, and Branden's hold over me would be broken irreparably...

But I won't.

I never will.

"I'm glad you agreed to come to hang with me," Liam says, awkwardly changing the subject. "The way your brother talks about you… I thought he'd kill me if he knew I liked you. He acts like you're a saint."

His voice is so gentle, and he means it as a compliment. I tell myself that over and over—but I can't stop hearing those words. *If he knew I liked you…*

My chair squeals as I push back from the table. "I should get back."

"Of course." Liam flags down the waitress and pays the bill. "Let me walk you."

He takes me all the way to my apartment building, and a cruel part of my brain whispers a taunt. *How long before he reports back to Branden?*

"Have a good day, Branden's little sis," he calls warmly. "We should do this again."

I smile and nod, but the second I'm trapped behind the safety of my apartment door, I'm shaking so badly I have to brace my back against the solid frame just to slide down to my knees without falling.

What the hell did I do?

If Branden finds out… Not if, but *when*. When he finds out, he'll be furious. Paranoid. He'll resort to his tired old tricks for keeping me in line. Always keeping me quiet.

Though maybe that's the point. My brain's sick, masochistic way of reminding me of the dangers of feeling. Or letting anyone get too close, be them a thug or a harmless beat cop.

I live the way I do for a reason. I am the way I am for a reason.

Otherwise…

There'd be nothing of me left.

A LITTLE AFTER DARK, my cell phone screen illuminates with an incoming message.

Have a good night. Send me a pic before you go to bed. I need to see your smile.

I grip my phone so tightly my fingers leave smears all over the screen. If Liam mentioned Lexi to him, his casual message doesn't reveal any of the telltale signs of his anger.

For now.

Night, I type back. I change into my pj's and snap a picture from my couch. Then I crawl into bed, struggling to find a comfortable position beneath my blankets. Minutes of staring up at the ceiling eventually turn to mindless scrolling on my cell phone.

Mara's stopped texting me—not much of a surprise, considering I've been ignoring her messages. *Sorry for being a flake,* I start to type. But it's like my fingers rebel, adding more onto the statement than I mean to.

Let me make it up to you. We should go out tonight.

I stare at the screen for what feels like hours before I finally set it aside, convinced she won't answer. The second I do, my ringtone pings, and Mara's message dominates the screen in a series of short, snappy sentences.

Hello, bitch who has been blowing me off. Go to hell.

Not even a minute later, another reply arrives. *Yes, I will go out, but you're buying my drink, skank.*

Despite everything, my lips stretch into an unfamiliar position. A smile? It remains as I sit upright and shrug off my blankets. My clothes are still scattered over my floor, but my gaze falls over my brown sweater with white bunnies.

Can I borrow a dress? I type, feeling my chest constrict even before her response arrives.

Of course. But now you owe me two drinks.

"We're heading straight to the bar first," Mara shouts against my ear. "I'll take two shots, please! Pay up, baby! You owe me."

I reach into my purse for my wallet. Or at least, I would if I weren't forced to fumble with a much different model than my trusty knitted bag—a leather clutch of Mara's. Its glossy black matches the dress she let me borrow. Said dress suspiciously resembles the one she wore the first night we came here—only on me, the effect isn't quite the same.

My appearance could be summed up with one word. Gangly. Every few seconds, the straps threaten to slide down my shoulders in rebellion of the lack of cleavage they have to support.

Mara, of course, looks stunning in a red mini, her hair swept into a loose knot at the nape of her neck, and her muted makeup flawless. I'm once again struck by her confidence over all else. I swear, every guy within a ten-foot radius has his eyes on her, and her sly grin betrays that she's well aware of that fact. Taking my arm, she drags me through the crowded dance floor and nearly lunges across the bar counter to get the bartender's attention.

"Hey, Tony!" she calls to the man in question who leans against the counter, wearing a black uniform. "Load me up!"

Minutes later, she's happily plied with her third shot when she frowns, her eyes narrowing at something behind me. "Dammit. I swear, chick, you have the worst luck when it comes to clubbing. You must be an asshole magnet or something."

"Huh?" I follow the line of her gaze over to a different set of private booths from the area we'd been accosted in last time. It's larger, furnished with a broad, leather couch, and a bar ledge stocked with liquor bottles.

A lone figure dominates the space, and this time, he's without the entourage. Regardless, he sits like a king, with his head cocked and his posture sprawling. The firm set to his jaw paired with those piercing eyes commands attention from nearly every woman who isn't here with a date.

I hate myself for watching him longer than I should. For noticing the tight fit of his shirt and how his short sleeves display his muscular, tattooed forearms. I hate myself even more for glancing at his fingers that are braced on his knees —I know I'm blushing.

And I especially hate the wry smile shaping his pink mouth as if he's aware of every rebellious observation sneaking into my head.

"I come here all the time, and he's rarely here," Mara says defensively between sips of her drink. "Though, he *does* own the place so—"

"What?" Only then does the club's name truly resonate. *Dragon's Head.* The same symbol that seems to crop up everywhere he goes. I'd been a fool not to put the pieces together before.

"Yeah," Mara says, rolling her brown eyes. "One of the reasons he gets so much ass. Desperate skanks." She eyes a group of scantily dressed women strategically dancing near his booth and scoffs. "Though...he *is* sexy, even if he is a total man-whore," she admits, her eyes drinking in the muscle straining against his shirt. "Sexy, loaded, *and* ripped." With a sigh, she turns back to the counter and slams her hand down. "Bartender, I need another drink, please!"

The summoned figure approaches our section. "Hey, Mara." He hesitates before leaning in, shooting me a wary glance. "Look, don't go spreading this around, but you might want to get out of here. Word is Gino's boys are on the prowl, looking for trouble. They might head here next."

"Dammit." Mara's face pales, and she nods solemnly. "Thanks, Tony."

He shrugs. "Sure thing. My shift's almost over, so I think I'll be heading out too." He winks and rakes his hand along his neon green Mohawk. "I'll make your drink first, though." He returns to the row of liquor on the other end of the bar.

The second he's out of earshot, I turn to Mara and attempt to appear more curious than alarmed. "Gino?"

"An asshole." She wrinkles her nose, waving me off. "It's nothing. Just dumb, wannabe gangbanger shit."

I feel my eyebrows shoot up. "That doesn't sound like nothing."

I picture Rafe and his uncanny confidence. His knack for violence. *Gangbanger* seems to be the most accurate term.

Mara sighs, leaning her hip against the bar. "God, bringing you here, I feel like I'm corrupting an innocent or something. Gino runs a club across town. One of those tittie bars that preys on young girls desperate for extra cash." She rolls her eyes. "I know a girl who worked there and hated it. She said it's nothing but rich guys who think they can own anyone they want. Sometimes, Gino likes to start shit with Rafe. Just to keep things interesting around this godforsaken place. But it's all talk. Rumors like that float around here all the time, but it's usually fine. Rafe is fucking crazy, so most bastards leave him alone."

We both turn back to the figure in question—only to discover him staring back. His eyes find mine as he inclines his head, beckoning with his finger. *Come here.* My feet twitch, disrupting my precarious balance in Mara's heels, but I don't move a single inch.

Because he's not beckoning me. A slender blond scampers from the crowd to answer the summons. With a familiarity that has my cheeks catching fire, he palms her waist over her hot pink mini, guiding her onto his lap. She bounces there, murmuring in his ear as a coy smile plays over his lips. But his eyes…

They find me again and linger, drilling in a silent message I can't ignore. *Watch and learn, bunny. You never attracted me to begin with.*

"Come on." Mara snatches my hand, turning her back to Rafe. "Let's dance!"

She drags me onto the center of the floor, muscling her way through a mass of writhing dancers. I can only stand awkwardly as she sways, undulating her hips in time to the beat.

Is this fun?

I don't know. My thoughts are scattered, buzzing in a million directions like a horde of flies, and they seem to converge on the one figure I can't stop glancing at.

He's still with his blond, leaning back against the couch as she straddles him. Their gazes are locked, their faces inches apart. Closer... From the outside looking in, they're enthralled with each other.

Or at least *she's* enthralled with him.

Because every time I risk glancing in his direction, he's always staring back. Shamelessly staring as if laying down a challenge with every cold, searching glance. *Come here.*

I look away, scanning the room for anything else to draw my attention. The flashing lights do at first, pretty and dizzying. As does the spinning DJ, crafting the pulsating beat.

But against my better judgment, my gaze always seems to find him again. This time, his lips part, and I can almost hear his laughter from here—his taunt. *Don't kid yourself into believing you don't want more.*

But he's content to get his fix with anyone he can. Such as by sticking his tongue down the blond's throat. I don't know why my throat tightens when he does. Why I find myself staring without even trying to disguise the interest. Disgust? Watching him kiss is a world apart from being on the receiving end.

He moves assuredly, letting his fingers sink through the blond's hair, drawing her into him. My own lips tingle, remembering the feel of his. That taste. That uncomfortable, forbidden sensation I still shiver at the remnants of.

"What is with you?" Mara grabs my wrist, forcing me to face her. "*You* wanted to come out, remember?" She purses her lips, eyeing me through narrowed slits. "Prove it. Go find some hot guy to dance with." She practically shoves me into a group of dancers nearby.

Before I can truly panic, she prances past me and sidles up to a blond guy in a sports jersey. "Have fun," she mouths at me before turning her attention to him.

Fun.

It's a foreign concept to me in a world devoid of books or quiet places to hide and read. My body moves woodenly with no chance in hell of ever copying her effortless grace. All I can do is lurk in her shadow and ask myself the same question over and over.

What am I doing here?

Making a fool of myself, I realize, feeling my throat tighten further. *Letting some bastard make a mockery of me yet again.*

Going against my tried and true instincts.

And for what?

The answer unexpectedly comes in the form of a grasping hand that cinches my wrist, yanking me deeper into the press of bodies before I can resist. I watch in horror as Mara disappears behind a crush of dancers, ensuring that I'm hidden from her view. Helpless, I feel my fingers twitch at my sides, but I don't pull away even though I know well before I spin around just who has me.

"Good to know you can follow the rules when you want to, bunny," Rafe says, his mouth near my ear, his grip still on my wrist. His thumb strokes my forearm, raising goosebumps over the flesh. "Very good."

"Get off!" I wrench my arm away, but for whatever reason, I don't leave. Yet. Curiosity? Or maybe pride.

He doesn't bother me. Not the fact that his lips are wet, his gaze unreadable, his jaw clenched. As if to spite me, my nostrils twitch, catching the cloying scent of feminine perfume wafting from his skin. *Hers.*

"Where's your little friend?" I hate how harsh my voice comes out sounding—an angry hiss.

"Where's yours?" he counters, his eyes blazing. I may shy away from diagnosing the hitch in my voice, but there is no ignoring the source of his growl—jealousy. "You know… I always heard it was the wild ones who fuck the cops."

I lift my hand without realizing it, but he grabs my wrist before I can connect with his face this time. His expression darkens, and he tugs, forcing me closer. Closer. When our hips collide, he places my hand against his shoulder while his opposite arm hooks around my waist, preventing me from moving away. His hips sway, and mine jerk away in answer, but he persists. To anyone looking on, we must resemble some disjointed version of the couples grinding together around us.

Not that Rafe seems to give a damn what anyone might think. He holds me assuredly, using any attempts I make to escape as an excuse to grip me tighter. "Nice dress," he murmurs, letting his gaze drift to my neckline. "You wore this for me?"

"I didn't," I snap, slamming my hand over his chest to push him off.

He chuckles, working his fingers through the thin fabric despite my resistance. Shivers erupt. My thigh shakes, and his palm cups the side of it, sensing the reaction and relishing in it.

"Sure, bunny," he tells me, guiding my movement through his touch—not away like I want to move. He makes me rock into him. The pulsating beat sneaks beneath my skin, and he uses it to control his motions. Hard when the beat quickens. Softer when it lets up. Then slower…

"And I didn't get a hard-on watching you struggle to hop just now," he adds against my earlobe. "You can't dance for shit. Still, there's something sexy about a wild little bunny."

I stiffen, breaking his rhythm as my cheeks flame. "You're disgusting."

"I'm honest," he counters. "There's no shame in that." His hands ghost my hips, drawing me back. Urging me to move again and feel him in time with the music. Feel…

I risk looking up to meet his gaze directly, but the mocking gleam I expect to find is absent. He stares back fearlessly, daring me to look away. Deny the heat he radiates with one look. Deny his honesty. Because, for whatever reason, he finds me sexy.

Because…

"You're a man-whore," I croak to him, parroting Mara's term—admittedly the cruelest one I know. "Why don't you go back to your blond?"

He doesn't bat an eyelash. "And you came all the way here to see me, bunny," he adds, forcing me to sway in time with his steps. "Why is that?"

"I'm here with Mara," I blurt out, craning my neck to search for her among the crowd. But it's too bright. Too loud. A giggling woman squeezes past, knocking me against him, and my hands scramble for purchase over his chest before I can stop myself.

"With Mara," he murmurs, his voice low, his breath on my throat. I don't know how he does it, but somehow, my arms are around his neck, and he's leaning in, letting his words brush my lips. "That's a damn shame, rabbit. Does she know you fuck police officers on your lunch break? She doesn't strike me as the cuckolding type."

"You *are* jealous," I declare, rearing back so that I can see the truth for myself.

But he doesn't try to disguise it. "*You're* the one with the boyfriend," he reminds me, his tone so soft I barely hear him above the music. "Innocent, sweet Hannah who let a stranger shove his fingers in her pussy—"

"Get off." I rip away from him, but he pivots to keep me trapped and pinned against him with his arm around my waist.

"At least I saw my competition," he says. "No offense, bunny, but I don't think he can fuck like I can."

I bare my teeth in a snarl. "You don't have *any* competition."

"Relax. I don't want to marry you, bunny." He inclines his head, inspecting my mouth while his tongue traces his lower lip. "I won't interfere with your white picket fence future as a cop's wife. I assume we'll fuck once or twice, at least, then part ways after that. I don't do relationships."

"Do you tell that to all the girls?" I croak, feigning confidence even though my face is on fire.

"Don't have to." He adjusts his grip to palm my waist with both hands. "They know it. I don't exactly present myself as the settling type."

"You sound so proud of yourself."

"I am," he admits, licking his lips. "Because I don't feel the need to be anything else. And you, bunny, *like* that about me. It's why you keep on hopping around."

I try to pull away, but he follows. "You like that I don't play nice," he goads against my scalp. "Because, deep down, that's all you really want from me. You just won't admit it out loud. A few quick fucks before you hop merrily on your way. I'm not offended, though. You were right. Girls like you only want one thing from guys like me."

"Nothing," I hiss. "I don't want *anything* from you."

"Wrong." He steps back, but his arm flexes to draw me with him. Impatiently, he pushes through the other dancers, dragging me along until I'm crowded in against a wall. His bulk alone is a prison that bars me from view and traps me here.

"You do want something from me," he declares, bracing his hands on either side of me, his mouth dangerously close to mine. "That's why you're here."

"I'm here because I was curious," I spit, barely aware of the words spilling off my tongue. "If you really were that desperate."

He frowns, his jaw clenching. "Oh?"

"Desperate enough to think that I'd ever be attracted to you."

I know the barb hits home merely by how he stiffens, but he doesn't release me like he should.

"Oh, really?" He lunges instead, and our lips slam together without warning, teeth gnashing. It hurts, but he effortlessly tilts his chin and takes charge. Swiftly, his tongue comes like a battering ram, prying my lips apart to force its way inside.

Making me choke on my taunt.

I start to bite down. I want to. My teeth clip the topmost edge of the invading flesh, but he's too quick and draws back. I don't even have the chance to gasp for air before he returns, shoving me against the harsh brick wall in a way I can't avoid, pressing his mouth to mine.

The assault hijacks my hardwired instincts, and my body reacts to him all wrong. I feel my head fall back and my lips part. Rather than recoil, I grab him, letting my nails taste the flesh beneath them, so hard he flinches with a groan. At this moment, I should feel powerless. Instead, my heart is surging, my pulse racing. I feel...reckless. Unstable. Unmoored.

The way he kisses me is dangerous. He doesn't want to scare me, dominate me, or control me—he just wants *me*.

To touch and toy with as he pleases. To taste, letting his tongue probe so deeply, I fear he'll choke me. But at the last second, he nips my lower lip instead until I jump. Squirm. It's sadistic. He makes me dance for him in this way, utilizing his body to electrify mine. My reprieve comes only when he stills against me, his nostrils flaring.

At the same time, his fingers grasp at my hips. My waist. Higher...

I gasp as he cups my breasts in both hands without permission. Squeezes. Kneads. Something in his touch makes it harder to panic like I should. Maybe how his fingers shake? They twitch, alluding to some indecipherable quality my brain struggles to name—*Possession*.

It's the only way to describe how he lazily tests my weight over his palms, stroking me with the very tips of his fingers, all the while gauging my reaction. My lips flutter apart, but he returns his mouth to mine before I can choke out a command to stop. It isn't long before I realize that this kiss is different from before—more teeth than his tongue. More pressure, more of his weight against me, driving my skull against the wall. Punishing. Polarizing.

And I fail to make him stop. My body rebels, quickening my breathing to match the unsteady pace of his. I writhe into his touch, goading him on. Craning my neck to feel his mouth on mine, roughening the contact. In response, his touch grows firmer, and his tongue probes hungrier.

It's like some sick, twisted game. Grunting, he shifts his weight, grinding his pelvis over my own to craft a cruel taste of friction—whatever he can to unnerve and disorient. But I'm quickly learning the rules and how to turn the tables…

By reacting instead of running.

My consent is an unexpected development. He shudders when I gasp into his open mouth, echoing his pants, and stop fighting. The second I clutch his shoulders, a startled grunt revs in his chest. That sound resonates through my spine, down to some secret place inside me that ignites. And my stomach flips with the knowledge that I've crossed a line. Gone too far. Too fast.

This corruption isn't debasing. With him, there's freedom in falling. In surrendering to base, vile instinct.

In doing more than just enduring.

In *feeling*.

But he takes it all away in a heartbeat when he rips his mouth from mine. Disappointment forms a pit in my stomach, mingling with shame. I expect him to mockingly leave me on the verge like last time.

My eyes flutter up to his, narrowed in anticipation. But he stares back, his gaze heavy-lidded and unfocused.

"Come with me," he grates, sliding his hands up to my neck, letting his fingers burrow into the fall of my hair.

"W-Wait." My brain sputters, struggling to remember something important. Several important somethings. Mara. Who he is. The fact that I shouldn't be allowing him to pull me across the dance floor toward the club's entrance.

I start to resist, tugging on his forearm, but it's too late. We're already passing the bouncer barring the entrance. Within seconds, my skin prickles in the night air, cooling the sheen of sweat glistening there that I wasn't aware of.

Neither was I aware until now that my hand is in his, his fingers grasping mine tight.

Until suddenly, he stops short.

"Shit." His gaze is fixated across the street where a red sports car skids to a tire-squealing stop. Three men climb out and approach the front of the club, cutting past the line, their posture bold and cocky. Alarm bells go off at the back of my mind, displacing my muddled daze. Something is wrong. I can sense it in the air...

A foreboding feeling that only grows as one of the men reaches into his pocket and withdraws something that glints

in the glow of a nearby streetlamp, unmistakable in shape—
a knife.

"Go—" Rafe shoves me aside so fiercely I careen into the
brick facing edging the entrance. Staggering to regain my
balance, I look back to see him lurch onto the balls of his
feet, his teeth clenched. "Get your little friend. Then go.
Now." His voice is too deep, devoid of any playful mocking.
The gruff baritone leeches into me, keeping my annoyance
at bay. He's not playing, for once, and I instinctively take a
step back, nearly running into a couple leaving the club.

They falter as well, fixated on the scene unfolding.

"Look who's here." The man in the center of the trio—the
one holding the knife—mounts the curb first. He's dressed
in a suit, crowned by a blood-red tie, which makes him
resemble some odd cross between criminal and
businessman. I suspect the effect is intentional to look like
one of the characters in my father's favorite mafia crime
dramas. "Little Rafie. The black fucking sheep, which says a
lot, considering your fucked-up family."

"What the fuck do you want?" Rafe growls.

"I hear you've been stepping outside of your zone," the man
says. "We've come to enlighten you as to why that might
not be the best idea." He brandishes the knife, and a gasp
erupts from the few patrons still waiting in line. Some of
them scatter, and one of the bouncers steps forward only to
halt as Rafe raises his hand.

"Hannah," he snarls without turning around. "Go!"

"That your new bitch?" the man wonders, nodding to me. He's tall with short dark hair styled into a slick coif. Cold, green eyes glare from an angular but handsome face, set with a Roman nose. "Funny. I thought you liked blonds."

"I do," Rafe replies. "Like Bonnie. Do you want to tell your buddies why she might be here crawling all over my dick? I thought she was fucking *you*, Gino. One of the few bitches who will without you having to pay for it first, from what I hear."

Gino laughs, but there's no humor in it. His eyes blaze, wild and unstable. "Funny because I *hear* that you're not as much of a hardass as you pretend to be. That you listen to whiny little whores who run their goddamn mouths. That you like to snitch, Rafie. My club got raided the other week. I wonder why?"

"Hannah," Rafe snaps in a tone that's like a whip, yanking on my attention. "Go!"

This time, he doesn't have to tell me twice. I whirl on my heel and race inside, searching for Mara. She's not at the bar or on the dance floor. Am I just too frantic to see her? It's as if every nearby face blurs into the same indistinguishable person until I'm blinded by panic. My attempts grow desperate. Sloppy.

"Mara! Mara?" Without meaning to, I stagger into another dancer who hisses in irritation.

"Watch where you're… What the fuck?"

Suddenly, the music dies mid-song. Bright lights flick on overhead at the same moment, and in the absence of ambiance, the fantasy is ripped away. Gone is the majestic allure, and we're left standing in a brick room, crammed with people who murmur in shock.

Then alarm, as a scream echoes in the distance, and the calm erupts into chaos.

It's as if everyone heads to the exit at once. In the resulting crush, my body is buffeted, a rag doll in the tempest.

I can't breathe. Can't think. A hand slams into my back as I grasp at flailing, lashing limbs, desperate for stability. Eventually, I find myself being shoved forward, back the way I came.

Outside is a different world from the typical, clubgoing scene I'd witnessed just minutes before. People stream from the mouth of the club, clogging the road and stopping what little traffic remains. Amid the shouting, honking chaos, a group of men stands before the entrance—Gino and his two thugs, and Rafe, who seems woefully outnumbered.

"Hannah!" Mara comes out of nowhere, clutching my wrist. Her hair is askew, her makeup smudged, her wide eyes darting around the crowded street. "This is bad. We need to leave."

I agree as my throat contracts to choke down a building sense of dread. The scene unfolding just paces away seems so surreal, like something out of a movie. A bad one where someone winds up dead in the end.

"I suggest you turn around and head back to that fucking shithole you call a club, if you even have any business left," Rafe growls. How I hear him above the noise, I have no idea. Scurrying patrons create a thin path through which I can make him out, standing tall. "Don't blame me if you hold on to your territory as well as you do your women."

I don't catch Gino's reply or anything else for that matter. Just my heartbeat, surging through my ears, pounding...*pounding*.

"Hannah! Come on!" Mara yanks on my wrist until I stagger down the block after her, away from the inevitable fight. Right before we reach the intersection, my steps falter. I can't stop myself from craning my neck and looking back.

And...though it defies logic, his eyes meet mine instantly, conveying a command I feel in my bones. *Go.*

"Hannah! We have to get the hell out of here—"

"Where's the rush, baby?" a man wonders, his voice cruel and unfamiliar, uttered near my ear.

"Hannah!" Mara's scream rings out ominously as her fingers slip from my wrist. *Ripped away.* Someone different has a hold of me now, yanking until I'm staggering after them, back through the crowd. Far too quickly, they shove through the center of the commotion. All I see is Rafe as hands slam against my back, propelling me toward Gino. Grinning, he hooks his arm around my neck, forcing me against him. The cloying stench of his cologne threatens to choke me, his touch crawling over my skin.

"Look what I found," the man who grabbed me growls—a tall brute with a round face and massive bulk.

"A pretty little thing," Gino croons. The ragged tip of his thumb scratches my cheek in a twisted caress. "Friend of yours? *Hannah?* Not blond, but who knows, I could get exotic for a change." He winks. "We'll see who does a better job of holding on to his women."

"Let her go." Rafe's inflection doesn't change, but his posture stiffens, his hands forming fists. "You don't want this fight."

"Is that so?" Gino laughs and brandishes his knife, tapping the edge of it against my throat. With each brush of the blade, he goes deeper, toying with the topmost layer of flesh. A sound bubbles in my throat that I don't recognize. A whimper?

But it has nothing to do with the man behind me and everything to do with the figure watching, his body poised on the balls of his feet. His body radiates power—raw, volatile rage—to the point that he seems to ignite with it, the flames on his arms writhing with every twitch of coiled muscle.

"Take this as a fucking warning," Gino snarls, oblivious to the unease I feel coiling in my stomach. "You stay away from my fucking district *and* my girls. Next time you get cocky, I'll pay this shithole another visit. I wonder if it's fireproof?"

"You should find out," Rafe goads, his smile alarming. I'm reminded of the dragon of his that I stole, a dangerous creature seconds from breathing fire. "I'll give you the fucking match. Make sure you stay to watch."

"Like your daddy stayed to watch your mother turn tricks for Shen just so he'd feed your ass?" Gino replies. "I bet it was quite the show. Your uncle is one cold son of a bitch, though he has nothing on your daddy. You should know that, though. Aren't you the one who turned his ass in?"

Every ounce of color drains from Rafe's face, enhancing the sharpness of his features—and how cold he can appear with just one look. "I don't think you want to bring mothers into this," he warns, his voice deeper than ever. "But the next time yours comes crawling into my bed, I'll ask her to send you a heads-up. Now let the girl go."

"Should I?" Gino sniffs near my neck, chuckling. "Tell me, Rafie. How is this one? She seems a little stiff, not that you have standards. I think she could make some money at my place. Maybe more… I don't think you'd mind sharing, considering you've fucked every other bitch in this goddamn shithole. Will she be worth the trip? I bet your mommy was. I think my old man took a few rides on that Mexican bitch—"

Rafe lunges, and I'm too stunned to react. I've never seen anyone move so quickly. It's as if he teleports to Gino, shoving him back. The man releases me with a grunt, and I stagger to keep my balance as the two men grapple. Sharing awkward glances, Gino's thugs look on without stepping in.

And they should because the fight is painfully one-sided. The winner reveals himself near instantaneously. Rafe moves like an animal in a graceful shift of muscle to deliver a series of blows that leave Gino hunched over and clutching at his mouth. It's clearly over.

But Rafe pivots, delivering another blow so violent it brings Gino to his knees in a spray of blood.

"Who's the bitch now?" he snarls, delivering a kick to his side. The force knocks the other man onto his back, leaving him open for another. And another, which lands with a sickening crunch. "Who's the fucking bitch now?"

"Fuck," Gino groans, his eyes rolling. He tries to crawl out of range, but Rafe pins him down, crashing a fist into his lower jaw. Over and over until blood speckles the pavement.

I barely recognize the attacking figure, his hair hanging wild, his eyes gleaming, his teeth bared. He's grunting with every blow, hunched over Gino's limp body like a predator. A monster…

"You're going to kill him, you fucking asshole!" One of Gino's lackeys finally starts forward, but his face suddenly flashes a peculiar blue. Then red. The wail of sirens fills the air, adding fuel to the already hectic scene.

"Shit." Rafe stiffens, looking up, and Gino finally moves to shove him off.

"You crazy motherfucker," he grunts, using the curb to stand.

Rafe staggers to his feet as well, clutching at his upper thigh, too distracted by the new arrivals to keep fighting.

Those who aren't in the process of running start to bolt as two police cruisers peel around the corner, blocking the nearest intersection. When I look back, the three men have seemingly vanished, leaving Rafe behind. But he's already standing before me, tilting my face for his inspection. I shiver at the heat imparted by his touch as his eyes bore into mine.

"Are you alright—"

"Hannah!"

I turn to witness Mara pushing through a throng of bystanders, hurrying toward me. By the time she breaks free, Rafe has already let me go.

"Are you okay?" she asks, her bottom lip trembling. "I'm so sorry—"

"Get out of here," Rafe commands, his gaze fixed on the police officers leaping from their vehicles to scan the crowd. "Shit."

My heart sinks in grim agreement. One of the officers draws my notice more than the others, tall and dark-haired. Liam.

"Tony!" Rafe flags down a figure racing from the club. "Take her home," he gently pushes Mara toward him.

"Wait!" She reaches for me. "Hannah—"

"Go," Rafe snaps. Then he grabs my hand, tugging me down the sidewalk and through an alley that cuts between the club and the adjacent building.

"What are you doing!" I pull at his grip only for him to tighten it, dragging me closer to him.

"Do you really want your boyfriend to see you here?" he hisses without turning around. "Dressed like that?"

My gaze falls to my borrowed dress, its neckline plunging unattended, and I don't say anything. Together, we move so quickly the streets become a dizzying maze, and his grip is the only thing guiding me forward. We eventually reach a part of the city bustling with nightlife where the foot traffic becomes too thick to run. Forced to slow, he pulls me beside him, throwing his arm around my shoulders.

My initial impulse is to resist, but then I realize how heavily he's leaning against me. I look up to find him gritting his teeth, his forehead glistening in the glow of a passing streetlamp.

"Rafe…" My nostrils flare, catching a distinct, coppery scent that makes my steps falter. *Blood.* "You're hurt."

"Not here," he says near my ear. "I'd rather not get arrested, bunny." He inclines his head in the general direction of his shop, but I doubt he can even make it that far.

With every step, he seems to slow, and I find myself having to support more of him. As we round a corner, a familiar street sign draws my notice, and I realize that one other destination is within just a few blocks. My heart pounds as I wrestle with indecision. Taking him home would be a bridge too far, with or without Branden's paranoia to contend with.

I shake off the idea, letting him pull me along, but as we descend a curb to cross the road, he groans. "Fuck…"

And something in me breaks. I hook my arm around him, pivoting on my heel. "This way."

It's his turn to resist. "You wouldn't be leading me toward your boyfriend, would you, bunny?"

I brush off the suspicion. "Trust me."

My initial impulse was right, and not even ten minutes later, we reach my apartment building.

Rafe eyes the front of it warily, not that he's in any shape to argue. He sags against me with every step until my knees are buckling beneath his weight, and I have to pry open the heavy front door one-handed. The moment we cross the threshold, my stomach drops through the soles of my borrowed heels. I can't shake the overwhelming sense that I've made a mistake.

He doesn't belong here. Too tall in this narrow space, he's too imposing, even while bleeding. Thankfully, the hall is nearly deserted, though the sounds of the other tenants drift through the walls like some surreal reminder of what normalcy *should* be. I can smell food being cooked in the next unit over as we ascend to the third floor. The faint notes of a radio playing echo from up above as does laughter and murmured conversations.

Beneath those deceptively normal sounds, I also hear drops of moisture striking the floor. Ragged, unsteady breathing. The squeak of rubber grating against metal as the figure behind me struggles to keep his balance on the next step of the staircase. I snatch at his clothing, but he shrugs me off.

"Keep going," he grunts.

There isn't time to think. I simply inhale as I power myself up the final flight of stairs to my floor and then hurry down the hall to my apartment. He stays upright until we reach my door. Then he grunts, slumping against my back while I fit my key in the lock.

Our combined weight sends the door flying open, and we both stagger in. Cold air tickles the back of my neck as he brushes past me for my gray armchair and collapses onto it.

"Fuck." His voice is gruff with pain, reinforcing just how much of his blood is all over my floor. I can't stop staring at the various scarlet puddles. It seems impossible that one person could lose so much blood and still be coherent.

I don't know what to do. My vision blurs, and the room starts to spin.

Focus, Hannah.

I race into my kitchen for a rag and throw it down. My heels catch on the terry cloth as I use my foot to drag the fabric across the worst of the blood. But there's too much of it. It's everywhere. Dripping over the threshold of my apartment. Leading down the hall…

"A-Alcohol." Rafe grits out the word from between his teeth. When I just stare, he snaps his fingers. "Do you have any alcohol?"

I shake my head. My family doesn't drink. Not after Mom's last stint in rehab all those years ago and Dad's constant insistence on "therapeutic" sobriety. And Branden's…issues.

"Shit," he hisses. "Can you get some?" He watches me carefully. I notice that one of his hands is clenched into a fist and presses down hard against his upper left thigh. The blood keeps appearing in random places—all over his hands and the armrests of my comfy chair. It's even pooling on the floor at his feet.

"Hey!" He snaps his fingers again. "Can. You. Get. Some?" His lips move slowly, each word carefully enunciated.

Get some. I bolt into the hallway, leaving the door to my apartment wide open. My heels slip on a puddle of scarlet, and I barely catch my balance against the nearest wall. *Focus!*

Somehow, I'm three units down and knocking on a door with peeling red paint and the scent of cigar smoke wafting from underneath it.

"Hi," I greet the man who answers the door brightly—a stranger I've never taken the time to meet before now. He's wearing a wifebeater stained with what looks like broth, and I can catch the hint of a naughty movie playing across the old-fashioned TV that dominates his living room.

"Yes?"

"Sorry to bother you," I start in a rush, "but I'm having some friends over, and I forgot to run to the store for some drinks—" I somehow choke out a laugh. "Do you have… any that I could, um, borrow?"

My fingers are shaking. My toes feel sticky, and *God*, I'm too terrified to glance down and see why.

The man—who I vaguely recall from a few awkward exchanges at the collective mailbox—eyes me for what feels like an eternity. Then he turns without a word and rummages through what sounds like cupboards out of sight. A moment later, he returns with two green bottles. "Enjoy," he grunts before pressing both into my hands and closing the door in my face.

When I finally re-enter my apartment, Rafe's still seated on my armchair, but his shirt is off. Most likely the wad of dark fabric he has pressed against his thigh.

"Good." He nods to the bottles of alcohol. "Bring them here."

I manage to get the door closed one-handed and stagger over to him. He snatches one of the bottles, rips off the cap, takes a sip, and then grimaces. "Sake," he announces after swallowing. His blood streaks the bottle as he settles it between his hip and the gap in the seat cushion. With one hand, he lifts his bloodied shirt, revealing the bleeding gash along the inside of his left thigh.

"He stabbed you," I hear myself whisper. It's a nasty wound, unfathomably deep, and I know right away that he'll need stitches. It isn't until he reaches out and bats my hands away —causing my phone to fall to the floor—that I realize I was already in the process of dialing 911.

"No," he growls. "No cops."

For once, it's easy to shrug off the voice that rumbles through my skin. "I'm not letting you bleed to death on my La-Z-Boy—"

"You don't have to." He grunts and tries to stand, but his knees buckle. I can almost see the color draining from his skin. "I can fix this. Get me a knife." His voice isn't so gruff anymore, lacking the spark I'm used to. He sounds exhausted and in pain. Weak.

911 feels like the only option.

"You need stitches," I insist.

"You're right." Surprisingly, he nods. "Do you have a needle?" His calm tone throws me off. "Do you sew?" he adds in response to my blank stare. "Do you—"

"I...I have a sewing kit." The admission drives me over to the hall closet, where I store my raincoat and umbrella. My fingers shake as I reach for the plastic Hello Kitty lunchbox resting on the topmost shelf and pull it down. Inside it are the remains of my supplies from a brief interest in embroidery a few summers ago. The only thread I have is in three shades of pink. A pincushion, shaped like a rubber duck, holds an array of needles, but my vision is blurring too badly to make out a single one.

"Any luck, bunny?" I sense Rafe watching me from across the room, but I don't look up when I finally bring the kit over to him and fish out a single sewing needle.

He eyes the strip of metal carefully but doesn't reach for it because his hands are shaking too badly to even grip the armrests properly. "Thread it," he prompts rather than admit as much out loud.

"You're not serious." I shake my head. "You're not going to—"

"Thread it."

I select a spool of pale pink thread, rather than argue—maybe the color choice will convince him more than anything else how insane he's being?

But it doesn't. "Hurry up, bunny."

I lick the end of the thread and attempt to shove it through the needle's eye. Once I finally do, I hear the cushions protest beneath a shift in his weight, and there's a sound like that of fabric being torn.

"Look at me..."

I don't. I can't. I'm oddly fixated by the process of carefully tying off the length of pink thread. *It's just a simple stitch, Hannah,* I tell myself while mentally running through everything I've learned about sutures from watching medical dramas on television. *Just a simple stitch...*

"Hey. Look at me."

The stench of blood sears the air when I finally gather up the nerve to obey him. Rafe's legs are spread far enough apart for me to make out the gash. God, it's about the length of my thumb and dangerously wide. It's laughable to even hope that a little bit of pink thread will make him whole again.

"H-Here." My fingers tremble as I attempt to offer him the needle, but he shakes his head.

"I can't." With a groan, he manipulates the bottle of sake and pours enough into the wound to make him howl through clenched teeth. "Fuck!" When he catches his breath, his eyes meet mine again, their expression fathomless. "I need you to do it. You can consider this paying me back, bunny."

He makes it sound so logical. *You do it.* Like *I'm* the irrational one for jerking backward, shaking my head furiously. "N-No! I can't—"

He spits out a single word as if uttering it pains him more than the injury itself. "Please."

That request alone shouldn't be enough to erase every trace of logic that warns me to run…but for some reason, I'm on my knees in an instant, crouched between his. The indecency of the position briefly runs through my mind, but by then, my hands are already covered in his blood. I can *taste* it—the smell is so thick. In the space it took me to grab my kit, he's torn the sleeve of his pant leg all the way down to reveal the skin around the wound. It's slippery and cool to the touch as I pinch as much of it closed as I can.

"It's all right," he coaxes, brushing my forearm with sweat-soaked fingers. "It's okay. Pick up the needle. That's it. Good girl."

I struggle to control the needle with my free hand, lowering it…

Doubt descends, scattering my thoughts as the insanity of this entire situation sinks in. I can't…

"Do it!"

My hand jerks, plunging the tip of the needle through flesh. I'll never forget the sound he makes. It's unrestrained and savage, despite being smothered beneath his fist. He bites his knuckles, sinking his teeth into the flesh. "Don't look at *me*!" he chokes out once he notices me staring.

I glance down and find that the needle is still in his skin. Almost robotically, I grab it and pull. Again. Again. After a while, the simple motions become monotonous. *Stitch. Stitch. Inhale. Stitch. Stitch…*

On the fifth one, he shifts, and suddenly, his hand is on my shoulder. The fingers squeeze, their nails gingerly raking my skin.

The next stitch comes out lopsided as a result, and I have to make another just to get the flesh to line up properly. Eventually, the surge of my own pulse drowns out the sounds he makes. The groans. The grunts.

I don't even realize my fingers are shaking until I finally tie off the last stitch and cut the thread with my teeth.

"Holy…shit." He mutters a few more words that are barely coherent. His eyes are unfocused, dancing around the room. "You did good, bunny."

The compliment feels hollow, all things considered. Almost on autopilot, I drop the needle onto the lid of my makeshift sewing kit and then carry the entire case into the kitchen. Streaks of blood splatter the basin of the sink as I methodically wash my hands beneath a stream of hot water.

Then the needle. It's almost laughable how easily the blood washes off.

But the same can't be said for the floor. Or my armchair. Or…

I inhale sharply and fish a bottle of cleaner from underneath my sink, along with a bucket. Then I fetch my mop from the gap between my fridge and the wall.

It takes me nearly ten minutes to wipe every trace of blood from the hallway. My heart pounds, but the overwhelming need to just *clean* erases even the fear that someone might stumble upon me. With single-minded determination, I follow the blood trail until it ends just near the entryway. By the time I finally return to my apartment, Rafe is already on his feet, hobbling across the living room.

"You'll rip your stitches open," I tell him while resting the mop and bucket against the wall. For some reason, my fingers don't want to let go of that bottle of cleaner, and I clutch it like a child might cling to a teddy bear. "Sit down!"

"You've proven lucky, rabbit," he says hoarsely, though he doesn't sound very happy about that. "If I were a betting man, I'd assume you'd let me die."

"You will, if you bleed out all over my floor," I reply. Common sense or *should haves* or *what-ifs* don't matter anymore. Everything I've ever known about myself is falling to pieces as I cross over to my bedroom door and hold it open.

"Just…you've got to lie down." I swallow hard and manage to regain some control over my voice. "I need to clean up the blood."

I nod in the general direction of my bed, but he doesn't budge.

"No can do, rabbit." His eyes dare me to challenge him, and the smart thing to do would be *not* to. Any other day, letting him go would have been an easy concession to make, but for some reason, I really don't want him to bleed out in my living room.

I don't want to descend the stairs in the morning to find his lifeless body at the bottom of them. I don't know why. I can't explain it…

I just don't.

"You've lost a lot of blood." I try reasoning with him, but my voice cracks, negating the effect.

He shrugs. "It's fine." The stubbornness in his gaze only intensifies as he draws himself upright. "I'll live."

He takes a step forward as if he means to blow past me for the door. He nearly makes it halfway before he staggers into my coffee table and knocks it off balance. I'm beside him in a heartbeat, and I throw one of my arms around his back, guiding him across the room while bearing most of his weight.

He lets me take him all the way to my bedroom door before he realizes just where we're headed.

"No." He tries to pull away, but for once, I'm stronger. It's easy to drag him inside and over to my bed, considering he seems incapable of holding himself upright. Somehow, I manage to get him close to the edge of the mattress before his legs give out completely, and he falls across it widthwise.

What to do, Hannah. What to do...

He groans. Swears. Somehow, he manages to seem more threatening while pale and sweating than he does at full strength. He tries to sit up but falls back down. With every attempt, his voice thickens until I can't tell if he's even still speaking English.

All I know for damn certain is that I can't let him leave in this state. And there is that illogical trace of concern once again, forcing me to care about what might happen to him if I even call the police.

My bed frame creaks, and I glance up to find that he's succeeded in shifting his weight to the end of the bed in an attempt to stand again.

"Lie down," I command while crossing over to him.

"No." He uses my support to stand, but then I surprise him by shifting him sideways and letting him fall. His head lands on my pillows, and I reach for his feet before he can push me away.

Grunting with the effort, I lift his legs so that his boots dangle over the edge of the mattress. His uninjured leg, I leave flat. The injured one—which I'm alarmed to find is still bleeding through the stitches—I prop on my pillow.

He's glaring when I finish. The dark irises of his eyes swallow me up, mirroring the snarling creature on his back. "You Florence Nightheart or some shit?" he snaps.

"Florence Nightingale," I correct, backing away while he flails over my bedspread, seemingly too drained to stand this time. "Keep moving, and you'll bleed out faster."

That seems to reach him. He gives in with a sigh, letting his head fall back against my pillows, his body limp. Those dark eyes blaze, however, seeking out mine. "You meant it, didn't you?" he says, his voice hollow again.

"Meant what?" I reply, crossing my arms as if the act alone can erase the insanity of this moment of him in my bed.

"That you weren't attracted to me." He chuckles brokenly while I just stare. Of everything that should be on his mind right now, my rejection isn't it. "But you *are* attracted to me, bunny. You just don't want to admit it."

"Why would I be attracted to someone like you?" I whisper. Why I choose to argue with him at all, I have no idea. Maybe it's the noise. His voice melds with the typical cacophony of honking cars drifting in through my window, creating a false sense of normalcy. Almost.

"Why? Cuz I'm sexy as hell." He chuckles again only to grunt, reaching for his thigh. "Shit…" He looks up, but his smile fades, leaving behind an expression so serious it transforms him into another man. Someone I can't dismiss so easily. "You want me for the same reason I want you," he tells me. "I'm the only one who sees you for what you are, bunny rabbit."

I turn away, fidgeting with the stained skirt of my dress. Poor Mara won't ever want it back.

"It's true," he says, unwilling to let me ignore him. "I noticed it the first night, little bunny, when you hopped right in front of me. You're sexy…but that wasn't what I saw."

I grit my teeth, but something makes me bite out a response regardless. "What did you see, then?"

"You looked like me." He makes it sound so simple. So… honest, even in the obvious throes of delirium—an observation so astounding it made him seek me out. "Those scared little bunny eyes…"

He falls silent for so long that I'm terrified when I finally turn back to find him slumped sideways, his lips parted, his breathing steady. He's asleep, thank God.

Though, should I?

I don't come up with a fitting response by the time I finally collect myself enough to escape into my bathroom and shower. Wrapped in a towel, crouched in the body of my tub, I try to regain my composure. My old instincts. Anything.

Nothing makes sense anymore. Not living in this apartment or moving out here to go to school for a degree I'll probably never use.

If I were smart, I would have stayed in Wellington. I would have fought to regain my perfect, old life. I would have never let Branden take control of it the way he has.

But no amount of wishing can change this reality. It reasserts itself with a telltale ping that I unfurl my aching limbs to answer, wearing only a towel. I grab my phone and hiss in alarm. Branden has sent at least twenty messages throughout the night.

But, surprisingly, he isn't the one calling me now.

"Oh, thank God!" Mara exclaims when I answer. "I was so worried. What a fucking shitshow."

"I'm glad you're okay," I whisper, leaning against my living room window, staring out into the darkness beyond.

"Are you?" she asks warily. "I can't believe that asshole had the nerve to—"

"I'm fine," I say. "Really."

"Thank God for that," she replies, her voice ripe with its usual chirp. "I say we turn this night into a positive. You got some damn good fodder for your essay, and as for me… I think I'm going to sleep with Rafe."

"Rafe?" I can't tell exactly how my voice sounds. Alarmed? Amused? "After everything that happened, your first thought is getting laid?"

"Yes." She sighs dreamily, though I can hear the murmurs of who must be her parents, arguing in the background. "He was so sexy. He basically saved your life. Though… What happened when I left? It looked like you might have gone with him."

I recognize the wary suspicion in her tone. "He just led me away from the club," I say. "I think he wanted to make sure I wouldn't go running to the cops like a goody-goody."

"Oh." She sighs, satisfied by the answer. "Well, as long as he didn't try anything. And if you want to call dibs on him, let me know now."

She pauses.

I say nothing.

"Then it's settled. He's mine. The guy may be a total asshole, but I think I'll give it a shot. Just for fun. I mean, did you *see* his body? I don't have a dick, but I think I know what they mean about blue balls—"

"I have to go," I say as a sudden thud comes from the direction of my bedroom.

"Oh…okay. Well, night."

"Night." I hang up and race into my room, only to find that he's lying on his uninjured side, drawing my sheets over him. Once he's settled, his eyes drift to me, widening. A whistle escapes through his teeth, low and strained. "Either I'm dead, or you're a sadist, bunny."

I glance down and feel my cheeks flame as I realize I'm still in my towel. "Neither," I snap, turning to my hamper. I grab an oversized shirt and carry it into my closet, dressing in the dark with the door cracked.

When I emerge, he's already out for a second time. It should be impossible for someone so big to look so…normal, lying there. He's almost too large for my basic full, his feet dangling over the end of it.

A part of me still warns that I should call 911, but I creep into my living room without indulging in it. Curling up onto my couch, I close my eyes.

It should be far harder to fall asleep than it is.

CHAPTER TEN

I peel my eyes open to pale, gray daylight streaming in through my window. It takes only a second for the memories to descend. What happened last night and after… The new monster in my bed, his scent flooding my small apartment—and the familiar phantoms still lurking in my wake. As I stretch out my sore limbs, I catch myself eyeing my phone, too wary to pick it up just yet even though my text alert keeps pinging.

Ping!

Ping!

Ping!

Instead, I enter the kitchen and rummage through the meager offerings in my fridge. Minutes later, I'm studiously frying eggs in what I'm sure is the only cooking appliance I own.

Golden light gradually floods in through the windows, and I can hear something stir from my bedroom. My one vain hope of Rafe deciding to crawl out via the fire escape during the night is dashed.

The only course of action preferable to facing that reality seems to be stirring the cooked eggs a few times and pouring a glass of water from the tap. Grim with apprehension, I carry both over to my bedroom door and peek inside.

He's still on the bed, lying with his face obscured by a mound of crushed pillows.

"R-Rafe?" I cautiously creep forward and set the cup down on the nightstand before observing him in full. God, he's too still… For a second, I consider the possibility that he's dead. His skin is pale enough to make out the bluish veins snaking underneath. The bleeding from his leg has stopped, but there's a sallow, grayish quality to the skin around the wound.

"Rafe?" Swallowing hard, I balance the eggs on one hand and nudge the edge of the mattress with my leg. "Are you awake—"

Without warning, his hand flies out and seizes my thigh, yanking me closer. The plate of eggs crashes to the floor, and I scramble to brace myself against the firmest surface within reach—his chest.

"Morning, bunny." His voice is still hoarse, but his sly grin conveys anything but weakness. I lurch off him, staggering back.

Unconcerned, he turns his attention to the cup on the nightstand. "You cooked for me?" With a thoughtful expression, he eyes the food scattered over the floor. Then he pulls himself upright and shifts to throw his legs over the side of the bed, groaning all the while. At least he can move. His injured leg is bare from his thigh down, exposing taut muscle that doesn't seem too damaged by the assault.

Wrenching my gaze away, I stoop for the eggs, scraping them into a pile. "Well, there isn't any more, so—"

"Not so fast." My arm is seized from behind, yanking me against a body that feels only *slightly* softer than a brick wall. "You may have helped me out of the goodness of your bleeding heart, rabbit," he murmurs into my ear, sounding partly amused, partly suspicious. "Or… your little boyfriend could be waiting out there to arrest me or some shit?" He inclines his head toward the living room. "What did you tell him, huh?"

The accusation takes a split second to land. When it does, I'm already whirling on my heel to face him. "Tell him?" My shrill tone makes him wince. "If I did that, I wouldn't have let you sleep here all night! I wouldn't have scrubbed your blood from my floor… I-I wouldn't have made you eggs because I don't know what else to do!"

"Alright," he concedes with his hands upturned apologetically. I can't tell if I imagine the genuine guilt in his voice or not. At least he isn't laughing. "Alright. I'm an asshole. I get it."

"You are," I hiss, feeling my eyes burn ominously. Nothing I do keeps the tears at bay. They fall regardless. "You're lucky you didn't bleed to death. What the hell was that?"

"That?" He glances away, raking his hand through his hair. "Just boys being boys, bunny."

"Stop calling me that!" My foot flies out, kicking the remnants of my plate across the room. I don't know why I'm so angry. Why my breathing hitches as I take in the scarlet smears staining my sheets. Why the sight of his mocking, taunting smirk enrages me now more than ever. "You could have *died*."

His expression falls flat, and he groans, using my bed as leverage to haul himself to his feet. "Come here—"

"Get off me!"

His arms go around my waist regardless, drawing me in. The firmness of his chest conforms to my body, and there is no escaping it. God, he's *too* firm, encompassing me easily with his bulk.

"You saved my ass, bunny," he murmurs. I'm alarmed to realize that his fingers are in my hair, stroking through the tangled strands. "I mean it."

I glance up to find him staring down at me. He's honest, even in his expressions. It's so rare to someone who comes from a family where smiles are used to mask any unseemly emotion that might ruin the mood at the dinner table. Or obscure lies. Tears. A smile is a mere token in my world…

But he's able to convey so much with only a frown.

In the face of such an expression, I feel brave enough to ask, "What did you mean last night? That I looked like you?"

He winces and turns his attention to his hip, flexing his injured leg. A grunt of approval resonates through his chest. "You stitched me up good, eh, rabbit?"

As if to keep me from asking more, his arms curve around me, making me a slave to his swaying, unsteady motions. In some sick way, they almost feel…comforting. At least until my gaze falls to his leg—and the pink thread holding him together—and I realize that the rocking is more a result of him fighting to stand at all than anything else.

"I bet that hurts," I rasp.

"Like a bitch." He runs a hand down the side of his thigh. "We could have picked a better color, though. Pink. That's gonna leave a mark on my soul, bunny."

"Don't tell me Bonnie's not a fan of the color," I reply.

He laughs but raises an eyebrow as if he's not sure why exactly he finds the response funny. "Who the fuck cares?" He sways again, letting his mouth brush the top of my scalp so that his words drip into my skull. "I don't let her, or anyone, ride my dick longer than it takes to come. But…" I sense him hesitate. "Your boyfriend certainly seems like the clingy type. Five a.m. is a bit early for a wake-up text, bunny. Does the fucker ever sleep?"

My head swivels toward the living room. Even from here, I can hear that telltale ping. Sighing, Rafe lets me go, using the wall for support. As the seconds pass, his strength seems to return, enough that he can limp past me without assistance.

"Thank you," he grits out, shooting a glance at the eggs still littering the floor. "I owe ya one, rabbit."

"Wait." I wring my hands together, unsure of why I just don't let him go right now. He should. After all, what might happen to him next isn't any of my concern. I wrestle with that logic, but in the end, it doesn't make a difference. "Do you… Do you at least want something to eat first?"

Racing to the fridge before he can answer, I grab a pack of cheese from one of the shelves and blindly snatch a loaf of bread from the counter. Within minutes, I have two sloppily made sandwiches. When I finally look over my shoulder, I expect to find the front door swinging on its hinges, and Rafe long gone.

Instead, my gaze meets one of darkness, and I simply blurt out, "Whole or halves?"

He extends a hand streaked with dirt and blood. "Give me a whole one."

I do, crossing the room on bare feet. He takes a bite while holding my gaze, and to his credit, he doesn't grimace at the bland taste. I mimic him, and within the space of a minute, we wind up on opposite sides of the room watching each other.

He eats slowly, almost robotically. I can't seem to take more than a single bite of my sandwich, though, and its remains rest limply in my hand. Rafe is on his last chunk of bread and cheese when I finally find my voice again.

"Who was that guy? G-Gino—"

"A dick," he says before taking another bite.

"You could have killed him."

He chuckles. "Could have. But I didn't, now did I?"

"It seems as though it was personal," I say softly.

"He's *personally* a dick, but that's not what you meant, is it? He hates me because I've fucked his bitch." He chews casually, almost as if daring me to react. I certainly don't disappoint him when I flinch.

"She must be lovely for you to call her that," I snap.

He grunts, licking his fingers. "She's a good fuck. A bit clingy for my tastes. Spends my money like a motherfucker, but she's real about what she wants. There are no games when it comes to her."

My cheeks flame. I want to be angry, but I sense that every word he's saying is designed to irritate me. Why? Because a tiny pinging tune keeps sounding every few seconds, drawing his attention to the couch despite my best attempts to ignore it.

"That's not why you attacked him, though," I point out, raising my voice over the noise. His mouth flattens into a firm line, and I wonder if I should even broach the topic. I shouldn't—but I keep seeing that look on his face. That rage. That pain. "He called your mother a—"

Ping! Ping! Ping! My phone is alive, practically vibrating across the floor where I left it.

"You want to answer that?" he wonders, his head cocked, a far different question visible in his gaze. *Why aren't you answering it?*

"You should drink something," I blurt out while heading toward the sink, determined not to let him get to me. "You could be dehydrated—"

"I'm fine," he says, but he doesn't ignore the glass I offer him, filled from the tap. After taking a measured sip, he wipes his mouth with the back of his hand and places the glass on the end table beside him. "You live here alone?"

I don't like how curious he sounds. "Why?"

"I'm trying to decide if it's you or your boyfriend who has such shit taste." He eyes my bare walls with a scoff. "You need flowers or some shit, bunny, to brighten up the place. It looks like a jail cell in here—" He eyes my door, and the series of locks affixed to it. "This neighborhood is shit," he admits, "but it's not bad enough for that. Or that." He nods to my television, namely the small camera perched on top of it. "You don't strike me as the video making type."

"Like you're the expert?" I hiss, only to belatedly realize he might be.

"I just meant that your bed is small, rabbit," he says. "I don't see us fucking in it. And as a rule, I don't bring chicks back to my place. I don't like my sheets smelling like pussy. Maybe this is a sign?"

"A sign of what?" I demand against my better judgment.

He shrugs. "That it's probably not a good idea for you to hop on my dick, after all. Hate to disappoint."

I feel my mouth drop open. "You are such an asshole." A shrill sound pierces the quiet, louder than my text alert noise. My ringtone.

I freeze, my eyes on the device. It's within arm's reach of Rafe, and he doesn't hesitate to grab it now. Deliberately, he crosses to me, shoving it into my hand, but he doesn't back away. He uses his body as a barrier to block me in against the window. "Answer it."

I don't even have to see the name flashing across the screen to know who's calling. I can practically read it written across Rafe's icy stare. *Bran <3.*

"Fucking answer it," he demands.

I do, scrambling to bring the receiver to my mouth. "H-Hello?"

"Hannah."

"B-Bran?" I nearly drop the phone as fear penetrates my voice. Rafe stiffens, but I do my best to ignore him by injecting false cheer into my tone. "H-Hey… W-What's going on? I…I was just making some breakfast."

"Yummy," he says flatly. "I texted you last night. You didn't answer. I've been fucking texting you."

"Oh, really?" I feign confusion. "My phone must have been on silent. I'm sorry." My voice sounds hollow, like a bad actress speaking too loudly on stage. "And yesterday, I was really busy. We got tied up at the shop—"

"Too busy for me?" he counters. "The one person who gives a shit about you? For fuck's sake, Hannah. All I ask is that you keep in contact with me. Is that so fucking hard?"

"I'm sorry—"

"Sorry? After everything I've fucking done for you? You know, you've been acting differently ever since that bullshit story made the paper. You think that means something? You're so damn selfish. Wasting all this money on a worthless fucking degree, and for what? To get fucking attention by leaving home? Unless that's not *really* why you came here. Take a picture," he demands. "Now."

"B-Bran…" The hurt pinching in my chest gives way to genuine alarm. My hair is a mess. Despite changing, I think there's blood on my clothing. Too many flaws to disguise even in a simple snapshot—not to mention Rafe, looming as if daring me to make him move. "I just got out of the shower, Bran."

He scoffs at the excuse. "Do it. Show me you're safe. That you're not fucking lying to me…" He pauses deliberately, and I have a horrible sense as to why he's really so angry. "I had Liam come by your apartment last night—*you weren't there.*"

I feel my thumb flinch for the red button at the bottom of the screen. Hanging up will only piss him off. Enrage him. But his prying is too much to take on top of my bloody sewing session last night and everything else crowding my skull for attention. My skill for enduring is nonexistent. For once, I can't play along.

"I have to go."

"Wait—"

"I love you. Bye."

From the corner of my eye, I see Rafe watching me, his expression unreadable as I stow the phone in the pocket of my sweatpants. Did he hear any of that conversation? I can't even look at him.

"You should leave," I tell him softly.

"Sure thing, bunny." Pulling away from the wall, he manages to keep his balance long enough to undo my series of locks and open the door. Right before he steps into the hall, his fingers reach out, grazing the jagged hole right beside the doorjamb—my breathing stills. Though, if he suspects anything at all from the sight, he doesn't reveal as much out loud.

"Let me know when you want that favor," he says, letting his hand fall. "Oh…and I hope your boyfriend doesn't mind the mess." Without ever looking back, he crosses over the threshold and slams the door in his wake.

CHAPTER ELEVEN

I'd been so naïve when I first moved into this place. To innocent Hannah from over a month ago, freedom could be found simply by scrubbing away the grime in her small, one-bedroom apartment to make it her own. Hope then had smelled like the dust and chemical cleaner that punctuated those first steps in reclaiming my life. Breaking away from Branden, I finally moved out, even if it were only a few minutes' drive away.

That fragile pride had lasted all of the ten seconds it took for him to visit with his "housewarming" present. It sits on my TV now, an electronic eye staring blankly as I tackle the mess scattered across my apartment.

The spilled eggs.

The stray thread.

The blood.

I rearrange my throw pillows to cover the stains on the chair I can't get out and sweep the wooden floors to no avail. It still looks barren. What had Rafe called it? A jail cell.

Desperate to ignore the phantom of him, I throw on a sundress and head outside, wandering aimlessly. I don't go to the bookstore just yet. Instead, I take a longer route, cutting through a part of downtown that extends my walk by nearly twenty minutes.

Halfway, I find myself pausing near a pop-up market of all places. I don't know why. Its offerings consist of fresh produce supplied by farmers from outside of the city. I grab some veggies with the idea of making them for dinner, but right before I leave, I snatch something else, leaving the money on the counter.

The bouquet of fresh yellow tulips smell, tickling my nose during the entire walk to the Paper Crane. I find a plastic cup and fill it with water, setting them aside, along with my veggies, while I get to work.

Today, I discover Mr. Zhang in the back room, poring over inventory. He spots me and nods in a silent greeting. "You're just in time." He points at a fresh box waiting to be unloaded. "You can help with this."

We work in friendly harmony during the entire shift—without a visitor who barges in unannounced.

It doesn't sink in until I leave that he never came. Is his leg still healing? Or worse…

Shaking my head, I try to dispel the worries. I shouldn't give a damn if he's in a ditch somewhere, suffering from an infection. He'd deserve it.

With my tulips and vegetables in hand, I force myself to head toward my building, putting all thoughts of him aside. But my legs rebel, and I keep going, eventually reaching a destination I should be doing everything I can to avoid.

It's open. The light is on, and a lone figure leans against the counter with his back to the window. To the world. But he's not alone.

Another man stands near the door, dressed in jeans and a leather jacket. From his size alone, I recognize him as the older man from the club. His voice is loud enough to hear from paces away. "You're just going to let that fucker go? Any other time, you'd crush those sons of bitches—"

"Not tonight," Rafe says without looking up. His voice conveys an authority even the older man seems to respect because he doesn't interrupt. "Gino's not an idiot. He's desperate. We go too hard now and tip our hand, then he'll have every right to retaliate. It's better if we bide our fucking time. Let him sweat."

"So you just let him off?" the man exclaims. "Fuck, Rafe. They could have killed your ass. If your uncle were here, he'd—"

"But he's not, is he?" Rafe hisses, lifting his head. I've never seen his gaze so hard. "And in case you haven't fucking noticed, I am not him—" He breaks off the second he spots me, his eyes narrowing. Almost imperceptibly, he shakes his head. *Go.* Just as quickly, he returns his attention to the man before him. "Shore up the club. If those assholes are dumb enough to come crawling back, then we can act. Got it?"

The other man whirls on his heel without comment and storms from the shop. He's too irritated to even notice me as he marches past and climbs into a car parked alongside the curb.

As he drives off, a shadow falls over me, thicker than the darkness cast by the setting sun. "You're a long way from home, bunny."

I turn in time to catch him loping behind the counter. He moves easily enough, despite leaning slightly to one side. The wound must be in a position that doesn't hamper his ability to walk. Or intimidate. "Back for more?" he wonders coldly from over his shoulder.

"More what?" I whisper, creeping forward until I'm standing in the doorway.

"Don't play dumb." He turns, shooting me a searching glance that leaves no doubt. He's furious. "You *know* what."

"I wanted to make sure you weren't lying dead somewhere." I hate how earnest I sound. "You didn't come by the store."

"No, no little bunny…" He wags a finger. "That's not why you're here. You wanted to play on the wild side a little more. Unfortunately, I'm too tired to play the role of a bad boy to your innocent nun right now." He braces both hands against the countertop, glaring at the polished surface. "Go run back to *Bran*."

"Nice." I blink incredulously. His dismissive tone shouldn't hurt. Maybe I could understand the hostility if the explanation weren't so…obvious. "So, I save your skin, and you turn into an asshole because you're jealous?"

"I'm not jealous," he counters. "I'm *bored.* Of you. Now hop along, I have shit to take care of." He shrugs me off and steps from around the counter, lumbering toward the back of the shop. "I said, get the fuck out."

I leave, picking up speed, my chest tight. By the time I return to my building, I'm shaking. I push open the battered front door and enter the foyer only to stop short.

Unease runs down my spine as my gaze fixates on the old, wooden staircase leading upstairs. I'd be kidding myself if I claimed not to sense the wrongness in the air even before I climb the four flights up to my apartment. Sure enough, my door is ajar as if someone let themselves in but were too irritated to close it behind them.

So irritated that they broke through all five of my locks.

An intruder? A thief or murderer?

One could only hope. Deep down, I know the truth even before I prop open the door with my foot while clutching the tulips in one hand. Flowers are so distracting—I think there's a reason people bring them to funerals, letting their bright colors and pleasant smells mask the stench of death and despair.

Amid all the pain, and fear, and horrible, cloying emotions…

There's something pretty to look at.

At this moment, my tulip's crisp scent mingles with the warm breeze blowing in through the open window and disperses throughout the space. The smell alone almost makes the tiny, cramped living room seem spacious and inviting. The secondhand furniture gleams in the flickering light of a fluorescent fixture hanging from the ceiling. I barely notice the scuffs on the hardwood floor or the peeling paint on the far wall, which the landlord swore were just "part of the charm."

It's perfect.

Until it isn't.

A tall, lanky figure crouches beside my television, fiddling with the supposedly broken camera perched on top of it. He frowns, his handsome features creased in concentration. His body propped on one knee as his muscular arms ripple with tension.

"Branden?" My other hand is curled around the bottom of a shopping bag that I have to keep bouncing higher on my hip. I can't even reach for the cell phone in my pocket as it continues to buzz incessantly with incoming text messages. Only now can I admit to myself that it's been going off all day.

"You weren't answering your phone," he says without turning around. He inspects the camera, gazing into its unseeing lens while inserting something into the back of the device.

Fixing it.

"You're supposed to be in Santa Barbara," I rasp.

Despite the gray T-shirt and jeans he wears, anyone with an ounce of deduction skills can tell he's a cop. It might take a bit more sleuthing, however, to figure out that—despite the stern expression and rigid posture—he's also supposed to be "enjoying" his two-week-long vacation.

"Where were you?"

"At work," I say. "Then, I went shopping."

He darts his gaze in my direction, honing in on my bag of veggies and fresh flowers. "Those are pretty," he says, nodding toward the tulips. "It's about damn time you did something to brighten up the place."

His hazel eyes sweep the narrow living room disapprovingly from the plain brown couch and gray armchair to the hardwood floors and minuscule kitchen space. *This is normal,* I tell myself. Most big brothers let themselves into their sister's tiny apartments uninvited. They install video cameras in their living rooms and request that their partners make drive-by visits in the middle of the night—but most big brothers don't have service weapons tucked into their back pockets.

Most brothers aren't Branden.

"Camera's fixed," he says, rising to his feet. "Try not to break this one, okay?"

"I thought you weren't coming back until next week?" It's a harmless question on the surface.

But his eyes flash, his fingers tearing through his hair. "What, you *liked* having me away?"

"N-No." I know better than to argue. Instead, I place my tulips on the end table near my door. Then I cross the four feet of space it takes to enter the kitchen. Inhaling deeply, I arrange my veggies on the counter, trying to decide what I'll keep in the fridge and what I'll leave out to ripen.

Tomatoes? Maybe out.

Peppers? In the fridge…

If I squint or squeeze my eyes shut, I can almost pretend I'm alone again. Almost. Branden's unease seeps into the walls, making them seem to close in, inch by inch…

"Kaitlin had some work to finish up for an assignment, so we came back early," he explains, referring to his wife's job as a consultant. "Try not to look so disappointed."

"I'm not." I turn to find him staring resolutely out of the window as if ignoring his surroundings makes them easier to stomach. "I'm g-glad to see you. I am."

His jaw twitches, though his overall expression remains neutral. "Why didn't you answer your phone?"

I palm a carrot, then a tomato. "I told you. I was shopping—"

"How was I supposed to know that? You could have been murdered or unconscious somewhere. I told you to answer your fucking phone when I call." His steps slam against the floorboards. *Thud. Thud. Thunk.*

The tomato I'm holding slips from my grasp, bouncing across the length of my kitchen.

And he stops. "I'm just saying that you're not used to living in this type of neighborhood… It's not like how it is back home. You're not living on Mommy and Daddy's property where a gate and a security guard keep the world at bay. Hannah—" His voice takes on that heavy edge that means he's about to deliver one of his trademark *"I'm just looking out for you"* speeches. "I just don't understand why you had to move out. You had a room all to yourself. A bathroom. Kaitlin didn't mind, and I could protect you."

"I'm twenty-one, Bran," I whisper.

But to be honest, I'm not sure why either after so many years of living under his thumb. Why now? Why this ratty place, as far from his as my budget—and fall classes— would allow. It certainly wasn't the only rental listing and definitely not the most spacious. I think the real answer lies in the fact that I scouted it out on my own. Met with the landlord and toured the dusty rooms *on my own*. In fact, I hadn't even told Branden I was moving out until I'd paid my security deposit.

And phoned my parents to get their approval.

If I let him talk me out of this apartment, it will be even easier for him to talk me out of the next one. And the one after. In the end, I'll be thirty, still living in his guestroom under his careful watch.

Even with the stupid camera, this is better.

"Are you busy tonight?"

Alarm shoots down my spine. This conversation isn't anywhere near over. Not that I'm in any position to stall. My throat constricts, but I force myself to keep breathing.

Stay calm.

"Are you?"

"No."

"Good." He crosses over to the door, pulling it open. "I'll take you out to dinner. We need to talk."

"Dad called." Branden casually tucks a piece of brown hair behind his ear and glances at the ornate mirror hanging on the wall across from where we stand. In lieu of his uniform, he's wearing a White Sox T-shirt and a pair of jeans. The casual attire cuts years off his age; he almost resembles a college student taking a break from finals.

And our resemblance is on display to its fullest effect—light and dark—two halves of the same damaged coin.

Beside him, I look sickly. My hair is an unruly mess coiled on the top of my head, and bloodshot eyes betray the lack of sleep I'd gotten last night. The only redeeming quality is my outfit—a starched yellow blouse and a gray skirt—but it's painfully obvious I overcompensated. Bright colors and neatly ironed lines can only disguise so much.

Like the scent of secondhand smoke lingering in my clothing.

The blood still caked beneath my fingernails.

The touch I still feel rasping over my skin.

"Hannah?"

"Oh?" I shrug, though my heart is racing. Random invitations to dinner simply aren't Branden's style.

He even let me pick the place, so we went to The Red Duck, a Chinese restaurant a few blocks away from my apartment. Despite how he sneers at the scenery, he has yet to make a single derogatory comment. It's like he's gearing up to broach one topic in particular.

His next words prove it. "So…Dad said you asked for some money?"

"Yeah." I do my best to muster up what I hope passes for another casual shrug. In the mirror, my failure is reflected. My eyes are too wide. Fearful.

"You did," Branden says cautiously. "What for?"

From across the room, a waitress approaches, wearing a bright red kimono-style miniskirt. She's pretty with long black hair accented with a sparkly butterfly hair clip and dark eyes that dart from me to Branden and widen. Her reaction makes me frown. Something about her face triggers a sense of recognition, but I don't know why. My attention keeps drifting to her hair clip, and that uncanny sensation grows stronger.

I know her somehow.

But her name isn't familiar. A name tag pinned to her chest reads, "Faith," which seems ironic enough to explain the unease. If only Branden had any faith left in me—maybe then I could avoid the interrogation that I know is coming.

Right on cue, he clears his throat. "You never ask for money. And since when are you into designer purses?"

Biting my lip, I say nothing while Faith leads us to a secluded booth near the back of a beautifully decorated dining room.

"H-Here you are," she says, cutting her eyes to the floor as Branden pushes past her and settles onto the bench. She's gone before I've even taken my seat.

"What did you need the money for?" Branden asks. He casually flips through his menu, but I recognize his tone.

"N-Nothing." My voice trembles, nearly swallowed up by the clang of silverware and murmuring voices.

I know that he heard me anyway when a fiery shade of red creeps along his neck. "Do not lie to me."

"Nothing! Just some stupid purse—"

"You suddenly drop ten grand on a purse when you wouldn't even look outside of a Goodwill for furniture for your own apartment?" He shakes his head, his eyes flashing. "Did Dad also tell you that he got a call from Karen Winacott?"

"W-Who?" I shrug again, but even I can admit that the motion is too fast. Too jerky.

With a sigh, Branden sits back against the wall of the booth, but the look in his eyes is anything but placated. "Someone from back home. You probably don't even remember her." His tone straddles the dangerous line between sarcasm and neutrality. I can't tell which reaction is real.

"So, where is this bag that you just *had* to have?" he asks, switching the subject. "Don't tell me that's it." He nods to the knitted bag resting on the seat beside me.

"I..." My throat contracts around a hard swallow. "I didn't bring it."

"Maybe because this money you suddenly needed..." He forms a steeple with his fingers and places his chin on the very tip. "Does it have anything to do with Mr. Zhang's 'problems' down at the Paper Crane?"

"H-Here you are!" Faith returns to set a jug of ice water down between us, but when she tries to fill my glass, she misses, and water sloshes onto the table instead.

"Dammit," Branden hisses as he snatches up a wad of napkins. "Just leave it. Fuck—"

"Sorry!" Faith squeaks before darting away, her face beet red.

"Bran, it's fine." I grab the pitcher myself and fill my glass. "You don't have to yell."

"Then answer my damn question," he counters, fixing the brunt of his wrath on me. His eyes blaze, and in slow motion, I see my fingers rip away from the pitcher. It falls over again, spilling water as fire lances through my arm. It's only when I try to reflexively draw it toward me that I realize why. He has my forearm in his grasp, the knuckles white. Bruising. "Zhang's bookstore got vandalized. Is *that* why you suddenly needed a couple of thousand?"

"I don't know what you're talking about," I insist, my voice high-pitched. Broken. "*Please—*"

"Hannah…" His eyes narrow, his grip tightening. "Don't lie to me. Liam was the one called out to Zhang's little accident. You didn't tell me. Why?"

I can't hide the surprise that crosses my face. "I…I…"

"You tell me everything. Unless someone got inside of your head. Like Karen fucking Winacott, running her goddamn mouth. Did you speak to her?" His voice is so cold, hushed so that no one nearby turns to stare. He's so good at this. From the outside, even his grip on me could pass for helpful. Supportive.

Not *hurting*. Numb, I stare down at my wrist, watching as my fingers flex over the table's surface. "You're hurting me."

He flinches, then tightens his grip… Then all at once, he lets me go, sitting back against his side of the booth. "I'm the only one looking out for you, Hannah. Do you have any fucking idea what I've done for you? Do you?"

I have an idea.

Terrorized me.

Followed me to another state.

Controlled.

Manipulated.

Always, always, always…

"I'll tell you. I looked out for you when Mom was too drunk to give a shit. When Dad was off fucking his secretary rather than caring for you. When everyone else bullied you and pitied you. I was there. I *always* defended you."

"You did," I admit hoarsely. But whenever I look back on those memories now, they don't feel so heartwarming or so valiant. "And you were tough, right?" I say. "Like when you pushed me down the stairs because I accidentally broke your skateboard that one time."

He rolls his eyes. "That was ages ago, Hannah."

"You broke my wrist," I say, eyeing the limb in question. "And when I tried to fit in. When I *tried* to stop being bullied for always being alone, you made me cut my hair. You started a rumor that I had lice. You told me that no one thought I was pretty. That's why I had to let you tell me how to dress. How to do my hair. How to act. Why you watched me shower—"

"What the fuck are you saying?" He slams his hands over the table, leaning across it. "Do you think this shit is funny?"

"You even made friends for me, right?" I blurt out, unable to stop. "Like Lexi? Pretty Lexi, who looked like me. Everyone said so—"

"Enough!" He slams his hand on the table in a way that doesn't draw notice from anyone else. But my body goes rigid. Before my eyes, he transforms. His entire body ripples with tension, his eyes flashing. "And you were always a liar, Hannah," he growls. "*That's* why Mom left you. Why Dad married some stupid bitch rather than take care of you. Why *you* caused every problem that ever plagued this family. You're a fucking selfish, stupid, ungrateful little liar. No one ever wanted you but me. No one ever gave a shit about you but *me*."

I look down at the table, biting my lip so hard I taste blood. But surprisingly? I don't feel anything.

"Am I wrong?" he demands. "Say it."

"I'm sorry."

"Good." His voice softens, and he sits back. "I want you to move back in. Tonight. I'll pay out the rest of your lease—"

"No."

He blinks. "What did you say?"

Nothing like always. But my burning lips contradict the instincts I've spent years honing to an art form. Silence. Endurance. Passive, obedient Hannah.

"It's not like you didn't pick one of the most dangerous fucking neighborhoods to live in," Branden snaps. In frustration, he snatches a neatly folded napkin from the table and unfurls it. "I've warned you, Hannah. Look, I don't know if you're just trying to provoke me or what. Moving into the center of territory owned by the fucking triad? Do you know what happens around here? I'll tell you. Murder, extortion, prostitution, and worse. This place is a fucking shithole and…" He releases a heavy sigh and picks up the menu resting on his side of the table as if hunting for a distraction. His ruse is slipping, his voice far too loud. Someone from the next table over glances in our direction, and he exhales, forcing some of the tension from his posture. "You know you can always come home, don't you?"

Home. That word affects me more strongly than I would have thought, and I shift on my side of the bench, curling my toes in their sandals.

"I know," I concede in a whisper, "but we've talked about this. I need to try living on my own. I know it's not ideal, but…" I bite my lip, keeping one more secret inside. Ironically, *he* is the only reason I found my apartment, renting at a steal. I'd noticed the torn page of rental listings on the kitchen table while living in his house, scattered amongst a bunch of case files on one of the rare nights he'd been too tired to lock them all away.

"Hannah?"

"I'm fine," I choke out.

"Fine," he echoes ominously while dragging his finger down the list of menu items. "But you deserve to be *safe*. What happened at the shop was the last straw. I've already called your landlord."

I want to be upset. Indignant…

I'm exhausted.

I'm *scared*.

"I don't—"

"Hello." A new waitress has appeared to take our order. With her eyes downcast, she disappears and returns with our food only a few minutes later. "It's on the house," she murmurs before retreating again.

Branden just grunts and snatches a fork. "This fucking place… Anyway, I've already had Kaitlin fix up your room. You can move in tomorrow—"

"Branden."

"Don't." He looks up sharply, his nostrils flaring, his neck that alarming shade of red. "I let you carry on with this bullshit for long enough. Coming all the way here was one thing, but now? You're pushing me, Hannah. You're fucking pushing me—again."

I inhale and clasp my hands together to disguise how they shake. "I'm sorry—"

"Sorry?" His gaze hardens, and I have to fumble for my bag as a woman walking past eyes my shaking fingers. For once, Branden is too fixated on me to care how he looks or sounds. Unrestrained, his voice deepens, touching on a growl. "You remember what happens when you act selfish, Hannah? The trouble you cause? What you make me do?"

A chill washes over me. *I remember.*

Memories too horrific to write down, at least in explicit terms. Instead, they lurk in prose and symbolism, caged in unsaid meaning. *Freedom's price paid with the blood of another...*

That phrase, in particular, weighs down one page in my journal. I'm holding it now, balancing my bag on my lap, but the thick pages don't impart the same sense of comfort I'm used to finding. I have to grasp for something else, nestled at the very bottom of the knitted material. Something small and firm sporting a roaring creature emblazoned on its surface.

"I love you," Branden says, his expression softening. "But sometimes it feels as though you don't love me. As though you don't respect me. Hannah?"

I'm on my feet without realizing it, scrambling from the booth. "I...I have to go to the bathroom," I stammer, racing to explain my own actions, but deep down, I'm just as puzzled as he seems to be.

What am I doing?

Not suppressing. Not relying on instinct. I'm not enduring —I'm running.

"Hannah?" He sits forward as I snatch my bag. "Do you need your purse to go to the bathroom?"

"I...I'm on my period. I'll be back." My heart pounds as I weave my way through the aisles too quickly for him to follow. The bathroom is at the back of the restaurant, but I seem to be heading in the wrong direction. Toward the front, past the hostess stand...

Out.

My speed picks up as I meld into a crowd of giggling partiers crossing the street. I can't stop. Panting, I keep going, scurrying from block to block until my neighborhood is entirely in the distance.

CHAPTER TWELVE

I don't know where I'm headed—or maybe I *do*, but I just don't want to admit it to myself as pieces of the city pass by in a blur. Bright lights. Featureless faces. A million different sights, smells, and sounds that barely register until I finally reach a building framed by the taunting visage of a dragon.

The main glass door opens easily when I pull on the handle, but the lights are dimmed inside, and the showroom is deserted. But he's here—I can smell him. Blindly, I stumble forward, through a darkened hallway and eventually reach a cavernous space illuminated by a single, harsh circle of light.

He stands hunched over a table strewn with loose sheets of paper. His shirt is off, and the artificial light above plays over the bare muscle sculpting his back, giving definition to the dragon. It coils with motion, breathing fire in my presence while he works. I come closer before I can stop myself, spying the work in progress from over his shoulder.

My breathing hitches—this drawing is different than the others adorning his walls.

Thinner lines and lighter shapes form a far different creature from his raging dragons. The sketching itself seems hesitant as if he loathes himself for every mark, but he can't help it. He draws her regardless. A girl with long dark hair and wild bangs; her guarded eyes wide but dark. Her gaze contains a million secrets locked within, seemingly impenetrable to anything or anyone…

Until her creator goes rigid, slashing an involuntary line through her face.

"What are you doing here, rabbit?" he wonders without bothering to turn around, demanding an answer to a question that I don't even have the nerve to ask myself. He drops the pen, and his fist forms a barrier over the face he's sketched, marring the details. "Answer the question."

But I can't. Maybe I'm just a masochist? Or I'm just spiraling because of one glaring fact that dashes what little harmony I've found. Branden wants me to move back. In theory, my brother's house represents everything safe that I've stubbornly left behind, and *this* space dominated by *this* irritating man has fucked up what little freedom I've strived to find for myself.

Because every time I imagine going back, I hear his voice. *You've seen a much worse monster. I want to meet that monster. I want to know what makes a little rabbit like you so damn hard she doesn't flinch when a man presses a knife to her throat.*

"You ruined my life," I shout, arguing against the incorporeal Rafe more than the real thing. I don't even recognize the voice echoing off the walls. Hannah Dewitt doesn't sound like this stranger—so bitterly angry. So insane. "You goddamn, selfish asshole!"

"I'm only going to say this once, bunny." He cocks his head back to face me, letting his fearsome expression drill in the threat. "Get the fuck out." His hair obscures most of his face, but those eyes lurk behind the jagged strands like predators hunting from the shadows. Only this time, I'm not sure whether or not I'm the prey.

"You ruined my life." I'm on autopilot. A broken record forced to bleat the same damn thing to anyone who will listen. "Everything is all wrong because of *you!*"

"Good. Because you hated living it anyway, little rabbit. Coming here… You must be fucking suicidal. What? Your boyfriend couldn't get you off? I don't think I'll give you the satisfaction this time. Get the fuck out."

I try to counter his hostility with a bitter laugh that comes out sounding broken. "You don't scare me. You're just a criminal—" I jab my hand into my bag and withdraw an object I've been carrying with me all this time. His lighter. "A stupid one who lets a little rabbit steal from him."

He chuckles. "So you aren't just suicidal. You're fucking crazy." The venom in his tone shocks me when paired with the look in his eyes; it's so cold. Terrifying.

I've been numb for so long, the fear shoots through me like a lance, different from anything I feel around Branden. It's electrifying.

He's a furnace, throwing off rage like heat. From how his shoulders are set in a rigid line down to his clenched jaw. Behind him, the drawing in progress spills out like an ominous warning. Wide-eyed Hannah, her lips parted. *Run.*

"Why are you here?" he demands, pivoting to block my view once again. "Fucking admit it."

He advances on me without warning. My back strikes the wall because I'm too unfamiliar with this layout, and he's too fast, closing in the moment I falter.

"Still bored, little rabbit?" His thumb prods my chin. The pad of it is wet and leaves behind something that smells sharp—ink.

I push away from him, desperate to ignore the way his heat eats through my skin. After a few shaky steps forward, I realize I'm not heading in the smart direction toward the door. I go straight for his table instead, toward the figure mocking me. I hate that she's beautiful in a way I could only dream of embodying. Her smile belongs to a stranger, and her eyes are so wide, they resemble camera lenses. Watching. Watching. Always.

But never fucking living.

Before I know it, the lighter is in my hand again, raised higher. My thumb flicks the spark wheel once. Twice. Like magic, a flame appears, promising destruction.

And I lunge, pressing it to the paper.

It ignites in a beautiful, horrifying display of color. Pale yellow. Brilliant orange. Tinges of red… All of it devours his image of me in an instant.

"What the fuck is wrong with you?" He grabs my arm—hard. A cry rips from my lips as the force spins me around. Desperate, I lash out with the one weapon I have on hand—the lighter.

"Let me go!"

"Fucking…stop!" He wrestles the lighter away from me and throws it. The fire has already died, smothered by his batting hands.

In a frantic search for another weapon, my grasping fingers find something thin and round lying on his desk. A pen. I throw it at his chest, and it breaks, splattering black paint across the dragon's wings. "I said, let me go!"

He retaliates by stepping in, gripping my shoulders and snatching me toward him. "Get the fuck out. Go run back to Bran—"

"Shut up!" Something inside me audibly *snaps!* I hear it. Feel it. Succumb. My nails are digging into any part of him I can reach, and I draw blood. I stare at the ruts in shock as he seizes my shoulders and shoves me back. I push him harder.

And it feels so fucking *good* to hurt him in any way that I can. Someone. Anyone. I want him to bleed. To ache. To know what it feels like to be so fucking raw on the inside and not understand why.

I hate him. God, I hate him.

When he reaches for me again, I clutch his arm and sink my teeth in.

"What the fuck?" He shoves me so hard that I go flying. My only salvation is I catch myself against a haphazard stack of boxes piled near the door.

"Psycho *bitch*," he snarls, but his stance is angled toward me, his weight balanced on the balls of his feet despite his injury. I'm reminded of a bullfighter purposely goading the beast he faces.

You want to fight? So fight.

My mind goes blank as I lunge at him, shrieking something wordless.

He grabs me before I can even touch him. *Wham!* My butt strikes the surface of the table, and then he's flush against me, holding both of my arms trapped above my head.

Memory descends for an awful second—the sheer terror that comes with being rendered immobile…but unlike him, I still have use of my legs. "Let go!" I kick him until my arms are freed. Then I scratch. Slap. Bite. Draw blood.

My heart races, the pulsing sound goading me. *Fight, Hannah. Fight, fight, fight. Kill. Kill. Kill.*

My advantage doesn't last long. He's too big. Too heavy. There's no recognition of the man staring down at me. Fire licks at the edges of those unfathomable irises while a sound like a growl rumbles up from his chest. I don't think he's even human anymore.

But neither am I.

"You're a bastard," I tell him. "I hate you! I fucking hate you!"

He doesn't even flinch. He braces himself over me, relishing the power of his position. The strength that makes my attempts to escape futile. Leisurely, his hands palm my hips, pinning me down…crushing me while he leans in. His breath sears my lips in a warning before his mouth is on mine.

He wants me to panic. I know he does. Instead, my lips part out of sheer instinct, and our tongues clash, wrestle, and attack. I bite down hard, but for some reason, my legs wrap around his waist so he can't pull away—not that he tries to. Grunting, he fists his hand in my hair and yanks. The pain is enough to make me release my jaw, and he eagerly takes advantage by plunging his tongue in so deep that I gag. Regardless, I copy the action, jabbing and striking.

Even that violence isn't enough. I flex my fingers until the nails succeed in piercing the skin on his chest. I can almost smell the blood, and it doesn't disgust me this time. I relish it. Crave it. I want more.

I hate him. *Hate, hate, hate.*

But when his hands go to my hips, I don't resist, and once he grinds his pelvis into mine, the friction has me breaking free of the kiss just to grate my teeth. My knees clench, gripping him tighter until my heels dig into the back of his thighs, and he's closer to me than anyone has ever been.

His heavy-lidded gaze warns that he knows as much. I can only gape as his hand dips between my legs and rubs through my panties. Once. Twice. Before I can fully adjust, he tugs the gusset aside and slides a finger beneath. Then inside me.

"Shit…" As if from far away, I hear him groan, echoing the gasp escaping my lips.

No one's ever touched me like this. Nothing has ever *felt* like this. Like being on fire yet submerged in ice at the same time. Conflicting. Intoxicating. My fingers flex greedily against his skin. I want more. With every stroke, the pleasure spreads. Muscles I never knew existed tighten in response, and before long, I'm undulating beneath him so violently that the table rocks in time with the motions.

My panties are soaked. His fingers are slick, and all I know is this all-encompassing burn has me reaching down to curl my hand around his wrist. Once again, he interprets my touch however he pleases, rubbing here…stroking there… all over.

I gasp when he withdraws his hand only for *both* to seize my shirt and wrench it open right down the middle. His eyes greedily take advantage of my bare breasts while he tears the rest of the yellow cotton away. My panties, he drags down my legs and tosses on the floor, in addition to my skirt. Then he's working on the latch of his jeans while I stare.

He makes it look artful almost. Like there's some hidden skill required to undo a zipper with a flick of a thumb. Then tug, freeing himself entirely in a fall of denim—but that's all he lets me see.

With a growl, he shoves me down, and then something new—something much fuller than his fingers—is between my legs. I only have a second to realize what's happening. To admit to myself that I *don't* want whatever it is to stop…

One thrust of his hips and a part of me gives way with a cry I can't even hope to silence. He's *inside* me, and the pinch is incredible. His heat is overwhelming. All consuming… I'm drowning beneath a million different sensations.

But his mouth finds my ear. "F-Fuck. You're so tight…" Confusion laces his voice as his fingers prod my chin, forcing me to meet his gaze. His eyes bore into mine, conveying a question I can't answer. So I arch up, sealing my mouth over his instead.

He groans, rocking into me as I lock my knees around his waist. It feels like I'll die if he doesn't move. Explode. Combust.

My voice rings out, a stranger's. "R-Rafe…"

He shivers at the sound of his name, digging his fingers into the backs of my thighs. An experimental buck of his hips draws another gasp from me, my teeth clipping together.

Then another. Another. Again, this time as he snatches me to him, thrusting deeper…

All I can do is dig my nails into his back and hold on. The sound he makes when I moan is so damn wild. Dangerous. Unrestrained, he pushes into me without hesitation this time. Hard. Harder. Beneath me, the table jolts with every thrust, sending an array of tools crashing to the floor.

It's the prelude to the volatile soundtrack we make together. I hear myself moan again amid the creak of the table and his own smothered curses. It's a tune as disjointed and complex as the music from his club. When his voice goes hoarse, he just settles for biting his lower lip, drawing another bead of blood alongside the gash I made.

Thrust after thrust, he picks up speed, using my own weight to enhance the contact. Every dose of friction carries some twisted emotion he's driving into me. I can name them all —*rage, hate, lust.* Like layers of ink, they transform my body into a creation of his own making. Something wild. Untamed. Free. Breathless.

All I can do is let him remake me, riding each wave until I break. It happens so fast, so violently. I claw at his shoulders, and our lips meet again, teeth gnashing until every sound I make is swallowed whole.

He finally pulls away, hissing as my body tightens, resisting his loss. I think it's over, but then he lifts me from the table and shoves me down. I hit the floor, face down, and while I blink in confusion, he hooks one arm around my waist and yanks me up onto my hands and knees. He enters me again before I even get my bearings.

I can't silence a cry—a whimper.

But he doesn't stop, and God…I never want him to.

Mindless, he rocks into me, crushing me with his weight while simultaneously inching our bodies across the ivory tile. *More. More. More.* With every thrust, we leave streaks of black ink everywhere. Ebony handprints. We're darkness, marring the light, and I let him swallow me up whole until nothing's left.

Just fire.

CHAPTER THIRTEEN

"Shit."

I roll over to face a pair of black eyes that reluctantly meet my own.

"Shit," he says again, but there doesn't seem to be any regret in his tone. Just shock. Maybe some confusion. Along with a dash of anger as his gaze cuts to mine, blazing with intensity. "I didn't use a condom—"

"I'm on birth control," I admit with a sigh. Thank God for the abnormally heavy menstrual cycles, which led my mother to suggest I take them all through my teen years, rather than out of any fears of unprotected sex.

Wincing, I brace one hand against the floor and push myself upright. The weight of everything we've done threatens to descend, but I'm too tired. Too tired to worry about the other implications of unsafe sex, such as a potential STD or...

I can't worry about any of it.

"You're a virgin," he rasps, sitting with his back to me. His tattoo looks different, and it takes me a second to understand why. Smears of ink streak his skin—which make the dragon seem more like a shapeless splotch of darkness with glowing red eyes than anything cohesive.

"Your boyfriend?" he asks next, his tone hard. "You haven't been fucking him?"

My lips part. Now could be the time to come clean and admit the truth. But as the breath escapes my lips, he scoffs, drowning out any confession I may voice.

"You were saving yourself, is that it?" he wonders, coming up with his own assumptions. "I've met girls like you before. You want to lose your cherry to some one-night stand you'll never meet again. Get it over with for when you meet that cop or doctor you want to marry." He chokes out a sound between a groan and a laugh before falling silent. For the longest time, he doesn't move. Then… "Did you tell him about me?"

This time, I can't maintain a lie. I shake my head. "No."

He stands in one swift motion, still unabashedly naked. His hand catches my wrist, pulling me upright as well. "Come on," he grunts.

Cool air tickles my skin as I let him lead me through a narrow hallway at the back of the shop, then up a flight of stairs. To another roof? No. The door at the top of this staircase opens into a completely different space. An apartment? Before we cross the threshold, he flicks a light switch that triggers the fluorescent bulbs built into the ceiling.

The glow illuminates a modest living room decorated in shades of red and navy. It's decently furnished with a degree of coordination I wouldn't expect from him. A leather couch and flat-screen television dominate the space, and I can make out a kitchen with modern appliances and plenty of windows with a view of the street below.

The bathroom we eventually enter is no less impressive, nearly triple the size of mine. Black tile flooring and silver fixtures create a sleek, modern style. He has a walk-in shower with a built-in bench, large enough to hold us both with room to spare.

Once I enter the stall, he follows, buffeting me back against the tiled wall. Only now does it sink in what we've done. I'm sore. His bottom lip is bleeding. There's blood streaked along my inner thigh—though I'm not sure if it's mine or his. A glance at his leg reveals that his stitches are intact for the most part, but he's bleeding freely through them, limping as he turns to the faucet and switches it on.

I watch him operate the nozzles, waiting for the regret. The shame. That's how intimacy should feel, isn't it? Shameful. Especially when his eyes are on my naked body, and mine are on his…

Yet all I feel is a sensation comparable to the moment I finally escaped Branden's. Like I can breathe again. Like every inch of my skin prickles with awareness, electrified, and not numb.

I can feel everything at this moment. Like the ice-cold water shooting from the faucet as he finally succeeds in turning it on. The shock draws me closer to his heat before I can stop myself. He goes rigid, only to grip my hips a second later.

And…I almost feel some semblance of the peace I've lost. There's no phone in here. No Branden. No guilt.

But around him, that clarity only seems to come in brief snippets. I'm left shivering when he pulls back, leaving me to stand on my own, and turns to a small plastic bin placed against the wall. From inside it, he takes out a bottle of generic body wash and a carefully folded piece of terry cloth. "Turn around."

I do. The spray of water plasters the hair to my head, muffling the sounds as he comes closer. I feel his touch first —a warm hand that runs down between my shoulder blades, trailed by that rough cloth. I glance down to notice that the water pouring from me is a purplish color…and then eventually a diluted gray as he continues to wipe the ink from me, erasing his marks.

When he's finished, he wordlessly hands me the cloth—my turn. I face him and swallow hard as I take him in. He's so *big* compared to me, seemingly invincible. As I drag the cloth along his forearms, I notice the scratches, though— the bite marks.

He might as well have been attacked by an animal. I finger a bleeding wound, in particular, and my teeth clench in guilt. "I'm sorry—"

"You're not," he snaps, batting my hand away. "You loved every fucking minute of it. Besides, I think I like you psycho, bunny." He strokes my cheek until I look up. He stares back, unflinchingly, once again, not bothering to hide the truth. "I think I like it too much…"

I don't know who moves first, but our lips collide again. We stay like this for a second. Longer. Then he breaks the contact to let me continue with the cloth.

It's harder to wash the ink off him. The swirls of his tattoo make it nearly impossible to know what's inked into his skin and what sits on top of it. I try my best anyway, observing him through touch with the same fervent concentration that my gaze takes him in with.

He's speckled with a million scars, most of them disguised by the harsh outline of the all-encompassing dragon. I can't stop myself from tracing the edge of one with the pad of my finger. When I toy with another, he gently pulls my hand away.

He has me pressed against the stall before I know it. Burning and soft, his lips feather over mine, hesitant at first, then firmer and hungrier. Steam floods the small space as our breaths devolve into pants. Soon, I feel him hardening against my thigh…between my legs.

It's a surreal sensation, and a part of me is too afraid to look. He feels massive. Like there's no way he could ever fit inside me or make this work. I shift, opening my legs to test the fit, and he groans, positioning himself against me.

He waits as if to ensure I won't resist. That I'm breathing just as heavily as he is with eyes just as unfocused. Right when the anticipation becomes unbearable, he pushes in. It hurts for only a second before my muscles expand around him. Grip him.

"Fuck, you're tight," he grates out, his mouth at my throat. Hungrily, his teeth nip at my flesh as he draws back and thrusts in again. "Spread your legs for me. Like this—" He palms my thigh, lifting my knee to his hip and rocks into me slowly, urging me to follow. I do so tentatively, marveling at the sensation. In so many ways, it's like the club all over again.

I do what I can to match his movements until we're writhing in sync. It's almost too easy, natural—as if he's in my head, knowing how I'll react before I do. How I'll arch. Writhe. Moan.

As though he knows me down to the bone.

The end comes quicker this time. Pleasure unfurls with the force of a kick to the stomach as he groans, stilling against me.

I go limp in the aftermath, catching my breath. He's still kissing at my neck, almost leisurely, and I recall the words he said to me on the roof. *I bet you taste sweet.* A groan betrays his thoughts on the result. Gradually, he lets his teeth rake a sliver of flesh—but I have enough sense to stop him. He'll leave a mark.

"D-Don't."

"No damaging the merchandise, huh?" he murmurs against my shoulder. "Can't let him see?" He pushes back from me, using the wall for support.

The water cuts off, dampening the heat of the moment, and I can't escape the sense that more than just the water is circling the drain. The mood has shifted, cooling the heat between us as we step out from the stall.

"Wait here." Naked and dripping wet, he lumbers down the hall into what I can tell is a bedroom and returns with a handful of fabric. He uses the towel to dry me off with an almost studious intensity. Afterward, he helps me slide an oversized gray T-shirt over my head and slips into a pair of sweatpants himself.

He inclines his head to have me follow down the hall, deliberately closing the door to what I assume is his room as we pass it. I guess he wasn't lying about his rule. Am I insulted? How many times have Bonnie or those other "desperate skanks" Mara mentioned been here in this spot?

I can imagine them following some unspoken cue. Once the fun was over, they left. "I should go—"

"You can't stay?" His expression is carefully stoic, but his voice is gruffer than it should be if he were gearing up to kick me out. Questioning. "Is he waiting for you—"

"N-No. I mean… I can stay." I bite my lower lip just so that the brief pain can distract from any panic. *Stay.* There are so many logical reasons to refuse. Branden might be waiting for me at my apartment, and this little voice at the back of my mind warns me to do everything I can to run and forget what just happened.

He should be taunting me to do just that. But for whatever reason, he isn't, and curiosity overrides the unease.

"Come here." He sinks onto the leather couch and pats the space beside him, leaving the decision up to me. Cautiously, I sit just out of his reach. I'm convinced the slight distance makes me safer, but he demolishes my peace of mind once again and reaches out to drag me closer.

Coconut and warmth encase me in a heavy and surprisingly comfortable shell. I don't resist when he lies back with me at his side. I don't think I've ever shared an intimate embrace like this with anyone who isn't related to me by blood.

I can only stare up at the ceiling at first before eventually trailing my gaze down to the rest of the room, and then finally to the chest beneath my chin rising with his every breath.

"I've never done something like this before," I hear myself admit. My cheeks sear with the million different implications of what that statement *really* means, but it's oddly relieving when he laughs.

"You mean do whatever the fuck you want, bunny? You're a natural." The hand that holds me to him trails down to my waist, and as if on cue, I feel that space between my thighs throb in the presence of him. Yep. A natural liar. A natural slut.

"Who are you?" The words come out on a heavy sigh that I don't really intend for him to hear. They're more or less directed at myself. *Who is the stranger you've just slept with, Hannah? What the hell were you thinking?*

"A sexy motherfucker," he murmurs.

I lift my head, spreading my wet hair all over his skin. "You're so eloquent," I say. My lips twitch into a grin that feels so out of place, given what happened earlier today. "So skilled with words. No wonder you go around stealing books and giving random women writing advice."

"A *very* sexy motherfucker," he reiterates. "Born and raised in this shithole of a city."

I let him take his time, watching his chest vibrate as he speaks. The dragon comes to life again, ruffling its wings while the remaining droplets of water drip down from our bodies.

"My mother was a house cleaner. My father was a… Let's call him a 'businessman.' He didn't stick around, so she had to rely on his family for help with me. They aren't the friendliest people in the fucking world, and it was hard on her…" He trails off, his gaze distant, and I recall what Gino said. *Watch your mother turn tricks for Shen just to feed your ass…*

"She did her best," Rafe continues. A faint smile shapes his lips, but just as quickly as it arrives, it's already gone. "But I was a handful. She died when I was twelve, and I got bounced around after that."

"I'm sorry," I croak when he falls silent. The genuine sympathy in my voice startles me.

"Don't be." His fingers absently stroke down my hip, slipping beneath his borrowed shirt. "Eventually, my uncle took me in. He's a tough son of a bitch, but he taught me to fight for what I want. That nothing in life comes for free. I'm who I am because of him. I can say that much. What about you?"

I glance away. That question sounds so innocent on the surface. "I grew up in a small town," I finally say. "My parents are fine. No horrific childhood trauma to speak of."

A lie, of course. All of it, lies. The evidence is all over my skin. My arm is still throbbing, though I avoid looking at the aching flesh. I prefer to eye him instead. Even scarred, he's still beautiful.

"Typical." He chuckles. "Let me guess, you had the perfect childhood in some big ass mansion with a servant and shit."

"Something like that…"

"And Bran?" His inflection shifts, setting off alarm bells in my mind. "When did you meet him?"

"I've known him all my life," I confess, a rare bit of honesty. "He's always protected me."

"Oh, really?" He grabs my arm, lifting it. Purple bruises form an unmistakable imprint; that of a grasping, gripping hand staining my flesh like one of his tattoos. "When did he start beating the shit out of you?"

I cringe at the question, clutching the arm to my chest. "It's nothing." And it's true, in a sense. The marks look so much worse than they feel now. A tickle in comparison to my heated lips and relaxed, languid muscles.

Without Branden here, it's so easy to embrace the selfish impulses I'm used to suppressing. One overriding urge drives me now. I don't want to lose this moment—this peace.

"It's nothing."

"*Nothing?*" He scoffs, but I'm startled by how vicious the sound comes out. He's angry. Despite my hands pawing at his chest, he sits upright, letting me go. "Yeah. And I wasn't fucking stabbed. That's not the first time I've seen your arm like that—"

"Don't do this right now. Please." My voice breaks. I'm begging. "Please—"

"Stop it. I'm not some fucking teddy bear you can use to make yourself feel better. Is that the plan? He beats the fuck out of you, and you come crawling to me? For what?" He glowers, only to sigh, his frown softening. "Wait… Come here." I'm in his arms, my face against his chest. He doesn't let me pull away, tightening his hold until I relent, sinking against him. I don't even realize that I'm crying at first. Not until I feel his fingers running through my hair, his voice low against my ear. "Go on, bunny. I don't give a shit if you cry."

And I do, clinging to him more than I have any right to.

CHAPTER FOURTEEN

I don't think I sleep at all. I just lie here, watching the dawn creep across the sky. His view is better than mine, including a breathtaking snippet of the skyline amid a backdrop of buildings and skyscrapers.

Gradually, he stirs beneath me, flexing the grip he has on my waist. His eyes are closed, his breathing easy. The noise creates a low, muted soundtrack to this moment, and it's the strangest thing…

It's like nothing else can intrude on this. Not the reality looming beyond this building. Not Branden. Not anyone.

After years of craving freedom, it almost feels ironic that I would find it on a narrow leather couch in the arms of a man who made his intentions clear from the start. This is all he wants. Moments. Sex, a cuddle, and then a hasty goodbye, and the ability to use this escapade the next time he needs to boast about his prowess to some punk.

I'm frowning as I picture it while my finger traces a

featherlight path across his chest. Out loud, I find myself musing, "Is this the part where you kick me out?"

"Yes." He answers me with his eyes still closed. When he finally opens them, they're cold and resigned. While I couldn't sleep, I suspect he did, reaching some internal conclusion during the night.

My finger freezes over his pec, and I slowly withdraw it. "So now we're done?"

He holds my gaze for so long that I'm dizzy when he finally turns away. "We're done." He sits up, shrugging me off him. I gape as he stands and pads down the hall into the infamous bedroom.

"I left my skirt downstairs," I croak.

He reemerges, dressed in a black shirt and jeans. Without acknowledging me at all, he opens the door and starts down the stairs. I have no choice but to follow him down into that narrow hallway. The larger room must be a storeroom in addition to his drawing space. He tosses me my skirt and shoes, and I find my bag in a corner behind a box of assorted supplies, along with a small, ombre lighter that I take as well.

I'm slipping on my last sandal when I notice a slender object peeking from beneath the table—a book. Recognition sears through me before I even step forward to read the title printed across the cover.

It's the one he stole from the bookshop—he kept it. I'm dumbstruck by the realization that a man like him has a stashed copy of Emily Dickinson, despite the bloodstains marring the pages.

"You should go before I open," he grunts from behind me, and I turn in time to catch him round the corner.

"You kept it," I say, knowing he can still hear me. "The book you took from the bookstore."

His steps falter until he stops entirely. "Take it." I'm starting to recognize the way his tone shifts like this, leveled like a dare.

"Have… Have you read it?" My gaze cuts back to the book, and my fingers twitch, aching to grab it—but only to discern as much for myself. Has he read it, something that looks so out of place in his world?

"I *can* read," he snaps, taking the question as an insult. "Like you. Though your comprehension must be a million times better given the shit you have to read—" He whirls on his heel, nodding to my bag. "Will you fucking shut that up?"

My cell phone. I fumble through my bag for the device, but rather than withdraw it, I turn it off.

The act doesn't placate him. If anything, it seems to infuriate him more. With a scoff, he turns his back on me, his shoulders rigid. "Get out, rabbit. Go scamper back to your boyfriend. I'm sure you're eager to ride his dick after riding mine—"

"You're being an asshole."

"I *am* an asshole."

"I can see that." My eyes burn as I push past him to the main storefront. "Have a nice—"

"Fuck!" He grabs my hand, dragging me behind him into the hall. At the same moment, I hear the bell above the door chime.

"Hello?" a woman calls.

I stiffen at the soft, sensual voice. *Mara?* I crane my neck as far as I dare to peek beyond the doorway. Sure enough, she stands before the counter, a breath of fresh air against the muted backdrop in a baby-pink top and skintight jeans.

"Rafe?" She cranes her neck back to eye the drawings on the wall. "You in here?"

"Fuck." Hissing under his breath, he pulls away from me and steps from the hallway, blocking me from view. "What's up, Chan?" His tone straddles an odd note between gruff and polite. "You here for your old man?"

"Hey!" She whirls to face him and smiles. It's one of her beautiful, breathtaking grins that score her a free bus trip whenever she "forgets" her fare. "No… I just wanted to say thank you for what you did the other night, helping Hannah." She leans against the counter in a way that makes her curves pop against the thin fabric of her shirt. "Let me buy you dinner later?"

"Um…" Rafe rakes a hand through his hair. Even from here, I can sense where his gaze drifts—where every man in her radius looks. Her hips. Her breasts. Her curves. "I have shit to take care of later. Don't worry about it."

"Oh…" Mara frowns but recovers with another smile. "Okay. See you around."

She slinks from the store, drawing glances from a random man walking by. My heart pangs at her posture, though, and how she walks with her head down and shoulders slumping in disappointment.

"She's gone," Rafe calls.

I creep from the hall to find him still watching her go. Irritation sears through my chest, startling me. Do I have any reason to even be upset? *No.*

After all, he set down the rules of the game well before last night.

"You know what the fuck that was about, rabbit?" he demands, his tone suspicious.

I push past him, shoving my way out the front door. "You're right," I tell him as I step out into the morning air. "You are an asshole."

The shop is still closed, and Mr. Zhang isn't inside when I enter it. I'm left alone with my thoughts and forced to replay the events of last night over and over again.

Work is my only salvation. I finish documenting and shelving new inventory, letting the tasks consume my focus. After, I file the insurance paperwork to finally work on replacing the window. Then I clean the shop from top to bottom without even taking a lunch break. Once I'm done, I clean it again…

It's like time is racing up to me, and it's time to leave before I know it. Too soon. My cell phone is still off in my bag, and whenever I think of going home, my breathing hitches. I can't. Not yet.

Food seems to be the only thing worth dragging me from the shop in the end. I head toward a familiar restaurant with my head low, jumping at any figure who resembles

Branden. My only consolation is that he hates this part of town enough to avoid it, even if searching for me.

Or so I hope.

Still, I nearly run inside the restaurant the second it comes into view. Inside is a pleasant dining room with red walls decorated with elegant accents of gold.

"Hannah?" Mara stands behind the hostess counter, though wearing a far more modest black dress than her outfit from earlier. "Finally come to take me up on that free food?" She winks. "Have a seat, and I'll join you."

I take a booth at the back, and minutes later, she saunters over with a plate piled high with assorted veggies and rice.

"It's on the house," she declares, sitting across from me. "Where have you been? I tried texting you."

I pause with a forkful of food near my mouth. "My phone is…dead," I say. "My charger broke."

"Oh, that sucks." She sighs, leaning back against her end of the booth. "I was just looking for reassurance, anyway."

I choke down a bit of rice. "Reassurance?"

She eyes me warily, biting her lower lip until she can't contain herself any longer. "Am I fat? Ugly? Anything that might not attract a total douchebag on the first try?"

"What?" I fumble with my fork, dropping it. Diving under the table for it gives me the chance to hide my expression. I struggle to regain control of my lips, forming a neutral line.

When I do, I haul myself upright, but Mara isn't even looking at me.

"I am, aren't I?" she declares with utter horror. "I'm a total cow."

"Of course, you're not! What are you even talking about?"

"Rafe!" She slumps forward, pouting. "I went to his shop in my fuck-me jeans. Don't judge me," she adds, shooting me a plaintive glance. "But he didn't even bite. No ass grab or nothing!"

"Maybe he was tired?" I blurt. "I mean, if you went early… Besides, why do you even want a guy like that? You're too good for him." My voice breaks. What does that say about me?

"Yeah, I know." She sits up, beaming, but her eyebrow arches as she eyes my chest. "What on earth are you wearing?"

I glance down and feel the color drain from my face. What am I wearing? An oversized man's dark T-shirt with an obscure rock band logo printed on it. "I…um, it's thrifted. I had a bleach escapade when I did laundry. Most of my stuff is wrecked."

"That sucks!" She shrugs in sympathy. "Well, I have some stuff for you to have if you want. You can definitely have my fuck-me jeans, for starters. They have failed me for the last time."

"Thanks."

"I'll be right back."

While I clear my plate, she dashes off, presumably to the Chan apartment that I assume is above the restaurant. After a few minutes, she returns with a pink duffel that she offers to me with a reverent bow.

"My much-loved but woefully out of season babies," she says. "May you treat them well."

She walks me to the doorway. "I plan on aiming for Rafe again tomorrow," she declares with a wink. "Charge your phone by then. I'll text you and let you know how it goes."

"Why do you want to be with him anyway? You said he goes through skanks. He doesn't seem like the boyfriend type."

"Duh!" Her eyes widen as she follows me down the block, ensuring we're out of earshot of her parents. "Bad boy sex is the best kind of sex. No emotions. No strings. And then I get to brood about it for many a novel when I'm a future bestseller. It's a win, win, baby! Besides, my dad would kill me if I actually dated him."

"Why?"

She cocks an eyebrow. "He runs in the triad, for one," she says matter-of-factly. "Well, this city's version of it, anyway. Not to mention, well... My dad isn't racist or anything, I swear, but he just has this fantasy of me marrying some rich Chinese businessman due to a promise he made to his mother on her deathbed about never forgetting his roots or something. He's dramatic." She rolls her eyes.

"Rafe isn't Chinese?" I ask, unsure of how else to phrase it.

"Rumor is his dad was, but his mother wasn't," she explains. "His dad was pretty infamous around here, from what I've heard. He ran things before his brother took over. But he went to prison, though I'm not sure why. Murder, I think."

"That's awful."

"For Rafe, yeah," she admits, frowning. "Could be why he's such an ass. Angry, damaged, and sexy as hell. A perfect candidate for bad boy sex."

"I guess so…"

"Night," Mara chirps, waving me off. "Hopefully tomorrow will be a *very* good night for me."

I leave, still mulling over that unique perspective. In reality, I don't think I match her enthusiasm. My bout with "bad boy sex" has just left me…

Cold. Tired. Alone.

I can't tell if I were ever heading to my apartment at all by the time my feet bring me to a different destination—The Paper Crane. I let myself in and head for the storeroom. Mara's duffel makes a decent pillow, and I curl up behind a box of damaged inventory.

CHAPTER SIXTEEN

I wake up feeling more exhausted than if I'd never slept at
all. I change into a pink sundress Mara gave me that I
can get away with wearing without underwear. Then I run
to a nearby corner store and buy deodorant and toothpaste,
and then return to the shop to wash up as best as I can in
the staff bathroom.

I'll go home later, when I have the energy to deal with the
potential fallout. Later...

Apart from that looming deadline, it might as well be a
normal day. I start on the tasks that still need to be done,
and Mr. Zhang pops in to tell me that the final
arrangements have been made to fix the window by the end
of the week. He merrily heads off to the insurance office for
the paperwork, and I do what I can to clear the space
around the window.

It's a little after noon when I happen to glance up and spy a
woman peering in through the front door. She doesn't seem

to notice the sign still affixed to the front of it. Or she doesn't care.

Sighing, I step from around the counter and open it. "We're closed—"

"Hello, Hannah." She's tall with short light-brown hair cut bluntly at her chin. A heavy coat sets her apart from the locals dressed in light clothing, as if she's woefully out of her element in this climate. But her face... I recognize it instantly. Though I'm drawing primarily off someone with similar, younger-looking features. Those bright blue eyes. Golden brown hair.

"Please," the woman pleads as I lurch for the door handle. "I just want to talk."

"I'm busy." I try to close the door, but she blocks it with her hand.

"Please."

"How did you even know I work here?"

She cuts her gaze away, biting her lip. "After the article on you... I thought I'd put it all behind me. But seeing your name again, I couldn't." She sighs and runs a trembling hand through her hair. "So I hired a private detective to help me find you. I just want to ask you one thing, and I need you to look me in the eye when I do."

I should slam the door in her face. Run. I don't know why I don't.

Guilt? Deep down, a part of me knows the truth I don't want to face. She doesn't deserve any of this.

"Do you know what happened to her?" she demands. "Do you know what happened to my daughter?" She holds my gaze with an intensity that makes me look down at the pavement.

"No." I try to close the door again. "Please, go—"

"Wait! When Lexi... She had a bracelet, but they never found it. She wore it everywhere. But seeing as how you were so close with her. Do you know what happened to it?"

"No. I'm sorry, but I don't." I step inside the shop and close the door before she can stop me.

"Hannah!" She knocks. "Hannah, please!"

The sound becomes insistent. I slam my hands over my ears, but I still hear her.

"I'll leave my card. If you remember anything, please. Just call me."

I don't move. Just when I think she's finally gone, the door shudders again.

"Leave me alone!"

"Hannah?" The voice isn't a woman's this time.

I whirl around to find Liam on the other end, his expression puzzled.

My hands shake as I wrench the door open and force a grin. "Hey…"

"Hey." He eyes me warily, his hands in the pockets of a navy jacket. I notice that he's not wearing his uniform today, swapping it out for a shirt and a pair of jeans. "Your brother seems to be worried about you," he says. "He wanted me to keep an eye out. Everything okay between you two?"

In some ways, it's alarming that Branden isn't here himself and sent a proxy instead. I may avoid him, but he knows I don't have it in me to shun everyone.

"We're fine," I croak.

Liam nods. "Well, if you're not busy, I could spot you for a coffee, and you can bitch to me about him."

"I can't…" Leaving the store at all feels daunting. Impossible.

But not because of Branden, a part of me hisses. *He isn't who you're hoping might come by. That's why you're here.*

"No worries. Oh, and is this yours?" He hands me something I crumple into a fist without looking at it—a business card. "Anyway, if you're busy, I'll leave you to it—"

"Wait." I head inside for my bag, dropping the card inside it, and fish out my cell phone. As it powers on, dozens of messages crop up, filed under one contact—*Bran <3.* If I were hoping they'd reinforce my decision to keep hiding, they don't. It's the same demands over and over again. *Where are you? Answer me, Hannah!*

But not every message is from him. As Mara said, she'd texted me the other day, but her most recent one is from barely an hour ago. *Wish me luck! ;)*

When I return to Liam, there's an ache in my throat that wasn't there a minute ago. "Can we just walk for a while?"

"Sure." He nods, letting me set the pace and direction, but it's somehow still a shock that we end up in the part of town we do. If he recognizes it, he doesn't say. Looking at his face, I can't discern if *he* was Branden's initial informant who spied me in a certain tattoo shop just up ahead.

Rather than pass it, we enter a sandwich shop across the street and split a sub.

Liam regales me with stories about his suburban upbringing and cracks jokes about what it's like on the force. His voice has a way of setting me at ease, lightening the atmosphere of even this dingy shop. His mood is infectious, and despite everything that's happened within the past forty-eight hours…this *almost* feels normal. Two friends grabbing food, just as it had with Mara—minus the figure who exits a building nearby, his head held high as though he doesn't have a care in the world. He's alone, and I don't know why the fact surprises me so much.

Mara hasn't texted me back yet, so I have no way of knowing if her seduction attempts succeeded this time or not. Is she up in his apartment right now, lounging on his couch, waiting for him to come back?

He's not wearing a haphazardly thrown together outfit, but instead a typical black shirt and jeans. His hair hangs loosely, obscuring his eyes, and he doesn't notice me at first. Not until he's almost completely passed the shop.

Our eyes meet, and I stiffen. The sensation I feel is a shock —electricity crackling between us as his brow furrows, his mouth tightening into a hard line. But he keeps walking…

And I turn to Liam, maintaining my easy smile. I listen to more of his stories. I nod along as though enthralled. I try to ignore, even forget, and pretend that this is fine, and my life is *fine,* and the world could truly be so simple. So nice.

Maybe it's not too selfish to hope for as much. Too petty. Spiteful. I could genuinely enjoy this.

Liam doesn't tell me to fuck off when we finish eating. He doesn't make references to sex or his dick as I follow him outside. It's chilly out, and when I shiver, he offers me his coat.

"This weather is a mess this time of year," he teases with a smile. But when he slips an arm around me, I don't resist. If anything, I lean into the embrace, racking my brain to describe what he feels like…

It doesn't take long to, and the results devastate me more than I would have ever expected. I feel *nothing.* No sparks emanate from his touch. No searing heat radiates in his breath. No anger. No rage. No conflicting, enthralling, electrifying emotions.

I feel like myself. Boring, enduring, sheltered Hannah. I'm no animal in his orbit, and he's a pleasant, predictable presence who would never goad me to that point.

"You okay?" he asks, eyeing me from the bridge of his nose.

I nod, still holding my fake grin. My mouth hurts from forcing the expression for so long. "I'm fine."

"Well, here you are," he says when we reach my building. "I'll tell Bran you're safe before he calls out the cavalry."

"Thank you," I croak as reality returns. For all I know, Bran is already inside, waiting for me.

But there's no point in running forever.

I do everything I can to steel myself as I head upstairs, holding my breath the entire time. I reach my door and test the handle.

It's locked. Once I get it open, I'm shocked to discover that everything is still in place. My furniture. My tulips. *His* camera. A blinking red light alludes to the fact that it's on and recording. He's watching. Waiting for me.

I barely register crossing over to it and swiping it off my TV, sending it crashing to the floor. It's not broken. I could salvage it, but I don't. A cry rips from my lips as I stomp on the tiny metal body until the insides spill out. Again. Again. Again.

The second my phone rings, I answer it, my breathing heavy. "Stay away from me. I mean it. I'm not moving, and if you ever touch me again… I'll tell. I swear to God, I will."

"Hannah…"

"I love you," I insist, my voice breaking. "I do. But you can't control me anymore."

I hang up, slumping against my windowsill. Tears burn behind my eyelids as I stare from the glass, desperate for a view of the scenery I usually take comfort in. But it's tainted tonight.

A stranger doesn't belong here, standing across the street, his eyes on my window—on me.

"Hannah?" The voice accompanies a knock on my door. Alarmed, I turn to it, my heart thumping. Could Branden be on the other side? No…he wouldn't knock. When I finally creep to the door and open it, I find Liam waiting for me.

"You have my jacket," he explains, smiling. "And normally, I'd love to let you keep it, but I think I left my wallet in it."

"Oh!" I laugh, and sure enough, I shrug his jacket from my shoulders and find a leather wallet in the pocket.

"Thanks." Taking it, he starts to leave. "You should keep the jacket. I have another at home. See ya, Hannah."

I don't know why I stop him. "Wait. Let me make you a cup of coffee. As thanks."

He smiles, and we sit on my couch while sipping from the last dregs of cold brew I have in the fridge. The conversation is nice, and it's surprisingly relaxing to enjoy the company of someone who isn't trying to intimidate me. Those reasons alone could justify letting him stay.

Or maybe I'm just a spiteful bitch. My eyes refuse to leave the window long after Liam finishes his coffee, and I place our empty mugs on the counter.

"I should get going," he suggests.

Smiling, I see him to the door, but I quickly find myself inching toward the window once he's gone. I use the pretense of arranging my tulips in the windowsill, adjusting their petals—but the angle from their vase gives me the perfect view of the street below.

I catch sight of Liam leaving, his hands in his jean pockets, his smile visible even from here. He walks toward where he must have parked—completely oblivious to the man lurking in the mouth of a nearby alley.

As if sensing my gaze, the shadowed figure cranes his neck, boldly meeting my stare through the panes of glass. He has a cigarette in his mouth, breathing out smoke in tendrils resembling the flames licking down his bare forearm. He's a veritable dragon, waiting for the right moment to attack.

Slowly, he lowers the butt from his mouth and tosses it aside, crushing it beneath his foot. Then he moves—but in the wrong direction. *Toward* my building and not away. My heart picks up speed as he disappears from my line of sight, near the entrance.

He won't, a part of me insists. *He won't...*

But he is. It's like I can track his ascent. Up one floor. Another. Mine.

I don't even hear his footsteps, but I know the second he arrives at my door. He never knocks. He doesn't have to—he merely waits.

And I'm drawn forward like a moth despite every nerve warning me to run. Rebelliously, my fingers fan out over the wood as if I might be able to feel him this way. I never have to open the door to benefit from his electricity. His heat. His nearness...

I can deny his presence and still feel alive.

But the simulation of his touch isn't enough. My fingers creep to the door handle before I can stop them, turning, tugging, and pulling it open.

There's always the possibility that he isn't here. Never was. But one inhale, and I know.

The scent of smoke floods my nostrils as my skin ignites with the awareness of him. But I don't look up at first. Instead, my gaze settles on the floor at his feet. The dark wood shifts beneath the fall of his swaying shadow as if it's taking all of his effort to remain still.

But not silent. "Look at me, rabbit," he commands.

I take my time, slowly inching my gaze higher, grazing over the fabric of his jeans and the contours of his chest. His face last…

Our eyes meet with a sensation that makes my breath catch. He should be angry, I think, but his brow furrows more in confusion than anything else. As if he doesn't even know why he's here. Just that he is, stepping inside without an invitation, grabbing for me. His fist seizes a handful of my dress, using it as a leash to tug me aside and press me up against the wall. Stunned, I can't even react before his lips claim mine.

My nails bite into his arms preemptively as he hooks his palm around my waist, but I don't push him off. I can't, and he doesn't move as if daring me to. Our breaths mingle, our lips hovering apart. Together. Apart. It's like we don't know how to maneuver if one isn't trying to bite the other. Finally, he nips, and I inhale, letting my hands find his shoulders, then his hair.

He copies me, sliding his hands over the straps of my dress. My arms go up as he draws the fabric over my head and pulls it off. As if watching this happen to someone else, I stare as he tosses the dress to the floor and tugs at the clasp of his jeans, kicking them off.

My view is blocked when he steps into me and fists his hand through my hair, making me face him. His eyes glow, blazing with a million different accusations he doesn't voice out loud. *You were with him. Did you fuck him?*

But I can't disguise my own curiosity. I lean in, flicking my tongue along his lip as if it would be that easy to taste someone else he may have kissed. Mara? Bonnie? All I sense in the end is ash and smoke. Him. His skin smells only like coconut, his clothing bone-dry, his boxers straining at the front.

I close my eyes, hating how much the thought of him with someone else bothers me. It's selfish. It's pathetic. It's primal, a raw feeling.

Even if it burns, it's so much better than nothing.

"Look at me." He snatches my chin until I do, his nostrils flaring, chest heaving as he turns, dragging me to my couch. He shoves me down and plunges his hand between my legs, extending a finger and slipping it inside.

I whimper, drawing my knees up to his hips as my body expands around the intrusion. He searches me ruthlessly as if by touch alone, he can tell what I can't just by looking at him. Have I been with someone else?

No. The answer makes him groan, his eyelids lowering, teeth skewering his lip. Satisfied, he withdraws, bringing his mouth to my throat. A fiery burst of pain makes me gasp, and he does it again—snatch a sliver of flesh between his teeth and grind. Bite. There's no chance he won't leave a mark—he *wants* to.

I shiver at the possession, clawing at his shoulders, but for whatever reason, I don't command him to stop. Not that he would—he's ruthless, raking with his teeth to create his own twisted version of a tattoo that spans the length of my collar. Anyone who sees will know what caused it.

Panting, he brings his mouth to mine. "Beg me to fuck you." He presses his lips as if in a demonstration. "Say it. 'Fuck me, Rafe'…"

I arch into him instead, brushing his lip with my tongue, plunging inside his mouth entirely.

He grunts, shoving me down, and urging my legs apart.

My nails sink into the couch as he guides himself inside me, inch by inch. He goes slow at first, but soon, he's forging a steady rhythm, and I stop thinking, letting my body move against him however it wants and needs to. Gradually, his tempo builds, driving him deeper, setting me alight.

Every thrust seems to sow a million invisible flames that converge into a blaze—an inferno. I can barely track how it happens—just that the pleasure swells, raging beneath my skin until it boils over and explodes.

Every nerve in my body seems to unravel at once. All I can do is cry out, my spine curving as he stills, grunting against my throat.

It's fire in its rawest, most destructive form.

And I never realized how good it could feel to burn.

CHAPTER SEVENTEEN

"Is he coming back?" Rafe's voice is hoarse, his eyes on my counter where even from here, two empty mugs are visible.

Bit by bit, reality returns, bringing with it a million painful observations. The smashed camera on the floor. The borrowed jacket slung over my armchair. The taste in my mouth and the stench of smoke in my lungs.

"Is he?"

To stall having to answer him, I turn into his chest, seeking out as much heat as I can take in case he leaves now. "No," I confess when my face is safely hidden. "He's not."

He relaxes slightly, a grunt revving in his chest. "You're a goddamn tease, you know that?"

Do I? *No*, I decide. He turns that word into something cruel, well beyond any hold I might have over him. Unconvinced by my silence, he laughs.

"What next? You bring him to the club? Fuck him on the dance floor to get my attention?" The venom in his tone doesn't match the gentleness with which his fingers pick through my hair, parting the strands. "I'm not someone you want to taunt, bunny. You keep playing with fire, and you're going to get burned."

He doesn't even know the half of it.

"Damn…" A sigh rips from his chest, and he adjusts his weight, drawing me against him. My couch is too small for us both, making our current position difficult to maintain. He has to brace one foot against the floor to support most of his bulk. Balanced on top of him, I've never felt smaller, in danger of slipping off at any moment.

"Is the bed off-limits, rabbit?" His tone makes it sound like such a dangerous question. A line he'll only cross with my permission.

He has his rule, but do I have my own?

I shake my head, and he stands, bringing me with him. I feel a definite shift the second he steps over the threshold of my bedroom. Nothing will ever be the same again.

But the cause of this momentous change doesn't even seem to realize the enormity of what he's done. His size alone makes him look huge in the narrow space, and he easily dominates my bed as he sits on the edge of it.

His eyes find mine, daring me to join him. When I do, he returns us to our previous positions. He lies on his back with me on his chest. My thin mattress creaks to protest the unusual amount of weight, and my blankets are no match for us both. I lie in his arms, half-expecting Branden to barge in. This peace feels too surreal. Too fragile. Too *good.*

"If you want me to leave, I'll go," he suggests, picking up on my unease.

"No," I say. "It's just… I'm wondering how many women you must have had in your bed to not want it to smell like them."

I inhale, imagining how he'll taint my sheets. The strange part? I can't see myself hating the effect, even after he leaves. If only his heat could remain the same way.

"There you go again." He grunts out another harsh laugh. "Playing with fire."

"I'm not jealous." Though it's not like I've been in any relationship long enough to feel the right to claim anyone. "I'm just curious."

"Enough to know that shit gets fucked up real fucking fast the second you let a bitch sleep next to you."

I lift my head, fixing him with a raised eyebrow. "Oh, really?"

He frowns. "Unless she already has a fucking boyfriend," he clarifies. "Then there's no risk."

"You don't want a girlfriend?"

He shakes his head. "Don't want my bed smelling like pussy, remember?" Ironically, the motion causes his hair to spill out around him, staining my pillow like ink. "I don't want to be owned, either—" He grabs my wrist beside the healing bruise. "Not by anyone. I don't want someone thinking they can control what I do or blow up my phone every five fucking minutes."

I draw my arm away and turn my gaze to the window. "Point taken."

"I didn't mean it like that…" He sighs, and I feel his palm slide over my hip. He lets it linger, his finger tapping as he mulls over whatever he wants to say next. Finally, he murmurs, "Explain it for me, bunny. Use those pretty words."

Explain it?

"I owe him." It's the only explanation I can give. The one reinforced since childhood by everyone from my parents down. "He protects me…so I owe him."

"You owe him." He sounds so calm. I don't realize the true extent of his emotions until I make the mistake of looking up. His eyes flash, and his hand flexes against me, radiating anger. "To hurt you? To call your writing bullshit? To control you—"

"He gave up a lot for me," I confess against his chest. "It was hard on him."

So hard that he'd lash out when the pressure overwhelmed him. When the weight of the world on his shoulders threatened to crush him. When I provoked him, and he felt compelled to remind me of just how much he'd sacrificed for me.

You're a selfish bitch, Hannah. If only you just listened. Everything I've done is on you. It's your fault...

"I owe him."

"That sounds like bullshit, bunny," Rafe says, and I remember that he's even here, judging every word I've spoken. Listening. "Does he tell you that? That you owe him just for fucking being there?"

"Please stop." I hate how pathetic I sound. Desperate. When he says it out loud, it doesn't seem as rational as it does in my head. And it has to stay rational.

Branden loves me.

He protects me.

I owe him.

And he owns me.

"Would you break up with him?" he asks next, his voice still level. "Not for me or anyone else. Just to do it."

It's my turn to sigh. "It's complicated."

"Of course, it fucking is." He lets his hand fall from me, fisting a handful of my sheets in lieu of my skin. "Let me guess. You know him better than anyone. He's not always a total dick. When he's not beating the shit out of you, he's a pretty nice guy. You know, for a writer, you use a lot of fucking clichés."

I eye him through my lashes, unsure of how much to read into his vitriol. Those words don't sound entirely of his own creation. Like he's heard them before, countless times—from someone else? "Why do you care?"

"Why?" He runs a finger over the lines of his tattoo as if the swirls of ink speak for him more than anything else—fearless power and vengeful fire. "I care because I know bullshit when I hear it and when I see it. I know you're miserable. I know from your fucking little journal that you feel trapped and want a way out."

My cheeks heat as I remember all the ways he's already invaded my head. My thoughts. My soul. Yet his overall impression isn't to mock me or even to call my musings bullshit. My brain can't rationalize it. His understanding is an enigma. "It's not that simple."

"Isn't it?" He cocks his head. "Don't tell me you feel happy with how shit is now."

"Happy?" I taste the word. It sounds like such a foreign concept.

"Happy," he snarls. "Hell, *normal.* The way you feel when you hold that fucking journal. Or when you stare wide-eyed around a club as if you're in fucking wonderland. When your nose is in a book. When you're in that fucking bookshop…" His voice deepens in a way that makes me shiver. *Run.* His hand lashes out, chasing me before I even process that I'm inching away from him. He captures my breast, kneading…

My spine arches, and my startled gasp nearly drowns out what he says next, his voice a rasp, "The way you feel when I'm inside you, and *he's* not in your head."

Goosebumps come to life over my skin with the heat of his touch. Dazed, I stare down at my bare limbs as if observing a stranger's. His fingers look massive on me, claiming any inch of my body he can reach. "Are you saying you're my way out?"

"No. I'm a distraction," he admits, his gaze cutting. "But I get bored easily, rabbit. I won't be around for you to play with for long."

It feels like a threat—and it is. "What do you want from me then?" I ask hoarsely. "If you think this is a game, what do you get out of it?"

"Take your pick." Deliberately, he flicks his thumb over my nipple until it hardens. "A tight, virgin pussy. A smart-ass mouth. A girl who thinks she can beat me at this… You *can't* beat me at this, rabbit. I invented this fucking game. What do I get out of it? The look on your face when you realize that."

My voice fades to a whisper, "Is that what you tell Bonnie and the other women you've slept with?"

He laughs and withdraws his hand from me. A second later, the calloused fingers return, inching between my legs as he rises to his knees and crouches over my body. Beneath him like this, I come alive, writhing over the sheets at his fingertips. Away from him. Toward…

"Bonnie? I could buy that bitch whatever she wanted. Fuck, I could give her every last dime I have, and she'd never get this fucking wet for me—" A thrust of his thumb punctuates the statement. He's not boasting.

And admitting as much aggravates him like nothing else. He glowers, his brows drawn together as his fingers ease inside me one after the other, testing his theory. A scoff betrays what he finds, and he leans down, ensuring I can't miss a single word.

"You must enjoy getting off on the attention, bunny," he bites out against my earlobe. "You're so goddamn wet…"

My eyelids flutter as I rock my hips against the invasion, relishing the fit. The feel of his chest rasping over mine, enhancing every inch of my skin.

"Look at me," my tormentor commands, going still. I shiver, bucking against him, but he's resolute. "Fucking look at me."

I have no choice. My eyelids flutter to him on cue, a pair of eyes watching me from above.

Satisfied, he pins me down, prying my legs farther apart. Shame unfurls, and I try to clamp my knees together, but he shakes his head, then growls until I go limp. "Stop."

He looks, but the more he stares, the less self-conscious I feel. His gaze sears with the same intensity as his touch, traveling from my heaving chest downward. With every inch gained, his expression changes. Darkens.

"Fuck," he grates, his throat working to swallow.

His hand slips between my legs again, and another finger eases inside me. Another. He moves them slowly, creating the barest tease of friction.

My breath catches, spine arching.

And he inhales as if empowered by some dark, dangerous secret. "Beg me to fuck you." There's no mocking in his tone this time. No game. Just a need to hear it almost as badly as my throat aches to say it.

"Please—"

He rocks forward, slipping his hands beneath my back to draw me close. I bite my lip to silence a cry as my body welcomes him. This time feels so different from the rest. Hotter, as if every touch is scorching. More frantic. Ruthless. Hard. Slow. Everything.

Panting, he lunges against me. Bracing one hand over my headboard, he jolts the entire bed with every thrust. The friction makes my toes curl and thoughts spin. I'm breathless, gripping whatever parts of him I can reach.

Until he turns the tables and flips me over. I'm on top of him before I know it, forced to maintain the tempo on my own. Breathless, I close my eyes as I feel every inch of him thrust in, then ease out as I lift, then lower myself on trembling hands.

He grunts, gripping my hips, biting out curses—and I stop caring about anything but moving. Taking whatever I want from him, however I can.

The pleasure reaches a tipping point and boils over. I slump forward, letting our lips meet, our bodies writhing until we collapse.

It feels like an eternity before I regain my senses enough to rationalize what happened. Just *who* lies beside me now, his body gloriously bare. One look at his face, and I know my confusion isn't unique.

"Fuck," Rafe rasps, his eyes on the ceiling. His hands rake through his hair, his expression puzzled. "Fuck, that was…" He trails off, letting his breathless silence speak for itself.

That was dangerous. Something he didn't bargain for in the rules of his game. He reacts by withdrawing his arm from around my shoulders. As the seconds pass, I try to imagine what thought has him frowning. What realization makes him look at me and grit his teeth. What makes him switch on a dime, closing me off and turning cold again.

As if to punish me, his hands return to my hair, tugging. Pulling. Petting. I slowly lower my head to his chest, pressing my ear against his flesh, sensing the heartbeat raging beneath.

And I know that seeing this side of him won't come without a price to pay.

One he'll demand in full soon enough.

CHAPTER EIGHTEEN

I don't think either one of us ever sleeps, but when dawn breaches the darkness of my room, he stands first, shrugging off my twisted yellow blankets.

By the time I stagger to my feet and throw on a dress, he's at my fridge, scouring the meager offerings. He's already discovered my loaf of bread when I approach the counter.

He eats a piece and shoves another toward me. I copy him, maintaining what little distance between us allowed by this narrow space.

At first.

Eventually, I can't resist the impulse drawing me toward him. That same need emboldens me to slide my hand down his bare shoulder even as he stiffens. Energy blazes from him, growing hotter the more of him I dare to touch, but I can't stop. My greedy hands brush his hips as my chest conforms to his back, bringing me face-to-face with that snarling dragon.

"Why this tattoo?" I ask.

Muscles ripple beneath his skin—recoiling against me only to relax a heartbeat later. "Do I need a reason?" His voice is low, containing an unmistakable dare.

For once, I feel brave enough to tackle it head-on. "Yes. Someone who has an elaborate explanation for calling a stranger 'bunny.' You wouldn't pick a dragon for yourself without a reason—"

"It's a fucking tattoo," he says dismissively. "Let's not get too deep about it."

But there's more to it. I can sense it in the way he keeps his face turned from me, and his shoulders tensed. This beautiful image beneath my fingertips means so much more to him than a meaningless ornament undertaken on a whim.

"It's beautiful," I say, watching the dragon coil and move with every flex of his shoulders. It's anticlimactic in a sense —someone who claims to be a writer should be able to come up with a better descriptor. Something worthy of the blend of color and swirls of ink. "It's beautiful… Where did you learn to draw?"

"Nowhere." His voice falls flat, devoid of emotion. "I've always done it. Where did you learn to write?"

"I've always done it," I say, parroting his explanation. But I'm not as guarded as he is. "Sometimes… Sometimes it felt like the only way I could get my thoughts out of my head without screaming. If I didn't have it as an outlet, I don't know what I would have done. It was easier to endure it all as long as I had an escape."

A safe place to voice the complaints my parents never wanted to hear.

The emotions enduring Branden's control forced me to suppress.

Everything.

"Endure?" he prods, his tone gruffer. "Don't tell me that talk about your innocent, perfect childhood was bullshit?"

If anything, he doesn't sound surprised. Did he suspect as much all along?

I incline my head, gazing at him with a newer perspective. However, his face is still angled away from me, keeping whatever emotions it may reveal to himself.

"Everyone has their problems," I murmur. "Writing was the one thing that always gave me…a way out? It got me a scholarship to come here. Chasing that dream gave me enough courage to leave. I still feel like it was worth it, even if Bran—" I break off, alarmed by how close I've come to slipping up. Confessing.

"He followed you?" He sounds so deceptively calm. So nonjudgmental.

I'm woefully unprepared for the spell his baritone can cast when uttered so gently.

"He followed me." I close my eyes and inhale, fighting back the wave of anger I'm not expecting. Pain. "I was stupid enough to think that he wouldn't. That he would ever let me go."

But he didn't, forcing me to leave the dorms the week I'd moved in. Using his career as a police officer back in Wellington, he'd had no trouble joining the local force, and I had no choice but to move into his home. *You need me,* he'd insisted. Even after he met Kaitlin over a year ago, it seemed like I would never get the chance to leave him.

Break free.

"If I didn't have my writing, I would have suffocated. I..." Confusion leaves me frowning. I've never admitted this to anyone.

No one's ever asked.

I've never met anyone so open in his own expression yet so secretive at the same time. Displaying his drawings for the world to see but tensing up the moment he's questioned on the meaning behind them. He told me once that his writing was in flesh. Pain. And I understand now more than ever what he meant. Hidden prose lurks within every inch of ink, locked away behind his silence.

And I can't stop myself from chasing his secrets with the same fervor he delved into my notebook with.

"You designed this," I suspect out loud, gathering up the nerve to trace the edge of the creature's contorting back. He may not have inked it himself, but the artwork carries all his hallmarks—bold lines, expressive subjects, elusive emotion.

I gaze into those glaring red eyes and see a creature staring back, one accustomed to viewing the rest of the world as prey. A monster poised to spit fire at a moment's notice.

"You were *angry* when you designed it." He pulls away, leaving my fingers hanging in the air. Slowly, I lower them to my side. "I'm sorry."

"Don't." A muscle in his jaw twitches, and he stops short. I've irritated him. "You always apologize." He makes it sound so strange, so aggravating. "Even for asking a fucking question."

"I'm sorr—"

"It symbolizes power," he says over me, but his voice is softer. Absently, he trails a hand along his shoulder, following the path my fingers had traveled seconds earlier. "Strength. A reminder, so I never forget what it fucking takes…"

"Takes to what?" I ask when he falls silent for good.

"To survive." He sounds hesitant, and I can assume why, using my own slip of the tongue around him as a precedent. He isn't used to speaking unbidden, not about this.

"It's beautiful," I repeat, unashamed by the awe tainting my voice. I inch closer, letting my hand fall between his shoulder blades. "Your drawings are beautiful."

"You sound surprised, bunny." He turns and deliberately lifts my hand, placing my fingers against the planes of his jaw instead. "Why?" he demands, letting me feel his mouth shape the word, how much tension such a simple motion carries. "Because I'm some illiterate punk? Too dumb for your lofty, artsy ways?"

"Because you're talented," I say simply. "But…"

His eyes narrow to slits. "But?"

"But it's like you don't want anyone to notice. Not really." A blind man could see his bravado for what it is. Defensiveness. I'm so confident of that, I'm willing to go a step further. "You'd rather someone see you as a punk than an artist."

"And you're the expert?" He fingers a piece of my hair and laughs. "The girl who smothers everything inside her fucking notebook? Tell me, bunny. How would you describe me now?" Releasing me, he leans back against the counter and strokes his chin. "Use those pretty words."

"You're talented," I reiterate. "You're cocky. You're…honest."

"Cocky and honest." He nods in approval. "Two out of three ain't bad, rabbit—"

"You're talented." I'm not even sure why I'm so adamant about it. Or why he frowns, his jaw clenched. "Did you ever think of pursuing art? As more than a tattoo artist?"

"Like what?" He grunts, turning his gaze to the window.

"I don't know… College," I say, picturing him lumbering around the campus. "Studying art. Running a gallery—"

"You see all of that in a few fucking sketches?" he counters. "Or is that what it takes to be valid in a bunny's world? College?"

I flinch at the hostility in his tone. "What I think has nothing to do with it. They're good. They are." Saying it out loud feels empowering in a sense. I'm the dragon for once, breathing out compliments that he interprets as fire. "Why does it bother you so much to hear me say that?"

"The same reason it bothers you to hear the truth about your fucking Bran," he snaps back. "*Hearing* it doesn't change shit, does it?"

Before I can respond, he pushes past me for his jeans and yanks them on, shoving his feet into his shoes without even bothering with the laces. He snatches his shirt next, and the ferocity of each action betrays how angry he truly is, sparked seemingly from nowhere.

"I don't know what I said wrong," I blurt out.

Moving toward my door, he wrenches it open without looking back. "I think we're done now, bunny. I'll save you the trouble of cutting me loose."

He leaves, slamming the door behind him, and I blink, alarmed as my eyes burn. It feels so childish and almost pathetic to care that I may have upset him.

I'm a moth again, fluttering too close to a blazing flame, only to be shocked when it burns. The pain feels different from the cold, numbed state it's used to flying in. One taste of something new, and it can't get enough, no matter how reckless the act becomes.

It would rather burn than continue to feel nothing.

My legs shake when I finally remember how to move. I stagger into my bedroom, falling to my knees beside the bed frame. Reaching under it, I withdraw the worn shoebox, throwing it onto my bed.

But for once, I don't feel each item individually. Pushing the faded article aside, I curl my fingers around one, in particular, holding it up to the light. The gold bracelet is so simple in theory. And in so many ways, it's more dangerous than Rafe's lighter, capable of sparking a raging fire volatile enough to destroy my life in the aftermath.

And Branden's.

I don't know why I've kept it all this time, hiding in plain sight even while I lived in my brother's house. Out of guilt? Regret?

Or maybe revenge? The vain hope that one day I'd be brave enough to spark that fire. Let it burn…

Instead, I do what I've always done in the end and return the bracelet to the box. Closing it, I shove the whole thing back into its hiding place.

My head feels heavy as I re-enter my living room, grab my bag from near the door, and find my pen. My journal. After flipping to a blank page, I start writing, losing myself in the swirls of ink gliding across the page.

Nothing else matters. Not the time dangerously inching toward when I need to be at the bookstore. Not the ache in my chest or the cramp in my hand that makes scribbling the next few lines a struggle.

The only occurrence capable of breaking through the impulsive trance is the thud of a fist pounding against my door. I jump so violently, my journal skids across the floor. My throat dries as my pulse surges.

Branden?

No. He wouldn't knock. When I finally creep to the door, I feel my nostrils flare, testing the air. Cloying cologne tickles my nose, and when I open the door, the man on the other side is only vaguely familiar. A figure I last interacted with the day I moved in.

"Hey," the man, the building's landlord, says. "You sure you gonna be out by the end of the month?"

The words seem to take an eternity to register. *The end of the month.*

"I've already got a tenant lined up for the place, so I'm gonna need you to give me notice when you're out if you want your deposit back. Got it?"

Somehow, I manage to nod, and he grunts, turning away. "You must be in some hurry to leave, girlie. I've never had anyone pay out a full year's rent just to get out of a lease."

He makes it sound amusing.

But it's not. His incredulous laughter is the sound of my fragile wings being clipped, one by one. I'm not like Rafe's invincible dragon. I'm just a pathetic moth, incapable of breathing fire to protect itself.

And where does such an insect inevitably end up?

Crushed underfoot.

CHAPTER NINETEEN

I get to work over an hour late. By the time I do arrive, a man is exiting the shop carrying an armful of tools, and the storefront is home to a brand-new, crystal clear window.

"We can do a soft reopen today," Mr. Zhang says when I enter the shop to find him standing at the counter, flashing a rare grin. "You're on the register. I'm going to head to the printer shop for banners. Maybe some flyers. I think a sale would be a good start, huh?"

"Yeah," I say, matching his smile.

He starts for the door and pauses. "Won't you be hot in that? It's supposed to warm up later today?" He nods at my neck, and the woolen scarf I have draped around it.

I shrug. "Fashion statement."

"Okay, then."

When he finally leaves, I find myself pacing the center of the showroom, struggling to adjust to the bright, newly lightened interior. I had forgotten how beautiful this place could seem once cleaned and whole. If only my life could be repaired with something as simple as replacing a window.

But it can't. The gaping holes stretch too far, too big to ever fill—or cover up with an itchy green scarf. And when a shadow falls over me from behind, I realize that any pathetic attempts to erase that reality have been like putting Band-Aids over a gaping stab wound.

I turn around slowly, just in time to catch a figure pass the storefront and enter through the main door. Two of them.

"This isn't what I had in mind when you said you'd take me shopping," a blond woman chirps in a high-pitched and breathy voice. Loose curls spill down her shoulders, complementing her beautiful features and heavy makeup. A black tank top strains over her cleavage, and her skirt puts Mara's "fuck-me jeans" to shame.

"Really, Rafe?" Her blue eyes dart around the shop with disinterest, and she sighs, playfully swatting at the man who practically looms above her because he's so much taller. "What about that shoe store I like?"

He shrugs her off. "I'm looking for something." He takes his time scanning the store—everywhere but in my direction. I might as well cease to exist. Matter.

As if he isn't the cause for the scarf around my neck in eighty-degree weather.

As if he didn't leave my apartment hours earlier.

As if everything that happened between us was nothing more than a game.

"I'm bored," the blond whines, eyeing her pink nails. "You said we'd have fun—"

"Go wait in the car then," Rafe snaps, seemingly enthralled by a shelf containing gardening books. He runs his finger down the spine of one, but the second she's gone, he pivots toward my corner.

His steps land over the floor, slow and deliberate, giving me every chance to run before he comes close. When I don't, he pins me in against the wall. His fingers brush my chin but then change direction, teasing the end of my scarf instead.

My lips flutter apart, a plea to stop lurking on my tongue, but I never voice it. Holding my gaze, he tugs once. Twice. Again. Each successive yank succeeds in unraveling more of the scarf's opposite end. More. After what feels like an eternity, the last bit of wool slips away, exposing the flesh of my throat beneath.

His eyes widen, raking over his handiwork—the marks I'd faced with horror in the mirror hours after he left. I expect him to puff up smugly. Boast. Taunt.

His nostrils flare instead, his exhale harsh. "How long until he finds out, bunny?" he wonders. "How long?"

His eyes flick up to mine, blazing with an emotion so unexpected I gasp in the face of it. More than rage. More than anger. Whatever it is glows white-hot as his fingers find my chin again, lifting it.

"You know, I didn't think I'd see it," he grates. "This look on your fucking face. Tell me how it feels, bunny…" He squeezes the corner of my mouth until my lips part. "To be toyed with. I told you that you're not the only one who can play this game."

He waits as if expecting something in particular from me. A reaction I don't give. I just blink. And blink…

He glowers, swiping something from my cheek with the pad of his finger. Moisture that he eyes in disgust. "You are such a fucking tease."

The doorbell above the door chimes, and he barely breaks away before another woman enters—someone who isn't his blond. I scramble to readjust my scarf, securing it with trembling fingers.

"Hannah?" Mara crosses to me, frowning in concern. "You okay? Did Mr. Zhang already tell you?"

"Tell me what?"

She lifts something in her hands. The flyer is of a smiling girl with dark hair held back by a silver butterfly clip. Beneath her picture is a glaring title—MISSING.

"Faith Wen didn't come home the other night," Mara explains. "Her parents are freaking out. My dad is arranging a search party for her tonight. We're meeting at the restaurant if you want to join."

"Faith?" Frowning, Rafe snatches one of the flyers.

"She's a sweet girl," Mara says. "She works at the Red Duck."

Alarm shoots through me, and I finally realize why the woman's smiling face looks so familiar.

"I know her," Rafe says softly.

And now I remember exactly how. She visited him in his warehouse the night I went there for Mr. Zhang's debt. *"He's fucking insane,"* she'd told Rafe. *"I have no idea what he's going to do now..."*

"She's been gone for over forty-eight hours," Mara adds. "Her parents are worried."

"I'll make some calls and have my boys join in," Rafe offers, returning the flyer to her.

"Thanks," Mara says, but I don't miss the slight change in her posture that has her angling herself toward him. "I think she has a boyfriend out of town, so she could have just taken off for a few days."

"Yeah," he agrees, but he doesn't sound convinced. His gaze turns distant as if he's miles beyond this space.

"Are you okay?" Mara asks, placing her hand on his shoulder.

He blinks and then nods. "Yeah. I'll keep an eye out. See you around, Chan."

She calls after him, "Maybe later tonight for dinner, after the search?"

He stops and looks back, but his gaze cuts straight over Mara's head toward me. "Maybe." With that, he exits the store.

"Are you sure you're okay?" Mara turns to me once he's gone, eyeing me skeptically. "You look… Oh my God!" She fingers the end of my scarf. "Is this what I think it is?"

I grab for it, but she's too fast, yanking it loose.

"I knew it." She gasps, her eyes widening at the sight of my throat. "Jesus, Hannah—"

"It's nothing." I lift my hands to obscure as much of the bruising as I can.

"Yeah, right, it's nothing! I pioneered the 'scarf to hide the hickeys' trick." She prods a mark on my collar despite my attempts to cover them. "But no one's ever gone at my neck like that. Was he trying to hickey you or eat you? God, I bet that was so hot—"

"Mara!" I grab the scarf from her and secure it. "It's a rash."

"So, I don't get any of the deets?" She pouts, crossing her arms over the flyers. "No fair. I dish to you about all my guys. Or I *would*, if I were getting laid. Who knew Rafe played hard to get?"

"No luck yesterday?" I try to sound as neutral as I can, but it's a futile effort. Nothing could disguise the unease in my voice.

"Nope. He said he was busy—*again*. I think I'm going to start going back to the gym." She eyes her slender frame with a frown. "Anyway, if you're going to join the search party tonight, hit me up. Maybe I can see if Rafe will let us into the club for free after—you know, once they find Faith and everything. What was he doing here, anyway?" Her brow furrows as if she finally realized our location, which is the farthest thing from a tattoo shop.

I turn to the nearest shelf, adjusting a section of books. "I don't know."

"Well… I have to hand the rest of these out. I'll see ya, Hannah!"

She skips off, and I make it through the next phase of my shift in a whirlwind daze. I barely notice when Mr. Zhang returns from his errands, bustling with excitement.

"You can go home early," he declares once we've hung one of his new banners over the front of the store. "Go on. You've earned it."

I hesitate, eyeing a row of books I could straighten. Anything to stall having to leave. I'm desperate enough to admit as much out loud. "I can stay—"

"Go. And take a bonus while you're at it as thanks for delivering this…" He slips me two envelopes and takes my position behind the counter, his head lowered to disguise his expression. "Go."

I look down, eyeing the material in my hands. One envelope is white, containing a few crisp bills. The other is a slimmer, starker red, and feels significantly heftier.

"Deliver?" I ask, though a part of me suspects his answer.

He sighs and shoots me a knowing look. "To him. I'd go myself, but…" He fingers his glasses, adjusting them nervously. "I cannot thank you enough for all your help. You're a good girl."

He hurries away as my lips part, but in the end, I don't have the heart to refuse. As I leave the shop, my feet carry me aimlessly, and eventually, I find myself standing before a familiar building.

It's closed with the door locked and lights off, casting most of his artwork in shadow. There is no mailbox, no sign proclaiming where one could leave his blood money. I consider shoving it beneath the door or throwing it in the street. Perhaps dumping out every last bill in a spiteful row right here for anyone to take?

If Mr. Zhang wouldn't be the one to ultimately suffer for my actions, I'd do it. I'd give in to the violent, cruel impulses only he ever seems to inspire in me. Maybe the emotions are my own psyche trying to warn me? Nothing good could ever come of him.

I should be glad he made that painfully clear. He belongs with someone like Bonnie, and I belong with…

Someone like Liam?

The question hurts too much to think about, so I shove the envelope back into my bag and start for my apartment. As I do, my fingers brush against a crumpled flyer. Something I don't even remember slipping inside.

I run my finger gently over the smiling face printed on the page, and then I change direction, eventually arriving at the Chan Noodle House. Unsurprisingly, it's packed with locals eager to show their support. There are more volunteers than the building can hold, and excess people spill out onto the sidewalk, craning their necks to hear the conversation taking place inside.

Mr. Chan stands near the front of the restaurant beside an older couple who must be Faith's parents. Tears streak their faces, and their hands are clasped in solidarity. But not far from their orbit stands a figure who seems out of place amongst the bright, if somber atmosphere. He has his arms crossed, his gaze scanning those gathered with a piercing intensity. I can't help but notice that a certain giggling blond isn't anywhere near him, though he could have switched her out for a different model of floozy.

And if he did? Why do you care?

"You came!" A warm hand gently brushes my shoulder, and I turn to find Mara easing through the crowd toward me. "I'm glad you're here. This is starting to get a little scary." She frowns, glancing worriedly in the direction of Faith's parents. "I thought she might just be out having a little bit of fun, but no one's heard from her. There are rumors going around that it could be payback from Gino's gang of idiots. My parents are freaking out. If there's retaliation…" She trails off, her gaze on an approaching car. It's a sleek luxury model out of place amongst the modest vehicles parked along the curb. "Speak of the devil," she murmurs. "It's Mr. Shen."

She's presumably referring to the tall, broad-shouldered man who exits the driver's side of the car dressed in a crisp black suit. His dark eyes sweep the assembled bunch, his impression indecipherable. Moving assuredly, he starts forward and almost as if in some bizarre synchronized dance, most of the crowd hurriedly parts for him, muttering greetings as he passes.

"Who is he?" I ask before I realize that I already know the answer.

"Rafe's uncle," Mara says. "Shit just got real if he's involved. Last I heard, he was supposed to be out of town for a while. He wouldn't come back unless this was serious."

Two other men exit the car in his wake, wearing suits in muted shades of gray. While lurking in the background, they scan the immediate vicinity like sharks on the hunt.

"I'll be right back," Mara says before inching forward. Her voice reaches me from over her shoulder. "My parents will kill me if I don't show respect."

I watch her slink over to Mr. Shen and bow her head in greeting. The man places his hand on her shoulder before turning his attention to her parents. There's a rehearsed quality to it all, and I can't escape the sense that so much more is playing out beneath the surface.

The reason Mara was so shaken the night Rafe first accosted us. Why Mr. Zhang would entrust me, a relative newcomer, to approach these people rather than do so himself. Why the locals shuffle warily in the presence of a man who seems to command so much power just by arriving.

He takes up the remaining sliver of space between the Chans and Wens, showing sympathy with a bow of his head. But I notice that another presence is suspiciously absent. Even when I inch forward to enter the restaurant proper, I don't find him anywhere.

But as curious faces glance in my direction, I can't escape the sense I don't belong here either. It's as if everyone knows I'm a sheltered interloper watching from the outside looking in.

Finally, Mr. Shen steps forward. "Here, we are family," he says, his booming voice easily reaching throughout the wide space. "We protect one another. Look out for one another. And we fight for one another. Tonight, we search for one of our own, and I have no doubt that everyone here will search for Faith with the same intensity you'd search for your own sister or daughter. We are family here."

As he falls silent, the Chans set out, passing out stacks of flyers along with suggestions of where to begin. I start forward, my eyes on Mara, but a heavy hand falls over my shoulder. Alarmed, I turn to find a stranger looming over me. I vaguely recognize him as one of the figures who arrived with Mr. Shen.

"What's your name?" he demands, eyeing me up and down. "You live around here? Or are you a reporter? Or…" He leans in, his eyes narrowing. "Are you a snitch for that fucker Gino?" His grip tightens, his nails digging in. "Which one is it—"

"She's with me." A different hand lands on my opposite shoulder, and my entire body resonates with the heat emanating from it.

The other man grunts, but when he eyes the figure behind me, he nods and lumbers off, joining the press of people breaking off into small groups to search.

"What are you doing here, bunny?" He sounds so cold. I can clearly predict his expression before I even turn to face him—guarded eyes and a mistrustful frown.

As if he has any right to be.

Saying nothing, I reach into my pocket for Mr. Zhang's red envelope. I shove it at him so fiercely he barely manages to catch it. Then I turn on my heel with my chin in the air and my shoulders back.

I don't even make it a step.

"Wait." He snatches my arm, steering me past the restaurant and into a nearby alley. From here, we have a decent view of the restaurant's entrance, but we're out of sight from those inside.

"This isn't the time or the place to hop around, little bunny." The words carry his trademark taunts, but his voice falls flat and lacks its usual flair. He sounds wary. I risk glancing at his face only to find his stare fixed on the nearby gathering—namely, the man commanding attention from the very heart of the commotion. "You're going to draw attention," he tells me, his jaw tense, a muscle twitching against the tan skin. "You have that face. Anyone could take one look and know you aren't missing a damn thing—"

"I'm not here for you," I say, my voice softer than I'd like. To bolster the statement, I step forward, searching for Mara, but I can't resist one last quip. "But I'm surprised someone like you can cease being selfish long enough to look for someone else."

"A search party isn't a good time to be jealous, bunny," he counters.

I feel my cheeks flush hot, but before I can sputter out a comeback, his grip tightens, pulling me deeper into the alley. With every step, my heartbeat quickens, and my palms sweat. Am I afraid?

Yes, I decide as my gaze flicks along his face. I'm terrified—but not of him.

"Get off." My hand forms a fist before I can stop myself and lashes out. My knuckles smart, harmlessly glancing off his chest, but he grunts, caught off guard.

"I said, let go." I try to tug my arm loose, but he doesn't relent, steadily pulling me along. So I dig my heels into the pavement. "I can take a hint," I snarl as loudly as I dare. "We're done, aren't we? Now you can go back to Bonnie, and I'll—"

He releases me so suddenly that I trip, forced to brace my hand against the nearest wall for balance. But his heavy sigh stops me dead in my tracks. My feet refuse to move, forcing me to watch as he wavers, raking a hand through his hair, his mouth twisted into an expression that transforms him into a different person. Guilt?

I'm so used to suppressing and enduring. It seems as if he's the only person in the world who stokes my worst instincts, breathing them to life.

Feeling.

Hating.

Spite.

"What you did was *cruel*," I snarl, feeling my upper lip pull back from my teeth. "I don't expect much from you, but I do at least expect respect."

I don't think it hits me until now, just how angry I truly am. The ache in my chest. The pathetic need to blink as my eyes burn with the threat of tears, but Bonnie's image isn't the one in my head, making my blood boil. It's him, always him.

If he were truly an asshole, it would be so much easier.

Anything but this hot and cold. Fire and ice. Interest one moment and callous uncaring the next.

"And stringing me along isn't cruel?" he counters. "Juggling fucking me between dinner dates with your boyfriend isn't cruel?"

I bite my lip. I could come clean.

But I don't.

"You don't do relationships, remember? Besides, I've never gone out of my way to rub it in your face," I croak, only to realize—as his eyes cut to me, flashing with rage—that I have in a sense. Why else would I bring Liam to his neighborhood, across from his place of work?

I'd wanted to see the look on his face, the same thing he'd taunted me with.

"Well, now we're done," I stammer, turning on my heel. "Feel free to bring your next fling by the bookshop whenever you—"

"I *wanted* to hurt you." He breathes the confession into the air in advance of his approach, giving me every chance to run away. When I don't, his hands find my hips as his breath heats the back of my neck. "I'm glad I did," he adds without an ounce of shame. "You were jealous. You felt *used.* Maybe now you'll know what it feels like. To watch someone dangle what you can't have in your fucking face. To have them toy with you. Pretend there's more…"

My breathing feathers, my chest tight. "You're the one who set the rules, remember?"

He laughs as if the answer is too obvious to even utter out loud. Instead, he spins me to face him, then lifts my chin until I meet his stare. "Search your soul the next time you write in that fucking journal. You set the pace yourself from the outset. A girl like you could never be interested in someone like me, *remember*?"

"And you'd rather play mind games than tell me the truth," I say, startled by how well my voice matches his harsh tone. "Wasn't it you who asked me to use my pretty words? Your turn. If you *want* me to be interested in you, then just say so. Stop pretending you don't care. If you want me, then don't be a coward and punish me for it. Just say so!"

"It takes a while," he murmurs, eyeing me with a skeptical tilt of his head. "But that bunny bite always comes out in the end. And this time? You didn't even apologize."

He lets me go and slips past me, exiting the alley. "If you say we're done, we're done," he says. "But since you're here, you might as well help." He extends his arm toward me, and I make out a stack of flyers clenched in his fist.

Spurning him is my first impulse, but then my eyes fall over Faith's smiling face. She must be my age or a little younger, and I can't stop seeing her the night Branden and I had dinner where she worked. Even then…she looked terrified.

But that wasn't my first time meeting her—at least indirectly. That was when I caught her leaving the warehouse of the very man standing beside me.

"How well did you know her?" I can't resist asking the question, though I didn't intend for it to come out so…hostile.

Rafe raises an eyebrow. "Enough to know that now isn't the time for petty fights. You here to help or not?"

Warily, I step forward, taking a handful of flyers, and he heads off down the street with his own stack. I don't know why I follow him. Curiosity?

He tackles the heart of the restaurant district, mingling directly with owners and patrons alike with unmistakable confidence that betrays just how well-known he is around here. Much like with Mr. Shen, those he encounters treat him with the utmost respect, promising to come to him with any news.

Or fear. A few acquaintances of his seem as jumpy and on guard as Mr. Zhang. But most aren't, treating him the way one might a brother or son. Someone they trust.

In his wake, I find myself handing out flyers to anyone who will take one, but when he moves on, so do I. He cuts a path through the heart of downtown, until eventually, the foot traffic thins, and the streetlamps grow farther apart, casting a sporadic glow. The darkened atmosphere makes me inch closer to him as I scan the nearby alleys.

Suddenly, he stops, beckoning me with a curt nod of his chin. I follow the line of his gaze to a girl leaning against a nearby building, illuminated by the dim light emanating from a bar across the street. A lit cigarette sticks out from her mouth, and limp dark hair hangs loosely down her back.

"You should put those pretty words of yours to the test," Rafe tells me, eyeing my thinning stack of flyers. "Give her one."

I start to question, but he shakes his head once. His expression shifts again, softening to reveal a hint of something new lurking beneath. Some elusive emotion that makes me cross the street against my better judgment.

My breaths feather with every step as doubt creeps in. I may be sheltered, but I know what it means to stand on a street corner at this time of night, wearing high heels and little else.

The girl stiffens as I approach. "Who the fuck are you?" She pulls herself from the wall and runs her hand along her bright blue minidress.

"Here." I hand her a flyer, but she stares blankly at the front of it. The back of my neck prickles with awareness. Rafe is watching me, but I have no idea what he expects me to do other than simply ask, "Have you seen her?"

Her lip trembles, her eyes widening. "No." She shakes her head as her eyes dart wildly around the deserted block. "Now leave me alone—"

"You sure about that?" Rafe comes up behind me, radiating that enigmatic authority. "Because she's missing. Her parents have already called the police, and they'll start looking into her personal life soon enough. Her friends. Any *jobs* she may have held."

The girl pales and flicks her cigarette onto the ground. "I have to go—"

"Do you think Gino will protect you?" Rafe calls out.

The girl falters. "I don't know what you're talking about."

"I think you do," Rafe says at the same time I feel his hand brush my shoulder. A cue?

But to what?

"I… You're afraid," I blurt as the girl remains standing, her slender shoulders heaving with every breath. "Of someone?"

"You don't understand—" She jumps as a car drives by, and its headlights wash over her. With a fearful glance over her shoulder, she whirls around and scrambles down a nearby alley. "Please leave me alone."

"Just give me a place to start looking," Rafe demands. "A street corner. A name. Someone who might want her gone. Anything."

"I know what you did, you know," the girl hisses back, crossing her arms over her chest. "Everyone does. You called in the raid. You don't have any idea what kind of people you messed with."

"Don't I?" Rafe demands, sounding anything but cowed. "You want to know the truth? Faith came to me because she was scared of the shit that fucker was getting up to. Gino has no idea who he's messing with. I know he set Faith up with a crazy fucker who terrified her and did awful shit to her. You want to be next?"

The girl stumbles, her chest heaving. "DW," she finally rasps. "That's what she called him. DW. She was afraid of him. I… I think he found her somehow. Where she lives. She texted me, but it wasn't like I could do anything. I just told her to stay away from him…but the last I heard from her was three days ago."

"Thanks," Rafe says. "If you think of anything else, you know where to find me?"

"Yes." She glances back, eyeing him warily. "But Gino won't like it if he hears that I talked to you." She scurries off, fading beneath the shadow.

"Come on." Rafe snatches my wrist, but I don't resist as he pulls me through the alley and down another back road. I sense the route is strategic, returning us to the restaurant district while drawing little attention from anyone else who may be on the main streets.

"What was that about?" I gather the nerve to ask him as the Chan Noodle House comes back into view.

He shrugs. "That was reality, bunny."

"You knew Faith," I say, letting my brain put the pieces together. "I think I remember her from your club the first night I was there." The girl who interrupted while he taunted me. "What happened to her?"

"A monster happened," he says, his voice low. He's not exaggerating for once. He means that word in the truest sense. "I tried to protect her, but…"

He crumples the remaining flyers in his fist, then hisses through his teeth, "Why don't you ask your boyfriend what some of his fellow officers like to do in their spare time?"

I look down at my final flyer, smoothing out the wrinkles with shaking fingers. "What are you talking about?"

He lets me go, lumbering in the opposite direction. By the time I whirl around, he's already half a block down, his shoulders hunched, the flames of his tattoo consuming his left arm. He's embodying every ounce of that dragon again, radiating rage like fire.

CHAPTER TWENTY

I don't know how long I stare after him before I finally manage to leave. In a daze, I wander down the next few blocks, and it seems as though I reach my apartment in record time—but the second I touch the doorknob, I falter. A smell tinges the air near my door, one that sets every nerve in my body alight. *Run.* I pivot on my heel, my sole focus on moving.

The door flies open before I can even go a step. A hand lashes out, grabbing my arm and dragging me inside.

"Just hear me out," Branden demands. He lets me go but blocks the door with his bulk. One-handed, he closes it, twisting the lock. "Don't I deserve that fucking much? Or are you going to stick your nose up at me too? Turn your back on me like everyone fucking else?"

"Branden…you're shouting," I croak. The light is on, casting his face in half-shadow. Part brother, part stranger who glowers at me with piercing eyes. "My neighbors will hear you."

"You'd like that, wouldn't you?" He winces, but his jaw doesn't lose the defensive tilt. He's not really here to forge a truce. "Get your stuff. Now. You're coming with me."

"Branden, it's late—"

"And you seem to be very *busy* at night these days, Hannah." His eyes rake over me with chilling intensity. "You make it seem so fucking hard just to take a picture of yourself lately. Could it be because you're naked, fucking some asshole—"

"Branden!" I grasp at the nearest wall for balance as the room starts to spin around me.

"An asshole whom you've aided and abetted after a *crime,* Hannah. You sheltered him here. You don't think I know where you've been? His club? His fucking shop?"

Those words… They're too specific. Too cold.

He knows.

"Deny it," he goads, his upper lip drawn tight, revealing his teeth. "Go on, Hannah. Like the little lying whore you are—"

"How?" I ask, my voice weak. "Are you following me? Stalking me?"

He scoffs. "I don't have to." He cuts his gaze to my bag, and a grim realization freezes me to my core. The phone. Has he been tracking my cell phone all this time? "How can I trust you when you lie?" he demands. "When you fuck around with a criminal? You need me, Hannah."

"I saw Karen Winacott," I blurt without realizing why. Maybe it's like Rafe said? Some sick, twisted part of me can't stop playing with fire. "I spoke to her."

"W-What?" Shock makes his jaw go slack, and his hands shake, tearing through his hair. "And what did you tell her?" He cocks his head suspiciously, stepping forward. "What the fuck did you tell her?"

I nearly trip over my own feet in my haste to back away. At the same time, my voice comes out stronger than I've ever heard it. "What if I told her the truth? That you *made* me be friends with Lexi. That you had me lure her into the woods. And then you—"

He moves so quickly, though my brain processes every frame in slow motion. His snarl. His hand forming a fist. Him raising it...

Pain. I see white. Black. When my vision returns, I'm on my knees, blinking until the blurred image of my apartment comes back into focus. Droplets of red drip from nowhere to speckle my floor, reminding me of Rafe's. But this time...

It's coming from me. My head. I feel dizzy when I attempt to stand. I can't without pitching forward, and my hands shake as I brace them against the floor in a desperate bid to stay upright.

"Oh, shit. Han… I'm sorry." Strong arms go around me, but they don't smell like smoke. They reek of cologne instead—a spicy wrongness that makes me twitch. Recoil. *Run.* "I'm so sorry," Bran croaks against the nape of my neck, stroking through the hair gathered there. "Why did you make me do that, huh? Dammit. You're bleeding, honey."

His hands ghost over my shoulders, finding my cheek. It's throbbing, and more blood drips onto the floor as he tilts it so that I face him.

"I'm sorry," he says, still stroking my hair back. "I never want to hurt you, you know that."

"Then, why do you?" My lip feels heavy, my muscles aching with every breath. Every blink. It should be easier than ever to stay silent. Endure. Suffer.

But for the first time in my life, I look at him, and I can't.

Use those pretty words, a mocking voice echoes inside my skull. *Explain.*

"Why do you do this to me?"

He frowns. "Han…"

"Why do you control everything I do. Why track my phone? Why—"

"Han." His voice turns cutting. "You're upset. I get it. Let me get you cleaned off."

"Don't touch me!"

But he does, gripping my arms, holding me against him despite my attempts to pull away. "You know I love you," he insists in my ear. "More than anyone. You're the only one who I can trust. Only you. I forgive you for what you've done. I will always forgive you…" His hands slide over me, triggering a reaction I don't try to suppress for once.

Anger sparks, catching fire in my limbs, and I push. Shove. Kick. Grunting in shock, he lets me go, and I stagger to my feet. Blindly, I race for the door, fumble it open, and then I keep running.

"Hannah!"

I start down the stairs too fast. My foot catches on a tread, and I slide down the next four steps, landing on my hip in a daze.

"Hannah!" I look up, spotting Branden racing toward me. He's paces away by the time I crawl to my feet and stumble through the door. Out on the street, a passing couple spies me, and the woman gasps, her hand over her mouth.

"Are you okay?"

I push past her, knowing I only have seconds to spare. The distraction buys me enough time to slip into an alleyway. Then another. Another.

I don't know if Branden's still behind me by the time I reach a building only to find the door locked. The lights out. Its owner isn't here.

And panic chokes me. I don't know where else to go. I don't even know why I came to him in the first place.

But then I glance up, spying a light in the window… Through it, I can see someone standing before it, his back to the world, his posture relaxed. A white shirt creates a contrast from his usual black, making him glow against the muted backdrop.

Relief blazes through me with such an unexpected intensity that I just stare. Gape at him. I must make some kind of noise, though. Move. Somehow, I catch his attention, making him venture closer to the glass. He stares down on me for so long, but then he turns away.

My feet twitch over the pavement. At this time of night, the traffic is moderate. Quick. Branden could be in his car by now, driving this way. He'll spot me.

But the light on the first floor switches on before the fear drives me to start running. A figure warily approaches, pulling the door open. His eyes are narrowed as he takes me in. Then they widen. "What the fuck?"

I don't know why or how, but the look on his face… It's like the trigger to the pain I didn't feel until now. Pulsating, burning, pinching agony.

He grabs my arm, pulling me inside without waiting for an explanation. The interior of his shop passes in a blur. It feels like I blink, and the next second, he's hauling me into that back room, making me sit on the edge of the table.

"Look up," he commands, gripping my chin.

My eyes burn from the artificial light as I comply. Something warm is dribbling down my chin, and I realize for the first time—as my body favors my right side—that the left is on fire. My knee is throbbing, and my shoulder feels stiff. With every passing second, the adrenaline wears off, giving way to a crippling sensation with each frantic beat of my heart.

Pain, pain, pain…

"He did this to you." He's not asking—he's telling. Branden did this to me, causing so much blood it coats his fingertips as he continues his inspection. My brother smashed his fist into my face, the same way the man before me now attacked someone else.

Like an animal.

I don't even register standing, but somehow, I'm limping into the hall, aware of him watching me. I feel like I'm moving underwater, weighed down, and clumsy. I keep my focus on the door, though who knows what I'll find waiting for me beyond it. I just know I have to keep moving. Leave now.

Because the prospect of what might happen if I don't scares me more than anything Branden is capable of.

Eventually, I make it to the door, grappling along the wall for support. My fingers curl around the handle, but a larger hand reaches from behind me, snatching my arm away. My feet leave the ground a heartbeat later, but my brain is slow to piece the reality of what's happening together until I'm being carried inside a familiar living room and shoved onto a leather couch.

I think I try to say something, but my voice is so garbled, I don't even understand the words.

But he does. "You can barely fucking walk," he snarls before entering the kitchen with an enviable display of speed.

Seconds later, he returns with his arms piled high with supplies that put my meager sewing kit to shame.

"Your face is going to scar if you don't go to a hospital," he tells me, prodding my left cheek, which aches the most.

Any other day, I'd react to that fact with more panic. More guilt. A scar would mean more questions. Questions would mean more chances to screw up and betray Branden, which would only lead to him trying to exert more control over my life in general.

But now?

I can't feel anything but the warm fingers smoothing the hair from my face. He dampens a paper towel and applies a cool liquid to my cheek next, holding it there despite how I flinch.

"Don't move," he warns. "You don't want this to get infected."

He continues to apply more liquid with a familiarity that makes me suspect this isn't the first time he's patched someone up like this. Bonnie? No. Something in his stern expression triggers the memory of what he said to me the night he was stabbed. *You looked like me. Those scared bunny eyes…*

"You need to take off your shirt," he commands, drawing back. He stands and exits the room, seemingly expecting me to comply on my own.

I stare down at my sweater, speckled red in places, but I can't seem to make my arms move. By the time he reenters the room, I haven't budged.

But he's already stripped off his bloodied shirt, leaving his chest bare. Dangling from his arm is a clean one, but he brings it to me rather than put it on.

"Lift your arms." His tone carries an authority that I'm too exhausted to argue with. Or follow.

In the end, he sinks into a crouch and tugs at the hem of my sweater, dragging it over my head himself. He swaps it for the oversized one of his, which hangs on me loosely, pooling over my waist as he tugs off my skirt.

Wary, his eyes meet mine, brimming with confusion as though he's contemplating some complex puzzle. "Get up."

To leave. I've already made peace with that inevitable outcome. I try to stand. Gingerly, I brace my feet on the floor, but when I attempt to rise from the couch, my muscles refuse.

He has to grab my arm and haul me to my feet. I stagger, forced to cling to him for balance. "Come on."

My fingers grip his forearm, but he sweeps his hand around my hip, keeping me upright. Then he lifts me entirely, taking me into his arms as though I weigh nothing. Instead of the stairs, he carries me down the hall, deeper into the apartment's layout. When he reaches a closed door, I can feel him hesitate before he finally pushes it open.

A spacious bedroom lurks behind it, one accented with navy walls and pops of scarlet. His sheets are red, his comforter black. Apart from a black wooden dresser, he doesn't have much furniture, leaving the space almost utilitarian. Somewhere he sleeps, savoring his time alone.

Time to read the battered book I spy on a nightstand as he sets me down on the wide mattress, double the size of mine. I'm too stunned by the feel of the blankets to fully process the action. This whole room smells like him, a haven of smoke and coconut. But my observation is cut short when he pushes me down.

"Sleep."

He turns, leaving the room and closing the door behind him.

Even now, he'll bend his rule, but he won't break it.

CHAPTER TWENTY-ONE

I wake up so disoriented I know I'm dreaming. The bed beneath me is far too soft to be mine. Too big. Soft blankets shroud me in swaths of fabric, and it feels as though I could lie here forever.

But raised voices intrude on my refuge, sounding as if they're coming from directly below.

"…said you told him to stand down," a man says, his voice so deep it seems to vibrate through the floor, up the bed frame, and into my very bones. "Since when do we cower in our territory?"

"He isn't worth it," a man replies, his voice so level I almost don't recognize it. Rafe. He must be down in his shop, and the sound must carry easily in this old building. "There's no point in—"

"No point in proving that we are not people to be fucked with?" the other man counters, his inflection conveying a dangerous implication. "I've given you more control than most men would," he adds. "Don't make me regret that, Rafael."

"You won't," Rafe replies.

"And now with the missing Wen girl. The police will be buzzing around, sticking their fucking noses where they don't belong. You need to get a handle on this. Now. Not toy with your fucking whores, or waste time doing whatever the hell it is you do in this shithole of a playhouse." The vitriol in his tone makes my skin crawl. It's cruel, directed at more than just this building, but at everything down to the drawings adorning the walls.

Every piece of art.

"I will," Rafe says.

"And if you don't… You know I don't give second chances."

The man must leave because I hear a bell chime as though the main door was opened. In his absence, heavy footsteps resonate, though muted from the distance. I recognize the slow, steady gait. Rafe. Pacing?

He must do so for what seems like hours, forming endless circles. Finally, the sound trails off only to be replaced by the louder thud of advancing footsteps entering the apartment. He comes close only to retreat without trying the door. Again, minutes later.

My brain reads into the action. His attempts to do what he did the first night I stayed here. Tell me to leave. Uphold his rule.

Pain shoots down my spine as I push back the covers and gingerly sit upright. I'm still wearing his shirt, my shoes removed, my bag nowhere in sight. I brace my feet on the floor and attempt to stand. My knees buckle, and I have to clutch the bed frame just to stay upright.

Bit by bit, I inch toward the door and push it open. My eyes scan the living room for my stuff. I find my bag on the couch and my shoes near the door. I start for them first and attempt to wrestle my feet into each sandal.

From this position, I have a clearer view of the apartment's common space—including the figure standing in the kitchen with his back to me. He sighs heavily, rummaging through a pile of assorted items. I can tell from the set of his shoulders alone that he's sensed my presence.

I don't wait for him to turn around scowling or to dish out his trademark kiss-off.

Limping with the effort, I start for my bag. I barely get my fingers around the strap when it's yanked from my grasp. A sturdy arm hooks around my waist, bringing with it the overwhelming scent of coconut. My feet leave the ground a heartbeat later, and before I can even blink, I'm being placed onto a hard surface while a muscular body blocks me in, preventing me from falling.

I'm on the counter, sitting precariously beside a loaf of bread and a jar of peanut butter.

"Eat." A sandwich appears beneath my nose, oozing peanut butter from the edges. "Eat."

I eye the soft, pale surface. Of all the scenarios running through my head, this one didn't even make the cut. A trick? A test?

"I'm not hungry," I finally rasp.

He makes a gruff sound in his throat, and I finally gather the nerve to meet his gaze. A single cocked black eyebrow transforms the cold, icy expression I expect to find. He looks more irritated than anything. "You slept through the night," he says. "It's two in the fucking afternoon. You're starving. Eat."

My brain short-circuits, and I can't argue. My lips part as he rams a corner of the sandwich between them. I bite down and chew.

The simple act triggers an avalanche of pain I'd been able to suppress until now. My throbbing left eye. My cheek. My jaw. My shoulder. Chewing hurts, and it's painful to swallow.

Taking a hint, he sets the sandwich aside and grabs a spoon from the drawer. He shoves it directly into the jar of peanut butter and brings the mixture to my mouth.

"Eat."

It's easier to swallow without having to chew first. I take a careful lick. Then another. After that, he switches up the rhythm by presenting me with a glass of water before one more spoonful.

His eyes scan my face as I choke down each sampling, hunting for something. Whatever he finds in the end, makes him set the spoon aside once I've licked it clean. He raises a hand to my face next, but his demeanor keeps me from flinching. I don't think I've ever seen this expression shaping his features, tightening the line of his mouth, and darkening those watchful eyes. The worst part? I can't even begin to name it.

My confusion only grows as his thumb glides beneath my eye, and the mysterious emotion shifts. *Now* I recognize it. Rage. "A little higher. A little harder. He could have killed you."

He says it so matter-of-factly and with a nonchalance that makes the overall statement even more chilling.

"Like you could have killed Gino?" I don't know why I turn it on him. Why a part of me squirms, hating his attention. Though I haven't seen my face yet, the need to minimize is ingrained within me as a mantra of sorts. *This? This is nothing.*

"Yes," he says without an ounce of shame. He teases aside a lock of my hair, exposing more of my injuries to him. "Like I *could* have killed Gino. But Gino's got a good hundred pounds on you, and I can tell you right now that he's not fucked up half as bad as you are."

I assume he's joking, at first. But no, his eyes stare dead into mine, daring me to question.

"Are you an expert?"

"I know my own strength," he counters. "What's that saying? Pick on someone your own size. If Gino were anywhere near *your* size? I'd know better than to touch him. Not unless I wanted fucking prison."

"He insulted your mother," I point out. "You were angry." I'm not sure whether I'm justifying his actions or pointing out the failure in his logic. There was nothing controlled about what he did. He lashed out purely on instinct. In rage.

He frowns, letting his hand fall from me. "He did," he admits. "And he fucking deserved a fist to the face for that. But using that logic, what did you do, huh? It must have been pretty fucking bad, bunny." He eyes me again in that indiscernible way, making my breathing hitch. "I wanted to shut Gino's ass up and teach the fucker a lesson. But what *he* did to you? He wanted to hurt you—"

"Stop."

"You know what Gino does to the girls who work for him?" he adds. "He treats them like shit. Makes them turn tricks to curry favor with whoever he wants. Rich fuckers. Businessmen. Even the cops. Someone like *that* deserves to be beaten so badly he can barely fucking walk, not—"

"I'm fine."

"Oh?" He rears back, an eyebrow cocked. His thumb finds my chin, manipulating my face so that he can view me from a different angle. "Fine," he echoes harshly. "You know that journal of yours… One of those little stories you wrote? Deceiver, I think you called it."

Alarm prickles down my spine. That story got me my first ever feature, submitted to a paper on a whim. I try to turn away, but his grip tightens just enough to keep me trapped without causing more pain. "S-Stop."

"It was really morbid shit, bunny," he tells me, snatching a fresh paper towel to dab at my lip with. "About someone haunted by a monster. One who got inside her head and threatened to destroy her from the inside out. The only way to save herself? Deceive someone else into becoming his prey—"

"It's just a story."

"I doubt that," he replies, sounding confident. "In fact, I think it's the realest thing you've scribbled in that little journal of yours. The one time you admitted it to yourself —you're afraid. Not of just him, but of the things he's done to you. Whatever twisted shit being with him has made you do—"

"Please stop." I squeeze my eyes shut, steeling myself for more. More anger. More vicious words. More of the truth…

He sighs. "Eat."

I open my eyes as another spoonful of peanut butter appears beneath my nose. His version of a truce? I'm too grateful for the distraction to care. Parting my lips, I let him shovel a spoonful inside. And then another.

He watches me swallow, his expression unreadable. When I've eaten enough to satisfy him, he rocks back on his heels, and I grip the edge of the counter, preparing to stand.

"I should go—"

"Stay." He grits his teeth, and I can practically see him wrestling with the decision to voice the next words to leave his mouth. "You should stay. Get some sleep."

He makes it sound less like a suggestion and more like he's granting a request I never asked out loud. Regardless, he's already tugging off my sandals without waiting for an answer. He tosses them into a corner near the couch, and then palms my hips, easing me down from the counter.

"I have to work," he says before pulling away, heading toward the door to the stairs. "In the meantime, you can come up with a good ass lie to explain your face before you go back to him."

My face? I watch him go, then I turn on my heel and find myself creeping toward his bathroom. It's dark enough inside it that I have to flip the light switch just to be able to make out my reflection.

But a monster stares back. Her eyes are bloodshot—one partially swollen shut. Bruises in various shades of purple discolor her skin. A gash slices beneath her cheek, dangerously close to her eye, and her neck is a patchwork of discoloration.

I can see that my mouth is open and my eyes wide, but I don't hear anything, just my surging heartbeat. It hammers against my eardrums, deafening me to anything else.

Until the door flies open, smacking off the adjacent wall. The figure behind it looks at me, his brows knitted in concern, his chest heaving as though he ran all the way here. I can finally name that elusive emotion creeping across his features. *Pity.*

He steps forward without a word, impossible to outrun. I'm in his arms before I can even think to react, burning alive in his heat.

And all I can do is surrender to the inferno.

CHAPTER TWENTY-TWO

"He's never hit you in the face before. When he abuses you." He makes it sound normal almost. As if he's so familiar with the ins and outs of such a dynamic. Abuse? A part of me cringes from the word, and the soft surface beneath me makes for a fitting hiding place from the reality of it all.

His bed. He's sprawled out beside me, his fingers in my hair, his eyes on the ceiling.

"He keeps it all concentrated on your arms," he continues. "Your legs. Back. Places that are easier to hide. Easier for you to ignore. But when it's on your face…" He sighs, bringing his hand to his right temple. His thumb traces the length of his eyebrow, bringing attention to a tiny scar slicing through it that I never noticed until now. "*That* makes it real. You can't ignore it then."

"Like you?" I tilt my face against his chest, just enough to make eye contact. "Your father?" I ask, recalling something

Mara mentioned. *He went to prison, though I'm not sure why. Murder, I think.*

He stiffens, and I don't expect an answer. His fingers are in my hair again, distracting me with their soft, gentle motions over my scalp. "He'll do it again," he tells me, ignoring my question. "You don't want to hear it, but he will."

Of course, I already know as much. I've made peace with it in a sense, but the fact never alarmed me before. My chest clenches at the prospect, my limbs trembling.

Why?

Because it's getting harder than ever to shut the pain off? Because the moth drifted too close to the fire, burning up her fragile shell. Now she feels everything.

And it hurts.

I hunt for another distraction and find one as I shift over scarlet silken sheets. "I'm in your bed," I point out, my voice broken and raspy. The change in subject makes him stiffen this time. "Your sheets will smell like me—"

"You have a boyfriend," he counters, his answer to every inch of his control he's let me take. "This doesn't count."

"No, I don't," I confess, feeling my throat thicken. "I don't have a boyfriend."

He grunts as if he's not sure how to process that statement. In the end, he just sighs, letting his fingers slip through my hair. And in the gentle motions, I lose the last bit of myself I've kept restrained.

"He hurt me." It's so surreal saying it out loud. Hearing my voice form those words I've expressed through my writing so many times. Through deception and prose. Through lies. "Bran hurt me. He's *always* hurt me...and no one has ever cared." Not our parents, who found it easier to let Branden oversee my life than do it themselves. Not my classmates, who overlooked the girl who always wore sweaters, even in the summer. Not his wife.

"My mother made excuses for my father," Rafe says, his voice so soft I barely hear him. "She always fell or tripped. She said she was clumsy, not that he'd smacked her with his fist when he didn't get his way or hit her with a wine bottle. Not when he left for three fucking years, fucking around while she did whatever she could to care for me. No matter what it cost her, she did it."

I brace my hand against his chest, feeling his heartbeat raging beneath my palm. He eyes the ceiling coldly, his teeth gritted, body rigid.

"And she always loved the fucker, though I don't know why. She always took him back, no matter what he did... No matter how badly he hurt her, she let him return again and again."

I shift against him, watching as those dark eyes flash with rage at the memories.

"One night, he got too rough after showing up again out of the blue. He shoved her around, but she didn't get back up. The asshole just laughed and passed out. She would never call the cops on his ass..."

"But you did," I whisper when he trails off.

He nods, his chin jutting proudly. "I did. Not that it made much of a fucking difference. She wasn't able to make excuses for him that time."

My gaze falls over his arm and the flames licking down the length of it—but I don't see a dragon's fire in the design for once. I see a little boy breathing out his rage in a world that ignored him. That hardened him, turning him into a monster who snarls at those around him with his teeth bared and guard up.

Anything to protect himself.

His art speaks for him in ways my writing never could, put on display for everyone to witness.

"What tattoo would you put on me?" I ask him, eyeing my bruised and battered limbs. "A rabbit?"

"No." He eyes me with an odd expression, pursing his lips in deep thought. "Roll over."

I do gingerly as he rises onto his knees beside me. Warm fingers lift his borrowed shirt and prod between my shoulder blades, testing out the quality of his canvas. Softly, he traces a path down to my hip, sketching an invisible design.

"I don't think I'll tell you, bunny," he decides, returning to my side and drawing me close. "You'll just have to find out."

"When?" I ask.

"When you don't have to hide it," he replies.

But that's not what he really means.

When you can stop hiding from him.

"I can't go back." It sounds so desperate when said out loud. So final. "I can't."

He nods as if unsurprised. "You got a place lined up?"

I shake my head. "There's nowhere to go."

He doesn't challenge that. He doesn't argue. He doesn't taunt. He lets me lie beside him, still stroking through my tangled hair. Then he stands, drawing the sheets over me before he heads for the door.

"I'll be back," he says.

Which leaves an unspoken invitation in the air. *Stay.*

I don't move, listening to him exit through the door and descend the steps. I sense rather than hear him leave the building entirely a moment later, but it feels so surreal. So strange to be here without him.

I can observe this room, invading his sacred spaces the way he's already invaded mine. For all his taunts about my décor, his is relatively just as plain. No posters on the walls. No drawings. No hanging photos.

The only picture I find sits framed in black wood on his nightstand. A smiling little boy with beautiful almond eyes and his arms wrapped around a dark-skinned woman who looks at him as though he's the only thing in the world that matters. Her sun. Her reason for living.

His mother? He has her mouth and her beautiful bone structure.

The mocking glare and cold eyes he must get from his father, but I don't find any pictures of anyone else, at least in here.

He keeps his room clean, much like his shop. It betrays a level of perfectionism I suspect he hides behind the gruff attitude and swagger. He likes things orderly. Neat.

He likes his sheets to smell faintly of fabric softener, devoid of any other scents that might intrude into his thoughts while he's lying here.

He likes to keep his private world empty, choosing not to display even his art. I can't resist wondering why. Does it make it easier for him to come here at night after everything he's done?

Or does the stark utilitarianism just betray how little he must stay here?

I can't decide by the time I hear steps ascending in the stairwell. By the time he enters the apartment, I've hobbled from his room, creeping to the mouth of the living room.

A peculiar smell reaches my nose first. *Food?* Almost in slow motion, I spot the brown bag clutched in one of his hands.

The other is supporting a cardboard box propped against his hip. He sets it down, and it's already open, giving me a glimpse of the items inside.

"The rest of your stuff is in my car," he says.

Stuff. The yellow bedsheets folded with care. The random assortment of clothing. The shoebox. The camera…

"This is mine," I blurt out, sinking into a crouch to better peer through the items. "You got them from my apartment."

He turns away to set the food onto the counter. "Were you lying when you said you couldn't go back?" His wary tone deepens.

"N-No." I can barely speak. "Thank you…"

I run my fingers over the rest of my things, overwhelmed by the emotion swelling in my chest. Terror? Gratitude?

But my hand keeps going back to one item in particular. Puzzled, I lift it, observing it in full. It's the same model of camera that Branden kept above my TV, only…it's unbroken. Newer, lacking any scratches or dents.

"Where did you find this?" Had Branden replaced his old one already?

"In your room," Rafe says. "You take your security fucking serious, bunny—what's wrong?"

I can't breathe. Can't speak.

In my room. Positioned near the bed?

Watching everything.

"Is it broken or something…" He breaks off, his head cocked. "Shit."

From down below, I hear a door open and slam loudly enough to rattle the entire building. Loud, a gruff voice calls out, "Rafael!"

"Stay here." He's gone in an instant, and not even a minute later, his voice drifts from below. "Uncle. What's wrong?"

"They found the Wen girl," a man declares. "Dead. In our territory. You know what that means?"

"It's a threat," Rafe suspects, but his voice is deeper than I've ever heard it, betraying a rare hint of emotion. Rage? Despair? Guilt?

"No," the older man says, his uncle. "It is a declaration of war. And *you* are going to dictate our response to it."

"How?" Rafe asks.

"In the only language these animals will understand," Shen replies. "You failed to react once to a direct challenge. I know you won't make that mistake again. The same way I know that the rumors circling about you are false."

A deliberate pause leaves Rafe no choice but to reply. "What rumors?"

"Rumors that say you've been running from fights rather than finishing them more often than not," Shen says coldly.

"That you've been taking it upon yourself to clear debts you have no business clearing. That you're too busy playing with your little toys rather than upholding the mantle of everything this family stands for."

Rafe scoffs. "I'm not—"

"I know," the older man says over him. "They're only rumors, right? Not worth wasting time entertaining. Now come."

Heavy footsteps retreat from the building, but the charged atmosphere remains, suffocating in its intensity. This time, Rafe doesn't pace, wracked with some internal dilemma.

He lurks below in utter silence, and it's like my body feeds off his tension. His anger manifests as nervous energy in me, and I find myself rummaging through my meager box of belongings.

At the very bottom, I discover my shoebox. I open it out of habit, reaching in for the assorted items inside. Nail polish. ChapStick…

A pang of alarm runs through me as I belatedly realize what wasn't there, lying on top of the other items—the newspaper clipping. And it's not the only thing missing. When I feel for the bracelet, I don't find its familiar round shape. Something sharp nudges my fingertip instead, and I look down, startled to find a different object glaringly out of place.

Small and silver, the hair pin is beautifully crafted.

One I recognize with an overwhelming sense of horror that strikes like a punch to the chest.

One in the shape of a delicate butterfly.

FLAME

Flame

Flame By Lana Sky

Copyright © 2020 by Lana Sky
All rights reserved.

ACKNOWLEDGMENTS

Thanks so much to everyone who supported this draft along the way, including the many beta readers who provided encouragement! Please keep in mind that this story includes dark, graphic and explicit content matter that may not be suitable for readers under the age of 18—or for readers who are uncomfortable with the following subject matter: explicit sex, mentions of sexual abuse, mentions of domestic abuse, and graphic depictions of violence.

CHAPTER ONE

I still remember the first time I ever put the tip of my pen to a sheet of fresh paper and scribbled whatever came to mind. What that felt like. In a word? Clarity. I went from voiceless to limitless. My words had power again, however little it might have been.

Amid the deepest depths of my brother's obsession and my parents' indifference, I had an identity all other aspects of my life had stripped away.

I became a *writer*.

For years it's been the one thing I've always excelled at. Creating. Crafting. Emoting.

And yet, lately, it feels like I've run out of the right words. My emotions can't be wrestled onto paper anymore. Gone is that defining identity, and once again, I'm a blob molded by my life circumstances.

So much for being a writer. I can't even voice the truth out loud—the event that, in so many ways, led to this present like the first in a series of falling dominoes.

A story that isn't really mine to tell.

Ironically, I used to imagine what life might be like outside of the cage my past forced me to craft around myself. I just never envisioned this—freedom found in a monster's lair, far different from the one I grew up fearing. *His* world is darker, stranger, lonelier…

And in so many ways, hauntingly beautiful.

I'm a moth, ignited by the intoxicating flame that tempted me to fly so near to it. In the aftermath, all I can do is lie on the ashes of my wings, blinking up at a beige ceiling as my brain struggles to reconcile everything that has transpired within the past forty-eight-hours, ending with me alone in the bed of a man I barely know.

Rafe.

The man embodies so many contradictions it's hard to keep track of them all.

Judging from the coolness of the sheets beside me, I doubt he slept here. I strain my ears, but I don't pick up any noise or footsteps throughout the rest of the apartment, either. The only clue of his presence I find at all, once I creep from his room and down the hall, is an empty cup on the kitchen counter beside a brown paper bag of leftover takeout from last night.

As I approach it, I happen to glance from one of the many windows at the street below. It's too early for rush-hour traffic, but several cars dart past at a steady rate—and my heart lurches at the sight of each one. No matter how hard I try to talk myself out of the growing paranoia, I swear every passing vehicle resembles Branden's.

Is Branden's. Though it's only a matter of time before he comes after me. Running was the stupidest thing I've ever done where my brother is concerned. He requires the same logic my father drilled into me around his hunting dogs— never turn your back. Never let your guard down.

And, most importantly, never give the beasts a reason to chase.

Not that he has to do much work to find me anyway. I spot my phone resting on the coffee table, though I didn't put it there. Ignorant of its use as a tracking device, someone even hooked it up to a charger he must have retrieved from my apartment—though he left it off. That little token of kindness isn't the only one I spy as I rise to my feet and start to pace from room to room.

I spot my shoes beside the door leading downstairs. My toothbrush and toiletries have been left for me on the counter in the bathroom. Three boxes of my belongings sit piled in a distant corner of the hall, rescued from my apartment. Out of consideration, some of my clothing has been neatly folded on the top box for easy access.

That same person probably left my bag within view too. Inside it, I find all those trivial reminders of a life that seems like a stranger's to me now. A crumpled business card and a battered gold lighter are just meaningless trinkets. Even my journal. Its pages are still filled with old writing, including my draft essay for the Fenwick program—my only hope for continuing school in the fall.

The proposed topic? Describe and conquer your inner demons.

I laugh out loud at the idea of it. How pathetic was that? To pin my entire success on a whim. My "talent." Scoffing, I flip the book open and scan the pages. All those pretty, carefully penned words read flat. Empty. Useless, emotionless lies. For the first time in my life, I'm numb as I stroke my thumb along a page. There is no spark.

But one person ensured that I wasn't without this possession anyway—an amount of caring that contrasts sharply with the dark-eyed figure dwelling inside my head. The creature capable of sowing the heavy footsteps I catch advancing up the rickety staircase leading to the apartment's entrance. I know even before the door opens who is behind it. I can smell him—ash and smoke.

His very presence is heralded by a shift in the air, like a drop in temperature warning of a storm. *Rafe.*

"You're awake," he grunts in acknowledgment while closing the door behind him. He's wearing a pair of gray sweats and a white beater top—a casual alternative to his usual jeans and black leather. In his hands is another brown paper bag and a faint aroma emanates from it, making my stomach rumble.

"Come here." With a curt nod, he beckons me into the kitchen where he unloads the contents of his bag on the counter—two steaming breakfast sandwiches wrapped in paper. He hands one to me, claiming the second for himself. As our eyes meet, his expression softens, his lips quirking into a frown.

"You bruise fucking easily, rabbit," he says, stroking my cheek with his thumb. His eyes travel down to my throat, fully exposed by the wide neckline of the shirt I'm wearing now—an oversized black one of his. The earnest sympathy in his tone makes me stiffen self-consciously. Apart from last night, I have no fresher mental image to compare my appearance to.

I can't even look in the mirror.

"Is it that bad?" I ask.

"Damn right," Rafe says, whistling through his teeth. "I doubt even the old 'sunglasses' trick will help you, bunny."

I brush my fingers along my jaw and barely feel any pain. It's like I'm numbed to everything but the here and now. His smell takes precedence over any other sensation, his nearness overwhelming.

Whenever I try to think about the million other pressing concerns in my life, only a few stick out.

"I have to work today," I say absently, though panic sets in at the thought of leaving. Branden will be looking for me, for one. My lease runs out by the end of the week thanks to his efforts. I have no idea how to navigate my usual routine, taking all of that into account. "*That's* what I'm worried about," I add with a tattered laugh. "I have to work today."

"I'll talk to Zhang," Rafe says, referring to my boss. He turns away from me and rummages through the fridge, withdrawing a brown bottle of beer. Despite the early hour, he pops the lid off on the edge of the door and takes a deep swig, throwing his head back.

For the first time, I step outside of my own worries and put myself in his shoes. He looks almost as bad as I feel. I have a sinking suspicion as to why.

"The missing girl. Faith," I say thickly. "You knew her."

"Yeah…" He swipes at his mouth with the back of his hand, his gaze distant. "She was a good kid. What happened to her is fucked up."

He sounds genuinely upset, and I hate the jealousy that unfurls when I try to imagine why. Just how well did he know her?

No better than Branden, a part of me snarls in response. *He's the one who had her hair clip, you idiot.*

Ashamed, I focus my attention to the window as another car drives past. A sharp pain in my hand makes me realize that my fingers are clenched, the nails cutting into my palms. "Do… Do they know what happened to her?" I whisper.

Maybe I'm a masochist, feeding off the weight of the heavy sigh he releases. His obvious regret drills in this reality like a hammer on a nail—this is real.

"Not yet. They found her body on the outskirts of the city, and—" he breaks off with a grimace. "I'll spare you the details."

Traffic is still moving down below, and another car zips by too quickly to inspect in full. I tear my gaze away and find myself staring down the hall instead, toward a stack of boxes. *Tell him,* my conscience warns. *Tell him now.*

"She was in trouble," I say, skirting around the truth again. *Trouble* that wound up with her dead and a piece of jewelry hidden among my belongings. My palms grow slick with sweat at the memory, my pulse increasing. "H-How?"

Rafe grunts, and I turn to find him taking another sip of beer. "She got caught up with the wrong motherfuckers and paid the price for it. And I couldn't help her…"

"Her friend," I say. "The one we saw the night of the vigil. She claimed a man, DW, was the one bothering her—" Not Branden for whatever it's worth. "Do you know who that is?"

"No," he growls. "If I did, I'd be ripping the sick fucker apart, wouldn't I?"

"And Faith never told you anything?"

"I know he's a cop," he says in an icy tone. "And that he was using her somehow. As a drug mule? An informant? I don't know. It's not like I can go ask Gino about it, now can I?" He slams the bottle onto the counter and takes a bite from his sandwich, an obvious clue that he's done talking about it.

For now.

But I can fill in some of the blanks on my own. Faith fell in with his rival Gino—a thug who owns what Mara deemed a "tittie bar." There she met a monster who supposedly made her do awful things.

A monster who found her silence well worth killing her for.

But that doesn't explain why her hair clip is in a shoebox in this very apartment. A threat? A warning? Branden isn't reckless. He took my only other piece of leverage against him, ensuring no one would believe me even if I came forward.

He wouldn't implicate himself in another murder so easily.

So why taunt me with that item in particular?

The more I think about it, the more confusing it all becomes until I'm rubbing at my throbbing temples, trying to make sense of the tangled web.

"Drink," Rafe commands, drawing my attention.

I blink to find the rim of the beer bottle beneath my nose.

"I don't drink," I insist, shaking my head.

"The fuck you don't." Rafe fixes me with another searching look, but one devoid of sympathy. An eyebrow raised, he tilts the bottle toward me again. "Trust me, bunny. You need a fucking drink. You look like shit."

It's the way he says it that makes me inch forward and warily press my lips to the bottle. *Shit,* some level of despair beyond any flowery prose or descriptor.

Satisfied, he manipulates the drink with one hand, allowing me to take the smallest, most cautious sip. It's gross, and I choke down the liquid as he pulls the bottle away.

"Did you sleep?" he asks next.

I shake my head, and he scoffs as though I've insulted him.

"Come on." Grabbing his sandwich, he pivots on his heel, approaching the door.

"Wait..." I contemplate coming clean now. Telling him everything. I *have* to. "I need to tell you—"

"Whatever you want to say, hold it," Rafe snaps with surprising intensity. "I don't want to hear shit until I've eaten." He heads for the stairs, leaving me no choice but to follow.

The second I cross over the threshold after him, paranoia plays a chilling game on my psyche. Branden could be lurking below right now.

Waiting for me.

"It's okay."

I look up to find Rafe halfway down the staircase. "No one's going to fuck with you here," he says.

"You don't know that." My fear isn't faked for the sake of drama. Branden always has a way of controlling me—no matter where I go. Nausea crawls up my throat as I recall the latest example. "He… He's been tracking me through my phone—"

"No one will ever fuck with you here," Rafe insists. "Trust me." He juggles the items in his arms to free up one hand that he extends to me. The fingers are bruised and riddled with scrapes, and yet it's still the most appealing sight I've been presented with all morning.

Finally, I entwine my fingers with his. Rather than head for the front of his shop, he takes me past the back room. There, the short hallway ends at the door leading into a narrow alley. Cool air raises goosebumps over my flesh as we step out into the morning, drawing attention to the fact that all I'm wearing is his shirt, nothing else.

"In here." He opens a nearby door that conceals another staircase. A doorway at the top of it exits onto a wide space beneath the open sky—the building's roof.

With a confidence that betrays just how often he must come here, Rafe guides me forward to a waist-high length of plywood spanning the edge of the rooftop. Below, traffic picks up, and I can't resist scanning every car, hunting for a familiar model.

"Don't," Rafe warns as if reading my mind. "No one can see us up here."

He sits with his back to the railing and arranges his food and drink beside him. "Sit."

Once I do, he grabs his sandwich and takes another ravenous bite. "Eat," he commands with his mouth still full.

I gingerly sample a bite of mine, registering the flavors of sausage, egg, and cheese. "It's good."

But he didn't bring me up here to eat. Blazing in the growing sunlight, his gaze contains a million unanswered questions. Much like a book with a blank cover, it's impossible to discern what he's thinking at a glance. I have to touch him—running my fingers along his forearm the same way I would flip through pages—and tension turns his muscles to stone.

"Damn right, it is," he agrees with my assessment, leaning his head back. His jaw tightens with a hint of seriousness he's concealed until now. "So, tell me… Those cameras I found in your place. Were they your idea or his?"

My cheeks catch fire. The cameras. One in my living room above my TV placed in plain sight. The other, presumably hidden in my bedroom without my knowledge or consent. God only knows what the footage might reveal—me dressing. Undressing. Sleeping…

With Rafe.

"It caught us, didn't it," he suspects in between swigs of his beer. "Is that what set him off?" He nods to indicate my bruised frame. "The fucker watched us."

The thought hurts to explore in full. I have to squeeze my eyes shut and digest it in pieces—Branden, watching me with Rafe. Watching. Watching. Watching.

It doesn't sink in until now as a mangled sound rips from my throat. A laugh? A scream? I'm not sure whether I'm cackling or crying as I bolt onto my knees and vomit.

"Damn." I hear Rafe sigh amid the clink of his bottle being set aside. A heartbeat later, he shocks me—his fingers are in my hair, smoothing stray strands away from my face. "The fucker must have gotten quite the show, huh? Come here."

In his arms, I find a surprisingly warm refuge. Heedless of the mess still dribbling down my chin, he sits back, guiding my head onto his lap.

"Don't let him inside your head," he warns. "That's what he wants. To disgust you. To shame you. He wants you to second-guess the person you are without him. Fuck that."

"You don't sound embarrassed," I croak, finally pegging the sole emotion coloring his voice. Pity for me, but surprisingly no unease for himself. No anger, either. A glance at his face reveals he's sporting his trademark stoic expression. "Or violated."

"I don't have shit to be embarrassed about—" he pauses in his petting of my hair and meets my gaze directly. "You don't either. We didn't do anything wrong."

Conviction resonates in his voice—he truly believes that.

But he doesn't know the awful truth still churning my stomach. Namely, the true identity of "Bran." The way he's watched me for so damn long. The horrible suspicion that planting the camera in my room wasn't done with the sole intention of catching me with someone.

He *wanted* to see me. Control me.

Exploit any part of my life that he could.

"We didn't do anything wrong," Rafe repeats, flexing his fingers as if force alone can drive that fact into my skull. "Sex is sex, bunny. You made your choice to fuck me. I made my choice to fuck you back—and it was damn good."

I flinch at how casual he makes it sound. Like he's said that line before—many times.

"You left last night," I point out, switching to a subject that makes him stiffen this time. He's right. I didn't sleep at all.

But did he?

"Were you with Bonnie?" Would I even have the right to be upset if he had been with the perky blond?

"I was up here," he admits softly.

I observe him more carefully, noting the shadows beneath his eyes I'd missed before. The slight redness to them. He's disguised it so well, but he's wrecked.

"All night?"

He nods. "All fucking night. Any more questions?"

"What were you doing up here?" I glance around the wide space skeptically, but I believe him.

"Thinking," he says, snatching his beer for another sip. His clenched jaw evokes troubles well beyond my personal issues.

"Thinking about Faith?"

He nods.

"And your uncle?"

Irritation flashes across his face. "What about him?"

I struggle to remember some of the conversation I'd overheard between the two. "He wanted you to do something about what happened to her. About Gino—"

"He wants me to do a lot of shit," he says, neither a confirmation nor a denial.

"I heard what he said to you the other night, too," I confess. "He thinks Gino had something to do with Faith's death, doesn't he? And he wants you to confront him. Attack him?"

Or worse.

"Don't worry about him."

"What if… What if Gino didn't hurt Faith?" I suck in a breath, fully prepared to confess the truth. "I—"

"Gino has a motive, but I hope the bastard wasn't that stupid," Rafe says. Going off the low note in his voice, he truly means it. "Whoever killed Faith, I pity the motherfucker. He's a dead man walking."

"Because of your uncle?" I blurt out. I recall how the older man had reacted to the news. As if Faith's death were some kind of personal slight against him.

Rafe shrugs. "Because, bunny, people who do bad shit tend to have it catch up to them eventually. Faith's killer is running out of places to hide."

I bite my lip. Despite everything Branden is, and everything he's done…

Some part of me won't stop clinging to that damn, pathetic phrase—*you owe him.*

"What the fuck were you doing eavesdropping anyway," Rafe demands, thankfully changing the subject.

"I couldn't sleep, and your uncle isn't exactly the quietest person in the world."

"And?" he adds pointedly. "What else did you hear?"

I swallow hard. "And… He doesn't appreciate your art." It seems so childish to point out—but the insult bothers me more than it should. I've seen his drawings. How he looks when in the throes of his craft. I know what the mere act of sketching lines on paper means to him.

Even now, he's tensing, his expression constricted as he chugs more of his beer. At his sides, his fingers twitch as if itching for a pen.

"My turn," he says, once again putting the focus on me. "So, you left him. Bran. What now?"

Any hint of vulnerability vanishes from his expression. His features harden, and a sudden thought strikes me—he already knows what I'll say, or at least he thinks he does.

I need to go back.

"I don't know," I confess, relaxing against the firmness of his knee. "It's not like he left me much of a choice, to be honest. He bought out my lease. The landlord already found a new tenant. I'm homeless. And if I don't figure things out soon, I won't be able to take the classes I want to next semester either."

"Why is that?"

I hesitate, but as his fingers sink through my hair, I find myself speaking. "I wanted to enter this program—the Fenwick program," I admit, fully aware of how childish it sounds now, all things considered. "If I'm accepted, it will mean an internship and a foothold into the publishing world. Otherwise, I'd be stuck taking random credits and waste a year. Though hell, it's not like I had a shot of getting in, anyway."

"Bullshit," Rafe coldly interjects. "You *know* you'll get in. That's what scares you. Getting in means leaving the fucker behind. Whether or not you even realize it, he's controlling you."

My lips part, but any retort I might come up with dies in my throat. He's right, and it's unnerving how easily he can read me. His fingers trace my scalp to reinforce the comparison, picking through my thoughts as though I'm an open book, turning my previous impression of him on its head.

"It doesn't matter if I can't get my entry written in time," I say.

Without some kind of academic pursuit to justify my father's funding, my entire quest for freedom might go up in flames as well. Not to mention if Bran decides to convince him to stop paying my tuition anyway. A tired laugh trickles from me, but inside? I'm screaming.

Branden's won again. Though, despite his efforts, I'm not back in his cage just yet. By pure luck, or by design?

And, despite all his faults, is he really capable of murder?

"You're worried about him," Rafe deduces, unable to hide the jealousy tainting his tone. "Bran."

"He's a cop," I reply. "He's been tracking my phone. He probably already knows I'm here. Any minute he could trump up a warrant and—"

"Cop or not, I won't let anyone touch you."

My body flushes warm in response to his confidence. It's more than a boast.

"You're sure of that?" I peek at him through my lashes, but he doesn't look smug. Just exhausted. "You don't know Bran," I argue.

"Stop. Look at me." He cups my chin, his grip firm but gentle. "I don't care who the fuck he is. No one will touch you while you're with me."

I should counter that. I know the opposite is more than likely—at the same time, I'm too tired to say a word.

In the resulting silence, his hands find my hair again, easing me down against his thigh. Somehow, he makes the position seem far from sexual. Natural, no different from lying in his bed.

Should that insult me?

Thrill me?

"Fine," I finally croak without deciding on an emotion to feel. "So…is this your way of asking me to stay?"

"Stay." He leans back against the railing, stretching out his legs. The motion provides enough surface area to rest on, should I decide to.

"Don't stay," he adds with a shrug. "It's your fucking choice."

I have several reasons to question that—Branden will do whatever he can to get to me, no matter who I'm with. I shouldn't expect so much from a virtual stranger. He's done so much for me already…

Rather than drill him for more answers, I let my eyes drift shut.

Something tells me, given his track record with the truth, I'll find out soon enough.

For better or for worse.

CHAPTER TWO

I will never understand how I manage to fall asleep on literal concrete with my only excuse for a pillow being a toned thigh. In awe, I find myself flexing my fingers over what must be the curve of his knee, resting beneath my chin. It's a marvel how solid he feels. Hard enough to put his fist through glass and pummel a gangster into a bloody pulp. And yet soft enough to comfort me.

In a sense, his body serves as the perfect comparison to his personality—as unpredictable in nature like a chameleon. Or a dragon.

And just like that, my thoughts turn to a far more dangerous topic that haunts me as I trail my hand along his thigh. Like how the contours of this very body felt when pressed against mine. The heat of his skin, slicked by a layer of sweat...

"I'm here for you and all, bunny," a voice cuts into my dreamy haze, constricted with obvious discomfort. "But I am *human*, and while I can tolerate having your head close to my dick for several hours, try to keep those hands to yourself, huh?"

I wrench my eyes open to a blindingly bright stream of sunlight. It's hot out, but my skin feels pleasantly warm. Despite being curled on my side, with my head—as stated—practically on Rafe's lap, I feel utterly content. Which is the complete opposite of how I *should* be feeling.

His mere presence infects me, robbing the seriousness of the moment long enough to almost forget it all. He's staring down on me wryly, his lips quirked upward, betraying a million observations that I suspect he's been stewing over while I slept.

And I did sleep, deeply. A fact that unnerves me when I inspect it too much.

"How long was I out?" I demand, batting my hair from my face as I rise onto my knees.

He shrugs, turning his attention to the brilliant blue sky above. Judging from the position of the sun, it's late morning or even early afternoon.

"About four hours," he says.

"I'm definitely late for work now." With a sigh, I copy his posture by positioning my back against the railing. "Mr. Zhang has a welcome back sale planned. He needs me to help out with the setup."

But I'm not moving.

"I told you—" Rafe fingers the rim of his now empty beer bottle. "I'll handle Zhang. You calling out sick for a few days won't kill him."

"I really do need the money," I add halfheartedly, another wrinkle in the growing web that my life has become. It's laughable how naïve I'd been to think I could extricate myself from Branden's control so easily. "I'll have to start looking for another apartment soon."

An alternate option is asking my father for more money, but I can't even consider it longer than a few seconds.

"You can work for me."

I look over to find Rafe still eyeing the sky, his lips pursed thoughtfully. "At least until you can wear sunglasses."

"Why are you helping me?" I'm genuinely curious—and skeptical.

Any minute, he should toss out some kind of sexual request. Anything to lessen the enormity of what he's really proposing—helping me yet again, for seemingly nothing in return.

"Because I fucking feel like it. Come on—" He stands and inclines his head for me to follow. Once we're back in his shop, he enters the backroom to dispose of our trash. When he returns to my position, his expression triggers a pang of alarm in my chest. I can't decipher it.

"I mean it." His thumb slips beneath my chin when he comes close enough, raising heat in a shiver-inducing swipe.

"You can work for me. At least until you can show your face at Zhang's. I won't even take a cut of your pay."

I raise an eyebrow and wind up wincing with the effort. "Why? And 'work for you' doing what?"

"Well…" He steps into me, and I crane my neck back just to hold his gaze. It's strange how intimidating he can seem when he wants to. Like flipping a switch—all the warmth vanishes from those dark irises, leaving them as unfathomable as the night sky.

"What can you do for me?" He reaches out—but I'm not his target. Instead, he snatches an object from the wall behind me and promptly shoves it against my chest.

A broom.

"You work," he says. "Unlike Zhang, I expect you to earn your fucking keep. I like the place spotless."

"Fine." I curl my fingers around the broom handle as an odd feeling weighs on my stomach, building with every passing second. God, I hate that he can do this to me. Meld fear and gratitude into a disarming mixture that heats my skin and upends my tried and true instincts. His nearness inspires a million nuanced reactions I've never acknowledged before. My frantically beating heart, the rapid breaths causing my chest to rise against the fabric of my shirt. *His* shirt. The rough cotton teases my nipples, hardening them.

And the worst part is that I'm sure he noticed every little detail before I ever did.

"Thank you," I blurt in a rush, still eying the floor.

"Don't." He lumbers into the hall, and I follow him, watching as the pale light emanating from the storefront plays over his skin, reflecting off the subtle hints of gold in it. "Just keep the place spick and span, and I'll… Shit—" he stops short, his shoulders tensing. "Get back."

In a fluid motion, he surges forward, blocking me from view. Through the glass in the door, I can make out the shape of an approaching figure on the other side. Someone tall, wearing a signature shade of navy blue…

My worst fear escapes my lips, uttered in a whisper, "Branden—"

"Hannah," Rafe snaps. "Get back."

His voice knocks some sense into me, and I manage to lurch deeper into the hall, just as he wrenches the door open.

"Officer?" Rafe greets tersely.

I strain my ears to catch the officer's reply, biting my lower lip to choke down any sound I might make. It's Branden.

"Morning," a man replies—but his voice is deep. Too deep to be my brother's. Relief hits me like a bucket of ice water, both bracing and chilling—it's not him. But then who? The silhouette of the figure flung over the far wall is too slender. Not Liam either, but another member of the force. "Are you Rafael Wei-Shen?"

"Figures," Rafe says with a chuckle. "They'd send some newbie who doesn't even fucking know me by name." He laughs again, but the gruff sound triggers an instinctive tug in my stomach. The one that reacts to danger.

Whoever the officer is, he doesn't seem shaken. His shadow doesn't waver, his voice resonating crystal clear. "Are you familiar with a club named Stella's?"

"And if I am?" Rafe replies, but the deliberate second he hesitated before answering alludes that he wasn't expecting this topic to be the cause of the visit.

"Well, are you aware that sometime after one a.m. this morning, a fire was reported at the club?"

"No. But that sounds like a damn shame, officer."

"It is," the officer replies, nonplussed. "Especially considering the club wasn't empty at the time. A man is currently in critical condition, a second barely escaped with minor injuries. And a family of four in a nearby tenant building reported to the hospital for smoke inhalation. Their newborn required oxygen therapy. So you can imagine our alarm that, according to preliminary analysis, it looks like the cause of the fire may have been arson, Mr. Wei-Shen—"

"Wow. That sounds like a *real* damn shame, officer," Rafe snipes. "And not to be rude, but I've got some shit to attend to, and it sounds like you've got some sick motherfuckers to track down. If I have an epiphany, I'll let you know."

"Do that," the man says. "You can also 'let me know' if you recall anything about a young woman named Faith Wen. Her body was found last night. I'm guessing she doesn't ring a bell?"

Rafe says nothing this time, but I can feel his tension even from here.

"I thought so," the officer admits. "Several other women have gone missing under similar circumstances. Were you aware of that?"

"No," Rafe growls.

"When was the last time you recall seeing Faith?"

"Can't remember," Rafe snaps. "Is that all?"

"Strange. Seeing as how you and Faith were so close, at least according to what we've heard. What happened to that poor girl was a real damn shame. We've yet to locate her cell phone either, but you wouldn't know anything about that, would you?"

Rafe scoffs. "That's a really interesting investigation tactic there, officer. Letting a suspect know that you're missing a key piece of evidence."

"Ah, but I didn't say you were a suspect, did I? Have a good day, Mr. Wei-Shen."

As the officer leaves, Rafe slams the door, forming a fist. Without warning, he draws back and slams it knuckles-first against the wall. Again. "Damn it!"

Panting, he pulls away, storming in my direction.

"Did you do it?" I'm standing in his way, but I can't seem to move. A sense of dread pools in my chest. Or maybe it's relief? I should be begging for a reason to hate him. Doubt him.

Will he lie to me? *Did* he lie to me?

"Did you set the fire?"

"I don't know…" He takes another step, towering over me, his gaze unreadable. "Did I, rabbit? Would I be sloppy enough to set a fucking fire that would bring the cops right to my doorstep? Or would I be a little bit smarter than that?"

His gruff tone differentiates this anger from his usual temper. Rather than rage and shout, he has his jaw clenched, his eyes distant. He's just as on edge as I am.

Why? His wary glance toward the front of the shop might give me a clue. "Those motherfuckers," he hisses. "What the fuck are they up to…"

It hits me—if his uncle's men were behind the attack, he didn't know. And the prospect caught him off guard. Did the older man leave him out intentionally?

Or was Rafe the one who stayed away?

The questions mount, but all I seem capable of doing is sighing, still clenching his broom.

Eyeing him, I press the bristles to the floor. "When do I start?"

"Huh?" He blinks and shoots me an odd look, only to recover a heartbeat later. His slanted smirk contains a mere fraction of his usual smug persona, however. He's distracted. "You start now," he says. "But change first. I'm not running a fucking skin bar."

He boldly rakes his gaze down to my bare legs before starting for the stairs. I follow him into the apartment and approach the clothing stacked on top of the boxes at the end of the hall. I grab a skirt and sweater only to draw a scoff from my audience.

"I don't run a nunnery, either," Rafe says, reaching around me to snatch the sweater away. His breath heats the back of my throat, his voice vibrating through my skin, "Trust me. You look better in my shit."

Referring to his shirt, I presume. The possession in his words requires further inspection—but later. For the time being, I squeeze past him and enter the bathroom, closing the door behind me.

He retreats, his steps storming toward the living room with a determination that alarms me. At least until I hear his voice, low, strained, presumably speaking into a phone.

"…If I hear you motherfuckers were involved, I swear to God," he growls. "You'll answer to me. I told you to keep out of this—I don't give a fuck what anyone might think.

Just be ready when those assholes come calling, because they will."

Judging from the next few seconds of silence, he must have hung up.

"Hurry up, bunny," he calls, raising his voice for my benefit. "I don't got all fucking day."

"I'm coming," I snap back.

Approaching the mirror is a grueling ordeal, but in the end, I don't even look at my reflection. I grab a washcloth from a nearby shelf and wash up blind. Once finished, I tug on my skirt and fresh underwear. I finally exit the bathroom to find Rafe standing near one of the windows in the living room with his back to me.

"What's the rush?" I ask, crossing my arms. "Are you—"

"Fuck." His posture alone conveys another alarming shift in his mood. Gone is the mocking, playful aura. "Shit's about to get real, bunny," he says coldly, his gaze riveted on something taking place below.

"What's wrong?" I ask.

As I inch closer to the window, I spot the problem for myself—a parade of three, flashy cars parking alongside the curb across the street. As if in some rehearsed motion, the driver's side doors open in sync, and the occupants stream out. They're dressed in suits—and I instantly recognize their leader.

Gino.

The other men with him are unfamiliar, but they approach the shop with a clear intent made obvious by their posture —clenched fists and rigid spines. Nothing good.

"Fuck." Rafe barrels into the kitchen, speaking to me from over his shoulder. "Can you shoot?"

"What?" I gape as he wrenches open a cupboard drawer and rummages through the various random items inside it. *Shoot* could apply to a milieu of different things—or so I try to convince myself.

At least until he slams an object onto the counter, leaving nothing to the imagination. A part of me knows what is inside the slim black case before he lifts the lid.

"Rafe…" I back away, but my alarm doesn't prevent him from curling his fingers around the hilt of the weapon and raising it—a gun.

I've seen one before—my brother's service weapon. This one looks to be a similar model, black and no less intimidating.

"What's going on—"

"You hear shit going down, you take this, and you run," he says as if I've never spoken. "Get the fuck away—but if you can't, get on the roof. Do you hear me? Listen!" He smacks the counter with his free hand. "Do you remember that place you brought Zhang's payment? Do you?"

I nod, picturing a musty warehouse on the outskirts of town, by the docks.

"Good. You get there, and you wait for me. If I don't show, you look for a red case. I already changed the combination to something you'll be able to guess, and you—"

"You're scaring me," I croak.

"You're damn right, I am." He returns the gun to the case, closes it, and sets it on the counter. "Remember this shit—"

A sound erupts from down below. One, ironically, we're both familiar with—smashing glass.

"Damn it." He pushes past me and wrenches open the door to the stairs. "Keep an ear pressed to the goddamn floor if you have to. You hear me say 'motherfucker' in any context, you run. You don't hesitate. There's a fire escape below the window in the hallway. Got it?"

"Rafe—"

"You fucking listen." He holds my gaze until I finally nod.

"Okay," I rasp.

Satisfied, he pivots and descends the steps, slamming the door behind him.

My pulse hammers against my eardrums, filling the silence left in his absence—but the quiet doesn't last long. A series of footsteps resonate through the building's very foundation, heading toward the shop's front.

"What the fuck do you want?" I hear Rafe demand.

"You son of a bitch!" I recognize the speaker as Gino, his voice constricted with rage. "Do you have any idea of what you've done? Who you've fucked with? Do you?" More glass shatters in a musical cacophony. The frames holding his drawings? Something bigger? Panic chokes me, and this sense of blindness only enhances my dread. I'm shaking, my knees knocking together, my gaze fixated on the floor as if I can see through it by sheer willpower. What did he tell me?

You hear me say 'motherfucker' in any context, you run.

I drop to my knees, bracing my hands against the floorboards. Too suddenly—I might be heard from down below. I hold my breath, fearing just that, and I strain my ears, listening for any hint of what's happening.

"…think you can fuck around with us?" another man demands. "You stupid cunt. You have no idea what you've started."

"I don't, do I?" Rafe sounds more distant as if he's speaking from the very front of the store now. "Tell the bitch holding your leash that he doesn't know what *he's* done. Faith Wen? That name ring a bell? The next time you whore out your girls for a dime, don't get so goddamn sloppy. I went easy on your ass once. No more."

"You think you know everything, huh?" Gino replies with a harsh bark of laughter. "Oh, this is well beyond Faith, you dumb son of a bitch. You have no idea who you've *really* fucked with, do you?"

"Do you?" Rafe snarls amid the sound of more smashing glass. Each tingling chime brings to mind a series of picture frames breaking one by one. "I know the assholes you cater to. Bastards who strongarm barely legal girls into sex. Who torture them. Then kill them to protect their fucking reputations—"

"Faith was a lying little cunt," Gino snarls. "She stuck her nose into where it didn't belong. But it's not like you have any *proof.*" He deliberately emphasizes the word with a hiss. "Do you, Rafael? Hidden in this rundown piece of shit? Keep looking," he snaps, presumably to his men.

"Go fuck yourself," Rafe snarls. "If she did give me anything, do you think I'd be dumb enough to keep it here?"

"You better hope not. Though maybe you need a little convincing to tell the truth? Boys. Hold him."

Thuds erupt, alluding to a struggle, but sheer terror roots me in place. I can't move. Can't breathe…

My gaze drifts to the counter, and the box resting there, as my ears strain for a key phrase. Would I have the strength to grab it even then? I try to make my hands move, but my fingers twitch in place and nothing more.

"Fuck," Rafe snarls, and the pain in his tone sets every nerve on red alert. He's hurt.

I'm already on my feet, scrambling for the counter. I wrench open the box and clumsily grasp the object inside it. As I turn to the door, a shout rings out.

"Fuck! You motherfuck—"

"Shit!" Another man says. "Someone must have called the fucking cops."

Cops. That word spurs my paralyzed limbs into motion, and I creep toward the window. Sure enough, a lone cruiser idles alongside the curb. I'm not sure if it's the same one that used to live in Branden's driveway, polished to shine.

From this height, I can't make out the driver or anyone in the passenger seat. Liam?

The sound of a door slamming reinforces the more pressing danger. Three figures trickle from the store and stroll across the street. One man, in particular, has his hands in fists, visible from even here. A substance glistens over the prominent knuckles, and my mind goes blank with recognition. Blood.

By the time I regain my senses, I'm already inching down the short hallway on the first floor, tensing in expectation of what I might find beyond it. The smell reaches my nostrils first—coppery, fresh…

"R-Rafe?" From my vantage point, I can only make out the shattered front door at first—the source of much of the glass scattered across the floor. Anxiety builds with every step I take.

Near the counter, I spot a sight that almost makes me drop the item in my grasp. Rafe—upright, clutching at his chin. Overwhelming relief blinds me to anything else. Like self-preservation. I pick through a sea of broken glass to reach him on bare feet, heedless of the risk.

"Are you okay?" The words have barely left my mouth when I realize that he isn't. Blood is gushing from his lower lip. A lot. He may need stitches, though I'm already setting the gun aside and winding up the hem of his shirt to use as a makeshift cloth.

"I'm fine," he grunts, shrugging off my attempts to dab away the blood—until suddenly he isn't. We're face to face, toe to toe, and I suck in a breath, my hands frozen with his shirt lifted high enough to expose my stomach. For once, he drops the bravado. His face reveals everything—every emotion he's hidden so well until now.

Fear.

"They were here about the fire," I deduce, dabbing at his jaw as I remember how to move again. "And Faith."

He dodges my touch, his eyes narrowing. "I guess I told you to eavesdrop this time, so the joke's on me."

"Yes," I say thickly. "So, stay still."

He grudgingly submits to the ministrations but snatches the gun and slips it into his pocket. Thankfully, a split lip seems to be the extent of his injuries. Not that knowing as much stops my fingers from running over his forearm without my brain telling them to, searching for any hint of damage there.

When I reach his shoulder, he gently bats my hand away, swiping at the remnants of blood with his bare hand. "It's broad fucking daylight, and those assholes came *here*," he hisses, sounding more incredulous than infuriated. "Even you were smart enough to grab a weapon, though I don't know how you'd shoot it with the safety on. Shit. You know it as well as I do—this is about more than a fucking fire, bunny."

"Tell me, then," I demand. The back of my neck prickles with an awareness of just how dangerous a request this is.

Some monsters and their secrets are best left in the dark.

Regardless, watching his dark eyes scan the carnage of glass scattered at his feet triggers the same instinctive pull that I felt the night when I stole his lighter. In a childish sense, I'd believed I'd been protecting it from him. What had my rationale been? Some monsters *deserve* protecting…

"I want to know," I insist. The hitch in my voice contradicts that confidence. To steel myself, I tiptoe back into the hall in search of the one task I can do as I await his response. I find the broom where I'd left it. Grasping it in both hands, I return to the front and get to work sorting out the pieces of glass too small to pick up.

It's monotonous work—nearly distracting enough to shield me from his presence. He's watching me, his gaze like a laser, piercing through flesh and bone.

"What do you want to know?" he asks, though I get the sense that he's mocking me.

I look back to find his gaze far more serious than I expect, though.

Sighing, I lift my shoulders. "Everything."

He leans against the counter, letting his lip bleed freely. Confidence enhances him, until he's a giant, invincible amongst a sea of destruction.

"My uncle calls his outfit 'red dragon' though he's not stupid enough to broadcast it. Most of the people around here know he's dirty. They just don't know how." His gruff inflection conceals a dare.

One I warily take him up on. "So how?"

"Extortion, money laundering. Worse," he says with a coarse laugh. Shaking his head, he runs his fingers through his hair. "I can't believe I'm fucking spilling the dark family secrets to a nosy little bunny. You still could be a fucking reporter."

But he's talking to me. Deep down. I suspect that he needs to do just that. Talk. To someone. Anyone.

"He has a protection racket going, but it's just pocket change," he says. "His real money comes from real estate these days. Cleaning up his image so he can make a jump into politics. To hear him tell it, he's too 'reformed' to get his hands dirty anymore."

"Do you?" It chills me to the bone that I don't truly know what I'm asking. Dirty hands could refer to so many things.

Judging from the distant, cold gleam in his eyes, I suspect that none of the answers he could give I'd find reassuring.

"I work for him," he says softly. "Take that however you fucking want. Does that make me his errand boy? Probably.

But he promised me he's getting out of the business soon. Besides, he's family."

But there's more to it, apparent in what he doesn't say.

"So what happened with Gino?"

"Gino and his pathetic excuse for a wanna-be-mafia have been muscling in on our territory for years," he says. "His old man worked with Shen back in the day. They were partners, but lately, the bastard's gotten too cocky. He has a deal extending from his shitty club all the way to the top. Cops. Politicians. They come to his club for pussy and pay through the nose for it—but that's just the start of it. You see these cops, in return for the shit they get away with, overlook whatever happens in Gino's part of town. Murders. Disappearances. Everything. The fish rots from its fucking head—they're all in on it."

Anger leeches into his voice that was absent when he spoke of his uncle. Whatever his issue with Gino is, it's personal.

And he seems to feel that same animosity toward the police.

"You doubt that?" he prods, sensing my discomfort. "Your precious Bran is one of them. You ever hear him talk about hanging around Stella's?"

His tone is cutting—he wants a fight. Rather than give him one, I turn my attention to a pile of toppled frames in the corner and stoop to salvage what I can. Which isn't much. Only one casing is wholly unbroken, containing the snarling image of a wolf with mistrustful eyes.

It reminds me of Branden. For all I know, he could be in the cruiser still parked outside. I'm torn between alerting Rafe to its presence or just letting the inevitable take place.

The more I run, the harder he'll give chase.

"This is beautiful," I murmur, spotting another drawing, clinging to the distraction it provides.

"That bother you?" Rafe calls, like a shark catching a whiff of a drop of blood. "That your perfect boyfriend—that *Bran* could be a part of that shit? Trust me, chances are more likely than not that he is, bunny—" a fact he seems to gloat over. "Maybe you don't know him like you think you do."

"I know Bran better than anyone." And *that's* why I'm shaking. Why the back of my throat feels tight with the threat of vomit. I know Bran.

Could he be involved in something so heinous? Ironically, Rafe hit on the answer himself—the chances are more likely than not.

"Come here," he commands.

As I advance toward him, he withdraws the gun, presenting it to me on the flat of his palm. I jump, but the look in his eye banishes any alarm I might feel.

"You think the bastard cares about you," he says, once again reading me like an open book. "But he didn't even teach you to fucking shoot? A cop should be good for that much." He jerks his chin, daring me to inch closer.

The second I'm close enough, he snatches my waist with his free hand, spinning me so that my back hits his chest as he lowers the gun before me.

"Grab it."

I do with both hands, hating the weight of it. The power conveyed in the trigger.

Disgust inspires another confession from me, "I never wanted to learn."

Rafe laughs. "Fuck that. You need to. Hold it like this—" he guides my fingers into the right positions. "The gun isn't bad, bunny. Just make sure that you never point it at something you aren't willing to destroy. Kill. It's the intent that matters. Like when you write those pretty little words of yours—but in this case, there is only one conclusion to take away."

"And what's that?" I whisper.

"That you decide what happens next," he says, coaxing me to aim at the wall near one of his still hanging sketches—a snarling dragon. "You are in control of good or bad. It's all on you. So, learn how to take the safety off at least."

He demonstrates how with a few flicks of his thumb. Then he pulls away entirely, and I turn to find him stowing the weapon behind the counter.

"You seem comfortable with that," I deduce as my brain taunts me with why that might be. "Have you shot someone before?"

He grunts, palming the counter. "Don't ask me questions you don't really want to know the answer to."

Fair enough.

"Do you teach all of your women how to operate a weapon?" I ask.

Let alone in, as he put it, "broad daylight," in the middle of his vandalized shop. The fact that the police aren't swarming this place stuns me. A glance through the shattered door reveals no one in sight. The city itself might as well be deserted.

And the idling cruiser never does anything more than that. Wait.

"Teach the others? No. Only the sexy little bunnies who play out the innocent shtick," he counters. But his tone is too hard to be mocking. He's still on edge. Worried.

"What's wrong?"

He meets my gaze from over his shoulder. "What happened just now? That was just a friendly kiss on the cheek, bunny —they'll be back. And if you do decide to stay, you better be ready for that. Gino is a ticking time bomb. It's only a matter of time before the idiot goes too far."

If I stay…

There are plenty of reasons why I shouldn't, but I can't dwell on the choice now—so, I retrieve the broom, and I perform the one task I have control over. I clean.

Ironically, there is some familiarity in the act where he is concerned. I'm transported back a few days ago when I dutifully scrubbed blood stains from the floor of my old apartment. Utilizing the broom, I push the smallest pieces of glass into the center of the room, letting the monotony lull my brain into a false sense of normalcy.

Nothing else matters. Like the fact that I'm essentially homeless, or the police cruiser slowly driving away without its occupant ever stepping foot from it.

Once I've made headway in sorting a majority of the glass, I finally take stock of the store as a whole.

"So much for your invitation-only policy," I state to Rafe, nodding to the remains of the front door. "You may have to take walk-in clients, after all."

He shrugs and lumbers down the back hallway, muttering over his shoulder, "I have plywood somewhere."

A few minutes later, he returns armed with sheets of the material while I set off in search of a dustpan.

Between the two of us, it takes only a few hours to have a majority of the mess either boarded up or filed away into trash bags. Only as I dump the last few shards of glass into a quickly filling bag do I gather up the nerve to broach the topic he himself left open for discussion, "You said I can ask you anything."

He's on the other side of the room, wrestling the larger frames into a trash bag. Stopping, he looks back at me. "And?"

I suck in a breath, mulling over how to phrase my next question. But there isn't a pretty way to put it. "Mara says you're a member of the triad."

"Triad?" Laughing, he approaches me and lifts my chin with the pad of his thumb, peering directly into my eyes. "Do you even know what that word fucking means, bunny?"

I don't break eye contact. "I know it sounds illegal."

"Illegal." His voice deepens, raspier than usual. "Do you even know what *that* word means, rabbit? It means I do shit like 'shake down old men for money,' right? Or it could mean that I pay off their debts when a little bunny bats her eyes at me once. It means…"

Suddenly, he's too close. Warm breath feathers over my skin, and with every inhalation, his nostrils flare as if straining for more of me. More, more, more. I eye the flames licking down his forearm, convinced the dragon suits him more than ever. This must be how such a predator chooses to devour his prey—through fire. One scorching exhale at a time.

He even resembles the creature. Dark, glowing eyes and a fearsome expression unbothered by the day's events. Jealousy bites at my fragile resolve. Even bruised, he looks unshaken. Untouchable.

I look…

Broken. A trembling little bunny shrinking from my own reflection. But in his eyes, there is no hiding from it. The real Hannah is laid bare in the center of his irises—a creature caught beneath his gaze with a wide, unwavering expression. Someone who makes his brow furrow and his lips part, glistening with wetness.

The motion draws my attention to the red gash there—no longer bleeding—and the trail of dried blood snaking down his jaw.

I don't know why I do it. Lick my forefinger and swipe at the smear. Maybe self-preservation? Scarlet suits him, feeding the dangerous illusion he struggles to maintain. Without it, he's no more intimidating than anyone else.

Though no one has these eyes. Dark, they meet mine unflinchingly as he gently captures my hand in his. And no one has his voice, inspiring goosebumps as it drips into my ear. "I'll tell you," he murmurs, picking up the thread of our previous conversation. "It means I'm capable of some fucked-up shit, bunny. Shit that would make your innocent little toes curl. It means…you should probably vet the people you fuck."

"You too," I counter in a tone I don't recognize. "You don't know me."

He blinks in surprise before releasing a low laugh. "I figured that," he snarls, lowering his mouth to the crook of my shoulder. "I knew from the second I first saw you, watching me with those bunny eyes—you're a head fucker. I've got my work cut out, don't I? Making sure you don't pull your tricks on me—"

He seizes a piece of sore, abused skin, and rakes his teeth over it. In the same moment, he captures my waist, anchoring me to him. My nails sink into his forearms, seeking out stability, but beneath the various aches and pains I still feel all over my body, something sparks to life, too foreign to name. Pleasure?

Whatever it is builds as his lips latch over my pulse point, his tongue lathing in slow strokes.

It's terrifying how easily I can forget everything else.

"You get off on this," he grates, exhaling against my collar. "The thrill of it all. But you should ask yourself, bunny… What happens when I decide I'm tired of playing with you?"

In so many ways, it feels like a rhetorical question. One even he doesn't know the answer to—because he's the one initiating this game. His fingers are already sliding beneath the hem of my borrowed shirt, drifting to the waistband of my skirt and grazing the flesh beneath. Then he changes tack and travels higher. His fingers find my breasts next, toying with my nipples until I can't silence a gasp.

Our lips meet, and it's electric. My skin flushes warm as his tongue coaxes my mouth open before slipping inside. At the same time, his fingers continue their slow, searching caress unabated. I find myself arching into him, extending every moment—his touch, his taste.

But right before the inferno can truly take hold, I draw back.

Good, a part of me urges. *You should stop. You have too much to worry about. Branden. The program. Everything. This can only distract you for so long…*

Rafe tenses as if expecting me to voice that very conclusion.

But around him, I can't even predict myself anymore. A question escapes my mouth without any input from my brain, "Is the bed off-limits?"

He frowns, his eyes narrowing. Abruptly, he snatches my wrist, pulling me down the hall and up the stairs into his apartment. We cross the living room, heading straight for an infamous door that he doesn't hesitate to push open.

The bedsheets are still rumpled from when I last slept in here, the room otherwise unchanged. I cross the threshold as a dominating figure steps into me from behind. His hands return to my thighs, gripping them tightly before inching up to my shirt. He drags the fabric along with his ascent, baring my body to the cool air.

Removing my skirt is his next task. Warm, his fingers curl around my wrists after, guiding me to the end of the mattress. He leans into me from behind, forcing me onto my stomach beneath his weight. The firm flesh of his chest rasps over my bare back as his lips settle into the crook of my shoulder.

"You want this, bunny?" he asks near my ear.

Eager, I reach back, digging my nails into his skin without remorse, relishing the dangerous sound that revs up in his chest. He doesn't need a violent invitation, anyway. A part of me shivers beneath the ominous knowledge of what's coming, but he surprises me by drawing out the gentleness a moment longer. His fingers dip between my legs and stroke me luxuriously, as if he's just a normal man, and this is a normal roll in the hay.

I almost believe it. I let myself go limp, shuddering on the edge of an orgasm, my lips pursed to smother any sound I might make. The first shudders begin to wrack my body when he flips me over onto my back and settles on top of me. Cool air replaces his hand while he rakes his nails over my torso. Hard.

"Watch." There's a dark note in his tone, and I tremble with recognition. The man who bathed my wounds is gone. A dragon comes to life in his place, its hot breath igniting my skin. Aware of where his gaze is traveling, I struggle to prop myself on both elbows and stare. My breath catches at the sight of his fingers between my legs, the knuckles threatening to push inside me. He's hunched over, his expression unashamed as he takes me in, sweeping his gaze along the naked length of me. "Don't look away."

He strips his shirt, and the lines of his tattoo consume his forearm, leaving snippets of golden skin. It makes him seem as wild and untamed as the creature on his back. Ethereal.

I can sense the restraint he uses to guide my legs further apart, leaving himself enough space to crouch down between them. Then his fingers return, dipping inside me one after the other. So damn carefully, it's like he knows I'll shatter beneath too much pressure.

Watch.

I can't seem to tear my gaze away, but the sight doesn't affect me nearly as much as the sound. The soft groans he grits out between clenched teeth. The way his breath catches when I arch my hips, urging him deeper. The creak of the mattress, protesting under our combined weight.

"Lie on your back."

I comply without complaint, and my eyes are on the ceiling when he slides two fingers inside me. Quick. Hard. The fullness is an entirely new sensation, burning painfully and pleasurably at the same damn time. I fumble for a fist full of the bedsheets and grab hold, just as he begins to thrust. In and out—more forcefully each time.

My thoughts splinter. My body quakes. Fire sweeps through my veins, and it's almost enough to make me forget.

Everything.

"Rafe…" His name is a prayer, but I don't know for what. For less? More? As if to punish me, he draws out the last thrust, forcing me to feel every inch of his presence. The firm ridges of each knuckle. The callouses. The scars. I'm drugged with the sensation of him, feeling his touch translate to the words he doesn't voice out loud—*I own you this way—only me.*

I gasp out loud when he finally withdraws them, and his hand approaches my mouth. "Open."

Disgust and alarm converge into a refusal that springs to the tip of my tongue—but then I see his face. Those eyes, burning with a fire that leaves me senseless.

My mouth opens, and he swipes the slick pad of a thumb along my lower lip. My tongue drifts up before I can help it, catching the edge of his nail. He lets me lap at his fingertips at first, while darkness consumes what remains of his irises. When the last drop of humanity finally fades, he shoves them all in so hard I nearly choke.

Gagging, I struggle to suck, tasting myself on him, along with sweat. Maybe a hint of blood. I don't feel as disgusted as I should. Perhaps I'm not at all. I can't make up my mind before he pulls his hand away, leaving a moist trail that splatters my chest, and rears back on his knees. Taking the back of my calves in either hand, he spreads my legs.

The muscles in his arms ripple as he wrenches down his sweatpants, and I take him in with greedy glances, grateful for the fading sunlight seeping in. The golden glow gives me just enough light to appreciate the definition in the muscles of his upper thighs as he finally settles over me and pushes in.

I bite my lip. He's still going slowly, and I'm grateful for the reprieve, almost as much as I'm anticipating what's coming.

It's the first time I've gotten the chance to savor him like this. To actually process the feeling of him inside me. The hungry way my body clamps over him. The way his jaw clenches in response, his eyes glowing. The sounds he makes in that beautiful voice as he eases the head of himself all the way in and then begins to thrust in earnest.

He continues to take his time, easing his length inside me, stretching me fully. There's one last shred of gentleness as he hooks his hand around the back of my head and brings his face in close. With heart-stopping tenderness, his lips seek mine out, but the kiss doesn't last long. My lips burn when he pulls away and flips me over, forcing me to prop myself up on trembling hands.

He uses his fingers to spread me apart and then enters me again. Hard. The friction burns, and I grit my teeth, my eyes watering as he pulls back and then thrusts again. It's rough. He loses the steady rhythm, causing the mattress to shudder beneath us. I have to reach for a handful of the sheet and bite down just to keep from crying out. One of my hands fumbles for the headrest and finds a groove between the wall and the headboard. I curl my fingers around the metal and hold tight as he rocks his hips, jarring me forward.

I count the harsh slaps of flesh against flesh. *One. Ten. Twenty.* Despite the violence, my body heats up. Already, I can sense another orgasm is just out of reach, licking impatiently at my skin. My toes curl. I gulp for air. He's still thrusting when his fingers return to my clit, rubbing, pinching, stroking...until the intensity of my release slams into me. It knocks me over. My cheek hits the mattress. My ass is in the air, my body still at his mercy.

For what feels like an eternity, I just let him use me. Each thrust carries his rage, filling me up. Overflowing from every pore. Drowning me with the emotion. I'm just a vessel for his anger, willing, and receptive.

Already my body starts to ascend again, and I hate myself for the fact that the harsher the thrust, the higher I climb. I swear my head hits the ceiling as his thumb maneuvers between my legs, flicking, stroking. Faster. Higher. I fly apart beneath his fingertips before he ever starts to fuck me in earnest.

Wordless moans spill into the cotton clamped between my teeth, and when he speaks again, he sounds miles away.

"Move." The command is bitten out against the back of my neck. The hand between my legs drifts up to grasp my shoulder, forcing my spine to arch so that he can hover over me, his chest against my back, altering the angle. I gasp when he swivels his hips, and the bitten sheet falls from my mouth.

The penetration isn't nearly as deep as before, but the sensation is harsher. Damn near explosive. Sparks shoot through my body with every exacting stroke of his, alighting every nerve.

Setting me on fire.

I've never been so raw in my life. So wet. I can't seem to find any air, but it doesn't really seem to matter. He slams life into me—marks me with jabs from an invisible knife that will never ever heal. And I relish every single wound. When he's inside me, I'm not some pathetic, helpless rabbit.

I'm not even sure I'm still human. I'm greedy. I'm restless. Reckless. My nails seize hold of a pillow, digging in as I flex my hips toward him, meeting every thrust and eliciting hungry growls that resonate in my skin.

"That's it." He voices his pleasure in a low groan when my inner muscles clutch him, urging him to spend himself. Empty every bit of emotion from his body that he can't control. *Use me.*

"Bunny." His fingers latch onto the back of my skull, tugging my head toward him. The moment I'm within reach, his teeth seize my ear, nipping while his other hand cups my breast, squeezing just on this side of pain. He curses when I moan, the foreign words he mutters somehow making sense in my lust-addled brain.

"You're mine."

My sweat-soaked fingers lose their hold over that groove in the headboard. I settle for bracing both hands flat on the sliver of mattress in front of me, riding him until it doesn't matter if we're silent or not. The headboard rams against the wall, and I can't muster the energy to care.

Doubt fades. Shame melts away, and I surrender to everything he has to give. The fingers of his other hand find my nipple, swiping it into a stabbing peak before doing the same to the other.

And then I feel him slam into me with a shudder and the world ceases to matter.

Noises crawl from my throat I've never heard myself make, melding with his deeper, gruffer grunts. It's a symphony of pure, primal pleasure. My fingers grip his forearms, tracing the path of the flames spewing from the creature on his back as his explanation for designing it echoes in my mind —*it's power. Control.*

Another word seems fitting enough to describe it as well— *it's freedom.*

But it doesn't last. His thrusts quicken, losing their punishing rhythm. He grits his teeth on a frantic pace toward release—but his hand slips between us, finding a part of me that makes my spine curl as if connected to an invisible tether. One he can command with stroke, after stroke, after stroke…

Until he finally stills, his mouth at my throat, his fingers twisting through my hair.

"Fuck," he hisses before rolling off me to collapse onto his back. "Holy fuck."

He doesn't sound happy, just exhausted. I look over to find him scowling up at the ceiling, his chest heaving in a ruthless tandem to match his panting breaths.

It's jarring how he switches out emotions. Fire one minute and ice the next.

"You had to fuck him." He chuckles to himself, wiping his hand over his injured lip. "It would certainly explain why he's so damn pussy-whipped. You had to fuck him…"

I don't follow the leap in logic, but the confidence in his voice unnerves me enough to let another piece of the truth slip free. "It was never like that with him…"

He frowns and shoots me a searching glance. "It was about control, then. Getting inside your head. Directing your every move. That's what he got off on."

"It wasn't like that, either," I whisper.

Though he's not far off. I've spent my whole life growing accustomed to Branden's control. One mantra above all was drilled into my head like a creed. I owed him.

"Our… My parents never really looked out for me," I admit, stretching out onto my back beside him. "They were successful. We were wealthy. But my mom had her issues, and she wasn't around much when I was growing up. My dad was overwhelmed and looked to other relationships to cope. Branden was the one left to look out for me." It sounds strange when said out loud. Dysfunctional. In reality, it was all we knew. "One day… I think I must have been five. I ran out into the street and was almost hit by a car. The fallout was bad. The police were called. They couldn't find my parents. Bran was twelve, and it hit him hard. Things looked worse than they were. The aftermath could have ruined his life."

"He doesn't sound like your boyfriend," Rafe says. Strangely, he doesn't accuse me of lying outright. His tone carefully straddles the line between confusion and irritation, leaving it entirely up to me whether or not to come clean.

But there's no point in denying it anymore.

"He's not. Bran is my brother," I confess, too weary to even see how that piece of information lands. I stare up at the ceiling, my thoughts like a sieve, leaking all of the dark memories I've struggled to suppress.

"So what? Your parents got busted for neglect. Why the fuck is that your problem?"

I hesitate to answer, squeezing my eyes shut against the past. "Because… I wasn't wearing any clothes." The silence that falls in the wake of those words is deafening. The only way to combat the awkwardness is to keep talking. "And I don't remember what I said when the police came, but they were concerned enough to start an investigation. I shouldn't have to say what kind."

"Shit," Rafe says.

I nod in agreement. "All of that because of me." It always surprises me how deep the guilt goes. How a child's innocent actions could lead to a whirlwind of chaos.

"Bran had to go see a child psychologist after that because of me. I was almost put into foster care. My parents were mortified. I could have ruined his life—"

"Did he touch you?" Rafe demands.

I flinch at how earnestly he asks that question. "No! Not like that. Not—"

"You were a kid." His anger startles me. I open my eyes to find him tense, his eyes darker than ever. "A kid who ran out of your house *naked*."

"It wasn't like that," I insist, shaking my head. "I was probably playing a game or something. I barely even remember—"

"And how many years later and the bastard beats you. He hides a camera in your fucking room. Shit, he *watched* you naked!"

I cringe. "Stop making it sound like…"

"Like what? Like he may have molested you? That he's still abusing you. Trust me, it's not that hard to spell it out."

I roll onto my side as if shielding my body from view can protect from his judgment. "Stop!"

But he's too riled. Hissing, he brandishes a fist at nothing, his eyes flashing. "And your parents? They let you go around believing that shit? That you owe him because of what he did?"

"It's not that simple," I insist.

"Bullshit!" He strikes the mattress so hard I jump. "The fuck it's not. And what about that story you wrote, huh? Deceiver? What the fuck is that about? Did he hurt someone in front of you?"

"Please stop," I plead as my voice breaks. "I've never told anyone this."

Because I know how it sounds—and I know what dark turn this story eventually takes.

"You don't know what it's like," I add. "To be chained to someone, and you can't explain why. But it's what it is."

"Is it?" he snarls. "Why the fuck did you have a heart after his name in your phone then. Huh?"

I feel my cheeks flame as I choke out the answer, "Because it was one way to remind myself that despite everything he's done… I shouldn't hate him. I can't hate him."

"Fuck…" Rafe sighs, and some of the tension drains from his muscles. Judging from his tight expression, those words resonated with him more than I expected. Finally, he cocks his head at me, his gaze focused. "You said he tracked your phone?"

I nod, alarmed as he stands and crosses to his dresser, still naked. The dragon on his back ripples, coming to life as he wrenches open a drawer.

"Well, let's give the fucker something to follow." He tosses me a wad of fabric—another shirt. "Put it on," he demands while stepping into a pair of jeans. By the time I remember how to move, he's already storming into the living room. He grabs my phone from the coffee table and marches for the door, snatching something from a small hook hanging beside it on his way out.

"Wait!" I scramble into my sandals, grab my bag, and follow. "Where are you going?"

Rather than head for the shop's front, he exits from the back into the alley leading to the roof. This time, he heads to the street opposite the shop's entrance. It's a quieter block, mainly sporting a row of parked cars. The black one he approaches must be his.

"Get in," he commands before claiming the driver's seat.

"Where are we going?" I ask, hesitating on the curb.

His answer is to slam the driver's side door, leaving me no choice but to open the one nearest me. The interior is black leather, and while I'm not an expert on cars, I can tell that this one is expensive. Very expensive.

A meticulous level of cleanliness alludes to the care of its owner. Or a desire for control—Branden keeps his the same way.

"Get in," Rafe demands, revving the engine.

Finally, I comply. "Fine. Where are we going?"

"Do you want to buy yourself more time?" He shoots me a searching glance I can't decipher, and I remain silent even as he starts to drive.

Eventually, we reach the city's outskirts, where the close-set buildings give way to sparser winding roads. Our final destination makes me do a double take.

"A bus depot?" I question, reading the sign affixed to the front of a nearby building. "What are you—"

"Wait here." He exits the car, slamming the door in his wake. All I can do is stare as he crosses the street to a row of metal bus shelters. They're mostly empty save for a lone woman slumped against a wall of Plexiglass, a duffel at her feet.

Rafe approaches her, reaching into his pocket. A second later, he withdraws what looks like cash, along with something else that triggers a glimmer of recognition—my phone.

The woman accepts both, tucking them into her duffel as Rafe returns to the car.

"What was that about?" I ask as he starts the car and takes off, heading toward the city.

"That?" He chuckles, his eyes glinting mischievously. "That was a fucking reprieve, bunny. How do you think 'Bran' will like Minnesota?"

It takes a second for it to click, just what he's done. I'm startled by the laugh that escapes my lips, but there's more pain mixed into the sound than amusement.

"That won't fool him for long—"

"It's not meant to," Rafe snaps. "But now you have time. Fucking time. So, use it wisely, bunny. Break away from him. He can't control you anymore. Even if it's only for a day, you're free."

How do I choose to spend the first ten minutes of said freedom? Seated beside him, my mind reeling as he drives us back to his shop. He parks in the alley but doesn't leave the car right away. Instead, he sighs, gripping the steering wheel so tightly his knuckles bulge.

"So why lie about him, huh?" he asks, his voice cold. "Did you get off on it? Watching me fucking squirm? Throwing it in my face that you were—" he breaks off and whirls to face me, jabbing his gaze into my own. "That seems to be your fucking favorite game—playing with fire."

"It wasn't like that," I stammer, though honestly, there isn't a better way of phrasing it. I lied to him, and the guilt feels way worse than expected. "I didn't mean—"

"Then what fucking was it?" His voice is deep enough to penetrate my skin and the bone beneath. "Did you like fucking with my head, is that it? By pretending you were fucking your brother. You know how sick that sounds? God, you sure played me like a motherfucker—"

"How do you think it sounds to say out loud that my brother controls my life?" I bite back, startled by my own ferocity. "That he makes me take pictures of myself every night? That he hid a camera in my bedroom? That he haunts me. That he took away the one piece of power I've ever had over him. That he has me *trapped!* How do you think that sounds?"

My own high-pitched voice mockingly holds the answer. It sounds insane. It sounds pathetic.

It sounds like a living nightmare.

"I'm sorry." Rafe brushes my shoulder, but I cringe from his reach. In this confined space, however, there's nowhere to go. Persistent, his fingers slip through my hair, easily finding my chin. "Look at me."

In the end, he has to grip my jaw and compel me to. His eyes gleam in the glow of a nearby streetlight, his face bathed in shadow. The lack of lighting denies him of his usual swagger. Armed with dark irises and an earnest tone, he's harder to write off. Ignore.

"He hurt you." He enunciates every word as if teaching me a foreign language. "I want to hear you say it. Right now. He hurt you, and you don't owe him a damn thing."

"He's my brother," I blurt out instead. "I *do* owe him. And…"

"And what?" Rafe demands, his eyes slits. "And you deserve to have him beat the shit out of you? Track you? I know men with records who aren't that fucking crazy."

"And… I'm afraid of him—" a ragged exhale robs me of breath. Admitting the truth feels comparable to ripping away the veil I've chosen to live under. As a result, I'm naked in the aftermath, at the mercy of his scrutiny.

"Tell me," he says.

"I'm terrified," I hear a stranger with my voice confess. "He hasn't come after me yet, and I don't know what that means. I don't."

When Branden stews, trouble always follows.

"You're afraid," Rafe repeats, his tone softer. "So, what are you going to do about it?"

What could seem like a cruel line of questioning at first, becomes something else the second I see his face. A dare lurks in his stern expression, one that makes me shudder even before he voices it out loud.

"I can help you be ready for him the next time he shows up."

"How?" I croak. "You teach me how to fight? How to shoot a gun? Very funny."

But he doesn't laugh, and as the seconds tick by, I start to remember something Gino insinuated about his father. *Your uncle is one cold son of a bitch, though he has nothing on your daddy. You should know that, though. Aren't you the one who turned his ass in?*

"I'll teach you whatever it takes for you to not be afraid of him," Rafe declares.

The intensity in his voice takes my breath away.

"You're being ridiculous." I can't even face him, so I stare through the windshield instead, watching the orange glow play off the brick siding of the buildings nearby.

"Tell me then," he says, refusing to let the subject drop. "What's your plan? What do you think it will take?"

What will it take to feel safe from Branden?

I'd naïvely thought that finding my voice might do that. Strengthening my writing enough for my own words to speak for me. I thought stating the truth, even as distorted as I could, might help nurture some small, distant part of me brave enough to stand against him.

Weeks later and that hasn't happened.

"I just need to get into the writing program," I insist as dryly as reading a script. "Keep my job. Stay away from him. Nothing else."

"The offer stands," Rafe says while muscling open the door on his end. He mounts the curb, leaving me to scramble after him as he strides ahead for the back door to the shop. Halfway there, he stops short.

"Shit," I hear him hiss as he raises a hand for me to stop. Low, his voice reaches me, barely audible. "Stay here."

CHAPTER FOUR

He inches forward, his posture hunched like a guard dog. The only thing I can make out to explain his unease is the tail end of a bright red car. I've seen it before. Where?

Rafe's already rounding the corner, but I can't shake the instinctive urge in the pit of my soul to move as well—in the opposite direction. *To run. Hide.*

The second I take a step back, Rafe's voice rings out, but directed at someone else. "Uncle. I was—"

"I know what the fuck you were doing," a man replies. I recognize his voice—a guttural baritone that invokes the image of a snarling lion in contrast to Rafe's figurative dragon. "Once again, you were shirking your responsibility. Making me look like a goddamn fool for leaving you in charge at all. A girl was killed in our fucking territory, Rafael. And yet you're off wetting your cock while threats to us mount."

"It's not what it looks like," Rafe counters.

"It's not? I heard what happened here," Shen says. "That you cowered while those thugs sent you a direct warning. Even if this fucking excuse for a hobby is just a game to you, this place is under my territory. Mine."

"Uncle," Rafe starts. "I was going to—"

"You never called for backup," the man says over him. "You never initiated retaliation. I had to find out about it from fucking rumors like it's goddamn amateur hour—" he breaks off. "Come. We need to discuss this. Now. And in the meantime, you can explain why you covered Zhang's tab in full. That son of a bitch doesn't have that kind of money. Did you do it to impress the little whore that works there? Don't look so surprised. Like father like son—easily distracted by a willing cunt—"

"I'm not some boy you can call to heel," Rafe says, his voice gruffer than I've ever heard it. "I told you—confronting Gino head-on is what that son of a bitch wants. He wants to draw us into the open. I thought you wanted to lay low? That petty crime was above you now, Mr. Politician?"

The startled silence from his uncle's end adds a chilling effect to the conversation. Despite not seeing either party's face, I can easily pick up on the shift in the atmosphere— Rafe crossed a glaring red line.

"The cops are on his dick," he continues more softly. "I know it. We need to—"

"We?" His uncle echoes. "You don't decide a damn thing until you get your priorities in order. I may not be able to 'call you to heel,' but I'll give you a choice. I have every intention of keeping *my* hands 'clean,' but you haven't earned the same right."

"What are you saying?" Rafe counters, his alarm apparent by the subtle inflection in his voice.

"I'm saying, either you take a job for me—now. Or I'll extract double Zhang's debt from the little cunt you covered for."

"Job… I thought you were out of the fucking game?"

"I am," Shen insists. "*You're* taking the fucking risk. Or will you do the smart thing, Rafael?"

Silence falls, but I doubt the conversation is anywhere near over. I imagine them facing off, symbolically wrestling over a decision I don't understand in full—but whatever it is, I sense it's momentous. Life or death.

"Where?" Rafe says finally.

"Get in the fucking car," Shen commands. "We'll see how far you're willing to go to prove your loyalty."

Two sets of footsteps advance in my direction but stop short of the alley. I hear a couple car doors open and shut nearby. Minutes later, the red car vanishes from my line of sight.

When I creep from the mouth of the alley, Rafe is gone too, the street deserted.

A job. The way both he and his uncle uttered that word doesn't bring to mind the image of a typical nine-to-five.

But whatever he's doing, it's because of me. That much is clear by his uncle's reference to Mr. Zhang. He's punishing Rafe because of me.

And I have no way of helping. I don't even have anywhere to go. My only option seems to be waiting for him in the alley, or on the roof.

But as a flicker of movement catches the corner of my eye, I realize that neither option may be available. Headlights ignite a block down, belonging to a vehicle I can't make out. It pulls away from the curb, heading toward me at a speed that sends my body lurching into motion. *Run.*

I turn on my heel and start walking, praying that the driver keeps going. I'm being paranoid, overreacting to any little disturbance. Instead, it slows, coming close enough for me to make out the model—a sleek black sedan, far different from Branden's functional cruiser.

The driver lurks behind a tinted window, hidden from view as the car stops. The back door opens, and a figure climbs out. Tall and bulky, he mounts the curb, his dark eyes cutting in my direction.

This time, I don't suppress my first instinct. *Run!*

I take off, careening down the nearest alley—an overreaction I could write off later in a brief moment of embarrassment. Or not. Footsteps ricochet off the walls behind me, creating a dizzying cacophony. As I increase my pace, so do they, even turning a corner after I do.

Following me.

I surge forward, following this back road onto a larger, busier street. Enough pedestrians crowd the sidewalks here for me to blend in. Panting, I slow my stride to match a gaggle of giggling teenage girls and risk looking back. A man staggers from the alley in my wake. His eyes scan the crowd, hunting. Within a heartbeat, they latch onto my position, and he lunges, pushing his way through the throng of people.

With no other choice, I step into the street, dodging the moving traffic. A driver narrowly misses me by inches, but I make it to the other side unscathed. The man, however, is already doing the same, skirting an oncoming truck.

I keep moving, sprinting around the next corner, and I nearly run directly into another person. They grab my wrist automatically, and I react purely on instinct. I don't even realize my free hand is forming a fist until I brandish it.

"Hannah?"

It takes me a second to recognize the man gaping at me. *Liam.* "Are you okay?" he asks. "What the hell happened to you?"

Judging from the way he's eyeing my face, he can clearly make out every detail of my bruises, despite the dark.

"What are you doing here?" I ask. Though when I scan the nearby street, I realize we're not far from the bookstore.

"I just got off," he explains, but his grip on my forearm tightens before I can pull away. "God. What the hell happened—"

"I'm fine," I lie, evading the hand he extends toward my face. "I… I'm just getting off too. I should go."

"I'll walk you," he suggests, looping his arm around my shoulder before I can refuse. "You were at work all day?"

The suspicion in his tone is painfully apparent, but I don't have another lie at the ready. So I nod, avoiding eye contact.

"Huh. Branden didn't come by? He seemed worried about you. You guys get into a fight or something?"

"No. Why?"

"He's been messaging me all day asking if I've seen you," Liam says. He has a cell phone in his free hand, but, as if aware of my gaze, he tucks the device into his pocket.

Was he communicating with Branden?

"It's nothing," I say quickly, forcing a smile. "Just family stuff. You don't need to bother him."

"Family stuff." He smiles in return, but the expression seems strained at the edges.

We're already back on the main street, though I don't spot the man following me. Regardless, I can't shake the feeling that I'm being watched.

Hunted with every step I take.

"I'm not trying to pry or anything," Liam explains. "It's just, he was really worried about you—"

"Hannah!"

That voice… I stiffen, sensing someone approaching behind me. I know without turning around who stands there now. His hand lands over my shoulder, bearing down with increasing brutality until I have to bite back a cry.

"I'll take it from here," Branden says, presumably to Liam. "Thanks for the heads-up."

"Wait." Liam swipes his hand along my jaw, narrowly avoiding the worst of the bruises. "What happened—"

"I've got it," Branden insists. "Thanks."

Liam frowns but backs away. "Okay. Let me know if you need anything."

"Let's go, Hannah." Branden tugs on my shoulder, but I don't move, digging my heels into the pavement. "You don't want to make a scene," he warns against my neck. "All I want to do is talk—" his nails bite down with renewed strength, and he tugs, positioning himself beside me so that Liam can't catch my pained gasp.

"You're hurting me," I croak.

"Good," he counters, muscling me further down the block and fully out of earshot. "Do you have any fucking idea what you've put me through? Do you? It's like you're a selfish little brat all over again."

There's no one else on this street, apparently a quiet residential roadway. Lights in various windows allude to populated homes, their occupants within earshot of a scream.

But I can't seem to voice one.

If I'm a selfish little brat again, then he's the same towering figure who's dominated my memories for as long as I can remember.

But I don't even recognize him now. And despite everything he's done, there are some actions I've never considered him capable of.

"You watched me," I say in a hoarse whisper, the loudest sound I seem capable of producing. "You spied on me, Bran. You saw me—"

"I've protected you," he hisses, nudging me forward. "I still am. Rafe Wei-Shen? Do you have any idea what that fucker is capable of? What he's done?"

His hissed tone carries far too much rage.

"Why don't you ask around? I hear you're not even the first girl he's seduced. *Or* manipulated into doing his dirty work, but it's not even you he's interested in—"

"And what about you?" I ask, finally turning to face him directly. "Who have you 'manipulated'? Faith Wen?"

Surprise visibly crosses his face, but it goes far beyond typical shock. I've only witnessed his eyes narrow like this a handful of times. He's afraid. "What are you talk—"

"You know what I'm talking about, Bran!" I wrench away, causing his nails to gouge at my arm in the process. Rather than run, it's like my body is controlled by someone else. Someone reckless, who makes me meet his gaze head-on.

I don't recognize the man staring back.

He's not in uniform, and his mussed hair proves Liam's story. He's been out for hours, looking for me. Despite his best attempts, his neutral expression fails to convince me. Again, his eyes give him away, flashing and cold, a hard reflective green. In his gaze, I see myself staring back, every bit as gaping and stupid as the bunny Rafe implies I am.

But no more.

"I found the hair clip," I rasp.

"Hair clip?" He sounds so convincing I almost fall for it. But his supposed confusion never reaches his eyes—if anything, they remain frozen. Ice-cold.

"It's silver, in the shape of a butterfly," I explain. "I found it in a box of my things, but it isn't mine."

"What makes you think I put it there?" he demands, raising an eyebrow. "It probably is one of yours. You just forgot you had it, and you're so paranoid about making me the bad guy you'll jump to any conclusion you can."

"So, you don't know Faith?" I ask him. "She was found dead the other day. She waited on us at the restaurant. She was seeing a police officer, and—"

"Who told you all of this?" Branden interjects harshly. "Honestly, Hannah, you sound ridiculous."

"Just tell me you didn't do it," I whisper, and I'm surprised by just how earnest I sound. Desperate. "Tell me, Bran. Tell me you didn't."

"Do what?" he hisses, advancing a step, his hands in fists. "Catch you fucking a criminal? Lie to our parents when you disappear for days, Hannah? Think you were on your way to only God knows where? If Liam didn't spot you when he did—" he exhales with a gruff sound akin to a growl. "Why don't you ask your boyfriend about who's been planting shit on you? You really have no idea what he's capable of. Do you? Don't tell me you're dumb enough to think he'd be interested in you for no reason. To him, you're just leverage. Don't believe me?"

A tendril of doubt sneaks into my brain. After all, Rafe was the one who moved my things from my apartment in the first place. He had more than enough opportunity to hide something in a seemingly random box of trinkets.

But…

"Something else was missing from my things too," I say, watching Branden for any hint of a reaction. "A gold bracelet. Does that ring a bell?"

"Jesus Christ, Hannah! Why are you trying to provoke me? Do you want me to fuck up again, huh? Like what you made me do the last time."

I stiffen at the reminder.

Last time.

A fit of violence triggered because of me.

Everything he does is *always* because of me, even now. I'm the reason for the flush of red creeping across his neck, visible even in the dark. I'm the reason why his hands are twitching as if he's having to physically stop himself from striking me again. I'm the reason for his lack of control.

"Answer me!"

"Did you hurt that girl?" I ask instead. God, I can barely get the words out.

But they ring hollow. Laughing, he rolls his eyes. "What girl? Or is this just another game, Hannah? How you avoid blame. There's always another girl, isn't there? Like Lexi?" He scoffs when I recoil. "Ah, but you wouldn't want to use that memory against me, Hannah? When it was your fault that she died. You wouldn't be trying to delude yourself into thinking otherwise, would you? Enough!" He snaps his fingers. "Come home—"

"You killed her." My voice breaks, robbing the accusation of any grit. Regardless, I think it's the first time I've ever said those words out loud.

Am I referring to Faith? Or Lexi?

I don't even know anymore.

Rather than react in anger, Branden just keeps laughing. "Hannah, stop it. You know how crazy you sound?"

He advances another step, and I nearly trip in my rush to put distance between us.

"Don't touch me—"

"Come home," he snarls. "Now. While Dad remains clueless about how much of a little whore you really are. While he's still paying for your fucking, stupid school. But will he if he knows the truth, Hannah?"

I blink in confusion. "The truth?"

His smile turns feral—I've taken his bait. "That you're out here selling sex tapes on the internet while he funds your education? Or your school… Do you think that liberal fucking college would like to know one of their students is an online video star?"

I can feel the blood drain from my face as I stop dead in my tracks. "You didn't…"

"I will," he says coldly. "Unless you come with me now. I love you, Hannah, but if you want to act like a whore, I will treat you like one. Now come home—"

"Why?" I demand, evading his grasping hand. "Why are you doing this?"

"Because I love you," he insists. "I do. So, make your choice right now. Come home with me, or learn the hard way—I'm the only one you can ever trust."

He reaches for me again, but I shirk his grasp. Again. Again. Eventually, several feet of space separate us, but he just watches me, stunned.

"Hannah—"

"I could still tell," I hear myself say in that stranger's broken tone. "Daddy. The police. Everyone."

"Tell them what?"

My heart despairs at the answer. One that's haunted me for the past ten years. "That you were never worth the benefit of the doubt."

"You little bitch… If you think I'm the liar, then where is your proof, huh?" He eyes my bag, his nostrils flaring. "Where is it?"

When he comes for me this time, I turn on my heel and run.

"Hannah!" His voice chases me as I dart between two parked cars and cross the street. He's on my heels. His heavy pants lash at the air, his footsteps slamming against the pavement—but with every step I gain, they grow distant, until only his shouts can reach me.

"I'll give you until tomorrow night, Hannah. One fucking night! You come to me when you're ready to learn your lesson, or the world will learn the truth about *you*—you were always just a lying little whore!"

Tears lash at my cheeks as I keep moving, darting from alley to alley and street to street. Eventually, I no longer recognize my surroundings, and only fear keeps me going, driving me further into an increasingly industrial area where warehouses and office buildings take up most of the real estate.

I'm too busy replaying Branden's threat to even care that I'm lost. Would he truly do that? Post whatever he recorded on the internet. Make it seem like I did it. Lie. Cheat. All to keep me under his thumb?

The answer sickens me to my stomach—he would. He will.

And I'm powerless to do a damn thing to stop him.

A sudden smattering of noise draws my attention, and I finally falter. At a glance, the street I'm on is deserted, but up ahead, I spot a building that may have been my destination all along—a warehouse near the wharf.

A battered door serves as the entrance, but it's unlocked. Musty air tickles my nostrils as I feel through the dark until I find a hallway leading into a larger space. The first time I came here, a light had illuminated much of the enclosed area ahead, but now it's pitch-black.

Something clatters as I stumble against it. I forge ahead until my hand meets a surface I assume to be a wall, and I gladly sink to the floor, bracing my back against it.

I keep as still as I can, listening for any other sound. If Branden is still on my trail, enclosing myself in here is a stupid course of action, but it's one that I can't seem to talk myself out of. Maybe because a persistent warning is echoing in my mind on repeat. *You get there, and you wait for me.*

I should still be running. Fighting. Or better yet, getting ahold of my parents somehow and telling them the truth—about everything.

A laugh escapes me, as if even my body knows what my brain can't face. I won't. I've spent too many years resisting those very actions—too many years obscuring the truth.

And as a result, no one would believe me. Hell, even I wouldn't.

But Rafe did, a part of me whispers. He believed me without question, displaying a disgust for my circumstances that I've never had the energy to feel myself.

Is it genuine? Parsing over his responses, I can't tell. For someone who claims to be so honest, he's more guarded than not, displaying his real emotions only through layers at a time. And one fact remains painfully clear—I hardly know anything about him.

His true profession. His history with his uncle. His past.

Branden could be right. Rafe could have planted Faith's hair clip. A good sister would want to believe as much.

Do I?

Rather than mull over the answer, I lean back against the wall, settling into the strange, darkened space. The building must be old, given the various creaking, cracking noises that form a backdrop to my own harsh breathing.

But soon, another noise joins the quiet cacophony—heavy, cautious footsteps.

CHAPTER FIVE

"Hannah?"

I tense at the sound of my name before my body registers the cadence of the voice speaking it.

"I'm here," I croak, feeling along the floor as I stand.

An overhead light switches on, bathing the room in an orange glow—as well as revealing the pile of chaos I've left in my wake. I'm standing on a stack of overturned documents, marred by a muddy footprint that looks suspiciously like it might belong to my sandal. Out of guilt, I shuffle the pages together and attempt to return them to the nearest table.

The topmost one catches my eye as I try to shove it inside a folder. It's a slip of paper with the city police emblem emblazoned across the top. Beneath that is a list of what seems to be names. Several of them have been crudely circled in red ink.

One, in particular, catches my eye, halfway down the page —Branden Dewitt.

"Hannah?" Rafe stands a few feet away, his back to me. "Where are you?"

I snatch the list, tucking it into my bag. "I'm over here!" I approach him slowly, sensing even before I come close that something is horribly wrong. "Rafe..."

He's leaning to one side, heavily favoring that leg. His left hand clutches at his chest, and a telltale smell tickles my nostrils, growing more potent by the second.

"You're bleeding," I say, scanning his frame for any other signs of injury—which I find in a spattered trail of blood leading from the hall, tracking his entry. "What happened?"

Groaning, he hobbles to a sturdy table nearby and braces his hands over it. "Give me a hand," he demands, his voice hoarse. "Black case in the corner."

With the words barely out of his mouth, he slumps forward, knocking the table off balance.

I lurch toward him. "Rafe—"

"Just get the fucking case," he grates, lifting a hand to ward me off. "Please..."

I whirl on my heel, struggling to follow his instructions. The room is a maze of stray materials. Stacks of canvases. Boxes piled high with random equipment. Stray slabs of plywood lean against the wall, obscuring a shelf in a far corner. On it, I find a black leather construct resembling a briefcase.

I bring it to Rafe, setting it beside him.

"You don't look good," I rasp. He's shaking, barely capable of supporting himself on trembling hands. Still, he risks that precarious balance to grab the case, dragging it toward him. For all the effort, he fumbles with the latch. "Fuck—"

"I'll do it." I unlatch the top of the case, opening it to reveal a sight that takes my breath away. Fear constricts my throat, and all I seem capable of doing is whispering, "Rafe..."

"Don't," he warns before overturning the case entirely, allowing the contents to spill out onto the table's surface. Money. Stacks and stacks of crisp bills, each secured with a rubber band. There have to be hundreds. Thousands...

But the amount pales in comparison to what falls amid the scattered stacks, its shape unmistakable—a gun.

Rafe grabs for it first, tucking it into his pocket. When he reaches for a stack of cash next, droplets of blood drip from his fingers, staining a handful of bills. "Damn it." He forms a fist instead, cocking his head in my direction. "I need you to grab it."

I barely hear him. More blood is dripping from his chin, flowing from his split lip. Fresh bruising around his eye alludes to yet another blow. From one of Gino's goons? From his uncle?

"Did you hear me? Hey, bunny!" He snaps his fingers beneath my nose, but he's so weak they barely make a sound. Scarlet streaks the tips of them, painting a blazing path up his wrist…

Finally, I notice the gash slicing through the flesh of his left arm.

I snatch at his sleeve in alarm. "What the hell happened to you?"

"It doesn't fucking matter. Listen to me!" He slams his hand over the table so hard I swear he dents the wood. However, the act drains him, and I lurch forward to grab his shoulder before he can pitch over entirely. His eyes flit up to mine, and I swallow hard at the agony I find in them. Along with anger. Volatile, infectious rage.

"We need to move," he says, gasping with the effort. "Now—"

"You can barely stand up," I hiss.

He shrugs to throw me off, but he's so weak, he winds up swaying without the support. So he jerks his chin toward the stack of bills instead. "Grab the fucking money. Put it in your purse. Do it. Now." Something in my expression makes him sigh. "Please."

I don't know why that single word affects me—his tone. Maybe the aftermath of confronting Branden has robbed me of the ability to think for myself longer than a few minutes at a time. I grab a stack of bills without realizing it.

Then another—but at the back of my mind gnaws this irrational sense of hurt. Betrayal.

He's making me do this but won't tell me why. So much for freedom.

"That's enough," he says when I've grabbed four stacks of bills. "Put the rest back. Good. Now… I need you to come with me."

He pulls away from the table and staggers a few steps toward the exit. He doesn't even make it halfway before he careens into a pile of canvas. A volley of curses erupts from him as they—and him along with them—crash to the floor.

Rushing to him, I hook my arm around his shoulders, hauling him to his feet. I spot a metal folding chair nearby, and I practically drag him to it, making him sit. My eyes latch onto the way he's still clutching at his side, and I seize the hem of his shirt, wrenching it up despite his attempts to stop me.

"Don't—"

"Oh my God…" I drop to my knees to get a better look. Where there was once unblemished skin, mottled bruising paints his ribcage in a medley of purples. He must have been struck by something—heavy enough to leave a cylindrical area the width of his chest. A bat? A larger weapon?

"God, Rafe. You could have internal damage." I can't stop myself from brushing my hand along his ribcage, and he nearly jumps off the chair.

"Fuck!"

"What happened?" My voice rings out stronger as I rise to my feet. "Tell me, or I'm leaving. I mean it—"

"I need you." He looks me dead in my eyes, leaving no doubt that he means every word. "I need you, bunny. Don't ask questions. Not now. I'll explain everything later, but for now… You've gotta trust me."

"No." I back away and nearly trip over an array of scattered pens that must have fallen from the table. "You don't have the right to ask me to do that. You don't!"

He wrestles his shirt into place, and I can tell from how unfocused his gaze becomes that he's barely on the verge of coherence. In essence, he's miles away, still running from whatever drove him here.

Lowering my voice, I try to reason with him. "You need a hospital—"

"If I don't do this, we're both dead." He says it so plainly that I continue to talk over him without registering the depth of his words at first.

"An ambulance. You could be bleeding internally… What are you talking about?"

He grits his teeth in determination as he grips the end of the chair. The damn thing nearly topples as he rises to his feet.

"Trust me." He extends a hand marred by blood, and only God knows what else. It's so repulsive I recoil—or I start to.

The second I flinch, his gaze locks me in place, paralyzing in its raw intensity.

I can read his emotions in every nuanced quirk from his lips, pursed and tight, to his brow furrowed with concentration. As well as the feeling making him sway to stay upright—fear.

That sole observation affects me like nothing else. Robotic steps propel me forward, and my hand extends without input from my brain, my fingers entwining with his. He tugs me to his side, utilizing my body as a makeshift cane.

"I need to get to my car," he grates through his teeth. "Come on."

We head for the exit surprisingly fast, but every few seconds, his eyes dart toward the shadows. Whatever he sees —or doesn't—has him tightening his grip, urging me into the closest speed he can come to an outright run. Which is little more than a hobbling walk.

"This way." Once we reach his car, he wrenches open the driver's side door, but rather than claim it for himself, he nudges me closer. "Can you drive?"

"Yes, but I haven't in years," I admit. And this modern dashboard looks far different from the hand-me-down family car I practiced with back in PA. "But—"

"Do it. Please." Without giving me the chance to respond, he limps around to the passenger's side, clinging to the car for balance. "We need to move." He shoots another wary glance over his shoulder, and unease drives me inside despite my instincts warning me to jump right back out.

I can't do this—get dragged into whatever this is. But then Rafe slumps onto the seat beside me, and one look at his face breaks my resolve. I've never seen him like this. His hands shaking, his eyes unfocused with pain. For once, there's no bravado.

"Please."

Defeated, I turn my attention to the modern console. "Where are the keys? And where are we going?"

He strikes a button on the dashboard, and the engine roars to life. "Just drive," he commands. "I'll tell you where to go."

Where winds up being an area roughly ten miles away, following the waterline north. I can't tell if we're still within the city limits, though the only buildings in sight are a few scattered warehouses. The road itself is sparsely populated—which is a blessing in disguise, considering I'm going roughly fifty miles below the speed limit.

"Damn, bunny," Rafe chokes out, the first thing he's said other than a few grunted directions. "My grandmother drives faster than this."

"Then maybe you should call her." God, I don't recognize myself anymore—a stranger apart from the fearful figure who cowered in Branden's shadow. This Hannah is angry. Seething. And worried.

For *him.*

All I can do is pour my energy into driving, recalling the few skills I learned before moving to the city. I won't admit it out loud, but it's a miracle we've made it this far.

"Turn here," Rafe demands, indicating a shallow, gnarled road that looks unwelcoming at best. "Trust me," he prods, sensing my hesitation. "But I won't lie to you, bunny. Shit's about to get real. Now park."

I slam my foot on the brake so suddenly, Rafe grips the dashboard to keep from flying out of his seat.

"Fuck," he hisses, clutching at his side. "Now… Do you still have the money?"

"Y-Yes." I scramble for my bag, which I find tucked beneath the seat.

"Good. Now I need you to take it over to that building—" he indicates a massive industrial complex that looks to be about several years past its prime. Some of the windows are broken, the interior darkened, and plenty of rust is visible in the dim illumination provided by a streetlight. "You'll find an old dumpster beside it," he tells me. "Open the sliding door. Put the money in, and whatever is inside, you take it and run the fuck back. I'd do it myself, but we gotta do this quick."

His tone alarms me more than reassures. "What are you—"

"I'll have your back," he says over me. "Trust me, I won't let anything happen to you. But you've gotta do this. Now."

He leans over me to wrench open my door.

"Go," he snarls.

I move entirely out of reflex, stumbling to my feet. It's quiet here. Every step echoes, amplified until it sounds like a million other people follow in my wake. Armed with only his money, I've never felt more exposed.

"Go," Rafe prompts from the window. "You won't be on your own. I've got you."

He's got you, a part of me hisses. *As a puppet. A fool. Just like Branden.*

But I rightfully ran away from that monster. This one? I blindly follow into the shadows, as stupidly as the bunny he mocks me for being.

Find a dumpster, he said.

The only one I find lurks behind the nearest building. From here, the car is hidden from view, and yawning shadows dance over a desolate pavement littered with broken glass and growing weeds.

The dumpster itself is rusted through in places, but sure enough, the door that, were it in use, would allow trash to be thrown through it opens when I tug on the handle. The interior has been modified—a wooden ledge provides a place to set the bills on, and resting in the space already is another case. As I reach for it, a flicker of movement catches my eye. I barely manage to pivot as a hand reaches out from nowhere.

"Who the fuck are you?" a man demands. A bittersweet stench tinges his breath. Alcohol? He's bulky, his face obscured by shadow, but I instantly recognize the object in his grasp—a knife. "I said who the fuck are you—"

"We're here for the drop," someone declares from behind me. "She left the money. We'll take what we're owed and then go."

"So, you *did* show, after all, you dumb son of a bitch," the man says, laughing. "I hear your uncle whipped your ass good. But here you are, doing his bidding like a good doggie."

"Leave." Rafe's voice touches on a note so deep my entire body vibrates in response. "Take the fucking money and go."

"You're in trouble from what I hear, mutt," the man snarls. "Shen's not too happy with you, is he? You must have pissed him off good for him to use you as an errand boy. But he gave you the wrong information. This shipment isn't for you—"

"What the hell are you talking about?" Rafe demands.

The man steps forward, and a stream of orange light illuminates his gaunt features. "I'm saying, you got bad information, mongrel. Now get the fuck out of here." He deliberately reaches for his pocket, but suddenly goes stiff as I sense Rafe step forward.

"Don't even think about it," he growls.

"Like you have what it takes," the man says with a chuckle, but he raises his hands in surrender.

Rafe's shadow thrown over the ground gives me an inkling as to why. He stands at my shoulder, a slender object held between his fingers.

"You think you scare me?" The man laughs. "Your own uncle doesn't even keep you in the loop. You have no idea, do you? The game he's been playing at your expense? Setting you up to take his fall like the little patsy you are—"

"I said go."

"You really want to fuck around like this, Rafael? Steal from me?" The man doesn't move for so long I lose feeling in my clenched hands. Finally, he backs away, his knife still raised. "You'll pay for this."

"Come on." Reaching past me, Rafe snatches the case, tucking it under his arm. His hand latches onto my forearm next, imparting a strength that keeps the fear at bay long enough to navigate the ruined buildings.

We return to the car surprisingly fast, but when I finally see his face, it's apparent just how much effort maintaining the façade cost him. He's pale enough to glow in the dark, swaying on his feet.

"Just drive," he chokes out before collapsing onto the passenger's seat. "Drive…"

But he never drops the gun. If anything, his grip on it tightens as if any second, he expects to use it.

And he's more than willing to do so.

"You're pissed," Rafe declares. In a stark contrast to his fearsome display near the dumpster, he's lying flat on his couch, his head propped on an armrest.

He's stripped his shirt revealing the full extent of his injuries. A makeshift towel bandage staunches most of the bleeding from his arm, but the bruising on his chest worsens by the second. With every inhale, he winces, but somehow manages to sport a guilty frown. "I'm sorry—"

"You used me." It isn't until I hear my own voice that I realize just how angry I am. Hurt. Betrayed. Humiliated.

Of course, he used you, a part of me hisses. *You made it so easy for him to.*

"I did," he bluntly admits. "And you helped me anyway. I owe ya again, bunny. I mean that."

One look at him, and I think he's telling the truth. He looks so tired. Exhausted.

But I stamp out any pity I may feel and cross my arms, shifting my weight in the direction of the door. Where I'd go, I have no idea. Just away. Somewhere far away from all of it.

"You owe me," I parrot with a scoff. "Good. Well, you can start by telling me the truth. No 'what do you think it is, bunny?' stuff. You be honest with me now, or I'm leaving. What the hell was that?"

"That..." He chokes out another sigh. "I believe the technical term is 'a drug deal,' but you can be creative about it if you want."

"A drug deal?" I brace myself against the nearest wall, but it doesn't feel anywhere near sturdy enough to support me.

"More or less," he says. His eyes meet mine, devoid of any mocking, and I know deep down, he isn't lying. "It might be slightly melodramatic to say it was life or death too, but I'm not far off."

"Who hurt you?" I ask, though I figure a part of me already knows the answer.

"That..." He groans, clutching his side as he starts to sit upright. "Well, I've gotta keep some secrets close to the vest, bunny—"

"No!" My hands find my hips, and I'm seconds away from stomping my foot in anger. "No more secrets. You tell me everything now, or I'm leaving. And while we're at it—" I reach into my bag and withdraw the list of names, brandishing it in his direction. "You tell me about this."

His expression remains blank, devoid of shock, or alarm. "And where are you going to go?" He doesn't sound threatening, just curious.

And it's a darn good question. Where the hell am I going to go with my face bruised to hell and back, no car and no money?

Though, his keys are still in my hand—a fact he only seems to realize as I lift them and consider doing the obvious.

"Anywhere is better than staying with a liar."

"Fine." Groaning, he braces himself against the back of the couch. "I fucked up bad. To make up for it, I needed to do a job for Shen, or he'd bring hell down on both of us. Trust me, this was the lesser of two evils. I bought us time. As for the list. I was working my way through the cops that patrol this area trying to find Faith's 'DW.'" He cracks a tired grin that doesn't reach his eyes. "Funnily enough, there aren't many officers with a first name that starts with D and last name starting with W. Go fucking figure."

I can't hide the way my shoulders slump in relief. He sounds honest—which means he hasn't zoned in on Branden yet. Or at least, I can't tell from his pained expression if he has.

"So, what is in the case?" I ask, crossing my arms.

His eyes dart to the object in question, now resting beside the door. In the glow of a hanging lightbulb, it looks more intimidating than ever, containing only God knows what.

"You know," I say hoarsely, "you bitched at me for lack of detail, but you suck at it."

"Fine. You want to know the truth?" Some of the cockiness deflates from his demeanor. "I'm in deep with the family business, rabbit. If I didn't toe the line, my uncle threatened to drag you into my mess and have you work off what I owed. Every penny, and I can tell you for a fact that it wouldn't be in a fucking shop. He's a petty bastard with a nasty streak, and I've already pissed him off one too many times. I can't fight him on even footing. All I can do is shut him up for as long as I can by toeing the line. How is that for detail?"

His face conveys so much frustration and rage that I'm infected by both.

"Driving a getaway car wasn't ideal," he adds, "but trust me, it's a better deal than what he had in mind."

Work off…

I let the wall support most of my weight as I sink to the floor, crossing my legs beneath me. "Why me?"

He shrugs, wincing with the effort. "You were around, and I was dumb enough to think he wasn't fucking watching my every move. Don't take it personally. He's always been a controlling cunt."

He glowers at the ceiling, and I can't ignore the part of me that aches in sympathy.

I recognize that look. It's the same one I see the few times I'm brave enough to look in a mirror.

"He hurt you," I deduce. He doesn't react, but I sense it's the truth. "Is that what he does to keep you working for him? Hurt you. Make you commit crimes at his say so?"

"He's getting out of the game," he says tiredly. "It's only until I can break away on my own."

"So, now what?"

"I bought us time," he snaps, his gaze on his hands, bruised and streaked with blood. One by one, he curls a fist, his frown determined. "That's what."

Discomfort congeals in the pit of my stomach, growing with every tidbit of information I wring from him.

But I can't resist asking for more. "What kind of drugs?"

"Bad drugs, bunny. The kind that goes up your nose or into a vein. Shen's been out of the game for years due to the risk —at least directly. He's been focusing on 'legal' revenue, buying up property and shit. Trying to stay clean for a pivot into politics, I guess. The drugs are petty change to him now. He just made me get my hands dirty to prove a point."

What kind of point takes this kind of risk to prove?

"How much money did you give up?" I ask him not out of curiosity—but a twisted need to keep this conversation going. As long as he's still talking, I don't have to process this. Not yet.

He wrinkles his sore lip, pondering the question. "A fucking lot of money."

"Money that you get by selling and buying drugs? And shaking down shop owners," I add, picturing his interactions with Mr. Zhang. "Is this what you do? Sell cocaine or heroin—" the two most dangerous drugs I know of, "and then shake down old men to stay 'legal'?"

He doesn't shy from my accusing gaze. "Bunny, where the hell do you think Zhang's debt comes from?"

"What... I..." Shock renders me speechless.

"The old man's had a problem for years, between that and gambling. That store of his has kept him afloat, but he's racked up more on his tab than you would think. But I let it slide," he adds, staring beyond me. "I thought I could make up the deficit on my own, but..."

"For me," I croak, filling in the blanks of what he doesn't say. "You let it slide because of me."

Silent, he glowers into space, but he lost his grip on the towel in the course of the conversation, letting his arm bleed freely again.

Cautiously, I stand and approach him, eyeing the wound. "He did this to you?" Up close, the viciousness of the injury is on full display. I can't imagine a family member doing this to his own nephew—though I'm not one to talk.

Given their shape, his injuries could be caused by a fist. A shoe. His body striking something hard enough to slice into his arm. Brutal, grueling punishment.

"Don't worry about it," he says, dismissing me with a wave of his good hand.

I don't move. "You might need stitches."

"I might." He cocks his head toward me and lets his hand fall. "You up for it, Florence Nightheart?"

"Nightingale," I correct through a lump in my throat. Sinking down beside him, I wad up the towel and press it against the gash, applying pressure despite his hisses of agony. "I have to stop the bleeding," I explain as he groans. "I'm not even pressing that hard."

"I'll let you in on a secret, bunny," he says, his voice tight. "I fucking hate pain. Hate it. Call me a pussy, but it is what it is."

"Your ribs could be broken," I point out, alarmed by the discoloration over his chest. Not to mention what might happen if the wound on his arm severed an artery. "Why do it? Work for him?" I ask without taking my eyes off the bloodstained towel. "You have money. You have your shop. You have your talent. Or is it all just a front?" I'm surprised by the sheer amount of anger leaching into my tone.

"Why?" He turns his gaze to the ceiling, frowning as if he never considered the question before now. Whatever conclusion he comes to makes him exhale dejectedly. "It's not that simple."

"Explain it then," I snap. "In 'pretty words.' Why?"

"I don't know… Call it genetics."

I pause in my ministrations. "What do you mean?"

"My father ran shit for him," he admits, wincing in pain. "Drugs. Getaway driving. Worse. You name it, I'm sure he did it all for good old uncle Shen. When he tried to get out? Shen cut him off, and—big surprise—the bastard, couldn't hold a stable job. He left my mother to come crawling back to his brother on her hands and knees just to get by."

"So what?" I ask softly. "You follow in his footsteps?"

His eyes blaze, warning I've crossed a line. "What else am I going to fucking do?"

"What you want," I suggest.

He scoffs. "Like you're the expert on that subject?"

But I'm not him. Brave and powerful, armed with an undeniable talent.

"I bet you could make more doing tattoos," I add, observing the flames licking down the length of the arm I'm treating. "You know, *legally*?"

"Is that a dare, bunny?"

I purse my lips, making up my mind on the spot. "You said you owe me? Well, that's how you'll pay me back."

"I thought you were supposed to be working for *me*?" His lip quirks into a genuine smile I'm unprepared for. Crooked and faint, it softens him despite the blood and bruises. He could be a different person—at least until he grits his teeth, closing up once more. "Unless you want to find another way to pay me back?"

Innuendo seeps from his tone. Hunting for a distraction, I peel back the towel, satisfied by the wound's depth once most of the blood is wiped away. "Your arm has stopped bleeding," I deduce, rearing back to meet his gaze. "You'll live. I guess you don't need stitches after all—"

"Shit, your neck." He lashes out, tugging aside the neckline of my shirt. I don't even notice at first what has him so upset—reddened skin quickly turning purple, marred by tiny imprints left by raking nails.

"I know that fucker at the warehouse didn't touch you," he says, scanning my face like a shark catching a whiff of blood. "Your turn for honesty, bunny. What the fuck happened?"

"He found me," I confess, tugging the collar back into place. I don't feel any pain, but Rafe is persistent, running his fingers along my throat.

"Fuck... Why didn't you come here—"

"The door was locked."

He growls and practically tugs me onto the couch beside him. My shirt is off in seconds, his hands spanning my back in its place. "What the fuck did he do?"

"Nothing, but…"

The words won't come, too twisted to voice out loud. His threat. His ultimatum. The fact that despite his deadline looming over my head, the prospect of going back feels as viable an option as learning how to breathe underwater. Impossible.

"He threatened you, didn't he?" Rafe deduces. His fingers slip through my hair and find my chin, urging me to face him. "That motherfucker. What did he want? For you to come back?"

I nod.

"But that's not all," he suspects as though reading my mind. His fingers part through my hair and form a fist, using the handful to tug me further against him. This way, his mouth has easier access to my ear, and his lips brush the lobe, imparting a taste of his heat. "He did something. Said something he knew would make you consider hopping right back to him, scared."

He waits for a reaction, but all I do is go limp, resting my weight against his uninjured side.

"I don't want to think about him," I confess. "Call it what you want. You hate pain, and I—"

"You hate facing him," he says with a dry chuckle. "I'll call that what it is, bunny—you're human. But if you get to make little demands, then so do I."

His expression is carefully blank, leaving me no clue as to his intentions. "What kind of demands?"

He takes my hand in his, lacing our fingers together before lifting them both for inspection. In a way, we almost resemble some twisted representation of a flame—a golden core with glimpses of ivory peeking through.

"You want me to make some money 'legally'?" He makes the idea sound like a cross between outrageous and amusing. "Fine. But in the meantime, I want you to tell me everything. Everything he's done to you from the very beginning. Your words. Your way. I want you to write it. Every last fucking thing."

He manipulates our fingers, encasing mine within his. "That sounds like a boring story," I say.

"*Your* story," he counters. "Give it to me. That's what I want."

"Why?"

He nestles against the back of the couch, making himself more comfortable. "I told you the first time we met—I want to know what goes on behind those bunny eyes."

More specifically—*I want to know what makes a little rabbit like you so damn hard she doesn't flinch when a man presses a knife to her throat.*

"Fine," I concede. "But I still think you'll find it boring."

"Trust me, bunny." His good arm crosses my chest, locking me to his side. "I could use a little boring in my life right about now."

He sounds so genuinely eager it unnerves me.

A man begging for some hint of boring normalcy.

While I'm running from it.

CHAPTER SEVEN

It's starting to become normal, waking up to the scent of coconut, wrapped in warmth. Like this, I can forget everything else. At least until a heavy body stirs beneath me.

"You're late," someone commands against my ear, his voice gruff with sleep. "I expect my employees to be on the floor by nine a.m. sharp. I should dock your pay. How are you going to convince me not to?"

I open my eyes, stretching out my sore limbs. Gray daylight paints the room in hues of silver, giving everything an ethereal glow. The warmth cocooning my body only enhances the serene mood. I feel a childish desire never to move from this spot.

Going off Rafe's relaxed expression, I think he feels the same —if only my hip wasn't resting directly over a particular part of his anatomy.

"Even unconscious, you're a cock-tease," he remarks, his gaze heavy-lidded. "You can't even have mercy on an injured man?"

I roll off of him, observing the rest of the apartment. While we slept, reality didn't recede an inch—his blood paints a trail across the floor, and that infamous case is still in the entryway. I toy with the idea of seeing its contents for myself. Facing the truth might brand the harsh reality into my skull—this man is dangerous—a criminal.

As if sensing my train of thought, he runs his hand down the middle of my back, contradicting the hard image of him I should maintain. "We're starting over," he declares. "I'm a new man, bunny. On the up and up, remember? I'm making money the legal way. After last night... Don't hold that shit against me, deal?"

I stand rather than answer, approaching one of the windows. The street below is mostly empty apart from the average passing car, but no police cruisers—for now. Still, I'm not comforted.

Branden's deadline rings loud and clear inside my head— *But will he if he knows the truth, Hannah? That you're out here selling sex tapes on the internet while he funds your education? Or your school...*

"You okay?" Rafe demands from behind me. I turn to find him on his feet, grasping an armrest.

"Are you?" I toss back. Some of his color has returned, but his chest looks even worse. I'd be surprised if his ribs aren't broken. The pattern of bruising makes it clear what may have caused the injuries, though. The unmistakable imprint of the sole of a shoe. Or a boot. "God, Rafe," I whisper in horror. "Maybe you should go to the hospital—"

"I'm fine," he snaps. To prove it, he staggers into the hallway, moving with the speed and gait of a seventy-year-old man.

I follow him into the bedroom, where he makes a show of fishing a clean pair of clothing from his wardrobe. Only to howl in pain the second he tries to strip his bloodstained pants.

"Son of a bitch!"

"Let me." I cross to him, dropping to my knees.

If I weren't already aware of how this position may look, his low, agonized grunt would reinforce the awkwardness plenty.

"Damn," he rasps.

I look up to find his lower lip seized between his teeth. "If I knew that getting fucked up was one way to get you on your knees, I would have gotten my ass kicked sooner." His voice is too husky to entirely be joking, his mouth twisted in a grimace most men might sport when having to choose between life and death.

I don't know what possesses me to run my fingers down the length of his inner thigh. He groans, his head shooting back. Then he sighs.

"Not nice. Sadly, I'm gonna have to take a rain check," he says. "But damn, do I intend to make it worth your while when I can move without wanting to cough up blood."

I shiver at the promise, but when he winces in actual agony, my brain shifts gears. I gingerly ease his jeans down his legs and help him step into a fresh pair. When I grab a shirt for him next, however, he scoffs and lumbers into the hallway with his chest bare.

"Give me a few minutes," he warns near the bathroom door. "If I scream, I have not learned how to piss one-handed. I've got a lot to work with when it comes to aiming."

I roll my eyes and grab a fresh skirt from my pile in the hallway. After stripping my soiled shirt, I find myself pulling on the one he discarded—a gray graphic tee with a local sandwich shop's logo on the front. When he staggers from the bathroom a few minutes later, I catch sight of my reflection in the mirror behind him.

God, I have to blink a few times to recognize this strange, different Hannah. She's a mess. Wide-eyed. Dazed. Visible bruises mar the flesh near my right eye, and my jaw is a colorful array of browns and purples.

My collarbone draws most of my attention, however. Tiny marks stand out against the flesh there, left by nipping teeth. Days later, they've settled into a deep burgundy reminiscent of a certain dragon tattoo. I finger one, trying to decipher my reaction. It would be wrong to call them beautiful. Logically, I think they should disturb me just as much as the state of my face does.

I can't even begin to fathom why they don't.

"Come on," Rafe calls from the living room. "I wasn't kidding when I said we were running late. If I'm supposed to be a new and improved motherfucker, earning money through legal means, then I need a shop to work out of, don't I?"

That question apparently ends in him limping down the stairs. He enters the front room and thumbs through an arrangement of flyers tucked beneath the counter.

"Where the hell did I put that fucking hardware brochure?" he mutters before withdrawing a handful of flyers with a triumphant grunt.

As he orders a replacement for the door, I sweep the remaining shards of broken glass.

"You'll need flyers, I guess," I tell him once he's hung up. A glance over my shoulder reveals him to be watching me, slumped against the wall in a position he must find the most comfortable. "That's what Mr. Zhang had made for his reopening."

"I guess I do." He shuffles to another corner of the space and fishes out a sheath of paper and a pen. He flattens the sheet with one hand and starts to sketch. I find myself drifting closer, trying to guess the creature he's forming with stroke after stroke.

Gradually, a woman comes to life. Her large, dark eyes stare from the page, full of questioning wonder. Frizzy bangs. Long, curling hair...

"Very funny," I choke out once his subject becomes painfully obvious.

He doesn't look up, his brow drawn in concentration. Soon, his entire posture shifts, as if he's transcended the pain, too intent on his work. His hand moves steadily, possessed by some unnatural grace that allows him to form delicate lines in one motion and harsher broad strokes the next.

"Rafe?"

He doesn't react, blind to everything but this. Drawing. Creating. Bleeding his thoughts onto paper, shaping reality with the swipe of a pen.

My irritation gives way to shameless awe. Some of the emotion swelling in my chest is pure jealousy.

But the rest?

At some point, I have to mentally separate the woman he's drawing from myself. She's too beautiful. Too mysterious, her gaze so penetrating it's impossible to know what she's thinking. Her expression could convey a million different emotions. Interest. Disinterest. Lust. Wonder. Hate.

She's the type of woman I secretly strive to be. Someone confident. Talented. Prideful.

"Done," Rafe declares, shoving the drawing aside. He reaches into his stash again, this time withdrawing two slips of paper and another pen. "I work. You write," he commands, shoving both toward me.

I bite my lip rather than argue.

He's already starting on another sketch, but I sense his intention is to deliberately provoke me this time. The outline is broader, spanning the width of the entire page. Like magic, a figure forms—someone feminine, slender with bare legs, and a delicately curved torso.

"Nice," I scoff, my cheeks flaming.

He has the nerve to meet my stare without an ounce of humor. "Get to work." He taps my untouched sheet of paper. "A deal's a deal, bunny."

He returns to his task, easily shutting out the world again.

Without taking my eyes from him, I pick up the pen. Hold it to the page. Stall…

Set it aside.

"Write," Rafe demands, dropping all pretense. "Tell me what's in your head, bunny. Right now. Don't hold back. Let me fucking have it."

Asshole, I scribble. But that word bleeds into another, and then an entire sentence. Before I realize it, I'm scribbling down a paragraph, the words disjointed and sloppy, the meaning unclear.

But watching him robs me of the doubt I'm used to fighting.

And I hate him for it.

Envy infects me instead. He's so shameless in his expression. My initial suspicion was right, and a lewd display quickly comes together—a naked woman, lying on her side, her gaze concealing a dare. A taunt. A refusal. A beckoning.

She's an infuriating contradiction, her shape etched with brutal detail. Slender hips, perky breasts, and a proud tilt to her chin. I'm frowning, and my pen drifts, forming a slash across the entire page until I drop the pen altogether.

"Stop!" I slam my hand over his sketch, but the look he gives me. It's utter confusion.

"What?" I don't miss how his hand flutters toward the page as if to shield it from sight before he curls a fist.

"I…" I'm insulted…I think. Why? Because… "That's not me." I wait for him to deny that it was ever supposed to be. "I don't look like that."

Like *that*. Bold, displaying naked, beautiful limbs and a sensual appeal that takes my breath away. My blood boils, heated by another jealous thought—how many of his previous conquests did he mash into that picture?

His frown, however, sends my pulse into overdrive. It isn't guilty, like that of someone caught in a bad joke. Head cocked, he runs his fingers over the creature he's created like a man scouring a map, hunting for where he took a wrong turn.

And it hits me like a punch—I've insulted him. Because, as foreign as this woman is to me, to him…

She *is* me.

"I… I mean." My words falter, stammered, and disjointed. In the end, I wrench my gaze back to my page, grab my pen, and keep writing, shutting off the part of my brain that craves to pour over every word. Every line.

I just spill whatever comes to mind, aware of him watching me.

Eventually, he does the same, adding more detail to his drawing until the glimpses I sneak of it leave me more breathless every time. In a childish way, I could call it magic. How he crafts something from nothing. In a few masterful blends of shadow, he has a window in his hands, displaying the world as he sees it.

And what a cruel, mistrustful, mysterious, watchful, magical world it is.

Sometime during the process, I lose track of writing again and just watch him work.

"You have a gift," I blurt out as he blends his final lines with the pad of his finger. "I mean it, Rafe. You—"

"Do the same shit a kid with a crayon would?" His voice is sufficiently harsh, but his eyes give him away. In them, I catch a hint of the vulnerability he works so hard to shield—rebellious pride for his art.

"Your vision is beautiful," I whisper. "It's so beautiful."

"This is nothing." He flips the page over, but before I can argue, he crooks a finger, beckoning me closer. "Come here."

Curiosity mingles with the thrill inspired by his dangerous grin. Warily, I circle the counter, approaching him with increasing anticipation.

"Turn around." He palms my hips to assist me, and then his fingers find the hem of my shirt. Slowly, he lifts it, exposing the curve of my spine to his touch. I go rigid, paralyzed by the sensation of his breaths warming the hollow between my shoulders before his fingertips land over my skin next. Carefully, he begins to trace a series of invisible designs, and my imagination goes wild.

I don't have to see his face to picture his expression. He'll have his eyes narrowed in concentration, his lower lip seized between his teeth. The same careful way he eyed his canvas.

"You asked me once what I'd tat on you," he murmurs, grazing my spine with the pad of his finger. "I'll show you."

"When?" I'm startled by how eager I sound, but he draws back, letting my shirt fall into place.

"When you let me inside that head of yours. I'll give you whatever you fucking want."

"How?"

I'm left reeling as he pushes past me, lumbering down the back hallway and up the stairs. By the time I manage to follow, he's already returning, fully dressed, wearing a pair of boots, keys in hand.

"Where are you going?" I ask as he shoulders open the door to the alley.

"I'm hungry," he says without looking back. "In the meantime, get to work. I want this place spick and span."

As the door closes behind him, I sense there's more he's left unsaid. Something to do with whatever I glimpsed as he drew, paired with his confession.

He wants to know what's inside my head.

But how, when I barely know the answers myself?

I return to the counter where the two drawings remain. Once again, I'm taken aback at how similar the figure he etched looks to me. At the same time, she's an enigma. I run my fingers over her features before folding the page and tucking it into my pocket.

Eventually, I return to his apartment and find my bag near the couch, my notebook still inside it. Curling up near the window, I press my pen to a fresh page.

Emulating him is harder than it should be. That abandon eludes me, his sheer, focused need to draw an alien concept. I'm left fishing for the right words, unsure of how to start.

He wanted me to show him what it's like inside my head. In essence, it's comparable to being a moth. One drawn to a burning, dazzling flame despite the risks.

It will gladly burn in the aftermath.

And, with that imagery in my head, the floodgates open.

A million different phrases spill out as my mind whirls with images of watchful dark eyes and a body like sin. Soon, the rest of the world fades. My universe narrows to a strip of ink, forming whatever is in my head, but it feels as though I'll never have enough time to get it all out—this confession. These words. This magic.

My only tether to the real world comes in the form of a smell at first—sharp and pungent, savory, and spicy. My stomach growls, shattering the trance, as I look up from the pages of my notebook, I'm so shocked by the sight I find, I drop my pen.

Rafe is in the kitchen, shirt off, back to me as he works at the stove. He's cooking, a realization that catches me off guard almost as much as his voice does—low, forming a jaunty, slightly off-key tune.

By now, the man shouldn't be capable of surprising me— but watching him perform such a domestic task serves that purpose and then some.

"What are you making?" I ask, rising to my feet. My legs throb in protest, and a glance at the sunset painting the horizon beyond the window reinforces just how long I've been writing—I've lost hours in what felt like mere minutes.

"Elotes," Rafe declares as I approach. He presents me with a steaming platter of food balanced on one hand. "And tamales."

"Impressive," I declare, and my awe isn't faked—scrambled eggs and salad is the extent of my culinary abilities.

His creation blows both out of the water. Intrigued, I sample the elote—corn slathered in a mixture of spices—and my eyes widen in genuine shock.

"Good, huh?" Rafe smirks, unabashedly smug. "It's damn good."

Too stunned to argue, I nod and attack my plate in earnest. The variety of spices and rich flavor make me suspect he didn't learn this from a random recipe. "Who taught you to cook?" I ask once I've nearly cleared my plate.

"My mother." His face falls, and guilt hits me like a punch to the stomach.

"I'm sorry," I blurt out, but he shakes his head.

"Don't be. She could make one hell of a tamale." He takes a monstrous bite of his and flashes a grin.

"Tell me about her?"

His eyes darken, growing distant again. In a heartbeat, he's miles away, staring into the past where I can't follow.

Just when I think he's beyond my reach, he sighs.

"She was good," he says softly. "Damn good. A good mother. A good woman. She worked her ass off for me. Anything I wanted, I got, whether or not we could afford it. Even if I didn't deserve it. Somehow, someway, she made it happen."

Obvious sadness deepens his voice, and I have a good idea as to why. Gino once mocked him with the awful truth of just how his mother provided for him—by doing whatever his uncle required of her. Anything for her son.

"I was a punk back then," he adds. "I gave her shit like you wouldn't believe, but she never once yelled at me. Never hit me. Never really punished me. 'You're angry,' she used to say. 'Don't pout or throw a tantrum. You let it out. You show me your pain.' Then she'd give me a pad or a pen and make me draw. No matter how shitty it was, she'd always act like it was a Picasso or some shit."

He laughs, and I feel my lips quirk into a smile.

"She encouraged your art," I say softly.

He frowns as if he never put the pieces together himself. "I guess she did."

"And your dad?" I don't know what makes me broach this topic, but his eyes cut to mine, brimming with an emotion that isn't anywhere near love or affection. It's pain. One so raw, he must normally keep it buried deep. Just as quickly, he smothers it with a hardened mask.

"He was a piece of shit," he says. "She cleaned up at one of Shen's clubs back in the day and was nothing more than a conquest to him."

There's more to it, though. Exhaling, he adds, "He wanted to be a singer or some shit. Break away from the triad. Make something of himself. He fed her so much bullshit about the life he'd build for her, all of it a fantasy. But she never lost faith in that lie, even when he turned his frustration on her."

"He hurt her?"

He strokes his bottom lip, lingering near the bruised flesh. "Yes. He hurt her. Damn near every fucking day during the worst of it. Until he went too far."

He's already told me this part of the story. *One night, he got too rough after showing up again out of the blue. He shoved her around, but she didn't get back up. The asshole just laughed and passed out. She would never call the cops on his ass.*

"You look like her. Your mother," I point out, recalling the picture of the woman I caught a glimpse of in his room. "You have her eyes."

"Her eyes." He scoffs, his upper lip curling from his teeth. I worry I've insulted him, until he brushes his finger along the ridge of his cheekbone as if memorizing the shape. "I have those," he admits, letting his hand fall. "But that's it. Nothing else. I don't even want to be like her."

He sounds too cold. Too bitter.

"Why?" I ask.

"Because she gave it all up for a worthless motherfucker. Everything." He turns away, his hands forming fists. "She sold her soul to a son of a bitch for nothing in return. Nothing but pain and bullshit. What good came of that—"

"She had you." I don't know what makes me say it, but he flinches. Gradually, the fire leaves his eyes, and he's ice in an instant.

"I think she'd be proud of you," I add clumsily. "I know she would."

Slowly… Very slowly, he sets his food aside and approaches me. Each step is deliberate, giving me all the time in the world to evade his reach.

I don't, and his arms go around me, his mouth finding my shoulder. I can feel his heartbeat racing, his breaths heavy and labored. Very gently, his fingers slip into my hair, and the soft, hesitant motions goad me into voicing a confession of my own.

"My mother didn't want me." It sounds so dramatic to say and yet so emotionless at the same time. After twenty-one years, I've made peace with it. The admission doesn't hurt anymore, as natural to utter as my own name. "My dad really wanted a boy, and Branden was her ticket to guaranteed alimony if they divorced. I wasn't part of her plan. I barely even have memories of her, to be honest. She didn't teach me how to cook, and she certainly didn't teach me how to write. She just…existed. Until one day she never came back."

He stiffens, and it strikes me that he may suspect the next part of the story before I even say it.

"She was angry after what happened with Bran. Humiliated. I…" I suck in a breath, self-conscious of the admission on the tip of my tongue. "I envy you. I wish I had your memories. I wish I had something of her to cherish. Something to love—"

"No." Abruptly, he pulls away. "No, you don't."

He heads for the door, and his posture alone warns me from following. His shoulders are tense, his steps stiff.

When he leaves, slamming the door behind him, I don't know what to feel. Something tells me that his anger isn't directed toward me—that doesn't mean I don't feel it.

CHAPTER EIGHT

I wake up with my heart pounding as I struggle to make out my surroundings. Something's wrong. The room itself isn't what has me on edge, but a noise. Persistent, heavy pounding from down below. Scrambling to my feet, I tear through the small layout of Rafe's apartment, alarmed to find that he's still not back.

The only item out of place lies on the coffee table—my journal, still open face down. Even before I lift it, I suspect what page it's on. Sure enough, I'm right—my latest piece.

Reading it over now, I'm struck by how different it reads from my usual writing. There are no pretty, careful lines. No abstract phrases.

In blunt, ugly words, a story forms, plain for anyone to interpret. That of a moth who ventured too close to an enticing flame. Given the horror she was fleeing from, the fire was a fitting end...

A rumble of thunder draws my attention as I set the notebook aside. From the window, I can see the sky, gray with a recent storm, the street still wet below. I don't spot Rafe outside either, but as I start for the stairs, I catch the sound of his voice.

"Ah, fuck!"

Downstairs, I find him crouched before the entrance of the shop, wrestling a new door into place. He spots me from over his shoulder and jerks his chin. "Give me a hand, would ya? Hold it here."

I step closer, grabbing the glass frame where he indicates. As he fiddles with a set of metal hinges and screws, I scan his face, hunting for any hint of emotion. Paranoia whispers cruel insinuations of where he could have been.

With Bonnie?

Someone else?

His hair gives me a clue—mussed, slightly damp, matching the soaked pavement outside that betrays overnight rain. He's wearing the same jeans from yesterday too, his chest bare, the dragon on full display.

"Hey!" He nearly drops a screw and shoots me a stern look. "Focus, bunny. I spent too much money on this piece of shit to break it now."

I comply, assisting until he finally has the support in place, and the door stands on its own.

"Good, now go change," he tells me. "You're on the clock, bunny. I spoke to Zhang. Starting today, you work for me, and I won't tolerate your bullshit."

He swaggers into the back room, but I sense from the distance he puts between us that he's still stuck on whatever upset him last night. I toy with the idea of prodding him to tell me what. Instead, I go upstairs, shower, and change into fresh clothing—all my own this time.

Rafe doesn't say a word when I return to find him in the shop's front, arranging materials over the counter. When he finally looks up, his eyes graze over my modest sweater without a reaction.

"Sort these," he commands, shoving a stack of documents my way. "Disclaimers and shit. Anyone who wants a tat needs to sign one, got it?"

He's already gone before I can reply, arranging his supplies and tools on a table across the room. Warily, I creep behind the counter and organize the paperwork. All the while, that awkward tension between us grows, seeping into every interaction. Him handing me a handful of pens feels equivalent to a challenger arming an opponent in a silent war.

He moves stiffly with more than just the pain from his injuries. Any step that takes him away from me is quick, but any that brings him closer carries a speed reminiscent of someone wading through quicksand.

It surprisingly isn't long before the door opens, introducing new people into our dynamic—customers. They look to be tourists, going off their oversized shirts and casual attire. They wander the shop aimlessly as Rafe points out various hanging designs and names prices.

I quickly lose track of my supposed task by watching him. In this instance, he sports a different mask from his cocky swagger or ice-cold aloofness. He's approachable and informative but stern, conveying knowledge of both tattoos and his capabilities to apply one in a way I don't expect. With a few words, he's able to soothe a jittery twenty-something who consents to have a design applied to her ankle.

"I need the paperwork," Rafe snaps to me.

When everything is signed, Rafe guides the client to a leather chair in the center of the room and gets to work.

He's slow and methodical, utilizing the necessary tools with the same care he does his pens. He cleans the area, marks out a rough outline before implanting the actual tattoo using a mechanical object eerily similar to that of a gun.

Roughly an hour later, the client is beaming at his creation, and he has one happy customer down. More are already in the process of following, streaming in and out of the shop to eye the artwork or for consultations.

His flyers must have done the trick. It feels like barely a few minutes go by before someone new enters. As the latest visitor leaves, Rafe cuts his gaze to me.

"What's wrong?" I ask, alarmed by his expression.

"Get out," he hisses. "Now."

"W-What?" I follow his gaze to the front door and spot the beautiful woman about to enter. I barely manage to scramble into the back hallway before the bell above the door chimes.

"Hey Chan," Rafe says. "How you holding up?"

I crane my neck as far as I dare and spot Mara near the front display, her eyes downcast and devoid of makeup. Even her outfit is relatively modest—a T-shirt and jeans.

"I can't believe she's gone," she murmurs, and guilt hits me like a slap to the face. Faith. I've been so worried for myself, I never stopped to think about what Mara might be going through. "I mean, I didn't know her that well," she adds as Rafe draws up beside her. "But it's just so awful. Everyone's shaken up about it."

"It sucks," Rafe agrees. "But don't beat yourself up about it. She wouldn't want you to."

"I know." She sheepishly meets his gaze. "Can I ask you for a favor, though? There's a memorial service planned for tomorrow night—I think your uncle is helping to host it."

Rafe crosses his arms. Is he surprised by that revelation?

"Well, her family wanted a private burial," Mara adds. "But they're allowing this one for anyone who might want to pay their respects. Could you go with me?"

Rafe runs a hand along his jaw, his hesitation apparent.

"My parents are going, but they'll be keeping the Wens company all night, and I don't think I can stomach that. I know it's pathetic, but I at least want to stop by. I would have asked my friend to come with me, but I can't get a hold of her. Please?"

"Alright," Rafe agrees. "I'll go."

Mara beams. "Thank you. I'll even buy you dinner after if you want. I truly appreciate it." She brushes her hand along his shoulder, but he backs away.

"Yeah, no problem." He adjusts the paperwork on the counter, extending the distance between them. "Don't mention it."

"You're probably really busy," Mara says with a nervous laugh. "I nearly passed out when I saw the flyers that you were opening up your client list. I think I can name at least ten people right off the bat who would love to sport a design by you. Myself included." Her cheeks flush prettily, her dark eyes gleaming. "Please tell me that you aren't already booked out for all of eternity?"

Rafe inclines his head for her to approach him. "I think I can make an exception. Here—" he snatches a portfolio from the counter and offers it to her.

Mara flips through the pages, and I figure my expressions must mirror hers every time I view his art. Wide-eyed. Mystified. Seconds from drooling. Admittedly, she seems more impressed by the figure who owns the book than by anything inside it.

"You are so good," she gushes, eyeing him through her lashes. "Do you do tattoos all over?"

"Where are you thinking?" Rafe questions, his gaze on whatever design she's eyeing now.

"Hmm… What about here?" She places the book on the counter and lifts her shirt to expose her sternum and the very edge of a lacy black bra. "I heard some guys find this location sexy."

I hate the jealousy that ignites in my chest, catching my cheeks on fire. A fire fed by the way Rafe's eyes skim the flesh in question.

"Ah… Those hurt like a motherfucker," he warns after clearing his throat.

Mara shrugs. "I trust you," she says. "You'd be gentle with me, right?"

"Right," Rafe says, shifting to a different area of the counter. "So, you wanna schedule? I can fit you in next week."

"So far away?" She pouts, somehow managing to look beautiful and playful at the same time.

They hash out the details until her leaving is finally signaled by the chime of the doorbell. The second I creep from the hall, Rafe sighs.

"Don't fucking look at me like that," he snaps.

"Like what?"

"Like…" He rakes a hand through his hair in frustration. "Like I just fucked her over the counter. And maybe I *should* have. As often as she's been sniffing around my ass, she definitely seems to want it."

"I didn't say anything," I point out—but I don't deny the jealousy either.

"You didn't have to." He storms to the front door and switches the sign from open to closed, locking it from the inside. "I can see it all over your fucking face. And why shouldn't I be attracted to her, huh? You know how many assholes would go for that? I told you once, bunny. I don't do relationships."

But his posture alone warns me that his mood has nothing to do with Mara. He's breathing too quickly, his shoulders tense, hands in fists.

"What's wrong?" I demand, cutting to the chase.

"Wrong?" He barks out a harsh laugh. "Maybe it's time I got some new pussy?"

It takes everything I have in me not to take the bait. He's goading me on purpose, trying to get me to snap, much like a bullfighter waving red.

"You've been like this all morning." I come close enough to place my hand on his back, but he jerks away. "Tell me what's wrong."

"What you wrote… Was it true?"

I stiffen at the heat in his tone. Anger? Judgment?

Was it true—everything I can remember spilled out onto a page.

"Was it?" he demands.

"Yes."

He whirls around and grabs my waist, lifting me off my feet. Two steps back bring us to the counter, and he sets me on top of it, stepping in between my legs.

"Where do you see this going, huh?" he demands, palming the contours of my body through my sweater. "After… Or is this just a fling? A game. You flout mommy and daddy's wishes for a few days and then go crawling back. To them. To him. To the rules, and the money and the boring fucking life you hate. What is this?" He gestures around us with a wave of his hand. "Rebellion? How soon before you go running back to Bran, brother, or not? Just fucking tell me so at least I'm not surprised."

"I can't go back." Hearing it out loud makes my chest tighten, and my eyes burn with the threat of tears. Hope? And terror. I've been lying to myself for so long. Admitting the truth feels comparable to ripping away a Band-Aid and reopening the wound underneath.

"I can't," I repeat. "If I wanted to, I'd be gone by now."

He frowns, still suspicious. I have no choice but to broach the one topic I've successfully avoided until now.

I tell him about Branden's ultimatum, and his expression transforms from rage to disgust.

"That's fucked up," he snarls. "That's—"

"I'm still here." I loop my arms around his neck, trusting him to support my weight. He does, sliding his palms beneath my butt as his heavy sigh rustles my hair.

"Damn," he says. "Do you really think he'd go through with it?"

I shrug. "He wants to control me. He'll do whatever he thinks he has to in order to do that."

He grabs one of my hands from his shoulder, interlacing our fingers. "I've got you," he says softly. "Whether it's for a day. A week. However long you need me, I've got you."

I'm not brave enough to ask him just what that entails. *Me*, with a side of Mara, or Bonnie, or whoever else on the side?

Speaking of Mara…

"I can't keep hiding here forever," I confess tiredly. "Sooner or later, Mr. Zhang… Mara. They're going to find out where I am anyway. How do you feel about that?"

"How?" He raises an eyebrow. "A sexy motherfucker with a sexy bunny at his pad? Trust me, I'll get over the embarrassment."

But he doesn't go further than that, refusing to define our relationship between any definitive boundaries. The sad part? It's not like I even have the right to question that.

So, I take the easy way out by changing the subject. "Do people really get tattoos here?"

I copy Mara by lifting my sweater, but his reaction is the difference between night and day. He strokes his chin, eyeing the bared flesh with renewed interest.

"Here?" He runs his finger down the center of my ribcage, rousing a million goosebumps. "I wasn't lying when I said it hurts like a bitch." But he continues tracing the flesh there, mapping out an invisible design.

I lift my sweater entirely, setting it aside.

Any unease I might feel dies the instant I meet his gaze. I have his full attention, and I lean back, exposing his "canvas" to use as he sees fit.

"Show me?"

A wicked smile shapes his mouth as he crosses the room for a pen. When he returns, however, his focus shifts. Even as he palms my breast, I sense that he's one-hundred-percent intent on the task at hand.

He's an artist at work.

Observing him hunched over paper is one thing, but this… It's an experience in itself. He manipulates the pen expertly, and the design comes to life, stunning in every sense of the word.

"Rafe…"

"Don't speak," he scolds while applying a bit of shading with meticulous care. "Just stay like this. Just like this."

The more he works, the easier that command becomes to uphold—I'm too awestruck to do anything but stare.

Even from this angle, the image spreading across my ribcage is beyond anything I could have expected. Not a bunny. Not even a dragon...

"You read what I wrote."

He's already admitted as much. It's still surreal to see it unfolding—that of the moth and her flame.

"I wrote about you," I whisper, bringing my fingers to his jaw. They're shaking—he feels hot enough to burn, tensing beneath my touch. "And you got what you wanted, right? A look inside my head."

He doesn't bother to say as much out loud. He just draws, utilizing every ounce of flesh at his discretion to bring to life the creature I'd centered my writing around.

A moth, its wings beautifully singed, its detail exquisite. But the feature that makes my throat tighten is something I didn't mention in my scrawled tale. He drew a large, watchful eye on either side of the insect's body, staring impassively at the world, guarding their secrets.

I don't know how much time passes before he finally sets the pen aside and stands, running his hands through his hair. "What do you think—"

I arch toward him, my lips finding his, silencing his startled grunt. Closing my eyes, I relax into the feel of this moment, blinding myself to everything else.

In so many ways, the mock-tattoo feels like the perfect expression of *everything*. Every obscure emotion and inane concept I'd never be able to put into words.

But it's also a warning—what awaits me at the end of this, whatever this is.

Broken wings and searing flame.

CHAPTER NINE

I wake up in Rafe's bed, but this time I'm not alone. He lies next to me, his hand thrown over my waist, his scent in my lungs. I can't resist stroking my fingers through his hair, marveling at the sight of him like this, vulnerable for once, his body devoid of tension.

Some of his injuries look slightly better in the pale dawn light, including the one on his chest. I inch closer, tentatively brushing my fingers over the ridge of his pec.

"Damn, bunny." He opens his eyes, focusing on me. "I thought waking up with your head near my dick was torture enough. You had to go and kick it up a notch."

His words trigger an impulse only he has ever inspired in me. I rise onto my hands and knees, inching back toward the end of the mattress, aware that I have his full attention.

His confusion quickly morphs into shock as I slip my hand between his legs, urging them to part. He does slowly, creating a large enough space for me to crawl in between them while lacing my fingers around the waistband of his sweatpants.

As I drag them down partway, my chest heaves, revealing the trail of dark curls shielding what lies below. I look up to find him watching me avidly, his upper body propped on his elbows.

"Keep going," he commands hoarsely.

I do, easing the fabric down as he shifts to assist me. I'm soon faced with a part of him I've felt in the most intimate way possible. He's beautiful—reddening flesh mapped by a crisscrossing of swollen veins. Carefully, I reach out, tracing the path of one.

I've barely gone an inch as he grits his teeth, his head rearing back against his shoulders. "Fuck, I need you to—"

He can't even put it into words. Instead, he lunges for my wrist and directs my hand downward, and it's as if I can read *his* mind for once.

Open your hands. Like that.

Grip me harder. Harder.

"Shit, bunny." He fists his free hand over the sheets. Soon, a request becomes apparent, written across his gaze as if in blazing neon letters.

Slowly, I sink to my belly with my legs dangling off the end of the bed. Any doubt vanishes the second I see his face. His wet lips slightly parted, his gaze so intent on me that I almost fear I'll combust from the force of it, honed like the full intensity of the sun.

It's cruel how long I make him wait, hovering with my mouth dangerously close to where he craves it the most. Needs it. A vein in his neck jumps the second I brush my tongue along the tip of him, and I'm startled by the taste. Musky. Powerful. Not offensive.

"Jesus," he groans, watching like a hawk as I take him in as deeply as I dare.

A list of supposed actions—all overheard from Mara in vivid detail—cross my mind, only to fade beneath a wave of pleasure that shocks me to my core. Electrifies. Emboldens me.

I stop thinking and focus on wringing every gasp and grunt from him that I can.

"Stop!" He cradles my scalp in his hands, urging me off of him.

My confused glance is met with a growl as he flips me over, straddling my hips. He makes short work of my skirt and shirt. Then, our lips meet, his easily overpowering mine as his hand slips between my legs, easing a finger inside me.

My readiness makes him groan as he rocks his hips to replace the digit with a larger appendage. He thrusts in hard, letting my body greedily adjust to his size.

It's a sinful cross between pleasurable and painful. Then he strokes out, and in again, and it's fire. My mind reels with how vital an act can seem, though you've gone most of your life without it. How a single touch, kiss, and bit of contact can rival any other desire life has to offer. It's like my body didn't know what *feeling* truly was until it learned to grapple with the invasion of his.

The sheer depth of what it can be like to be known by someone else so deeply.

How dangerous it can feel to burn beneath another's body heat.

How good.

How reckless.

How destructive.

It's only in the early afternoon when Rafe finally drags himself from the mattress long enough to heat up some food. We devour leftover tamales at the counter, and he eyes the time on the microwave with a curse.

"I've got some shit I've gotta take care of," he says, setting his plate aside. His eyes cut toward the door, and I wonder if the 'shit' on his mind has anything to do with the ultimate destination of the briefcase we took from the warehouse.

"And Faith's service is tonight. I should really go see Mara," I add, forced to face the reality of just how terrible a friend I've been to her.

"And what are you going to tell her?" Rafe wonders. His back is to me, obscuring his reaction. From his tone alone, I can't tell just what he wants to hear. For me to keep our fling secret? Or save him the hassle of having to avoid Mara's attempts at flirtation.

"I don't know."

"Do you want me to drive you?" he asks. "In case you run into him?"

I suck in a breath and try to imagine what could be worse. Facing Branden alone, or pitting him against Rafe? I quickly decide on an answer and shake my head. "I'll be fine."

"Fine," he repeats before turning on his heel and padding down the hall as I gape in alarm.

"Rafe?" I start to follow, but he's already returning, an item in hand.

"Take this." He hands me a small device that takes my brain a second to identify—a cell phone, a much more modern style than my old one.

Gratitude is a living thing, threatening to crawl up my throat. "Thank you."

"My number's in it," he adds, starting for the stairs. He's already thrown on a fresh pair of clothing and donned his boots. Clenched in one of his hands is the handle of that infamous case. "I'll see you tonight."

He looks back as if to gauge how I'll respond to the invitation.

"Okay," I say with a nod. "Tonight."

He heads down the stairs, taking them two at a time. From the base of them, he calls back, "And take the spare key. It's on the hook."

Sure enough, I spy one, hanging from the same spot he kept his car keys.

I take my time showering and getting dressed before arranging my hair in the best way possible to cover most of the bruising. In the end, I leave it down and sigh in defeat. To be honest, the worst of the bruising is already starting to fade, leaving brownish splotches around my eye and down my chin.

Ironically, my neck looks the most ravaged, sporting fresher, bright red spots from this morning. When I finally leave the shop, I take the back roads to the restaurant district, jumping at any sudden noise to pierce the quiet.

I'm not ready for the true depths of paranoia that descend the further I go. Every person passing by morphs and transforms into someone else. Branden. Then I blink, and they reform into a businessman, a passing child, or another stranger. And each time, it's like I can hear him, scoffing at my attempts at normalcy.

You're a video star now, Hannah. You're a fucking slut. A liar. A whore. Say cheese…

"Hannah!" I blink and nearly run into the smiling figure who races forward to greet me. "I've been looking all over for you, girl!" Mara explains, throwing her arms around my shoulders. "It's like you fell off the face of the earth. Where the hell have you been?" She draws back, and her expression transforms as her mouth drops open, her eyes widening. "Oh my god. What happened to your face?"

She runs her finger across my cheek, but I gently evade her touch and force what I hope passes for a smile. "Would you believe that I ran into a door? I'm so clumsy."

"You ran into a door," she says, deadpanned. Her raised eyebrow betrays her true thoughts on that explanation, but I race to change the subject before she can say as much out loud.

"I heard about Faith. I'm so sorry."

"Yeah." She frowns, real sadness shaping her features. "It feels kind of weird to be pushing noodles, all things considered."

This time of day, foot traffic is light, the lunch rush over. Judging from her outfit—a black blouse and skirt—she must have been manning the hostess station of her parents' restaurant and saw me approach.

"So, where the hell have you been, Dewitt?" she demands, placing her hands on her hips. "I've tried calling you. Don't tell me your charger is still 'lost.'"

"Try my phone, actually," I say. It isn't a complete lie. To prove it, I withdraw the one Rafe gave me. "I have a new one."

"Nice," Mara says with genuine admiration. She snatches it and programs her number in before handing it back. "I wanted one of those, but they're fucking expensive. Anyway, where have you been?"

"I decided to go with my brother to the beach for a few days." God, it's almost terrifying how easily the lies come. *Because it's all you're good at, Hannah,* a part of me hisses. *Just like Branden says. You're a liar.*

"Oh, well… Now that you're back, we should totally hang out. I know it's kind of morbid, but Faith's memorial service is tonight—not like a funeral or anything. You don't have to dress up. Rafe said he'd go with me, but—"

"I'll go with you."

She smiles. "Thank God. At least I'll have a wingman for if I fall flat on my face again. Like damn, I know it's utterly trashy to try to pick up a guy at a memorial, but I just don't get this one. I mean, from what I hear, he's fucked half the girls in this town. But *I* practically flash my titties at him and…" She trails off, blushing. "Never mind. But damn, it's like some kind of personal conquest now. I will fuck that asshole or die trying. It's the principle of the matter."

"You're too good for him, Mara," I blurt out. "Besides, you could have any guy you want."

"But I want that guy," she declares, stubbornly jutting her chin. Her teeth seize her lower lip as she groans. "And he is so sexy. And nice—I heard from my parents that he offered to pay for Faith's funeral expenses as well as the reward for any information on her case. Five thousand dollars."

"He did?" I don't know why the thought surprises me.

Maybe because it brings one good point into question—what was the nature of his relationship with Faith in the first place?

"He did," Mara insists with a nod. "Let me tell my folks I'm on break, and then we can catch up on all of the gossip. You've missed a lot, girl. And I want to hear all about this 'vacation' that left you with even more hickies on your neck than before."

I feel my cheeks catch fire as I brush my hand along my throat. Even with the high neckline of my sweater, the marks are obvious.

"I hope the same culprit isn't responsible for the 'door' you ran into," she adds pointedly. "I know you don't have a lot of experience with guys, Han, but trust me. Anyone who puts their hands on you isn't worth the dick."

"It's not like that," I say, brushing my hair forward to cover most of the bruising. "But I will take you up on that lunch offer."

"Great!" She skips off, entering the Chans' restaurant, and I instinctively start to follow her as the back of my neck heats with awareness.

A glance over my shoulder reveals no one in sight—but I feel it. He's here, watching me...

"You ready?" Mara asks, appearing by my side, a black leather purse in hand. "Let's go. I'm starving."

I follow her, but the uneasy dread in my gut only intensifies, lasting through our entire walk to a nearby café.

And I swear that this time, the figure I catch as I glance behind me isn't a figment of my imagination.

"So, who are you fucking, and for how long?" Mara questions from over the rim of her latte. Winking, she smacks her glossy lips together and leans over her pink place setting. "Tell me everything."

We're seated at a table near the front windows, which provide a good view of the main street—and anyone who might happen to walk by. I can't stop my gaze from darting to it every few seconds just to scan the foot traffic. So far, I've only noticed a few workers dressed in business attire or the average tourist. No Branden. Yet.

"Hey!" Mara reaches over the table to tap my shoulder, and I reluctantly turn my attention back to her. "Spill, bitch," she demands. "I've told you about all the assholes I've fucked. Your turn."

"He's…" I swallow hard as the truth sticks to the back of my throat. Coming clean now would be the smart thing to do. The right thing. For whatever reason, I can't make myself form the words. "No one."

Mara raises an eyebrow. "No one. Damn, I didn't know the 'air' was into rough sex. I guess I've been masturbating all wrong—"

"Mara!" I steal a sip from my coffee if only to disguise how my cheeks flame. "You are so bold." Forcing a laugh, I fake a smile that she doesn't return.

"Fine," she snaps, rolling her eyes. "We'll leave that topic—for now. So how is the writing going? You get your essay done yet?"

"Not yet."

"The deadline's coming up," she warns. "Not that I'm one to talk. It feels like I haven't written anything good in ages. Like my sexual frustration is translating to a creative block. Damn Rafe Wei-Shen!"

"You said he's slept with everyone?" I ask only to instantly regret doing so. It's a dangerous topic to broach.

Dangerous, and at the same time, too tempting to ignore.

Mara nods. "Almost everyone. The sexy people, anyway. One could say he has a type—big tits and a bigger ass. But he's strictly transactional. His conquests give him what he wants, and he'll give them a shopping spree or two. Maybe some cash. I hear he's even into threesomes." She giggles. "Hey, maybe if I text him to come over with *you* here, he might bite?"

"Don't," I croak as she brandishes her phone for emphasis.

Still giggling, she stows it beneath the table, though I can't see if she's typing a text from here.

Her eyes meet mine, suddenly stern. "Though… On a serious note, rumor has it, he was seeing Faith before she died. Bad boys, I can do. Murderers? No go."

"What?" It's like the universe narrows to this table, and everything else disappears. I'm biting my lip, so hard I taste copper though I don't feel anything.

"Yeah," Mara says, sounding miles away. "Someone I know said he saw them together a lot at his club. And he helped in the search for her, and now that he's paying for her funeral, well it makes sense. But baby boy isn't the sentimental type. He must have really liked her. Or," she adds, lowering her voice conspiratorially. "He feels guilty. It's not public knowledge, but I heard from my parents—who have been trying to keep the Wens company with everything going on—that Faith's phone is missing. Maybe someone didn't want it found? Like, she could have had tons of nudes on it or something, though Rafe doesn't strike me as the type to be embarrassed by that. Hey… Are you okay?" She snaps her fingers beneath my nose until she has my full attention. "You went all space cadet there for a minute."

"I'm fine," I insist, but I'm already scanning the window again, this time in search of a distraction. Anything to get my mind off the selfish, sordid thoughts circling my brain.

But as a familiar figure comes into view, I realize that I got my wish.

"Good," Mara says, oblivious to how I stiffen in my seat. "Because I need you to help me plan the sexiest outfit ever that one could realistically wear to a memorial service—"

"Oh, no." The exclamation slips out the second I realize that the specter crossing the street doesn't disappear when I blink. *Liam*, heading straight for the café's entrance. He must be off, sporting a plain white shirt and jeans instead of his uniform, but he looks anything but relaxed.

He's angry.

"Hannah?" Mara exclaims as I lurch to my feet. I don't even think I choke out an explanation to her as I scramble for the exit.

I'm so focused on making it outside that I nearly run into someone on my way out of the door. He grabs my arm before I can pull away. One look at his face and I can tell he isn't here by accident.

"Hannah?" Narrowed and focused, his eyes latch onto me with an intensity I've never seen from him.

"Liam…" I croak. Self-consciously, I lift my hand to shield the worst of the bruising, but it's too late.

Without invitation, he brushes his thumb along my cheek, gingerly prodding the skin. Concern unfurls across his face, hardening the already stern tilt to his mouth. He doesn't look surprised. Just resigned. "Damn, Hannah. What happened? Branden said you were okay, but—"

"What did he tell you?" I demand, unable to keep the alarm from my voice. I whip around, hunting for any hint of my brother lurking nearby.

The street is nearly empty, and when I return to Liam, he looks taken aback. "He didn't say much," he admits. "Just that you were in some kind of trouble."

I suck in a breath to disguise my unease. Just how many lies is Branden spinning about me?

"I tried to check on you at the bookstore," Liam adds. "Luckily, I happened to see you walk this way. Are you okay?"

"I'm fine." I try to pull away, but he's persistent, trailing his thumb beneath my injured eye.

"That's not what I'm worried about," he admits. "I'm not an idiot, Hannah. These days you look like you're haunted. I've been worried about you. If you tell me what's wrong, I can—"

"I'm fine," I insist more forcefully this time. "I promise. Thank you for worrying, but you don't have to. But... Maybe you can help me with something else."

Rafe's suspicions keep bouncing around in my head. Now seems like as good a time as any to get some answers.

"What?" Liam asks.

For a second, I toy with the idea of how to spin the question as sneakily as possible. How to lie. Deceive. In the end, I come to the honest truth—there is no other way to put it than bluntly. "What do you know about the Wen murder case?"

His brow furrows as his thumb stills near the corner of my mouth. "Not much," he admits. "It's considered high profile due to all the exposure. Most of what I know is just gossip."

But his eyes flicker away from mine, suddenly evasive.

"I heard there might be other girls who have gone missing," I say, trying a different tack. "And Faith worked at this club. I think it's called Stella's. Do the police know anything about—"

"Stella's?" His tone is a fraction harder. Definitely more suspicious than shocked. Slowly, he withdraws his hand from my face, letting it fall to his side. "Hannah, what is this about?"

"One of my friends knew Faith," I say, which isn't technically a lie, and I allow my real desperation to leech into my voice, strengthening the claim. "I want to give her whatever comfort I can regarding the investigation. Is there anything at all you can tell me? Even something small. Please."

He sighs and shoots a glance over his shoulder before leaning in toward me.

"Well…I know they have one suspect," he admits. "I don't know who exactly. Just that he sent the last known message to her phone."

I feel my eyes widen as I recall what the officer told Rafe the other day. "I thought they couldn't find her phone?"

"They're keeping it hush for now," he says, stiffening as a group of people walk by, none of whom seem interested in our conversation. Stepping closer to me, he adds, "Her phone was wiped. They were able to pull some of her texts via her cloud, but not everything. Some of it was encrypted, I think. They also questioned one of her friends. A Lylah, something, about some guy who might have been giving her trouble."

It takes everything I have to keep any ounce of recognition from my face. Lylah. Was she the same girl Rafe and I talked to? If so, the police could know all about the mysterious DW. "What did she say?"

Liam shakes his head. "Look, I shouldn't even be telling you this stuff. Now you tell *me* something. What happened to you?"

I force another quick smile and pivot on my heel toward the café. "It's nothing. I should really get going—"

"Then let me ask you about something else," Liam says. "I googled her. That girl you told me about. Lexi Winacott."

My feet stop listening to my brain, and I nearly trip before stopping short entirely. "You what?"

I sense his steps approach before his hand settles over my shoulder. "I'm so sorry you had to go through that, Hannah. I'm so sorry. If you need to talk about it, I'm here. I mean that. About you. About Branden... About anything. I'm not saying this out of duty, either. I care about you—"

"Branden," I rasp, whirling around to face him. "Did you tell him? About Lexi? Did you?"

He tilts his jaw, his eyes unreadable. "No. Should I?" He scans my face as if hunting for a certain reaction. Whatever he finds makes him ask in a softer tone, "Has he told you what's been going on with him lately? I know it's none of my business, but..."

"What do you mean?" Dread builds in my stomach, impossible to hide any longer. Licking my lips, I once again aim for the truth. "About his suspension?"

From the way he purses his lips, he looks almost...relieved. "He told you then," he says with a sharp nod. "He made me swear not to say anything, but I've been worried about him lately—what's wrong?"

I can only imagine how I must look.

Horrified?

Behind Liam, a living shadow darts from across the street, heading straight for us. My brain identifies him instantly, but I'm nowhere near fast enough to head him off.

"Rafe!" I shout uselessly. "Don't!"

It's too late.

Too enraged, he doesn't seem to hear me. In a blur of motion, he rams into Liam from behind, nearly taking him off his feet with one blow. His fist already poised for another, his upper lip drawn from his teeth in a mask of sheer rage.

I stagger between them, trying to brace my hand against Rafe's chest. Solid muscle ripples beneath my palm, impossible to control. It's like trying to stop a charging bull. With little effort, he pushes past me, singularly focused on his target.

"Don't," I shout, clawing at his forearm. "Rafe, don't! It's not him! He's not Bran!"

He draws back suddenly, his fist still raised, eyes blazing without a shred of confusion contributing to the anger. Just rage. Fury. Betrayal. The second they fixate on me, I realize the truth. He *knows*. Whether he figured out before he hit Liam, or after, doesn't matter, he knows now.

And his rage hits me like a blowtorch, scorching whatever pathetic excuses I had prepared for this moment.

All I can do is reach for him, sick with guilt. "I'm sorry. I'm so sorry—"

"Fuck you." He squares his shoulders, turning on his heel despite the commotion swirling to life in his wake. Alarmed bystanders gape as Liam swipes at his nose. It's bleeding.

"Let me help." I rush to him and fish through my purse for a spare napkin. "Here."

"What the hell was that about?" he demands, staring after Rafe, who's already halfway down the block. "Do you know that guy?"

I say nothing, and when the worst of the bleeding stops, Liam shrugs me off. "I've gotta get to work," he says, swiping at his nose. With his free hand, he snatches something from his pocket and presses it into my hand. "Here. If you need me, I'm on tonight. Damn it, that asshole's lucky I don't press charges."

"Don't," I plead, but he's already crossing the street, still clutching at his nose.

It isn't until I finally turn to face the café that another realization hits with the strength of a gut punch. *Mara.* I race back to our table only to find her already gone. The check has been paid but scrawled across the bottom of the receipt is a simple message—*Thanks for being such a good friend.*

Feeling slapped, I leave the café and start down the block, hunting for any sign of her. What I'll say if I do find her, I have no idea.

But she's gone. I don't even find her near the Chans' restaurant. Desperate, I try texting her, but minutes pass without a response.

I keep walking as I wait for one, melding with the afternoon foot traffic. I'm halfway across town before I realize—I have nowhere to go.

Rafe's feels off-limits, and my old lease runs out in just a few short days. My only haven is a building I find myself approaching out of habit.

I nearly sigh in relief once I find the Paper Crane is open, blazing with light as the sun starts to set. A few customers litter the shop as I enter and see Mr. Zhang at the counter. He eyes me warily, lingering over my bruises.

"I heard you were taking off for a few days," he says without broaching any other topic.

"Yeah, well… I'm back," I say, unable to come up with any reasonable excuse. The pity in his gaze warns that I don't have to, and I feel bold enough to ask for the one thing I don't have a right to. A distraction. "If you want me to close up, I can."

"Hmm." He eyes me for what feels like a solid minute. Then he nods and grabs his bowler hat from a hook on the wall. "I'll head home early. You can close out the register too. And there's an envelope," he adds, his voice low with double meaning.

Too grateful to argue, I watch him go, mulling over what Rafe revealed about him. Could such a kind, hardworking man have a darker vice?

Though, who is anyone really beyond the façade they present to the world? To so many, Branden is the perfect gentleman, an upstanding citizen. The paragon of goodness and an inspiration to people like Liam.

But inside? Darkness dwells within him, too entrenched to overcome.

Speaking of Liam…

I'd shoved whatever he'd given me into my pocket. Unfurling it now, I realize it's a business card, complete with his number. Despite the chaos that unfolded today, my brain keeps coming back to one image again and again. The way he looked at me when I mentioned Branden's suspension.

That strange, unexpected reaction flickered across his face too quickly to appreciate in full then. Pouring over it now, I'm confident enough to name it for what it was.

Hope. Like he wanted to say more but wasn't sure how.

My brother is good at maintaining his façade, but what if even Liam has seen through it?

A conflicting array of emotions wash over me, setting my skin on fire and making my hands shake. The doubt is the worst part, the uncertainty.

For a dangerous second, I play with the prospect of telling Liam everything.

But even trying to imagine Branden's retaliation makes me shrink from the thought. As I settle behind the counter, my mind turns to another topic I've been deliberately avoiding —the video. Would he really upload it? Has he done it already?

I scan the various patrons perusing the bookshelves. Will one of them happen to stumble across a video of a girl having sex in her bed with a man adorned by a dragon tattoo?

The act itself isn't what makes me feel so helpless; I have to blink back tears. It's what it conveys. The lack of control over my own body cuts deep, more violating than any other action Branden's taken so far.

Except, maybe in the old days. In those memories, I've spent years avoiding. They feel as foreign to me now as old, dusty photographs tucked into a box at the back of a basement or attic.

The days of Lexi, and Branden, and the twisted ending to that saga.

"Excuse me?"

I startle to awareness and find a woman standing before me, holding a book.

"I'd like to buy this, please," she says.

"Sure." I ring her up and turn my attention to the remaining customers. By the time closing approaches, I've seen a steady stream of business, more than enough to distract from my thoughts. When the store is finally empty, I take my time cleaning up before stepping out into the night.

Now what? A part of me wonders.

A glance at my phone reveals an absence of text messages from either Rafe or Mara. All I can do is stare at the clock, pouring over my options. Should I go back to my old apartment? Wait for Branden to track me down, if he isn't on my heels already?

Or go to Rafe…

He's probably with Mara now, heading to Faith's memorial. I don't have a right to feel a damn thing about it, especially not jealousy.

Not that he'd need a reason to move on, that hateful voice in my head taunts. *He told you before—you're just a fling—a diversion.*

Even so, they both deserve an apology in person.

I exit the bookstore and find myself heading toward the park Mara mentioned. The service itself isn't hard to spot— a circle of ethereal orange, the result of the assembled crowd, and each attendee holding a lit candle. As I approach, a woman hands me my own as well as a brochure sporting a smiling photo of Faith. I flinch at the image. She looks so happy. So innocent.

Could Branden really be responsible for her death?

I squash the thought without deciding on an answer and creep closer to the circle of mourners. It's too dark to make out anyone from this distance. I have to wander from person to person as a speaker recites a list of Faith's attributes.

I listen avidly, caught off guard by the depth of emotions each speaker conveys. It's a beautiful if somber service. But I don't see Mara or Rafe. It isn't until my third trip around the gathering that I spot two figures who make my heart sink with recognition. The first thing I notice is a pathetic, selfish observation—they resemble a couple. The man is taller, his arm protectively thrown around the woman's shoulders. It isn't until they pass the glow cast by a lit candle that my suspicions are confirmed.

Rafe spots me first, his gaze rigid and indecipherable. Without taking his eyes off me, he murmurs something to Mara and pulls away. Deliberately, he takes a step in another direction, but a sharp jerk of his head warns me to follow.

My heart pounds with every step I take, letting him lead me away from the gathering to a quieter section of the park. The second I'm close enough to touch him, I rush to speak. "I'm sorry—"

"Save it," he snaps. In the dark, his features take on an angular, fearsome appearance. In a way, he seems more like his dragon than human. "I don't want to hear your fucking excuses. I'm done. You want to fuck your 'brother,' then, who am I to stop you?" A harsh laugh punctuates the taunt, making my cheeks flame.

"I wasn't lying about Bran," I say in a rush. "But… The man you've seen me with isn't him. His name is Liam. He's just a friend."

He rolls his eyes, hissing in annoyance. "Where have I heard that line before? A friend. Like Mara is your 'friend,' right? The one you've let try to fuck me left and right? Well, maybe it's time I finally did."

In a blur of motion, he surges past me in the direction of the ongoing service.

Eyeing his retreating back, I've never felt so damn pathetic. "I'm sorry," I say.

He stops mid-step, but if I were to hope I've convinced him, the glare he aims over his shoulder proves otherwise. "No, you're not," he growls. "You're a liar, *Hannah*. I'm done being your little fuck boy. You don't trust me, and I sure as fuck don't trust you. Oh, and just in case 'Liam' doesn't take your ass in, feel free to stay at my place. I certainly don't plan on sleeping in my own bed tonight."

He stalks off, and the pain I feel piercing through my chest shouldn't come as such a shock. Nonetheless, I have to bite my lip to silence another word. The worst part? I can't even blame him.

Or the figure sauntering toward me now, her head held high. Her cold, hard stare warns that she's fully prepared to finish what he started.

"So, just how long have you been fucking him, huh?" Mara demands, her hands on her hips. Several people turn to stare, but she doesn't bother to lower her voice. "He denied it," she adds haughtily. "But he didn't have to. I just wish my so-called friend would have been the one to tell me so that I didn't make an ass of myself, trying to seduce a man who's already taken. I knew you were an ice-cold bitch, Hannah. But that's low, even for you. Why are you even here?" she adds, gesturing around us with a wave of her hand. "It's not like you give a damn about Faith. Or is it because of him?" She jerks her chin in Rafe's direction as he departs. "You're so desperate to stay on his dick, you'll chase after a dead girl? That's sick, Hannah."

"Mara!" I start toward her, but she spins on her heel and marches away, drawing disapproving glances from those on the outskirts of the service.

As the attention turns to me, I set my candle aside and start across the park. Shame sears my eyes with the threat of tears and tightens my throat. Deep down, I know I don't have the right to be upset.

I *am* a liar. One who's gotten so good at it, she fools herself most of all…

"I don't know what you're talking about," comes a voice that freezes me in my tracks, snapping me from my thoughts.

Rafe. His tone is even colder, but I sense that even before I turn in his direction, he isn't talking to me.

However, he's close only a few feet away near a swaying copse of trees—and he isn't alone. A taller man stands across from him, his silhouette stiff and formidable. Even with his face in shadow, I recognize him instantly—Rafe's uncle.

"Don't play games with me, Rafael," he growls. "First, you pussyfoot around our enemies. Then a girl is murdered in our territory, and you do nothing. Fucking seems to appeal to you more than upholding your duty."

Rafe remains rigid. Frozen. I'm too far back to see his face clearly, but I have no trouble picturing it—watchful eyes, terse frown. The way he suddenly shifts reveals even more. He's on edge.

"I don't understand why you're itching for a fight so badly," he says in a tone that rings out firmly. Cautious. "Gino's just a punk—"

"You don't decide that," Shen snarls. "I do. And I think it's time I stop coddling you, the same way I had to stop enabling your father's bad habits."

"What are you saying?"

"I'm saying if you want to play at independence, then fine. Start with repaying Zhang's debt, you can repay me for your little shop as well. Consider yourself financially independent. I'm done bankrolling your ass."

"I earned my money," Rafe says so fiercely my gut clenches in response. He sounds the same way he did when he spoke of his mother. When he swore he was nothing like her. "I've done everything you've asked of me."

"Have you?" Shen cocks his head in a way I can only describe as smug. "I don't think so, boy. You shy away from using force to protect our territory. You balk at anything that might offend your pathetic idea of morality—but you forget. Everything you are, everything you have is because of me. Do you really think you can stand on your own?"

He turns, leaving Rafe to follow.

Which, despite a second of hesitation, he eventually does.

Dread rips through my chest as I watch him go, his shoulders hunched. In contrast, his uncle moves leisurely, radiating confidence in a way that makes me shiver, though I have no idea why.

Several seconds pass before the realization slaps me in the face—he walks the same way Branden does. So sure of his control, he doesn't doubt for a second his hold on the person under his thumb.

Like a predator.

They're barely out of view when another sound catches my ear—a persistent, musical ping. It's coming from my bag, and I reach inside. Instantly, my hand falls over Rafe's phone, the culprit of the noise. It's pinging with incoming messages. I scan them warily, feeling the air leave my chest as I register the topmost one.

Where are you?

From Branden? Somehow, he got ahold of this number, always one step ahead. I whip around, eyeing the shadows. I'm so ready for him to jump out from behind a tree, eager to corner me again. As I open my stance, I try to tell myself I'll fight this time. Scream. Run. Anything but stare and wait. And wait...

Heart pounding, I look down and realize that the sender's name is already programmed into the phone.

Sexy motherfucker.

Confusion robs my body of tension as another message appears on the screen from that same sender.

Stay at my place tonight, he warns. *Don't be a dumbass. Your "brother" isn't the only asshole looking for you. Gino's been running his mouth. You'll be safe at the shop.*

I swallow hard as a million different emotions hit me all at once. Somehow, I manage to compile a reply, fighting against my shaking fingers. *Where will you stay?*

Wherever the fuck I want, he responds within seconds. *With whoever the fuck I want.*

I clench my jaw, knowing that I'm reacting just how he wants me to. Hurt.

All I can think of to type back is a pathetic plea. Bonnie would make a fitting rebound, but…

Don't use Mara to punish me.

Don't play the victim, he counters. *She's a big girl and can handle herself. But can you? Gino's men won't fall for those bunny eyes. Don't. Be. A. Dumbass.*

He's right—and knowing that stings more than any insult. Sighing, I look up and try to guess my location in relation to his shop. I head there slowly, not out of guilt or a sense of duty. Mainly pure self-preservation and a niggling, selfish impulse that won't let my thumbs leave the cell phone's screen.

Liam is a friend, I find myself typing. The excuses keep coming one after the other, written without any pretty prose —just stark honesty. *I used him to make you jealous. I won't deny that.*

Holy fuck, Rafe snipes, his hostility palpable even through the screen. *Is that the truth? Give the woman a goddamn medal. Now, if you'll excuse me, I aim to be balls deep in some pussy. Preferably one belonging to a bitch without a "Liam."*

Again, I flinch as his barb hits its target.

Beyond the cruelty, I have to admit that I'm impressed by the extent of his vocabulary. In fact, I think he's deliberately trying to provoke me on that front, proving once more that he's not the punk he pretends to be.

So in the spur of the moment, I drop my own guard and copy his tactic.

I express the one thing I don't think he expects from me—the truth.

You scare me, I confess, hitting send before I can rethink the message.

His next reply—if he's preparing one at all—doesn't come right away this time. Tearing my gaze from my phone, I spot a familiar street sign and feel some shred of relief. I'm near his shop already, and I slip into the alley, approaching it from the back instead of the front. It takes me a few seconds of fumbling with his keys before I get the door open and enter his apartment.

When I sink onto the couch, he still hasn't replied. I exchange my clothes for a nightshirt and enter his room, crawling onto the bed.

Still no answer.

Because I do trust you, I add, letting my fingers linger over every letter until I finally hit send.

Judging from how quickly his next reply comes, he's been anticipating as much.

Lying. Fucking around. Treating me like a dirty little secret. Some definition of trust, he says.

While being "balls deep in pussy"? I can't tell. It startles me just how much the prospect stings. Him with someone else. Another woman tracing the swirls of his tattoo with avid interest. Someone else moaning into his ear. Clawing at his back. Someone else in his arms, relishing his heat.

Mara?

Bonnie?

An entirely different woman?

It doesn't matter. In this arena, he's resorting to his preferred weapon of choice—sex.

I don't want to be with Liam, I admit, fully aware of how pathetic continuing this conversation might seem. Someone like Mara would probably block his number and go on with her night. She wouldn't beg.

But Mara never saw the man he is beneath the mask. Even if I wrote off his bravado and swagger, I couldn't escape one glaring image in my head—his face when he saw me with Liam. That rage wasn't faked. Or the pain.

I hurt him.

So I keep typing, even at the expense of my pride. *I don't want you to be my dirty little secret. I want to be with you.*

I see the flashing symbol indicating he's responding in real-time. My breath sticks in my throat, staying there as the seconds pass before the symbol vanishes without another message. For a minute. Longer.

Ironically words are supposed to be my medium. My outlet. My one way of getting my intentions out into the world unfiltered.

But there's no pretty way to spin what I've done to him. No way to wiggle out of this web of lies. In a moment like this, I can only show him.

My heart races as I sit up and strip my shirt without thinking through the consequences. Adrenaline feeds through my blood, but doesn't provide any extra confidence. I'm scared. Niggling paranoia mocks me with all the ways this moment could be violated. Branden could have snuck in somehow and hidden another camera, spying on me from a distance.

It would certainly explain why he hasn't already broken down the door and dragged me back to his home by my hair.

But for the first time in my life, another fear takes precedence over my apprehension of him. It's simple and selfish at its core—I like being free. I relish every minute spent away from him.

And even if he's done with me, I don't want to lose the one person who made this possible. Sucking in a breath, I manipulate the camera to face me and strike the shutter button. A heartbeat later, the resulting image floods the screen.

She's a world apart from Rafe's beautiful, stylistic image.

This figure is one-hundred percent how I see myself. Me. Wide-eyed and unsure, my shirt off, breasts bare. My body exposed.

All of the reasons not to send it race through my mind, forming a mantra of sorts. If anyone could use this against me, it would be him. As blackmail when he grows bored of me. As leverage over my brother and his position as an officer. As pure fodder to feed his stud reputation.

The list goes on and on.

But the more I stare at myself, the more nuances I pick up that I'd overlooked at first. And I come to one startling conclusion—I was wrong. The look in my eyes isn't shame or fear. Instead, it's a mirror image of the one he crafted in his sketch of me.

Guarded. Mysterious—but with a hint of the emotion, he exudes in spades—honesty.

Any doubt I had vanishes as I hit send and slump onto my back, staring up at the ceiling. He could reply with some cruel comment or never at all. He could be fucking Mara or who knows who else.

He could be doing whatever he can to hurt me back. To punish me for lying to him.

I still don't think I'd regret it. For the first time in my life, I caught a glimpse of the Hannah I never see in my own reflection. The woman he's been taunting me with all along.

She's real.

I'm more than some fearful, little bunny.

As the seconds tick by without a response, I'm resigned to the fact that this is all I'll get from him. Maybe I can live with that. Grow from that. Even his rejection would be well worth the new perspective.

There's more to me than cowering, and lies, and fear…

I've barely finished the thought before my screen lights up.

More.

I shiver at that sole command. I can imagine him voicing it against my ear, his voice gruff, breath like fire against my earlobe.

Alight with his encouragement, I reposition myself and raise the camera, aiming lower. This time, I don't have to wait for his reply, brusquely succinct.

More.

Excitement electrifies me in ways I never knew were possible. My brain shies away from the comparison at first —only to cling to it ferociously. It's the same thrill that infects me whenever I write. The inane belief that anything is possible as long as I will it to be. That my actions can shape the universe, for good or bad.

That I have control.

Power.

But for how long? A lump in my throat warns me that I'm standing on the ledge of some massive precipice. One wrong move and a few bruises won't be the outcome—I'll be decimated. At the same time, by taking this leap, I may finally unfurl those damaged, singed wings I've kept suppressed for so long.

It doesn't take long for me to settle on a response. Tumble or fly?

When I finally lower my fingertips to the phone's screen, a part of me knows deep down that he's waiting for it, eyeing his phone avidly. In this moment, I have power over him, whatever that means in the long run. Even if it's for a few, sordid seconds. My words. My images. Me.

I have him.

But there's an alarming realization wrapped up in that reality, one I don't even want to explore in full just yet.

I may have him for now, but...

I don't want to let him go.

Shifting onto my back, I draw my knees up to my chest and take a photo. Then another. Another.

They dance across the screen one by one, each near instantaneously garnering a "seen by" caption. Soon, the indicator that he's writing back flashes at the bottom of the conversation.

Damn head fucker, he says, and even trying to envision his expression makes my belly clench. I can practically hear his groan from here. *Show me what a bunny does when she's very, very sorry.*

Just like that, the tables turn. Yes, I hurt him.

And he's delighting in punishing me.

This time, I slump against the pillows and take a picture of my face, my expression weary. No fake smile. No sensual mask. Just me.

I'm sorry you're with Bonnie and not with me.

I see that he received the message, but there's no reply. Silence stretches on for what feels like an eternity until I finally hear it—the distinctive click of a door opening down below. I bolt upright, torn between the horrific possibility that Gino's men have returned, or an even more terrifying prospect.

That *Rafe* is the one boldly creeping through the lower level. The unsteady figure climbing the stairs with deliberate slowness, each step resonating loud enough for me to track. He's methodical to the point of torture, giving me more than enough time to mull over what his quick arrival means.

That, even if he were still near the park, he started driving here early in our conversation. Maybe before the pictures. The banter. All this time, he was already on his way to me.

My mind is still reeling as the intruder enters the apartment and advances down the hall, creeping ever closer to this room. Then, the door itself opens, revealing a realm of shadow and a figure who dominates the center of it.

Something strikes the floor with a thud, making me jump. His shoe? Then another, followed by a lighter swishing noise. His clothing. He steps forward, allowing me to make out the hint of his motions through the dark.

Gleaming muscle reveals he's already shed his shirt, cording in his forearms as he works on the clasps of his jeans. Unable to tear my gaze away from him, I rise onto my knees, staring avidly as he tugs them down, down, down…

Then he steps forward, robbing me of my view, as his fingers shoot out to trace the line of my jaw. "You want to be with me, huh?" His husky murmur sets my blood on fire.

Before I can answer, he snatches both of my hands, raising them above my head. Under his control, they form an x over my chest as he leans in, shoving me onto my back. Breathless, I can only gape as he nudges my legs apart with his knee.

"Prove it," he goads against my exposed collar. "Prove you want to be with me."

How? He doesn't leave it up to my imagination to figure out. His hands pin me in place as he juts his hips forward, entering me with a desperation that has us both gasping out. Eyelids fluttering, I marvel for the umpteenth time at the fit—the feel of him.

Perfection.

Greedily, I claw at his back, locking my knees around his waist.

And I show him exactly what I want from him.

Everything he has to give.

CHAPTER TWELVE

He doesn't let me sleep; I wake to the sensation of his fingers sliding inside me, wringing a moan from my throat. This round winds up moving into the shower, and by the time we're done, the hot water runs ice-cold.

Afterward, we get dressed—him in a pair of jeans and a black shirt, while I wear a similar shirt but paired with a loose gray skirt of my own.

On his way into the hall, Rafe snatches something from the dresser and holds it out for me to see. His cell phone.

"Watch," he commands before brushing his thumb across the screen, flicking through several images. Each one makes my cheeks grow hotter until I can't even meet his gaze.

But he's persistent, his voice so low the vibration resonates in my bones. "Look."

As my eyes flick up to his hand, he strikes a button, and the current picture vanishes. Then he proceeds to do the same until each one is deleted.

"Give me your phone," he says next.

I find it coiled within the bedsheets. Without hesitation, he does the same on my device, deleting every single picture I sent him last night. When I finally gather the nerve to face him again, he shrugs at my look of confusion. "Those belong to me. Only me."

Meaning he won't hoard them for ammunition later, or so I assume. I'm confident enough to believe he won't share them either. Those intimate pieces of me will dwell within his skull for only him to enjoy—no one else.

When he hands me the phone, I can't take my eyes off the now blank screen. It seems that he's accepted my written apology, but I might as well say it out loud.

"I'm sorry for lying to you," I blurt in a rush. "I'm sorry. There isn't anything between Liam and me. And I'm sorry for putting you in an awkward position with Mara."

His laughter is such a shock, I whirl to face him. He's watching me in return, his lips quirked, his eyes gleaming. "I never thought I'd hear a woman apologize for that," he murmurs, stepping close enough to flick his thumb against my chin. "I'll tell you how you can make it up to me."

"How?" I ask in a whisper.

"From here on out, you tell me everything," he says. "Everything. Like why you were looking at Liam like he'd just punched you in the face."

I stiffen. "That… I was asking him about Faith's case," I admit. "I thought he might know something."

He blinks, his overall expression unnervingly blank. "And?"

"They have a suspect," I confess. "They found Faith's phone and they think that whoever sent her one of the last messages before she vanished might know something about what happened… What's wrong?"

Suddenly, he's staring off into space, his jaw clenched, and a foreboding knot forms in my stomach. After days in his orbit, it's becoming easier to read him.

And know when he's on edge.

"Rafe?" Tentatively, I brush my hand along his shoulder, lingering over his forearm. "What's wrong?"

Finally, without looking at me, he says, "If their suspect was the last person who messaged her, then I know who it is."

His voice is too deep. Too cold. A heavy sense of dread washes over me, but there's no point in running from the truth now. I need to know. "Who?"

I suck in a breath as he meets my gaze in that brutally honest way, holding nothing back.

"It was me," he says. "I messaged her."

CHAPTER THIRTEEN

For what feels like an eternity, all I can do is stare straight ahead, desperately trying to process my emotions. Confusion. Terror. Shock.

He could be a suspect in Faith Wen's murder.

The scariest part? Branden hinted at as much.

Was he lying to hide his own guilt, or is Rafe every bit the criminal Branden's insisted he was from the start?

Turning to face him, I can't tell. He's an enigma, his eyes a stormy black, glowering into the distance. A tiny voice at the back of my mind warns that Branden is right.

I have no idea what he's capable of.

Do I even have what it takes to find out?

"What do you mean?" I ask, taking a steadying breath. My voice shakes anyway, betraying any attempt to sound brave. "Tell me everything."

The look he sends my way doesn't ease my fears one bit. "I'm pretty sure I might be the last one who texted Faith before she went missing," he says. "But I know for a fact that she had two phones."

I feel my brow furrow. "I don't understand. How do you even know that?"

He shrugs, but his eyes maintain that distant, elusive gleam. He's hiding something. "Trust me, I know."

His confidence triggers that niggling sense of jealousy again. I do my best to swat it aside and focus on the information at the forefront. Faith had two phones. A fact that even the police don't seem to know. Liam hadn't mentioned it either.

But why?

"What did you text her about?" I ask, scanning his face for any hint of emotion. Love? Lust? His jaw remains stubbornly fixed, giving me nothing—not that he has to. My brain skips ahead, wondering if they spoke about way more than her problems with Gino and DW. "Why would that make you a suspect?"

"Because I was trying to get her to meet me," he says.

"About?"

His heavy sigh triggers another wave of unease I can't suppress this time.

"Tell me," I prod.

When he finally looks my way, he's more cautious than I think I've ever seen him. Like someone judging whether or not to strike a match over a lit puddle of gasoline. In the end, I guess he has no choice.

"About—" He breaks off, his head swiveling toward the front windows. "Shit."

"What's wrong?" I start to ask, but then I hear it—loud, steady pounding coming from below. The front door?

Above the racket comes a voice, ringing with authority. "Police! Open up, Mr. Wei-Shen. We have a warrant."

Rafe doesn't look anywhere near as shocked as I feel. Without so much as flinching, he grabs my arm and shoves me toward the hallway. From the couch, he snatches my bag and tosses it to me. I drop my phone into my purse before wrestling it over my shoulder

"Get down the fire escape and get to the warehouse," he hisses, already racing for the stairs. "Wait for me there. Go!"

"What..." My brain is slow to process everything at once. All I can do is stupidly ask, "Why are the police here?"

"I said go!" he snaps back without turning around. "Now. Trust me, they won't knock again."

You know why they're here, a part of me whispers. *Because Rafe is their number one suspect.*

Or...

They're here for the same reason Branden hasn't come after me. Because, much like his planted cameras, he's hidden another piece of cruel insurance…

Horrified, I turn to the pile of boxes down the hall and picture the item lurking inside one of them—*the hair clip.*

The muffled chime of the front door snaps me back to the present danger.

"Officer?" Rafe inquires, his voice seeping through the floor. "What the hell is this about?"

"We have a warrant to search the premises," a man replies. I vaguely recognize his voice—the same officer who came the other day about the fire. Judging from the commotion, he didn't come alone this time. I can make out at least four other figures marching in through the shop's entrance. "We'll need access to both the shop and your private residence, Mr. Wei-Shen. We'll try not to make too much of a mess."

From his tone, it's obvious they aren't here on a whim. They're looking for something.

And I think I have a sinking suspicion as to what.

As quietly as I can, I lunge toward the box of my belongings and dive into the first one. Inside is just a random assortment of clothing and books. The second one is no different.

Panic urges me to keep searching as muffled footsteps emanate from the lower level, moving toward the back of the shop with a purpose that leaves no doubt as to where they're headed next.

Gritting my teeth, I double my efforts, ripping through my belongings as quickly as I can. It isn't until I reach the third one that I finally discover my old shoebox of trinkets. I grab the hair clip and wrench open the window just as a cadre of footsteps ascend the staircase.

There isn't time to think or plan. Without barely a glance downward, I scramble onto the windowsill and aim for the fire escape below.

With a heart-stopping thud, my feet land on the rickety structure, which squeals in protest. The sharp noise is loud enough to be heard across town, and I can't stop myself from glancing at the window. If the officers noticed, I only have a second or two to react.

So I move, blindly scrambling to the lower level where a steep drop separates me from the ground. There isn't time to unfurl the nearby ladder. Clutching my bag, I close my eyes and jump instead, landing in a crouch on the pavement.

Staggering upright, I scramble deeper into the alley. Another glance over my shoulder reveals no one is following me—yet.

But a sudden movement from the corner of my eye dashes that hope—it's already too late. Someone grabs my forearm, dragging me around a corner before I can even get my bearings. Alarm shoots down my spine as a familiar smell itches my nostrils.

I know before I even spin around to face him, just who has me.

"Wait," Branden warns in a low tone before I can say a single word. "Don't do something stupid. Just hear me out."

He's not wearing his uniform. Instead, a nondescript black shirt and jeans help him blend into the shadows of the alley. His hair is mussed, his chin coated in fresh stubble. One look at his gaze, and I feel an instinctive impulse too strong to resist.

Run!

"Let go of me!" I tug my arm, discretion be damned. In fact, I should want to bring attention to myself, police or not.

But just as I open my mouth, he tightens his grip.

"Think of your little friend," he warns, dragging me closer to him, his nails gouging at my flesh. "What's her name, huh? Mara Chan? She hangs around the same pieces of shit you do, isn't that right? It would be a damn shame if she wound up like that other girl."

I go limp as my heart pounds. I can't even tell if he means it as a threat or just an observation. It's pathetic how a part of me desperately wants to cling to the latter option.

Even though I know which one is the truth.

"Like 'the other girl.' Like Faith?" I hiss, hating how my voice breaks.

"Hannah..." I'm too slow to cringe from the hand he swipes along my cheek. "I would never hurt you," he says. "All I want to do is protect you. Even if I have to protect you from yourself."

"I didn't hit myself," I point out, swatting his hand away. "I didn't hide cameras in my room, either."

His eyes narrow, unreadable from this angle—but the subtle shifting of his posture sets every nerve in me on red alert.

"Why don't you ask the bastard you're fucking about that, huh? I'm sure he's already bragged to every gangbanger in the city what an easy piece of ass you are—"

I lash out without thinking. My hand harmlessly glances off his chest, but the violence leaves me stunned anyway. I hit him.

And in retaliation, he snatches my wrist so hard I cry out. "What the hell has gotten into you?"

"Who's there?" a voice calls from the direction of the shop.

Hissing under his breath, Branden yanks me deeper into the alley he's in. From behind me, I hear cautious footsteps ring out, creeping in our direction.

They're so close. A scream would be enough to draw their notice. Determined, I opened my mouth...

At the same moment, Branden brings his mouth to my ear. "Do you think he really gives a fuck about you? Hannah, don't be so damn naïve. You think you're the only one he's been fucking? They found the dead girl's phone, Hannah. I'm sure you can guess what was on it?"

I feel my cheeks flush. Rafe told me himself—messages.

But Branden's tone is way too smug to be referring to something strictly platonic in nature.

"Look," he snaps. I crane my neck back despite my better judgment, in time to see him withdraw a handful of crumpled papers from his pocket. At a glance, all I can make out is walls of text. And…

Images. One, in particular, makes me freeze in place—a woman bared from the neck down.

"We need to talk," Branden says, sounding miles away.

You need to scream, the logical part of me warns. Run. But I can't stop staring at the pages in his grasp—those pictures.

They trigger a milieu of different emotions in me, almost too many to explore in full. Disgust. Dread. Familiarity.

But fear wins out. Twisting on my heel, I try to wrench my arm free. "Let go of me—"

"How soon before your little friend gets tossed into a dumpster next?" he warns. "Or even you? I'm trying to help you, Hannah. Fuck! Be quiet."

His hand falls over my mouth, triggering a wave of pain. I squirm, but he only presses harder, his head cocked, his jaw tight. Soon I realize why—a smattering of footsteps echo off the nearby walls, increasingly loud.

"Is anyone there?" the officer questions again, sounding alarmingly close this time.

Cautious footsteps creep toward this part of the alley, and before I know it, Branden's already dragged me further away.

A van parked near the main street is his destination, but I don't recognize it. A rental? Without explaining, he wrenches open the passenger-side door and shoves me forward.

"Get in."

I barely manage to catch myself on the rim of the door. "No." Craning my neck, I hunt for any sign of the officer. If he's still within earshot, he'll hear me. "Help—"

"Fine," Branden warns as the shout leaves my throat. "I didn't want to scare you, but you leave me no choice. You think it's a coincidence that Rafael Wei-Shen went after you?" My expression must give him exactly what he wants —doubt. He laughs coldly, shaking his head. "Oh no, Hannah. I tried to tell you once, but you wouldn't listen— he knows damn well who you are. The fucker's been blackmailing me over it. What? You don't believe me? Here's the proof."

He withdraws that handful of pages and shoves them beneath my nose.

"That same asshole has been talking to the dead girl," he says. "Take a good look, Hannah. This is the kind of monster you let into your bed."

Every ounce of logic I possess warns me not to look, but I'm already scanning the top page, anyway. The exchange reads like a typical correspondence between acquaintances. That is until a series of images creep into the conversation, one by one. The star barely shows her face, but I can guess her identity from her dark hair and pale skin. My chest clenches, my heart pounding with recognition.

Faith.

Whoever she messaged, she sent him images of her face. Her breasts. More…

"You want to know about Rafael Wei-Shen?" Branden taunts as my cheeks catch fire at the sight of every sordid image I come across. "Well, he's had a vendetta against me ever since I busted him for dealing a year ago. He pulled some strings and got off on probation, but he's had it out for me ever since. Enough to set me up for a suspension and fuck my little sister while he was at it. Don't think for a second that he didn't know who you were when he picked you out."

I replay my first meeting with Rafe over and over. The way he looked at me then. How he had singled me out, haunting my footsteps ever since.

Maybe his very first boast to me held the truth all along. *"I want to know what makes a little rabbit like you so damn hard she doesn't flinch when a man presses a knife to her throat."*

All along, he could have known exactly who that monster was…

"You know I'm right, Hannah," Branden says as if reading my mind. "I've always been the only one you can trust. I know you better than anyone."

But the Hannah he's referring to isn't proud or mysterious. She's a world apart from the figure Rafe sees. She pretends to be a captive, but her own lies form the shackles holding her back.

Gritting my teeth, I try to deny it. "You're lying."

"I'm not. The worst part is that you know I'm not. You were dumb enough to think he wanted you, Hannah?" Scoffing, he snatches the pages from me and tightens his grip on my arm. "I'm the only person who will ever care about you. Who has ever cared about you. Now get in the goddamn van."

He shoves me into the seat so hard I lose my balance. Clawing at the door frame, I try to get out, but I'm too slow. Before I know it, he's slamming the door after me, nearly smashing my bag in the process. When I tug on the handle, it's already locked.

My wide-eyed reflection watches me from the window glass, waiting for my next move. But I'm frozen. The panic I know I should feel is dulled by sheer confusion. What was Rafe's real motive if everything Branden says is true? To use me to get back at Branden?

Or use me in another way. Could he have been the one to plant Faith's hair clip after all?

No. I shake my head to banish the doubt and try the door again, fumbling for the button to unlock it. A door does open, but it's the driver's side.

"Don't be stupid," Branden warns as he climbs behind the steering wheel. "We're just going to talk. You're going to listen and give me the respect I deserve. Hell, I'm not just your brother, Hannah. It's always been you and me from the start. Just the two of us, right?" His expression softens as he attempts to touch my arm, but I cringe out of his reach.

"Just the two of us," I croak, pressing myself against my door, as far from him as I can get. "Because you won't let me do anything on my own."

He laughs at the mere idea while turning onto the main street. Then, he rounds another corner so quickly I'm thrown against the dashboard. My wrist smarts as I brace my hands for stability. Amid the hum of the engine, I sense our speed increasing by the second until we're peeling down the streets, heedless of the posted limit.

"On your own?" he parrots nastily. "So that you can keep ruining your life and spewing your lies?"

He cuts in front of another vehicle before darting across an intersection. My stomach lurches, threatening to jump up my throat. "Bran," I croak. "You're going too fast."

God, I can't tell if the last light he passed was even green. All I can do is grip the edge of my seat so tightly my nails bite into the leather. "Slow down!"

"You know," he says in a chillingly calm tone. Without taking his eyes from the road, he wrenches on the wheel, weaving through the thinning traffic. "Liam said something strange the other day. About you."

Pinpricks of alarm bite at my nerves as I race to recall just what he's referring to—Lexi?

He doesn't answer right away. With a shuddering jolt, the van bolts across two lanes, turning onto the highway amid a smattering of honking horns.

I can barely breathe as terror clenches my chest in a vice grip. "Bran!"

"He asked me if 'that' was why I'm so protective of you," he says in that eerie tone. "What happened 'in your past.' He didn't say what," he adds. "But he didn't fucking have to. What did you tell him?"

I choke out an answer without thinking. "N-Nothing."

"Oh? Then why did he have that kicked puppy look on his face? The one that dumb little whores like you inspire by telling lies. What did you tell him?"

He peels down a busy lane, and I scramble to engage my seatbelt. As I shift, something firm stabs against my outer thigh. Alarmed, I swat at it, only to remember the object in my pocket. It's been there all this time.

"Hannah," Branden growls and—despite the chaos of the moment—I marvel at one grim fact. Any other day I'd react to the authority in his tone the way he wants me to. I'd jump. Cower. Confess.

But with Faith's butterfly clip cradled against my palm, I'm reminded of another piece of jewelry. One that Rafe would have no interest in taking.

"Answer me, Hannah," Branden growls. "What. Did. You. Tell. Him?"

"The truth?" I blurt, though I don't know why it comes out as a question. Or it could be a dare. "That you've always looked out for me, haven't you? You've always protected me. And you've always been there to guide me. Control me. Manipulate me. Guilt me into being silent about the things you've made me do. Because it's always my fault, isn't it?"

An emotion flits across his face too quickly to name. His eyes dart from the road for a split second, and the van drifts dangerously toward the oncoming lane.

"Watch out!"

A truck darts out of his path, narrowly avoiding a collision.

"Truth? Don't be ridiculous, Hannah." He throws his head back, laughing. "What are you even talking about?"

"I'm talking about when you made me be friends with Lexi Winacott." It's a strange way to delve into these memories. Like ripping out a knife that's been embedded within me for so long, I've deluded myself into thinking that I'd healed around the intrusion. That I could go on living with the weapon still there, buried deep.

All I had to do was ignore its existence.

But at the same time, I wasn't just protecting myself. Everyone from my parents to the rest of the town drilled into my head that someone else always mattered more.

"She was nice to me," I say softly, watching as the speed dial gauge ticks higher. Higher… For whatever reason, I don't feel the fear anymore. It's as if speaking forms a boundary between my brain and my emotions too thick for anything to puncture. The only way to maintain it is to relive these memories.

Every last one.

"You said you wanted me to have a friend, but that wasn't it." Even back then, he'd kept me isolated, but I had been so desperate for someone to interact with. I'd have done anything. "You had a crush on her. She was pretty—"

"Stop it, Hannah," Branden snaps.

I stare through the windshield, seeing nothing but images of the past. "And you… Dad caught you lurking around the bathroom while I was in the shower. You took pictures of me, then. Polaroids. You kept them in a box in your room, and you always told me that you did it to protect me—"

"You're crazy," he snarls. "Fucking crazy. Do you hear yourself?"

But I do. For the first time in so long, I can finally hear myself speak.

"You told me to be friends with Lexi, and I was. Then you asked me to bring her to the lake, and I did. But you were there... You told me to take a walk." I sound so detached. It's as if I'm narrating a scene from a movie or play—not my own life. "But when I came back…"

"Do you know the damage you could do, spreading those fucking lies?" Branden demands. "Is that what you want? For me to end up in fucking prison because a little liar couldn't keep her goddamn mouth shut?"

"You always made it sound like it was my fault," I say, turning to look at him directly. In profile, he doesn't even resemble the brother I've known. He's a stranger, snarling over the steering wheel. "And I believed you. I believed that everything I did affected you. But that's not the truth, is it? Did… Did you do that to Faith?" I hear myself ask. It's as if my body has taken over, cutting off all input from my brain. "Hurt her because she pushed you away—"

"Why don't you ask your fucking Rafe what happened to Faith?" he demands.

The engine whines as the van lurches forward even faster. Genuine alarm creeps through the numbness, and only now do I realize how tightly I'm gripping my chair. So tight, my knuckles are white.

"Branden, stop—"

"One good fuck, and you already care about him more than me, huh?"

"Look out!"

Another car cuts into his path, and he barely manages to swerve in time to avoid it.

"Slow down!"

"Come home," he counters. "Say you'll do it. Now." He wrenches on the steering wheel, cutting directly into the path of another car.

"Branden—"

"Say it." The engine revs to enforce the threat.

"Slow down!"

He raises his voice to easily drown out mine. "Come home."

We're going too fast. The vehicle sways, fighting to stay in the same lane. Only God knows what the drivers nearby are thinking. Who he's putting at risk.

All of this to make a point.

He's always in control.

"Come home," he goads to reinforce the thought. "Everything will be like it was. All you have to do is come home. Because I'm worried what will happen if you don't. Your friend Rafe thinks he's hot shit, but no one is untouchable, Hannah—and he isn't the one calling the shots. You have no idea what you've stepped into—"

"Then, just tell me!"

"Come home," he insists in a softer tone. "I'll tell you everything if you do. I mean it."

It's easier than ever to sense the lie in his words. I've known him long enough to catch that telltale dip in his inflection. A denial springs to my lips just as another van comes into view.

He speeds up until we're rapidly approaching it, able to see the white stickers plastered on the rear window—a small sticker family, down to a little dog.

"Come home," Branden warns, a dangerous note in his voice. "I mean it, Hannah."

He breaks into the next lane, speeding even more, most likely to cut the other van off.

"Fine," I whisper. "I'll come with you."

"Good." The vehicle gradually slows to a normal speed, and he signals to take the next exit. "This is the best way for everyone," he says. "You've made the right choice."

But my hand is still resting over my pocket, sensing Faith's hair clip beneath.

What choice had she made when it came to him?

And did she pay the ultimate price?

CHAPTER FOURTEEN

The setting sun provides an ominous backdrop of shadow as we pull into the driveway of a scenic, two-story home in the heart of a peaceful, idyllic neighborhood. Children play in the distance, and their laughter is audible even with the van's windows rolled up—a mocking, twisted soundtrack.

"This is where you belong, Hannah," Branden says while shutting off the engine. He braces his hands on the dashboard, his knuckles cracking with tension. "With your family. With me."

An ironic boast, all things considered. This place is a world apart from my crappy apartment or a flat above a tattoo shop. A pale yellow Victorian-style townhouse, guarded—quite literally—by a white picket fence. The imagery symbolizes my childhood perfectly.

A beautiful image when glimpsed from the outside. But what lurks within those four walls? A cage.

I can feel the bars of it closing in as Branden exits the car and circles around to my end, wrenching open the door before I can do so myself. In the same motion, he snatches my wrist and tugs me to my feet.

At the back of my mind, I realize I could always scream. Resist. But I don't. As he hauls me up the front steps, I ask, "So you'll tell me the truth? About everything?"

He shrugs, unlocking the front door. Inside, the narrow foyer opens onto a short hall extending past the living room and into the kitchen. Memories descend, reminding me of how trapped I felt here. How desperately I longed for an escape.

"Honey, is that you?" A blond woman peeks through the doorway, her expression wary.

"Yeah, it's me," Branden says, muscling me forward. The door slams behind us, and I can't disguise how I flinch at the sound. "And Hannah's back like I told you."

"Hey," Kaitlin says with a strained smile. Her blue eyes flit over my posture and linger on my face before drifting away to a painting hanging on the wall. I can only speculate as to what lie Branden told her to explain the bruises. "I'm glad it's you," she says to him with unmistakable relief. "I was worried they had come back and—"

"We'll talk about it later," Branden growls, cutting her off. Just as quickly, he flashes a strained smile and inclines his head down the hall. "Why don't you make us some lunch?"

"Okay." With a terse nod, she scurries into the kitchen while Branden pulls me into the living room, effectively blocking the doorway with his bulk. He meets my gaze, and for the first time, I see a hint of the brother I recognize. The caged, suspicious one willing to do anything to stay in control.

"You promised," I say lamely, but I don't expect a damn thing from him. Mentally, I scan the room, spotting one of the large bay windows overlooking the back garden. It's low enough to jump from.

"I will," he snaps, his voice low. "But first you tell me something. Where is it?"

Real confusion makes me blink. "What are you talking about?"

Belatedly, I sense a telltale weight in my pocket, and the answer becomes obvious. Something small enough to fit within his grasping, flexing hands.

"You know what," he says. Nervous energy seeps through his confident exterior, and he starts to pace, his shoulders hunched. "*You* mentioned a hair clip. So, where is it?"

He eyes my bags, and I instinctively back up a step.

"W-What hair clip—"

"You know what," he growls.

Maybe I do. A certain hair clip that he should have no interest in if Rafe planted it. Perhaps he wants to bring it in as evidence to have him arrested for Faith's murder?

Or…

He wants it for another reason entirely.

"Did you put it with my things on purpose?" I ask, cutting to the chase. At the same time, I inch a step back. Then another.

"Don't play dumb, Hannah." He advances a step, and I sense that distracting him is my only option. If he keeps me here, I suspect I won't ever leave again.

So I choke down any fear and say, "Were you the one seeing Faith?"

He stiffens, his eyes widening.

"You were," I say, taking another step back. "Weren't you? When she went missing, you hid her hair clip. Why?"

I'd assumed he'd wanted to scare me. Threaten me. That everything led back to me—but I was wrong. Foolish.

I can see everything from a different viewpoint now, and the real answer becomes obvious.

"Could it be traced back to you? I know why you were suspended. If something of Faith's could be tracked to you, it would make you their number one suspect, wouldn't it?"

"Shut up! You have no fucking idea how high up this goes. If you keep running your goddamn mouth, he'll come for all of us. I don't even know how they traced her to me—" He breaks off, his eyes cutting wildly around the room. Copying him, I realize why. It's been so long since I've been here that I've missed the scattered cushions thrown haphazardly across the couch. The piles of documents and books scattered among the bookshelves that line the back of the room. Trinkets and knick-knacks clutter the coffee table, and overall, the entire space is a mess.

Which could explain Kaitlin's unease. She had been worried about "them" coming back. Who?

Maybe the same people currently tearing apart Rafe's shop.

"Who will come for us?" I ask, picking up on that one word. How he said it—uttered hoarsely with undeniable terror. "Who are you afraid of?"

"Where is it?" Branden demands, advancing toward me again. I snap to awareness and stumble toward the window.

"You weren't trying to scare me, were you?" I croak. "You were just trying to hide it. Weren't you? Because eventually, the police would come searching for it. Is that why they were here?"

He stiffens, but I don't think he even really heard me. He's too busy fixated on his true aim. "Where the fuck is it, Hannah?"

The hair clip. But if he hid that in advance, then he knew the police would come looking. Meaning anything else that might incriminate him—like a certain series of tapes—must not be in this house either. And then I remember the other unfamiliar object I found among my things.

"Were the tapes on the camera this whole time?"

That catches his attention. He turns around to face me, but I stand firm. For the first time—maybe ever—his glare has no effect on me. I can see through it to the real emotion lurking beneath.

Not concern for me.

Just fear.

"What did you do, Bran?" I ask. "Because whatever it was, it wasn't because of me. Was it?"

His gaze darkens ominously, and I barely catch the moment he surges toward me. I pivot out of his range, tripping into an end table. An array of materials crash to the floor in a jarring cacophony.

"Is everything okay?" Kaitlin calls from the kitchen.

Branden curses under his breath, and I look up to find him alarmingly close, his hand raised inches from my face. "It's fine," he hisses, curling the fingers into a fist.

Soft footsteps start to advance down the hall. "Are you sure, because—"

"Stay in the kitchen, baby." He starts for the doorway and hesitates, obviously torn between threatening me and maintaining his charade. In the end, his façade wins out. He lunges into the hall, hissing at me from over his shoulder, "Stay here. If you leave, I won't protect you anymore, Hannah. I mean it."

I watch him go, and I give myself a second to wallow in the pain. The self-pity. The aching, crushing reality. Those emotions have barely washed over me before a new feeling overrides everything else—the need to run.

I race to the bay window overlooking the backyard. Wrenching it open feels dramatic in so many ways. At least until a set of heavy footsteps approach from the hall. As quietly as I can, I climb onto the ledge and slip through, landing hard beside a hedge.

The noise triggers a flurry of commotion from inside the house, but I don't stop to see if anyone is behind me. I spot the gate leading from the fenced-in yard and tug on the handle. It's locked.

"Hannah!"

At the sound of that voice, I scramble over the waist-high fence in a flurry of motion. Pain lances through my hip, and a ripping sound comes from my skirt as the edge of it catches on a spoke of the fence. Wrenching free, I race down the side of the house. My sandals slam against the pavement as I start running, with no real destination in mind but getting away.

Only when I'm out of Branden's neighborhood, do I finally stop to get my bearings. A series of trees and manicured lawns make up what seems to be a small park. After moving as far from the main road as possible, I adjust my bag's shoulder strap and nearly choke on a sudden realization. Sure enough, I fumble through it and easily find my cell phone.

All this time, I could have called the police—someone else for help.

Could not doing so be written off as fear? Or is the need to protect Branden too ingrained in my being to overcome so easily?

Even now, my fingers shake with indecision as I consider calling one contact in particular. Rafe really was behind those texts for all I know—he even admitted to communicating with Faith.

Trusting him could be running into another trap.

CHAPTER FIFTEEN

As if to test my resolve, a string of texts flashes across the screen. *Where are you?*

Choking back the doubt, I hit the call button, and it barely rings once.

"Where the hell did you go?" Rafe demands. His voice sounds muffled as if he's speaking far from the receiver. "Where are you?"

I rattle off the street name I spy on the nearest sign, feeling the back of my neck prickle with every step I take.

"I don't know how long I can wait here—"

"I'm already pulling up to you," he replies.

Not even a second later, a black car peels around the corner, skidding to a stop across from my location. I race to it and finally risk looking back.

In my head, I'd imagined Branden chasing after me on foot, always one step behind.

But I don't spy him or his van anywhere.

"What the hell are you doing out here?" Rafe demands, eyeing the residential street with a frown.

I slip inside, locking the door after me. Facing him, I raise an eyebrow. "How did you find me?" Call it a hunch, but I doubt he frequents this part of town.

A harsh sigh betrays his guilt. "Fine." He nods to the cell phone propped against his dashboard. A map is displayed on the screen, with two blinking dots in close vicinity. "I tracked your phone's GPS. Cops show up at my place, and you go missing. What was I supposed to think other than—"

"You thought I had told them something?" I ask, too stunned to feel truly insulted. "Tipped them off?"

He flinches and snatches one of my hands, gripping it tight. "Hell no. I thought some dickhead tried to drag your ass away in the chaos. Was I right?"

I clench my teeth rather than answer him right away. Scanning his expression, I try to picture him on the other end of Faith's messages. Receiving those pictures from her. Asking for them…

"Were you seeing Faith?" I ask bluntly.

He nearly swerves off the road and pulls his hand away to steady the wheel. "Not like that." His tone deepens, fully serious. "I swear it on my fucking mother. I wasn't fucking her if that's what you're asking."

Relief goes to war with doubt until my head spins with the potential outcomes. "I saw the texts," I say lamely.

"I can explain that," he counters, grimacing at the thought. "I was frustrated. She kept giving me the fucking runaround, and all I wanted was—"

"Nude images?" I snap. God, I can't get them out of my head.

But when I finally face him, he doesn't look like someone caught in a lie. Instead, shock displaces any hint of deception.

"What the fuck are you talking about?"

"I saw the messages," I say. "All of them."

He frowns. "Then you saw me cussing her out. That's it. She promised to meet me at my shop but never showed... I should have gone looking for her, but you showed up instead."

I remember that night. He'd been on edge, but I'd been too wrapped up in my own issues to notice.

"So, she never sent you pictures?" I ask.

"No." He risks taking one hand off the wheel to brush my cheek. "It wasn't like that with us, I swear."

"But, the police were looking at your shop for a reason."

"The fuck they were," Rafe hisses. "Luckily, the bastard cops could enact their 'warrant' without me being there. Sons of bitches—"

"Do you know what they're looking for?"

He shrugs. "Anything they can use to pin it on me if I had to take a guess."

He could be lying, but I'm tired of living in doubt.

"I think I know what," I admit, reaching into my pocket. "I think they were there because of me. Because of something I have."

He shoots me a skeptical frown. "What?"

"This." I hold the hair clip up to the light, awed by the detail. Delicate and light, it must have been expensive. Something Faith wouldn't lose easily.

But if Rafe recognizes it, he's an expert actor. His face reveals nothing.

"It's Faith's," I say without beating around the bush. "She was wearing it a few days before she died."

Still, he says nothing. When I gather up the nerve to look at him, he's staring forward, gripping the steering wheel so tightly the car starts to drift and nearly crosses into the oncoming lane.

"Watch out!"

"Shit." He rights the car easily, but his expression is more distant than ever. Even after a few days in his orbit, I can clearly identify the emotion responsible for the tension hardening his jaw. Mistrust.

"How?" he demands finally. "How the hell did you get a hold of that?"

I look at the hair clip again and try to see it how someone like Branden might. Not as a threat meant to terrify me, but as a desperate ploy by someone who probably thought I wouldn't recognize it. Or know who it belonged to.

"Someone planted it in my apartment," I confess. "I think he was trying to hide it in case the police searched his place. I think... I think he hurt Faith, but I don't know why."

The silence between us is deafening. I squirm, feeling my heart race as I try to interpret his reaction. His eyes are dark and thoughtful. Like while this wasn't exactly the plot twist in the narrative he expected, he had been anticipating something similar.

"Your brother?" he asks coldly.

"Yes," I admit. "But now it's my turn to ask a question. Branden Dewitt. Did you know who he was all this time?"

His brows snap together, and he strikes the steering wheel so hard the horn blares. "Branden Dewitt? *That's* who your brother is?" He looks at me so incredulously that I know it's not an act. He didn't know.

"You said his name was Bran," he says, pulling over to the side of the highway. "Though, fuck, I guess I'm the idiot for not putting it together. Branden."

"So, you know who he is?" I ask thickly. "I'm guessing his name wasn't circled on your list by accident?"

He swivels his head to face me. "You want to know the truth? That list was the name of every cop Faith knew had come through Gino's place—but there were about ten different names, and none of them started with D. She wouldn't tell me who was just there looking at tits or who might have been on Gino's payroll."

The irritation in his voice is too real to be faked. "Gino's payroll?" I ask softly.

"I know that fucker's up to something." A muscle in his jaw twitches, his eyes blazing. "Gino's club is a front for something. Faith hinted that it was illegal, but she wouldn't tell me exactly what. I know that it dealt with the girls, though."

"But there's more to it, isn't there? You know him personally?"

He sighs. "When Faith wouldn't give me any straight answers, I decided to get some of my own. I called one of those anonymous tip lines, and the cops actually followed through. They raided the club, but whatever they found wasn't enough to make any arrests. Just get a few unlucky cops who got caught there that night on suspension or some shit. Quietly, of course, as a fucking formality."

Like Branden.

"Let me guess, you've had that this whole fucking time?" Rafe asks, nodding toward the hair clip. "I thought the cops might have been looking for the phone, but that makes sense too."

"Phone?" I suddenly recall what he revealed about Faith having more than one.

"I figured someone would try something to get even," he says, ignoring my question. "Pinning Faith's death on me sure is a start, but it's a damn good ploy. The motherfucker…" He forms a fist and slams it against the steering wheel, making the horn sound a second time.

"Why?" I ask. "I mean how did you know—"

"Faith came to me scared." His tone makes me go silent. I've never seen him like this—posture so tense he's trembling, his lips pursed in thought. "She thought I could pull some strings to get her out from under Gino's thumb. Her parents owed a lot of shit on their house. He gave her the money in exchange for working at his club."

"But you didn't give her the money?"

"No," he admits, his frown deepening. "I didn't. I pressed her for information instead. And when I learned about the asshole she was dealing with… I called in the raid."

"And me?" I can barely get the words out. "You knew my 'boyfriend' was a cop. Is that the real reason why you were interested in me?"

He sighs. "Don't look at me like that. This isn't some fucking soap opera. I was interested in you because I could take one look at you and know there was more to you than some fucking bunny sweater."

"More," I echo. "Like my brother being on the police force?"

I'm holding my breath before I realize it, dreading what he might say. As the seconds tick by in silence, I don't have any other choice but to ask him directly. "Did you want to use me to get to him?"

"And how would I do that, huh?" he demands, raising an eyebrow. "You tell me."

"Manipulate me," I say. "Pump me for information. Use me to get back at him. I don't know—"

"I didn't know he was your brother," he insists. "This whole shit was a lot less creepy when you had a fake boyfriend."

"So, now what?"

"Now?" He inhales, gripping the steering wheel, his gaze determined. "We figure out what the asshole is planning. I don't think the police are at my place just for some fucking hair pin, bunny."

He's right. "You're their suspect."

"I can't even blame them," he says with a cold laugh. "I'd suspect me too. But they're looking in the wrong direction."

"Because Faith had another phone," I finish for him. Another realization dawns on me as I watch him nod. "And you know where it is."

"That night you saw her at my place? She gave it to me then. The phone that matters anyway."

I can clearly recall that moment in his warehouse.

"Why didn't you turn it in?" I ask. "Why didn't you—"

"I'm not turning shit in until I know for sure what's on it," he counters. "I'm not letting anyone whitewash this case."

"So, what did you find?"

He grits his teeth in a rare display of vulnerability. "Nothing. It's locked. Password-protected, and I'm already on my last try. She never actually told me what it is. I thought it might be the guy's name, but DW hasn't worked. Go fucking figure."

I suck in a startled breath. "Is that really why you had the police roster?"

He nods, oblivious to my shock. "Call me Sherlock Holmes, bunny. But DW must be an alias or some shit. Or she was lying about him being a cop at all."

Or 'DW' didn't stand for the culprit's initials in the way he expected.

"Her phone was supposed to hold whatever information she had," he adds. "Don't ask me what. She was vaguer than you when it came to detail."

"Show me?"

I can't describe the way he looks at me. Impressed? Guarded? "You think you can crack it when I couldn't?"

I don't answer. Maybe because if my hunch is correct, it could change everything, the final nail in the coffin.

If I'm right, my life, or my family, will never be the same.

"Bunny?" Rafe prods, nudging my shoulder.

"Just show me," I whisper. I don't sound confident in the slightest. Just resigned.

"I'll take you there. I put it somewhere safe," Rafe says, putting the car back into gear.

Warily, I ask, "Where?"

But I can guess the destination before he even says it out loud.

The one place he seems to frequent even more than his shop.

CHAPTER SIXTEEN

Unsurprisingly, we wind up in the same rundown area as his warehouse. Given the instructions he gave me the day Gino's men attacked him, this place must mean a lot to him.

"Is this your safe house?" I ask though I don't even know if that's the right term.

Apparently not because he laughs as he exits the car. When I copy him, he's still laughing, his eyes gleaming with a hint of something that could be amusement in another setting.

"You've been watching too many cop dramas, bunny," he says. "Come on."

He leads the way inside and switches on a lamp before venturing deeper into the space. From the assembled chaos in the far corner, he withdraws a red toolbox, and I'm reminded of something he told me once before. *"You get there, and you wait for me. If I don't show, you look for a red case. I already changed the combination to something you'll be able to guess..."*

"Here's your trial run," he declares as if sensing my train of thought. He approaches a wooden table in the center of the room and beckons me closer with a crooked finger. Then he slams the case down before me. "If I weren't here, how would you open it? Don't look at me for any hints, either. Use that bunny brain."

I wordlessly accept the challenge and observe the lock in question. It's similar to the kind I used on my high school locker, though instead of numbers, five letters make up the combination.

"Most people use their birthday," I point out, running my finger across the width of the device. "But I don't know yours, and it's not numbers, so..."

"And I'm not most people." He grazes my lower lip with the tip of his thumb, catching me off guard. "Be serious for a minute. If I didn't show the other day and you found this, what would you try?"

I think for a long moment before I finally make my attempt. As I turn to the lock, he pulls away, and I sense his gaze with every move I make. Knowing that, I'm deliberately slow, allowing him to see each symbol I land on before moving on to the next. Finally, as I near the very last letter, the lock clicks open.

"You used bunny," I say softly, eyeing him through my lashes. In a sense, it's humorously cliché, but the seriousness of his gaze belies another reason for the password, other than a joke. The thought ignites a heat that blazes beneath my skin, growing hotter the longer he maintains eye contact.

"I think I have a soft spot for them," he says in a tone that makes me shiver. He's disarming like this, and my body reacts to him in ways I can't deny. Or ignore. More fire creeps into my cheeks, and I glance down, hunting for a distraction. I find one instantly in the form of a slim, pink item resting on the bottom of the box.

Faith's phone.

Rafe starts to power it on, but I grab his hand before he can.

"Won't the police be able to track the GPS?"

He shrugs. "I doubt they know about this one. She only recently got it before she died, and she gave it to me not long after."

Supposedly to give him whatever information she knew— only she never got the chance to provide him with a way to access it.

Could the key really be what I think it is?

My thoughts are still swirling as the phone comes on with a musical jingle. It opens onto a bright pink screen that houses a demand for a password, and I grit my teeth in grim anticipation.

"So let's see it," Rafe says, handing it to me. "Show me how that bunny brain works."

Carefully, I press my fingers against the screen. Even as I type out the series letters, I'm praying that I'm wrong. Every clue leading to this conclusion is just an awful coincidence. I've been wrong all along…

But with a musical ping, the phone unlocks, opening onto an even pinker home screen.

"Shit," Rafe snaps, snatching the phone from me. "How did you—"

"Not yet," I plead, blinking back any tears that might form. "Let's just find out what she was hiding. Please."

He turns his attention to navigating to the sole icon visible on the screen. Once tapped, it opens onto a list of various numbers and letters.

"Are they dates?" I guess attempting to make sense of the data.

"I think so," Rafe says, his eyes narrowing. "Or… GPS coordinates? God damnit, Faith. What were you trying to tell me?"

"Why GPS coordinates?" I ask, seizing on that possibility rather than focusing on the obvious—Branden was DW.

"Could be to stash houses," Rafe suspects, his head cocked. "For whatever Gino is *really* serving at his club."

I swallow at the venom in his tone. "So how do we find where they lead? Google?"

"Probably." He nods, stroking his chin. "But we'd need more than just the locations. Who owns them? What happens around them. That sort of shit. Something specific the police wouldn't be able to ignore."

"Just what do you think Gino is up to?"

"What we need is answers," he says without addressing the question directly. Tucking the phone into his pocket, he starts for the exit. "I think I know how to get them."

His tone triggers a chilling sense of déjà vu. It's the same way he looked right before roping me into a drug deal. Like he's trapped inside an invisible cage with no clear way out but to resort to desperation.

Staggering from around the table, I race to catch up to him. "Meaning…"

"Meaning I know a guy who could give us that information," he says from over his shoulder. "But it wouldn't be cheap."

"How much?"

He scoffs. "A lot more than money. A lot fucking more."

I shiver, hating that my intuition was spot on. "We have to get justice for Faith," I say, even as I inwardly balk at what that might mean for my family. I'm not the only one with something at stake, though. "Especially if you're a suspect."

"Let's go," he says, leading the way from the building. "But don't say I didn't warn you."

2

OUR DESTINATION GIVES me a horrific flashback to the warehouse we went to for his uncle. Only a few key differences provide any ounce of reassurance—we're still in the city, for one. Though, this desolate street strewn with stray pieces of garbage doesn't instill much confidence, even before I look at Rafe. He's hunched over the steering wheel, wearing the same tense expression he did as he held the gun on the dealer.

Like he's toying with a decision from which there is no turning back.

"Sit tight," he tells me, slipping from the driver's seat. "Give me ten minutes on the fucking dot. I don't come out? You go back to the shop and pretend you were there all fucking night. Got it?"

"No!" I'm already unfastening my seatbelt. To his annoyance, I wrench open my door and place one foot on the pavement. "You don't get to drag people into situations like this with no explanation. *Again.*"

He winces at the reminder. "Fine. The guy here cracks video, phones, laptops. You name it, and he can probably rip into it, among other things. If anyone can help us make use of what info Faith had, he can."

"You don't look very convinced," I point out, eyeing his hands. They're clenched so tightly the knuckles protrude.

"A better option would be going to the police directly, but who knows how many are up Gino's ass? This is the next best thing."

But his tone alone gives me doubt. "Can you trust him?" I ask.

He switches off the car, and muscles open his own door. "He's damn good at what he does. Not to mention, if it's illegal and risky, he doesn't care."

Admittedly, those actions sound just a step below a drug deal.

"The more you elaborate on this plan of yours, the less enthusiastic I feel."

"Look." When we're both out of the car, he grabs my arm, spinning me to face him. "I won't lie to you. It's not ideal, and he's a sneaky son of a bitch. Usually, he wants a favor. A tit for tat sort of thing. He does an illegal favor for you; you do something for him so you can't rat him out. It's why he's lasted in this business for so damn long."

I suck in a steadying breath. "So, is this your way of asking me to cooperate in another drug deal?"

He flinches. "No! This is my way of asking…"

"For what?"

Sighing, he cups my chin, urging me to face him. "I'm asking you to trust me. And I'm asking you point blank—do you want to go in and get involved in that shit? Or wait here like a good little girl?"

I answer him by turning to the nearest building and craning my neck back to observe it in full. "This the place?"

Together, we approach it, following a desolate back road. At a glance, it looks like nothing more than an abandoned brick building. Any windows appear to be boarded up with plywood. An array of colorful graffiti mars nearly every inch of the side sporting a single battered door.

"Last chance to stay out of it," Rafe warns, meeting my gaze. When I say nothing, he sighs again and knocks once. Not even a second later, a voice comes from an unseen speaker.

"What the fuck do you want, Wei-Shen?"

"I'm here for business, Ace," Rafe replies. "Open up."

"You've been banned," the man snarls through the speaker. "Now get the hell out of here."

"Trust me, you won't want to miss this 'business,'" Rafe hisses through gritted teeth. "I promise I won't kick your ass this time. Now, open the damn door."

"I doubt that. Nothing you have could be worth the occupational hazard of working with you."

Rafe raises an eyebrow, inclining his head. "Not even if it could bring down Gino?"

A reply doesn't come for so long I figure we've been ignored after all. I look to Rafe, but he lifts a finger before I can say a word. A second later, I realize what has his attention—

footsteps. They approach sounding muffled as if from the other side of the door.

Then, with a metallic squeal, it opens from the inside amid a muttered curse from a figure I can't make out clearly. He's slender from what I can tell, leaning against the wall of a small, narrow hallway bathed in shadow.

"What kind of business?" he demands.

Rafe wrenches the door open wider and surges inside without an invitation. "Preferably now. So go on and name your price and take me to your little office."

"Hey! You can't just barge in here," the man sputters, attempting to block his path. He's short, with shaggy dark hair and large glasses that make his eyes seem comically wide. Shock doesn't begin to describe what I feel. I'd been steeling myself for someone like Gino or his uncle.

This man, however, doesn't seem to match Rafe's caution.

At all.

"Hey!" he exclaims, barring the hallway with his outstretched arms. "I said, stop! And I don't even know if I should work for you. Not after the last time—"

"Get over it," Rafe snaps, easily pushing past him. "Now cut to the chase. Can you do it or not?"

He's already rounding a corner, and I scamper in his wake as Ace has no choice but to close the door behind us.

"Who is she?" he demands, referring to me.

"No one you need to worry about," Rafe calls back. "Now, answer the question."

I find him in a cluttered room, his arms crossed. I have to blink several times just to make sense of the chaos. It's like a pawn shop exploded. Shelves and mismatched bookcases line nearly every available inch of wall. Each one is filled to the brim with old television sets from various decades, as well as boxes filled with assorted electronics—computers, radios, and pretty much any related device under the sun.

"I'm not doing shit for you without insurance," Ace says, squeezing past me. "Something good enough that if you ever so much as think about touching me, I could bury you."

Rafe forms a fist but doesn't lift it. "Name it."

"You must really want this job done," Ace surmises, a hint of smugness seeping into his tone. He approaches a desk wedged in between two bookshelves and throws himself into the swivel chair before it. A honeycomb of computer monitors, each displaying a different scene, loom behind him.

Swiveling toward Rafe, he steeples his fingers beneath his chin. "What's the job?"

"I need you to crack a phone for me. Every message. Every phone call. And decode some of the information on it." He pulls Faith's phone from his pocket and dangles it by a sparkly pink charm.

Ace raises an eyebrow. "Something tells me that there's more to it than that. So what are you offering for collateral?"

"Scan the security footage from the other night around the west side. You'll catch my car in the vicinity of a drug deal gone wrong. There. You have leverage over me against the police."

"That's it?" The man laughs, throwing his hands into the air. "Petty crime? Oh no, Rafe. I need something more than a tiger showing the same old stripes. Something good, or we're done here. You and your 'friend' can show yourselves out."

Rafe hisses through his teeth. "Like what?"

"I don't know," Ace says, stroking his chin. "Wow me. Something good."

"What about attempted murder?" Rafe says with deliberate malice. "Only it hasn't happened yet."

He takes a step forward, and Ace draws his knees beneath his chin, looking even smaller in comparison. "Hey! Don't touch me—"

"What about a sex tape?" I blurt out.

In hindsight, I have no idea why I brought it up at all. My chest is heaving, my pulse racing, but with every heartbeat, I feel less petrified than I should.

Rafe, however, goes rigid, while Ace scoffs, his mortal peril forgotten.

"With you?" He looks me over and sighs, unfurling his long limbs. "Nice, I'm sure, but not exactly worth my time—"

"Not even if it's Rafe with the sister of a cop?"

"Oh, ho!" Ace sits forward, his grin mischievous. "Now, that sounds interesting."

"No." Rafe grabs my arm, but his touch isn't anywhere near restraining. More protective. A warning. "That's not for sale."

"Too salacious?" Ace wonders, cackling. He spins to face me, stroking his chin. "Tell me more."

Rafe shoots me a warning glance, but I ignore him.

"Would that cover it?" I ask, stepping forward.

Ace continues to spin in his chair, seemingly mulling it over. "This information must be pretty pricey. Maybe I'm lowballing? What else do you have, pretty girl?"

"Take it or leave it, you greedy son of a bitch," Rafe growls. "You have five seconds to decide."

Ace's bravado lasts all of three. "Okay. Okay," he says, raising his hands in surrender. "Give me the phone."

Rafe hands it over, and Ace whirls around to the computer monitors.

"Well, I can tell you one thing," he says after a few moments of typing and navigating various screens. "The GPS coordinates all trace to various locations around the city—"

"Give the man a medal," Rafe says mockingly, clapping his hands. "I could have fucking told you that without playing hacker."

"That's not all," Ace snaps. "Check it out." He prints a sheet of paper that he hands to Rafe. "Read it and weep. Those locations correspond directly to incoming shipments from a supposedly defunct import. The owner's identity is cloaked in a layer of secrecy and obfuscation up the wazoo. Damn, do you know what this means?" A real hint of trepidation seeps into his voice, making Rafe take a step closer.

"Why don't you enlighten us?" he suggests, his irritation apparent.

Ace continues his computer search, switching from various screens to another. Suddenly, he pushes away from the desk so quickly he nearly barrels Rafe over. Spinning to face us, he crosses his arms over his chest. "It means you're in some deep, deep shit, Wei-Shen," he says. "Shit that even a sex tape won't be able to make worth the risk. Our deal is off."

He snatches the phone from the desk and tosses it to Rafe.

"What the hell? You can't—"

"I don't fuck with human trafficking," Ace says, squaring his chin defiantly. "So beat me up if you want to. If you make me go down this rabbit hole, I'm going to the cops. Shit, the FBI would probably be better."

"What are you saying?" I ask, feeling my eyes narrow.

"I'm saying that whoever had that phone was meddling into some deep shit. The information speaks for itself, but don't expect me to spell it out."

I turn to Rafe, and our gazes meet. One look at him and I know he's just as confused as I am. "What the fuck are you talking about?" he demands, speaking to Ace.

The smaller man shakes his head. "Trust me, Wei-Shen. If you know what's good for you, you'll turn tail from this too. Now get out. Now, before you're fucking seen."

He bounds to his feet and ushers us into the hall with a jerk of his chin. "Out."

Rafe doesn't move. "What do you mean human trafficking?"

"You heard me," Ace snaps. "Now get out before I call the police with an anonymous tip about your extracurricular activities."

"Why you little shit—"

"Let's just go," I say, grabbing Rafe by the arm. "Come on."

Surprisingly, he relents to my touch, allowing me to guide him down the hall and out of the building.

Once we're back in his car, he grips the steering wheel tightly, his head bowed. "What the fuck was Faith into?" he demands.

I don't know what to say.

Eventually, he sighs and starts the engine, but he doesn't drive.

"You didn't have to do that," he says in a softer tone, this time speaking to me. "Though it was a damn good bluff considering you don't even know where the recordings are."

"I think they're still on the camera you found," I say.

His eyebrows shoot up, but slowly he nods. "Damn. It's smart, though. But it's a good thing Ace didn't get his hands on whatever is on those tapes. I know he looks harmless, but you have no idea what that motherfucker might have done had you gone through with it."

I face ahead and try not to let my unease show. "Were you worried about me?" I ask him. "Or yourself? Scared of what might happen if Ace got to see you naked?"

He laughs, but his eyes widen as if he's shocked he's doing so at all. "For you, not me. Ace is a goddamn creep. He wouldn't just have leverage over me, and don't doubt for a second that he wouldn't use it over you too. The bastard has no shame. Then again, you do fucking love to play with fire."

He sits back and fingers a lock of my hair, his gaze thoughtful.

We sit in silence for so long, droplets of rain start to splatter the windshield in a quiet cacophony. As thunder rumbles in the distance, I finally gather the nerve to speak again. "I just want to know the truth," I admit. "About Faith. About everything. And if my brother was involved…" I trail off, unable to even finish the sentence out loud. "I want to know the truth," I say instead.

"Do you think you can handle that?" Rafe demands. "Doing what needs to be done, even if your brother is involved. Turning him in?"

"I don't know," I admit, looking down.

"If Faith were just upfront with me, we wouldn't be in this shit. If she trusted me." His voice is a rasp, revealing just how much that bothers him. "Maybe I could have helped her if she did."

"What about her friend?" I ask, picturing the girl we met after Faith went missing. "The one we spoke to in the alley."

"Her?" He strokes his chin with one hand, looking more puzzled than ever. "Maybe... We could—" he breaks off sharply, shaking his head. "Never mind. Forget it. I don't think she knows anything, and…"

I look up to find him watching me, his brow furrowed. "How did you know how to open her phone?" he asks. "You never told me what the password was."

It's a question he has every right to ask, but I cringe in the face of it nonetheless. My eyes burn, watering before I can even think to blink the tears back. In vain, they spill anyway.

"I used DW's real name," I admit. "Who I think he is, anyway."

Slowly, understanding dawns over Rafe's face. His eyes widen, his jaw clenching. Finally, he growls, "Branden *Dewitt*. I'm such a fucking idiot!" He forms a fist, slamming it into the steering wheel, but I brace my hand over his shoulder, sensing the tension coiled within each muscle.

"I think Branden was DW, but I don't think he killed Faith by himself. He mentioned someone. He said someone would come after us. He didn't know how the police had even traced him to Faith—they searched his house too—"

"Did he hurt you?" Rafe grabs my hand, drawing it onto his lap. Heat shoots down my spine as he uncurls every finger, inspecting the small scrapes and scratches I hadn't noticed until now.

"No," I say. "But I'm scared. And if he hurt Faith… He deserves to be punished."

Rafe jerks his chin in agreement. "If Ace is too chickenshit to delve into this, then we need more. Something to tie it all together. We know this 'DW' got Faith into deep shit. All of it ran through Gino's. And now with the fire? His place is ground zero."

"But, I'm guessing Faith didn't leave behind a full confession?" I nod to the phone still in his hand.

"No," he admits. "But I think I know where we can get something close to that."

I raise an eyebrow. "Where?"

"It's a stupid idea," he warns, averting his gaze.

"But it's not like we have a better one. You're a *suspect*," I point out. "We don't have a lot of options. And if Branden—" I can't even say it. The pain is still there, waiting to overwhelm me at any moment. The tears are still falling.

But I choose to focus on what I can change. I'm tired of cowering in my brother's shadow. Sighing, I stroke my thumb across the back of Rafe's hand. "Do you have an idea or not?"

"Everything points back to Gino's club," he says finally, his tone grim. "The motherfucker is hiding something, and if Ace is anywhere near right…then, it's bad. The kind of shit I'd have to be an idiot to get you into. No—" He snatches his hand away, gripping the steering wheel. "I'm not getting you involved in this."

"I want answers as much as you do." I'm surprised by how desperate I sound—and I am in every sense of the word. Desperate for clarity. For the truth. For answers. With a trembling hand, I swipe at my tears and fight to keep my voice steady. "I can't live like this anymore. So tell me what you're thinking."

"Fine," he growls in defeat. "You mentioned Faith's friend—"

"Lylah," I blurt, remembering the name Liam had used. "I think she spoke to the police as well."

"Well, if we can get her or one of the girls still working there to talk to us, maybe they could give us something worth taking to the cops. Something worth dragging Ace by his hair until he gives us everything we need, at least."

I wince in sympathy for the scrawny hacker, but then another thought comes to me. "Wasn't there a fire? Won't it be closed—"

"Like Gino would let that stop him," Rafe remarks with a harsh laugh. "I'm sure he's holed up somewhere. If we could find out where and get in, we could…"

"But Gino would never let you walk through his front door," I point out, envisioning how their last meeting went. For emphasis, I brush my hand along Rafe's still bruised jaw.

"You're right," he says softly, stroking his fingers over mine. "He wouldn't let *me*. But if we could use a decoy…"

"Like me?"

He glowers at the mere idea of it. "Hell no. You clean up nicely and all, bunny, but no. Don't even think about it—"

"I'll do it."

"No." He palms the steering wheel while shifting the car into drive. From the set of his jaw, I can tell that he's more than ready to leave this conversation behind.

But something inside me won't let him balk so easily. "Are you afraid that I'll succeed where you couldn't?"

His shoulders slump in defeat as he shakes his head. "I'm afraid you'll get hurt."

"Then we can do this together," I suggest. "To keep you out of jail and get justice for Faith. Or we sit around and let Gino, and whoever else is behind this, skip away scot-free."

Or allow Branden to get away with murder a second time.

As stubborn as he is, even Rafe scowls at the prospect. "Okay. But first, we need to do some shopping—" he casts a disapproving glance my way. "You won't be needing a sweater where you're going."

I try not to flinch at the ominous tone. Instead, I wipe away the rest of my tears and face forward. "I'm ready."

CHAPTER SEVENTEEN

Gino chose the most uninspired venue to reopen his business—a warehouse just a few blocks down from the original site. We pass the hollow, burned-out shell on our way there. The brick façade is blackened with soot, any entrance cordoned off by a maze of yellow caution tape.

I can't imagine the blaze that caused so much damage—especially considering the residential buildings nearby. Whoever was behind the arson didn't give a damn for anyone who might get in the way.

But why?

"I wouldn't be this sloppy," Rafe remarks, gazing at the destruction in the rearview window as we leave it behind. His hand finds mine with a reassuring squeeze. "If you've changed your mind…"

"No," I say, forcing down a nervous swallow. "I want answers. How did you even find out where the new club is, anyway?"

As if on cue, said building comes into view. Even if he hadn't told me beforehand—judging from the steady stream of people entering and leaving this seemingly isolated place —I could take a guess at what kind of establishment it might contain.

"Ace turned out to be good for something," Rafe says while parking a few blocks down from the club. "I had him track down what other property Gino owned. And guess what? The price wasn't a sex tape."

My cheeks flame at the reminder. "Lucky you."

With sudden seriousness, he braces his hand over my bare knee. His touch is electric, and I grit my teeth at the sensation. I can feel the ridge of every finger, radiating heat.

"You don't have to do this. I mean it, bunny. You may like playing with fire, but this isn't a game."

I have no doubt that he's probably right. But in the grand scheme of everything that's happened with Branden and Faith, I can't ignore a chance to seek out answers. No matter how dangerous it may be to find them.

"It's too late," I say, shouldering my door open. As I step out onto the curb, unease worms its way into my stomach, countering my resolve. Technically, as far as nightclubs are concerned, this is only my third experience entering one.

Faint music emanates from the distant warehouse, audible even this far down. Overall, this is a relatively desolate part of the city, especially compared to Rafe's Dragon's Head venue's busy location. Winding alleys snake through tall brick buildings, most of them seemingly abandoned, making the crowd of people gathered on the next block far more conspicuous.

I'm so caught up in recalling the basics of our plan over and over that I almost forget the presence still beside me.

"I've got your back," Rafe calls from the driver's side of his car, picking up on my unease. "Just keep your phone on you at all fucking times. I'll be listening. The second anything goes wrong, I'm coming in. Remind me again what the goal is."

I sigh before reciting the rigid criteria. An easy feat, considering he's told me at least a million times. "Get in and out. Keep my phone on. Only talk to one of the girls."

"Right," he agrees. "All you're doing is trying to *talk* to one of the girls. Got it?"

"Yes." I start forward, sensing that he's on the verge of attempting to talk me out of it—also for the millionth time.

"By the way, you look sexy," he adds in a low tone that makes me stop short, my cheeks flaming. I look over to find him nodding in approval, biting his lower lip. "You might have to roleplay as a redhead every now and again."

I eye the neckline of the tight black minidress he procured for me. It's the polar opposite of my usual style, along with a wig composed of synthetic curls. A cakey layer of makeup obscures the worst of my bruises, and I'd barely recognized myself in the mirror.

"You have ten minutes," Rafe warns, switching to a more serious baritone. "I mean it. Now set up your phone."

"Okay." I grab my phone from my purse, dial his number, and speak directly into it. "Got it."

Undertaking his role seriously, I sense him trailing in my wake with every step I take. I spy his car lurking a few yards away from the corner of my eye as I approach the front doors where a bouncer stands guard. Tall, bulky, he wears an ill-fitting suit and has a cigarette sticking from his mouth as I submit to his inspection. As Rafe predicted, he takes one look at me and inclines his head to the door.

"Next time, remember that dancers go in through the back," he growls on my way past.

A short, darkened hallway separates the entrance from the club proper. One step inside and I'm bombarded by an arrangement of pulsating, blaring rock music. Blue strobe lights create a chaotic atmosphere similar to the inside of Rafe's club.

The only difference?

The Dragon's Head didn't sport several scantily clad women dancing on various platforms spread throughout. It's such a culture shock. I don't know how to react without giving myself away. Or where to look...

Like a fish out of water, I linger on the outskirts until a flash of a brighter blue draws my attention to a girl walking past. She's tall, thin, and despite the turquoise wig, her features are strikingly familiar. I start to follow her, and something in her posture triggers a memory.

She's the girl Rafe, and I talked to the night Faith went missing, Lylah.

I follow her into a back hallway and then a dingy bathroom that contains only two stalls. In any stakeout movie I've watched, the pursuer would wait and observe before making up a well-thought-out excuse to strike up a conversation—but they had way more time than I do. I figure there's no better way to do this than to take a few shortcuts—I grab her arm on our way in.

Whirling on me, she glowers, her eyes rimmed by a layer of thick eyeshadow. "What the hell?"

"Do you remember me?" I ask. After the whirlwind chaos of the past few days, I'm too exhausted for tact. "I need to talk to you about Faith Wen."

She narrows her eyes, wrenching her arm away. "Who the hell are you?"

"We've met before," I say in a rush. "Does this trigger a memory?"

I reach into my purse and draw out a phone, but it isn't mine.

"Shit." The girl's eyes widen, and she reaches out seemingly by impulse before pulling her hand back halfway. Her trembling bottom lip makes her look far younger than her skimpy black dress would imply. "Where did you—"

"Just tell me what it means. What was Faith trying to expose before she died?"

The girl whips around, glancing over her shoulder as if expecting someone else to come jumping from a stall. "You have no fucking clue, do you?" she hisses. "What kind of shit you've stumbled into."

I grind my teeth helplessly, wishing I had some of Rafe's blunt honesty to draw on. Instead, all I can do is beg. "So help me."

"Fuck off." She storms away, dashing into the main club before I can stop her.

Even faint, I hear a voice issue from my cell phone. "Get out of there, bunny. Now!"

But I can't. Not yet. It could be because of Faith—or sheer curiosity. All of this time, I'd thought Branden's actions were based on me. Because of me. What I did. What I made him do.

But if they weren't, then he had another reason for killing Faith. Another reason for putting her hair pin in a box of my things.

My fearsome, tormentor of a brother was afraid of *someone else* for once.

Who?

And why?

Ignoring Rafe, I stagger down the hall and try to blend in, a surprisingly easy task. There is no main dance floor like Rafe's club. Just a bar, and a series of leather couches positioned around the various stages. As a result, most patrons are gathered around those attractions, leaving the walkways fairly free.

A flash of blue hair catches the corner of my eye, and I surge toward it, spotting the girl darting around a bar counter. "Wait!"

I slip around a scantily dressed dancer, fighting to keep the girl in view. I've barely gone another step when someone grabs my arm from behind, dragging me to a corner booth.

"You think I don't recognize Rafael's little slut?" a man hisses against my ear. "What the fuck are you doing here?"

Terror grips my heart in a vice, and I don't even have to look at him to put a name to that gruff rasp. *Gino.*

I crane my neck back to find him grinning ear to ear, but his eyes are wild. Unsteady. Despite his crisp black suit, instability reeks from him as strongly as a cloying cologne.

"You and I should have a little talk, shouldn't we?" Without giving me the chance to answer, he shoves me against a leather cushion, sliding in beside me.

"About Faith Wen?" I counter, scrambling to put as much distance between us as possible. At a glance, it seems as if we're alone—none of his minions are nearby, at least.

But I don't trust it.

Seated across from me, Gino looks more cartoonish than ever. The club lighting robs most of his features of any definition, and the overall neon blue glow gives him a ghoulish effect. With his teeth bared and eyes narrowed into slits, he's intimidating enough to more than justify Faith's obvious fear of him.

But is he capable of murder?

"What about that little bitch?" he snarls.

I swallow hard, bracing my hands over the circular table between us. Cutting my gaze to the exit, I realize that it would be easy to run. Or grab my cell phone and call for Rafe like anyone with sense would.

But for some reason I'm not even fully aware of, I'm compelled to keep talking. "She was going to expose something about your business," I say bluntly. "Then, she wound up dead."

I marvel at the steady voice issuing from my throat.

Gino, however, sneers at the sound. "Was she, now?" He throws his head back for a loud, barking laugh that has no real amusement in it. Fixing me with a raised eyebrow, he questions, "And what was she going to expose, huh?"

"You tell me," I snap back. "Like…" Glancing around, it's unsettling to realize that many of the dancers resemble Lylah. All are wearing skimpy dresses, and nearly every last one looks too young from the wrong angle. Scared. "Like what kind of business you might be offering other than just lap dances."

Blood rushes through my ears as I belatedly process the dangerous game I've just started—and with an opponent like Gino, who seems to have no trouble breaking into people's property and beating them bloody.

His eyes meet mine with an intensity that warns me he's more than capable of doing worse. So much worse. "Oh, really?" he murmurs. One by one, he cracks his knuckles.

"The p-police are already investigating," I point out, though I find myself eyeing the exit again. The impulse to escape strengthens, and my toes twitch anxiously in their borrowed black heels. "And if anyone else goes missing—"

"Like Faith?" he interjects. His green eyes flit over me as he cocks his head. Whatever impression he has of me makes him scoff. "You really suck at this whole 'Nancy Drew' shit, don't you?"

He slams a hand over the table, so suddenly I jump, but all he does is pointedly flex each finger. "The police, huh? You really think they can do shit?" His cruel smile widens, exaggerating his appearance even more. "Ask your little boyfriend how well the cops around here operate."

But Rafe already told me as much—they're under Gino's thumb. Even Branden admitted as much.

"You want to talk about *Faith*?" Gino says. "Fine. Let's talk, starting with one little question. You look like a smart girl —who do you think led her to Rafael?"

I feel my eyes widen before I can disguise any reaction.

Still smiling, Gino reads me clearly and nods. "Oh, yes, baby. And the dumb motherfucker couldn't even sell me out right." His upper lip curls back from his teeth, his eyes unfocused once more. A part of me shies away from the assessment at first, but there's no way around it now. He's desperate.

And terrified.

"Why?" I ask, more confused than ever. "Were you trying to set him up?"

It would make sense, fitting his cartoon villain persona, but his brow furrows to betray an emotion I least expect. Not smug pride. Just grim irritation.

Hoarsely, I propose another option, "Were you trying to warn him?"

He leans forward, fixing me with a chilling stare. "And if I were?" I can barely hear him above the pulsating rock music —by design, I suspect. His eyes flit around the room, revealing the same paranoia as the girl in the bathroom.

"So you sent Faith to warn Rafe. Why?" I can barely keep the disbelief from my tone. "Why attack him then? Unless you really believe he set the fire."

Any minute, I expect him to laugh or break into some super villain sermon.

Instead, he looks down at his hands, his jaw clenched. "Because some shit isn't worth it. And as much of a pansy fucker Rafael is, I know he's a boy scout. Though, apparently, not a very fucking good one."

Some shit isn't worth it...

"I guess this wasn't all your idea?" I surmise, deliberately skirting naming the topic outright. Again, I keep staring at the various dancers with increasing dread. Despite Gino's confession, I can't ignore the obvious—if he attacks me now, there isn't much I could do to stop him. "Why tell me all of this?"

He lifts his hands tiredly, his smile lopsided, teeth bared. "I'm dead anyway," he says simply. "I'm in this shit too fucking deep. But thanks to your boyfriend, I no longer have a choice."

"Why?" I ask hoarsely. His tone unsettles me more than him attacking me would. Gone is the cocky swagger I'd expect. All that remains is an emotion that eerily mirrors how Branden had looked pacing his living room.

Raw, open helplessness.

"Who are you working for?" I ask.

"Who do you think?" he snarls, practically lunging across the table.

I jump back, scrambling for the end of the booth, but he doesn't make a move to stop me.

"Are you that fucking dumb?" he demands, curling his hands into fists. "I'll give you a hint. Someone who wouldn't want his lackey to know where the real money comes from. Not the same darling nephew who put his own father in prison. Someone with a lot more to fucking lose than me. You mentioned the fire? Ask yourself who benefited from it. Maybe the guy who could spin it as retribution for a dead girl when in reality, he hasn't done a damn thing about it?"

The answer is elusive, and I'm tempted to call his bluff—he's trying to confuse me on purpose. But then something in my brain clicks.

"Rafe's uncle?" I rasp, unable to disguise my shock. "That doesn't make any sense."

"Doesn't it?" With a smug grin, Gino sits back, folding his hands before him. "Rafe plays it as though he's a tough, hard-ass, but deep down, baby? He's a fucking pussy. With him in charge, Shen has a loyal soldier, but one who plays by the rules. Since he's had the reins, the triad has retreated from the game in every sense of the word. What do they do now? Shake down business owners for chump change. There's no real money in that. But Shen knows that no matter how hard he tugs on his little puppy's leash, Rafe won't hesitate to bring him down if he goes too far. The only problem? All the money he funnels into his life, including that nice political run, doesn't come from nowhere."

And maybe he's right. Despite his bravado and tough persona, Rafe had allowed Mr. Zhang to rack up a sizeable debt—only to pay it off himself. That act reveals more than what he made it seem. He'd deliberately avoided extorting the money another way.

Then he took the loss, opening himself up to his uncle's retribution.

"I thought Mr. Shen wanted to keep his hands clean," I blurt, parroting Rafe's own insistence on that fact.

Gino chuckles. "Bullshit. When his precious nephew bailed, Shen just found another fucking patsy."

I don't think he's lying. He's too tense, hunched forward, frustration coiled in his posture.

"You?" I ask, stating the obvious.

He sits forward again, but this time I don't react, even as his breath hits me full in the face. "You have no fucking idea. And if you think me telling you this shit changes anything, then you're wrong. It's already too late, baby. For you, your precious Rafael, and—" He breaks off suddenly, his gaze cutting over my shoulder. "What the hell?"

The back of my neck prickles in warning before I even turn to see why. A tall figure is barreling toward us like a storm, shoving his way through anyone who tries to slow him. In his wake, two bouncers stagger, one clutching his stomach. Only now do I remember the phone in my purse, still relaying everything we've been saying.

And Rafe looks like he's heard every last word. His eyes blaze like fire, his hands curling into fists.

I'm stepping into his path before I realize it, bracing my hand against his chest. "Rafe, don't!"

He easily shrugs me off, heading for the booth where Gino eyes him warily, still seated.

"You think this is funny?" Rafe asks. He forms a fist and punches the table so hard it jolts against the floor, its joints squealing. "Playing fucking games. Spreading this bullshit?"

Gino blinks, his gaze unwavering. "Do I look like I'm laughing, mutt? Maybe it's about time you got your head out of the fucking sand. Look around—" he gestures to the rest of the club with an outstretched hand. "If Shen really gave a shit about some dead girl, do you think he'd let me open up shop so soon? Not unless he needed somewhere to stash his precious pussy—"

"Enough!" Rafe nearly lunges across the table, snatching a fistful of his suit collar. "You work for Shen? Let's call and ask him?"

Gino's eyes practically glow in the dim lighting. "Fuck, yes. Call him, mutt. Ask him why he's cut you out. Made you do his dirty work. The way I hear it, the old man's all but left you for dead."

"Rafe, don't!" I grab the fist he starts to form before he can lift it. Tension ripples off his body like a wall of heat. I grit my teeth in the face of it, and it takes everything I have not to give in to the raw, instinctive need to back away. "Don't do this."

He snatches his arm from me, but in the same moment, grips my wrist as he turns on his heel. I have no choice but to follow him. When I look back, Gino is watching us, his arms crossed, lips still quirked.

And his warning seems more ominous than ever.

"Run little mutt," he calls. "But you know the truth, don't you? You never meant shit to him, and still don't."

Rafe tightens his grip on me rather than answer. As we pass the bouncers, they let us go without a word, and his car is already parked directly out front.

"I thought we had a deal, huh?" he snarls once we're inside it. "Ten minutes, and if I say you bail, you bail."

"I don't think Gino killed Faith," I blurt in a rush. "But he knows who did. I think he's afraid of them."

I hesitate to admit anything more, gauging his reaction. He's staring straight ahead, still furious. Would he even believe that his uncle was capable of such crimes? Though perhaps he'd deluded himself like I had.

But the truth is inescapable. Branden's reasons were well beyond trying to intimidate me.

The silence between us extends as Rafe says nothing, but he doesn't have to. He heard Gino's tirade himself through my phone. Even knowing that I can't bring myself to name the prime suspect out loud.

But I don't have to.

"No," Rafe says, starting the car. "No. He wouldn't… He wouldn't. Not him."

His uncle.

I thought I knew what it felt like to be helpless—but this moment somehow tops any other.

Watching Rafe pace his kitchen, his hands clenched into fists, his head bowed. "No," he growls for the countless time. "No. My uncle may be an asshole, but… No. No. He wouldn't be into that shit. He wouldn't. And Gino? The motherfucker's been gunning for me since day one. He's just fucking with my head."

He has a point—but I can see the situation from a different angle. That of a man who desires only control, willing to do whatever it takes to exert it over his nephew. Like, goad him into a gang war for seemingly no benefit.

Or beat him.

Force him to commit a crime.

Torment him.

"If you went after Gino directly, what would happen, hypothetically speaking?" I ask, picking the less volatile topic to start with.

"Nothing good," Rafe says bluntly. He sighs, bracing his hip against a counter, his gaze distant. "It would escalate fast. Besides, Gino's territory isn't worth the risk."

"Why?"

"We'd have to muscle into his business. You can't rely on sheer force to accomplish something like that. You need allies."

"Allies that your uncle can't associate with if he's supposedly 'clean,'" I say.

He swivels toward me. "What the fuck are you getting at?"

I flinch, but I don't cower. Meeting his gaze, I say, "I think he's been lying to you. I think he's the one pulling Gino's strings, and I think he's about to do something worse."

Something so bad that even Gino was alarmed by it.

But…as his expression transforms into a grim frown, I come to a startling realization.

"You knew," I say quietly.

"I *knew* he could be a petty son of a bitch," he corrects. "So, what are you getting at? He used Gino to run his titty bar?"

I sense it's better not to say anything. Whatever he's going through is personal. A dilemma that no one else can unravel but him.

The same way I have to face my brother's part in this scheme.

"So what?" he demands, though I suspect he's speaking to himself more than me. "He dabbles in human trafficking now? He wouldn't. Why?"

He glares at the wall as if it might give him an answer. A muscle in his jaw quivers and I can almost see the struggle taking place in his brain between logic and loyalty.

"Rafe…" I finally step forward, placing my hand on his shoulder.

"Don't." He shrugs me off, crossing over to the couch. "I don't need you to look at me with those bunny eyes right now. I need…"

"Answers," I say, finishing for him.

"Damn right." He inclines his head, fixing me with a cold stare. "Let's start with the obvious. Your brother's name unlocked Faith's phone. Don't tell me that's a coincidence."

Tears burn behind my eyes, and I don't even try to keep them from falling. Nodding, I cross over to sit beside him.

"It wouldn't be the first time," I admit, hating the way my throat tightens. I've kept these secrets in for so long…

But in a hoarse whisper, I finally spill them. I tell him about Lexi. Her death. The bracelet.

When I finally finish, Rafe is glowering at the floor, his jaw clenched, expression unreadable. I can't move, sick with anticipation of how he might react.

In disgust?

Horror?

"Shit," he hisses, grasping my hand. I go limp to find there is no judgment in his touch. No hate. Only warmth emanating from his fingers, radiating reassurance.

And my head swims with relief.

"I think he may have hurt Faith," I say.

"Look at me." Honed with intensity, his eyes bore into mine. "Were you going to let him get away with murder if he did do it?"

"No!" I say. But my voice sounds flat, even to me. I've let Branden get away with so much. And why? For one pathetic reason. "I thought… I thought it was my fault."

Rafe scoffs. "Because he's fucking brainwashed you."

I don't counter that. "But I don't think he was working alone."

He stands, crossing to the window. Watching him from this angle, I can fully appreciate his strength in every sense of the word. His size, his muscle, and namely his ability to think critically. To push through his own rage and betrayal and see the truth at the heart of the matter.

"Fine. So Shen's dirty," he says, glaring at the street below. "What do we do about it? He must have the cops in his back pocket."

"Not all of them," I say quickly. One person, in particular, comes to mind.

Rafe fixes me with a raised eyebrow. "Let me guess," he says. "Your fake boyfriend?"

I try to ignore his obvious hostility. "I think he learned the truth about Bran too. Maybe he can reach out to someone else in the department? Someone your uncle doesn't control."

"It's dumb," Rafe says bluntly. "It probably doesn't have a chance in hell of working. But we don't have any better options. And… I trust you."

I shiver at the heat in his voice, but I don't allow myself the chance to decipher it. Instead, I fish through my bag and grab Liam's business card.

With a harsh exhale, Rafe snatches it from me, withdrawing his own phone from his pocket. "We have nothing left to lose."

"There are about a million reasons why I shouldn't even be here right now," Liam says, warily eyeing the drawings hanging on the walls of Rafe's shop. I doubt he can see much, considering the lights are off—a detail Rafe insisted on to avoid anyone from the outside being able to look in.

Another precaution is Liam's lack of a uniform. A nondescript sweatshirt instead helps him blend into the shadows.

But his presence here at all is jarring regardless.

"What is this about?" he asks, finally looking from me to Rafe. All I can make out are the whites of his eyes and the firm set to his jaw.

Was calling him here a mistake? Even so, it's not like we have any better options. Taking a deep breath, I decide to forgo any pretense. "Before, in front of the café… You were trying to tell me something about Branden." I hesitate before adding, "I want to know."

Liam's silent. Even with part of his face illuminated by the glow cast by an outside streetlight, he's unreadable. Doubt creeps in with every passing second, and sweat is beading at the nape of my neck by the time he finally sighs.

"I think you should tell me exactly why I'm here before I jump to the wrong conclusion." He cuts his gaze to Rafe, who is lurking near the hallway, his arms crossed guardedly.

Before I can open my mouth, Rafe steps forward. "Lee Wei-Shen," he says gruffly. "Does that name ring a bell?"

Liam cocks his head toward the window, and the extra light reveals his raised eyebrow. "Your uncle? What is this about?"

"Tell me the truth," I say, taking a step closer to him. "You can trust us."

"You go first," Liam counters, turning to me. "Tell me about your brother. The truth." The hardness in his tone warns that he has one topic in mind.

And there's no point in running from it any longer.

I tell him everything. Lexi. Faith. The rest. At the back of my mind, I hate how it sounds out loud, not to mention the risk may not be worth it at all. But when I finish, Liam looks anything but surprised.

"He's been under investigation for months," he admits. "I didn't know about the Winacott case, but there has been suspicion regarding him and corruption stretching back at least a year. However, there's been no solid evidence yet."

Dread congeals in my stomach, as painful as jagged shards of glass. It takes me several tries to form a coherent reply. "What can we do?"

"And how do we know your boss isn't dirty too?" Rafe pitches in. I flinch at the hostility in his tone, but Liam doesn't seem to take it to heart.

He meets my gaze directly, his eyes gleaming in the dark. "Because I'm not really a member of the police." Before the shock can fully set in, he says, "I'm with the FBI."

Rafe hisses. "I hope that's a joke."

"This area has been under surveillance for a long time," Liam says without addressing him. "But we need proof. At least a confession on tape, and I shouldn't have to say that consorting with a suspect's sister and a local criminal wouldn't be cleared by my higher-ups."

"I'm guessing Branden doesn't know, either," I croak.

Liam nods. "Look, if this information gets out, it won't be corroborated by my department, but we suspect some officers have been participating in illegal activities involving a local club and one Lee Wei-Shen." He nods pointedly toward Rafe. "That same club is at the center of a parallel special victims investigation involving suspected human trafficking. Again, we've yet to find any solid proof."

"How the fuck do we get that?" Rafe demands. "Ask him nicely?"

"Or I could," I blurt without thinking the plan through. "I could be the one wearing a wire."

"No," Liam says. "This isn't a TV show. I shouldn't have to tell you that involving civilians would never be approved by my superiors."

Rafe scoffs. "Well, you can give them this." He approaches the counter, placing an object on it. Even in the dim lighting, I can make out its shape. "That's Faith's phone," he adds. "We think she hid GPS coordinates on it. Maybe your 'superiors' can find something useful on it."

Liam nods. "It's a start."

But I can sense what he doesn't say out loud. "But it isn't enough."

"It could take weeks to analyze—which is good for supplementary information, but we suspect that Lee Wei-Shen will make a move soon. Either to liquidate his assets entirely or cast suspicion somewhere else to cover his tracks."

Which would explain why Gino was so shaken.

"He's just one player among many," Liam explains. "This ring stretches nationwide, but we've never been able to crack any of the cells."

"And yet you keep shooting down any suggestions," Rafe points out, his suspicion obvious. "So what do you propose,

Mr. FBI? Though hell, you could be up Shen's ass like the rest of them."

"I could," Liam admits. "And while I can't authorize you to wear a wire and garner a confession on audio—or better yet, catch Shen in the process of covering his tracks—that would be the best piece of evidence I could use to quickly advance the investigation far enough to make an arrest. But it's dangerous." He faces me directly, and for the first time, a hint of concern displaces his otherwise serious expression.

"You said the force here is corrupt," Rafe says, but I don't miss how he moves to my side. His hand lands over my shoulder, anchoring me to him. "My place was searched the other fucking day. I don't think that's a coincidence."

"Branden's was too," I add, frowning.

"If anything were found, there would be an arrest by now," Liam says. "We're at the end of the rope. A few more days without a solid lead, and this ring just moves to another city."

"So, what do we do?"

Rafe inclines his head. "If you won't 'sanction' anything, then what good are you?" he demands.

"I can analyze the cell phone, for one," Liam says, reaching for the device. "And, while I can't participate in any official capacity, I can be on standby. And if I happen to misplace some equipment in the meantime, then so be it."

"Good," Rafe says, his teeth flashing in the shadow. "I have an idea."

CHAPTER NINETEEN

Despite the time I've spent away, Mr. Zhang's shop feels the same. Here, amongst the dusty bookshelves, I can ignore the rest of reality. I even volunteer to finish out the business day, allowing Mr. Zhang to leave early.

But I can't ignore the tension lacing the air with every passing second. I'm jumping at every noise to break the quiet, and when the bell above the door chimes, I stiffen in anticipation even before I turn to face the figure standing near the entrance.

Shock hits me like a punch, but not in the way I've been expecting. "Mara?"

I stagger around the counter to meet her, stopping a few feet away. She's wearing her black uniform from the restaurant and must have just gotten off. Her arms are crossed, her gaze wary.

"What are you doing here?" I ask, but I can't stop myself from scanning the view of the street behind her. Apart from a few pedestrians, no one else is there.

"I'm sorry, were you expecting your boyfriend?" Mara asks, turning on her heel. "Let me just leave, then—"

"Wait! I'm sorry," I blurt in a rush. Awkwardly, I fiddle with a stand of pens beside the register, unsure of what else to do with my hands. From over my shoulder, I say, "I am just surprised you're here."

"My dad needed me to pick up a cookbook for him," she snaps, crossing over to a section of glossy new recipe books. She grabs one seemingly at random and flips through it, her back to me. After a second, she pointedly clears her throat. "Isn't this the part where you grovel for forgiveness?"

"Um…" I blink in shock and promptly knock over a row of silver ballpoints. I scramble to rearrange them, but when I finally face her, she's watching me, her head cocked expectantly. "Yes. I'm so sorry—"

"Good." She sets the book aside and places her hands on her hips. "Holding grudges can give you wrinkles, and I just don't have the energy to expend on dumb boy drama. Besides, it looks like you have more than enough of that for the both of us," she adds, raising an eyebrow.

My cheeks catch fire. Only God knows what the chaos outside of the café looked like to her. "It wasn't like that."

"So what was it like, then? Just you gloating over the fact that you were screwing Rafe despite encouraging me to go after him? That's fucked up."

I don't deny it. Finally, she sighs.

"The least you can do is spill the drama. I might be able to forgive you for keeping Rafe your naughty secret, but two sexy men? Who was that boy scout?"

I choke out a sound that might be a laugh. "Someone who I can assure you is all yours."

"I'm off this weekend," she says, heading toward the door without the cookbook. "You owe me dinner. My parents' place, and you might want to borrow lover boy's wallet. I plan on eating big."

"Deal."

I watch her go, feeling a weight lift off my shoulders. The relief lightens some of the heavy mood from before. When I finally finish my shift and head out the dread returns. I've barely put the key in the lock when I sense a presence approach me from behind. "You think this is funny?" a man snarls against my ear. Alarm shoots down my spine, but before I can even think to run, he snatches my forearm in a vice grip. "You go and jump out of a fucking window? What the hell has gotten into you?"

I turn to face him, steeling myself for what I might find— but nothing could prepare me for this. Branden, but in a state I've never seen him in before. His eyes are wild, hair mussed, and unkempt. Instead of his uniform, he wears crumpled sweats and a T-shirt, and his breath sears my nostrils, unmistakably tainted with alcohol.

"Why are you here?" I ask.

His eyes narrow. "You really want to 'talk'? Then come with me. Now."

He tugs me after him, but I don't resist, letting him shove me into a nearby van. It's the same one from before, and he instantly engages the locks.

I don't bother to hide the fear from my voice. "What do you want?" Fighting to keep my breathing steady, I crane my neck to watch him. "Where are we going?"

"Somewhere where you can't run away," he warns, pulling away from the curb. "So you want to talk? Who have you been running your mouth to, huh?"

His inflection varies wildly, his eyes unfocused as they dart around the road.

Inhaling deeply, I pose a question of my own. "Did you hurt Faith? Were you the one she was really messaging?"

He snorts out a harsh laugh, his nostrils flaring. "That little cunt. Why would I be speaking to her, huh? You ask yourself that."

But the answer is obvious in the way Faith had reacted to the topic of her mysterious DW. She was terrified of him, and I'd been so stupid not to recognize it. The last time I saw her alive, her haunted expression stuck with me for a reason—it was the same exact one I saw every day in the mirror.

"She was someone you could control," I hoarsely point out. "Until you couldn't anymore."

"You think you're so damn smart, huh?" he hisses through his teeth. "You tell me something. Where is the fucking hair clip? Where did you put it?"

I keep my hands in view, neither confirming nor denying that I have it. "Did you hide it in my apartment on purpose?"

"Don't play with me!" He slams his fist over the steering wheel so hard the horn sounds. Wild-eyed, he scans the road, his knuckles protruding from how tight his grip becomes. "Where is it?"

"You recognized her at the restaurant, didn't you?" I say, recalling that night and how angry he'd been. I'd assumed that I was the source of that rage, but someone else would pay the price in reality—just like with Lexi.

And me. My face still smarts if I focus on it. Absently, I trace the bottom of my lip, observing him from the corner of my eye. His expression isn't far from the fearsome snarl he wore the night he attacked me, and a grim sense of recognition strengthens my resolve.

"Did you follow her when I left? Is that when you killed her—"

"You don't have any fucking idea of what you've gotten into. Do you? No fucking idea. Now I have to fix it just to make sure you don't wind up—" He stiffens, and an emotion flits across his face that I recognize instantly. Fear.

A buzzing noise gives me a clue as to why. A ringtone?

"Shit." He fumbles through his pocket, withdrawing a cell phone. "Dewitt. Are you following me?" Whoever he's speaking to says something that makes him glance over his shoulder. "Where do you need me to go?"

He hangs up, shoving the phone into his pocket, and I sense the mood shift as drastically as if the temperature dropped several degrees. Branden, without his cocky swagger, is a stranger to me. He's shades paler, practically glowing in the dark. A sheen of sweat glints off his brow, and I know the alcohol stench isn't a coincidence.

"Who was that? Where are we going?" I demand as he swerves around a corner. "Tell me!"

"Shut up," he hisses. "Just shut up! You have no idea what kind of shit I'm in. No clue!"

"So tell me," I say, scrambling for my seatbelt as the van picks up speed. "Are you working for Lee Wei-Shen? Is that why you hid Faith's hair clip in my things."

He whips around to face me, so suddenly, the entire van jolts with the movement. "What the hell are you talking about?"

"Did you kill Faith?"

Shaking his head, he looks to the windshield. "You think you know everything, huh? Do you have any idea what I've done for you? The shit I've had to do to protect you? But it's too late now—" He releases a harsh bark of laughter that chills me to the core. "He won't let you off anymore."

"He?"

"I tried to warn you, but you couldn't fucking listen! You had to poke your damn nose into everything, didn't you?" He sounds hysterical, and I can't ignore a growing sense of alarm that has me digging my nails into my palms.

"What do you mean?"

He doesn't answer, still laughing maniacally, seemingly too distracted to even keep his eyes on the road. We barrel through an intersection, missing any oncoming traffic by a miracle. Logic warns me to shut up, save the questioning for when our lives literally aren't on the line. But fear and curiosity override anything else. "How long have you worked for him?" I ask, failing to keep my voice steady. It breaks, but I keep speaking, raising my voice until he flinches. "Why? Is that why you had to kill Faith? She found out about what really goes on at Gino's club—"

"Shut up!" The car comes to a sudden stop, and I'm thrown forward so violently my seatbelt cinches my chest. Dazed, I brace my hands over the dashboard and look up. We're in an unfamiliar part of town, far from any main street.

"Just shut up," Branden warns as he climbs out, circling to my end. He grabs my wrist, yanking me from my seat. "I'm warning you, Hannah. This isn't a fucking game. Now, where is the fucking hair clip?" he demands. "Give it to me!"

"I don't have it," I insist.

"Oh, really?" He grabs my bag, wrenching it from my grasp. He rummages through it and tosses it aside. "No!" He warns the second I take a step toward it. "Come on."

His nails rip into my shoulder as he shoves me forward, toward a narrow alley that cuts between two nearby buildings. Dark windows and abundant graffiti allude to them being abandoned, and my breaths quicken, my throat tight.

"Where are we?"

"Shut up," Branden snarls, pushing me forward. Eventually, we reach a battered door leading to one of the buildings. It's dank inside, the air so thick I can taste it. Coppery, like metal. Rust. Wet.

My steps falter, but Branden shoves me further down what appears to be a narrow hall. The pitch darkness is broken only by a faint glow emanating from a doorway up ahead. When we reach it, Branden forces me inside—a wide space littered with wooden crates. A row of large, dusty windows allows some of the outside light in, but it's barely enough to make out Branden's grim frown.

"Just stay here," he says, raking his hands through his hair. "Fuck! Let me handle this."

"Handle what?" I ask. "What's going on, Bran? Where are we?"

He doesn't answer.

The sound of a door opening makes him stiffen, and another man enters the room, his shape recognizable instantly. He looms against the narrow doorway, casting a shadow that seems to encompass everything in its path. But he isn't alone. Someone stands beside him, only his outline visible in the darkness.

Even Branden seems to shrink, whirling to face the newcomers. "I did what you said," he stammers, displaying an unease that shakes me to my core. "Everything. Now—"

"I didn't think you would be this foolish," Shen says, his voice a deep, unsettling rasp. "First, you get sloppy. Then careless, and now you seem determined to amplify your fucking mess."

Branden stiffens. "No! You don't understand—"

"I understand that you stepped right into a trap," Shen says. "And you brought a viper right into our midst—" He nods to me. "She's wearing a wire."

"N-No..." Branden turns to me, his gaze flashing. He grabs my hand, eyeing me with a ruthless flick of his gaze. "I took her bag. She wouldn't..."

"Search her," Shen commands.

I stagger back, but I'm not anywhere near quick enough. Branden snatches my wrist, tugging at my sweater with his free hand. "I don't feel anything," he declares after a moment.

But Shen steps forward, his head cocked. "Then you didn't search hard enough," he growls. "Luckily, I was alerted to your stupidity beforehand."

The man behind him enters the room fully, allowing the dim lighting to cast him in faint relief. At the sight of a familiar pair of dark eyes, I suck in a breath.

"Rafe?"

His gaze is fixed straight ahead, his expression unreadable.

"You can consider our arrangement over," Shen says to Branden, his upper lip curled in disgust.

"What the hell do you mean?" Branden demands. "I did everything you fucking asked!"

"You were sloppy," Shen snarls. "And now I'm forced to clean up your mess. Rafael."

On cue, Rafe steps forward, withdrawing something from his coat pocket. It's small enough to fit the curve of his palm, aimed straight ahead—and its purpose is undeniable.

Branden pales, backing up so clumsily he nearly trips over his own feet. "What the fuck?"

"To clean up your mess with the Wen girl, I have to take matters into my own hands."

"You told me to do it!" Branden shouts, clenching his hands at his sides.

"I told you to toy with the merchandise?" Shen growls. "I told you to run your mouth to that little bitch? Enough of this. Now you have another girl's death to answer for." His dark eyes cut toward me, devoid of any emotion.

"No," Branden growls. "Leave her out of this—"

"You don't have a say anymore," Shen says with a cold laugh. "As far as the police will know, you killed her to cover your tracks. Overcome with guilt, you then turned the gun on yourself. Rafael." He inclines his head toward Branden before turning on his heel to exit the room. "Clean this mess."

Rafe raises the gun, and the world slows to a crawl. I see his face. Those beautiful, unfathomable eyes narrowed with focus. Suddenly, he pivots, aiming in an entirely different direction.

"Don't move," he warns.

Shen stops short, glancing over his shoulder. It seems to take him a full second to realize just where Rafe is aiming. Anger colors his cheeks, his eyes narrowing. "What the hell are you doing?"

"Don't move," Rafe repeats, his voice steady. "I won't ask again."

Shen laughs, an eyebrow cocked in amusement more than alarm. "Don't tell me you've grown a pair, boy?" he taunts. "Put that toy away before you hurt yourself—"

"You really think I'm that dumb, don't you?" I can't even begin to classify Rafe's tone. My stomach clenches at the low, harsh notes roughening his baritone, even as his face remains expressionless. "*That* stupid," he adds. "That afraid of you that I wouldn't catch on. What the fuck was I to you, huh? A patsy? A fall guy?"

"Family," Shen growls, his eyes flashing. "But I suppose I should have known from the time you were a goddamn child how little that means to you. My brother may have shacked up with a worthless whore, but you are his real failure."

"Like he was so great, huh?" Rafe takes a step forward, still training the gun over his uncle's back—but his grip seems steadier. Determined. "I spent my life thinking I had to make up for his mistakes—but that was my real 'failure.' Thinking I owed your ass anything. You don't give a fuck about him, and you certainly don't give a fuck about me."

The other man whirls around, his face reddening with fury. "You think you have what it takes, Rafael? Do it then. Shoot me. Do it!" He holds out his arms, his smile feral.

Rafe doesn't move an inch, but I can feel his anger from here, radiating off him like a furnace. His eyes blaze with an intensity to match the creature inked on his back. When his fingers twitch, I step forward. "Don't—"

"Hannah!" Branden grabs my arm, yanking me back, but Rafe's eyes flicker in our direction. I swear I see him nod once—*I'm okay.*

But Shen just laughs. "You can't even betray me right," he declares, turning for the door again. "I... What the fuck?"

His gaze is directed at something beyond the doorway, but what has him so startled quickly becomes apparent. Footsteps—belonging to several people, racing in our direction all at once.

Loud, a voice rings out, stern with authority. "FBI! Hands in the air!"

I comply automatically, backing up against the far wall as several figures stream into the space. From their posture alone—and the navy jackets with a blazing emblem emblazoned on the front—their identities are obvious—FBI agents.

A slim figure I recognize as Liam spearheads the group, his focus purely on Shen.

"Lee Wei-Shen," he declares. "You're under arrest for suspicion of blackmail, extortion, and conspiracy to commit murder. You have the right to..."

My own thudding heartbeat drowns him out, surging through my ears as I watch two agents wrestle Branden to the ground. One of them pulls out a pair of handcuffs, applying them swiftly.

"Don't look," someone warns near my ear, his voice soft. Before I know it, Rafe is blocking my view, his hands on my waist as my cheek settles against his chest. "Just hold on to me."

And I do, gripping him so tightly my fingers ache. Adrenaline leaves me in a rush, and I'm forced to cling to him, trusting him to support my weight, which he does without a shred of hesitation.

I eye him through my lashes and wince in sympathy. He looks worse than ever, his bruising apparent even in the dim lighting. Carefully I stroke my fingers over the unmarred skin along his jaw, letting the sight distract me from everything else.

And somehow…

It does.

CHAPTER TWENTY

If I were to write my essay for the Fenwick program now, I know exactly what I'd center it around. *Fear*, the most insurmountable of inner demons. For so long, I've let it choke me. I've run from the truth and caused untold damage every step of the way.

To Lexi's memory.

To her mother.

Even to my parents, who have no choice but to face the truth now. My dad hasn't spoken to me in over a week. When and if he will again? I have no idea. In a sense, I can't even blame him.

Living in fear is comparable to hiding beneath a security blanket, pretending all the while that if you never remove it and look beyond, the reality can't touch you. Until that blanket is ripped away, and you're forced to face everything all at once.

"I don't pay you to stare into space," comes a mocking taunt that snaps me from my thoughts.

I look up to find Rafe watching me from over the counter, his head cocked, eyes a stormy dark hue. "You're slacking."

I startle to awareness, glancing down at the same section of the floor I've been sweeping for the past five minutes. He's right—if "slacking" is synonymous with *"contemplating the current state of my life."*

Compared to just a few weeks ago, the difference is night and day.

My brother is in prison.

My family is in shambles—between Kaitlin having to reconcile the truth of her marriage, and my parents coming to terms with present events and the past...

And amongst it all, I may have to testify in an upcoming trial, not to mention that I am still technically homeless.

In so many ways, I should be in a much worse state than I actually am—wearing a borrowed, oversized graphic tee and shorts, broom in hand. But for the first time, I don't feel that weight on my shoulders. That fear constantly lurking at the back of my mind has vanished.

I'm not under Branden's thumb any longer—and while my relationship with him is forever altered, at least I still have a handful of others to fall back on.

The man standing across from me, for one. And Mara. Once the news of the arrests hit the media, she was the first person to call me, even before my parents.

"Look alive, bunny," Rafe goads. Setting a stack of documents aside, he circles around to meet me. His hands find my waist, drawing me closer despite the broom held between us. "With my uncle in the slammer, I've got no choice but to be a stand-up citizen now."

"A stand-up citizen on conditional probation," I point out softly. It's the best terms, according to Liam—in exchange for him testifying against his uncle, he'll be looking at a lesser charge for any participation in criminal activity.

Which is a far brighter outlook than his uncle is facing. Branden, too, for that matter. Parallel to the investigation into his actions with Shen, the police back in PA have reopened Lexi Winacott's murder case. If everything proceeds toward its likely conclusion, then that's yet another trial I'll have to participate in.

But finally, I'll have the chance to give Lexi's mother some ounce of closure.

"So, a semi-criminal," Rafe corrects, his lip quirked. "Some people would find that a turn-on."

"A semi-criminal and a college dropout," I say with a wistful sigh. "What a pair."

He frowns. "You never mentioned anything about dropping out."

I lift one shoulder in a halfhearted shrug, but I can't meet his gaze directly. "The deadline for the Fenwick program passed. I'd rather not waste money on a useless semester."

Still frowning, he pulls away, returning behind the counter. "Funny you say that," he murmurs, lifting a stack of what looks like old mail from a drawer. From it, he withdraws a single envelope. "This came for you the other day."

Wary, I take the slim envelope, and I nearly fall over when I spy the name of my college admissions office—and judging from the fact that my old address is printed beneath my name, someone went through the hassle of collecting it for me. Whipping my gaze to Rafe, I feel my eyes widen. "You didn't."

I can't even say it out loud—turn in my essay to meet the deadline. And I have no doubt which piece of mine he chose. The one I wrote while watching him draw, feeding off his creativity.

"How did you even—"

He silences me with a kiss that takes my breath away. "You're technically still in college," he says.

Overwhelmed, I can't even challenge that assertion. "And what about you?"

"I'm an average joe with a fucking tattoo shop. The club is gone, though." He winces with genuine disappointment.

"There goes your chick magnet," I murmur. But I can't take my eyes off the acceptance letter, and the gratitude builds in my chest until it almost hurts to breathe. "I can't believe you did this—"

"I did," he says, stepping into me. "And I'll tell you how you can repay me."

My breath feathers in my chest. "How?"

"Let me tat you for real," he says against my mouth. "And then you work for me in between classes. You've got a debt to pay, remember?"

"I do," I admit, relaxing into the almost-kiss. A sudden thought makes me draw back and meet his gaze. "What kind of tat?"

He purses his lips, thinking it over, and raises one of his hands. With the tip of his finger, he traces a design over the front of my shirt. Thin, soft lines that creep down to my hips and then dip beneath the fabric entirely. My breath catches as he grazes my bare skin boldly, inching higher by the second.

"A little moth," he declares, referring to my story. What feels like his thumb grazes the flesh beneath my breast, arousing a shudder so violent my teeth chatter. "With big bunny eyes. As for the rest of your debt? You can start with writing me something new," he says, nipping my lower lip in between words. "I'm talking something way more than an essay."

I jump as he palms my breast entirely. The sensation is so distracting I can barely keep up with the thread of the conversation. Fighting for breath, I try. "Oh?"

He nods. "About you. About me… And I plan to give you more than enough fodder."

He tilts his head, deepening the kiss fully.

And I suspect that whatever story he has in mind, I'll have a wealth of inspiration to draw from.

Hey there!

Thank you so much for reading! If you enjoyed the story, please leave a review and recommend the book to any friend you think would love this twisted world. You'd have my eternal gratitude. Even a short sentence goes a long way!

Then, come join the rest of us dark romance lovers in my Facebook Group where you can get snippets, sneak peeks of upcoming books and even help vote on aspects of future novels.

Come to the dark side:
https://www.facebook.com/groups/lanasbeautifulmonsters/

WANT MORE STUFF TO READ?
Join my newsletter and get a **free book**! Plus, you get to stay updated with any new releases, random giveaways and exclusive sneak peeks!
https://www.lanaskybooks.com/newsletter

Other Novels: https://lanaskybooks.com/

Lana Sky is a reclusive writer in the United States who spends most of her time daydreaming about complex male characters and parenting her Cockapoo Joey. She writes dark, twisted romance across several genres. Her titles include everything from mafia romance to vampires.

facebook.com/AuthorLanaSky

twitter.com/lanasky101

amazon.com/author/lanasky

pinterest.com/lanasky101

goodreads.com/lanasky

instagram.com/lanasky101

bookbub.com/authors/lana-sky